OXFORD WORLD'S CLASSICS

THE ODYSSEY

By its evocation of a real or imaged heroic age, its contrasts of character and its variety of adventure, above all by its sheer narrative power, the *Odyssey* has won and preserved its place among the greatest tales in the world. It tells of Odyssseus' adventurous wanderings as he returns from the long war at Troy to his home in the Greek island of Ithaca, where his wife Penelope and his son Telemachus have been waiting for him for twenty years. He meets a one-eyed giant, Polyphemus the Cyclops; he visits the underworld; he faces the terrible monsters Scylla and Charybdis; he extricates himself from the charms of Circe and Calypso. After these and numerous other legendary encounters he finally reaches home, where, disguised as a beggar, he begins to plan revenge on the suitors who have for years been besieging Penelope and feasting on his own meat and wine with insolent impunity.

Nothing is known for certain about Homer—not even whether that was the name used by the poet responsible for the *Odyssey* and the *Iliad* in their final form, if indeed a single poet is in question. But if there was a Homer, he probably lived in the eighth century BC in Asia Minor or the Aegean islands. By tradition he was blind, and so most of the portraits of him that survive from antiquity represent him.

WALTER SHEWRING, for fifty years a master at Ampleforth College, has written on classical and Italian themes, has translated Latin hymns, and like his friend Eric Gill has constantly defended a traditional view of art. In his epilogue to this book he discusses the special difficulties of translating Homer.

G. S. KIRK was Regius Professor of Greek at Cambridge, and has worked on Greek myths and philosophy as well as on Homer. His books include *The Songs of Homer* (1962) and *Homer and the Oral Tradition* (1976).

OXFORD WORLD'S CLASSICS

For over 100 years Oxford World's Classics have brought readers closer to the world's great literature. Now with over 700 titles—from the 4,000-year-old myths of Mesopotamia to the twentieth century's greatest novels—the series makes available lesser-known as well as celebrated writing.

The pocket-sized hardbacks of the early years contained introductions by Virginia Woolf, T. S. Eliot, Graham Greene, and other literary figures which enriched the experience of reading. Today the series is recognized for its fine scholarship and reliability in texts that span world literature, drama and poetry, religion, philosophy and politics. Each edition includes perceptive commentary and essential background information to meet the changing needs of readers.

OXFORD WORLD'S CLASSICS

HOMER

The Odyssey

Translated by
WALTER SHEWRING
with an epilogue on translation

With an Introduction by
G. S. KIRK

UNIVERSITY PRESS

OXFORD

UNIVERSITY PRESS

Great Clarendon Street, Oxford OX2 6DP

Oxford University Press is a department of the University of Oxford.
It furthers the University's objective of excellence in research, scholarship,
and education by publishing worldwide in

Oxford New York

Athens Auckland Bangkok Bogotá Buenos Aires Calcutta
Cape Town Chennai Dar es Salaam Delhi Florence Hong Kong Istanbul
Karachi Kuala Lumpur Madrid Melbourne Mexico City Mumbai
Nairobi Paris São Paulo Singapore Taipei Tokyo Toronto Warsaw

with associated companies in Berlin Ibadan

Oxford is a registered trade mark of Oxford University Press
in the UK and in certain other countries

Published in the United States
by Oxford University Press Inc., New York

Introduction © G. S. Kirk 1980
Translation and epilogue © Walter Shewring 1980

The moral rights of the author have been asserted

Database right Oxford University Press (maker)

First published as a World's Classics paperback 1980
Reissued as an Oxford World's Classics paperback 1998

British Library Cataloguing in Publication Data

Data available

Library of Congress Cataloging in Publication Data

Data available

ISBN 0-19-283375-8

9

Printed in Great Britain by
Clays Ltd, St Ives plc

CONTENTS

NOTE

REFERENCES to the *Odyssey*, which was composed in Greek dactylic hexameters, are customarily given by book and line (e.g. VI 102) of the traditional text, a system with the advantage that it makes it possible to look up a reference in any translation of the poem where it is recorded with tolerable frequency which line of the original has been reached. In the present version the left-hand running headline states the span of lines rendered on the relevant double-page spread. References to the poem in the introduction, in notes to the translation, and in the epilogue are also on occasion given in the conventional form; but cross-references intended primarily for internal use are given to the pages of this book, in the belief that they will thus be more quickly consulted.

INTRODUCTION

G. S. KIRK

'GODDESS of song, teach me the story of a hero. This was the man of wide-ranging spirit who had sacked the sacred town of Troy and who wandered afterwards long and far.' The hero is Odysseus, one of the greatest (and certainly the most resourceful) of the Greek heroes who had fought for ten years before Troy. The Trojan War itself had been bad enough, but Odysseus' real sufferings came in the ten years that followed, which he spent in wandering and hardship before finally regaining his island home of Ithaca in the far west of Greece. Others of the Greeks, too, had had terrible homecomings. Agamemnon himself, leader of the Greek contingent and brother of Menelaus, whose wife Helen's abduction by the Trojan Paris had caused the whole war, had been brutally murdered by his adulterous wife Clytemnestra – Helen's elder sister, incidentally. Odysseus at least is still alive, but he, too, faces mortal danger when at long last he sets foot again in Ithaca. His wife Penelope is a paragon of loyalty, the very opposite of Clytemnestra, and he has nothing to fear from her. But she has had for years to hold out against the arrogant and violent importunity of a whole crowd of unwanted suitors, princelings from Ithaca and the surrounding regions who have crowded into the palace and are trying to force her to give up her husband for dead and marry one of themselves. Her only defence is stratagem (like the web that she weaves by day and undoes secretly each night); the ordinary people are helpless, and her son Telemachus is young and immature. Such is the background to the *Odyssey*, and it is the tale of Odysseus' wanderings, homecoming and triumph over the evil suitors that is the epic's main narrative theme.

It is a commonplace that *this* masterpiece of world literature, at least, can be read without having to try too hard and without special preparation. Yet there are certain considerations that the reader might, none the less, like to keep in mind, since they may increase his enjoyment still further. For the conventions of the *Odyssey* are obviously different from those of a modern narrative. That is illustrated, for example, by its unexpected variations of pace and detail, caused often enough by an ancient taste for repetition, for formality, for major digression, for long scenes of gradual recognition. The fundamental difference, however, is this (and it makes questions about the poem's mode of composition less than pedantic ones): that the *Odyssey* like the *Iliad* was designed to be heard in public performance, not to be read in private. That has all sorts of effects. It explains, to begin with, why the poem is so dramatic in essence – why characters display themselves in speeches or through actions and not primarily through discursive analysis by the author. We have grown used to this last method of approach, which has had special success in the novel, sometimes on planes to which no ancient author would aspire. Yet the dramatic approach, which often exacts more from the reader or audience, has its counterbalancing merits, and in the *Odyssey* we can observe the art of formalised but purposeful conversation, now devious, now urgent, now flattering or charming or deprecating, carried to heights occupied by Jane Austen or the Milton of *Paradise Lost* rather than by most writers for the modern stage.

In Homer's hands the dramatic epic is far from simple. Once again its complexities can do with preliminary identification, since their form and motives are different from those of modern literature – or, for that matter, of ancient Greek tragedy. The *Odyssey* is less severe in its structure and focus than the *Iliad*, which takes place mainly on the battlefield and by the Achaean ships, occasionally in beleaguered Troy itself, and only fleetingly, by simile or reminiscence, elsewhere. For the *Odyssey*'s action moves over three separate landscapes: Ithaca mainly (and almost wholly in its second half), the Peloponnese in the striking third and fourth books with a brief recall in the fifteenth, and mythical lands – Calypso's island in V and the coasts and islands of Odysseus' adventures, including the underworld itself, in VI to XII. Even Ithaca is sharply divided into town and country, with the palace and Eumaeus' hut as their centres; two wholly different ambiences with different rules, conventions and moralities. Odysseus' movements between the two lend tension and diversity to the second half of the poem, which again, as a whole, stands in counterpoint with the first. Geography is paralleled by grades of reality; for 'real life', itself divided between palace and countryside, suitors and honest men, is parodied or re-enacted at a different level by the gods and goddesses on Olympus, and more mysteriously by the inhabitants of lands of fantasy, the Laestrygonians, the Lotuseaters, the Cyclops, the Phaeacians. Finally there are strong social contrasts (we expect them, perhaps, but the heroic taste generally did not): aristocratic and proletarian (Odysseus and Philoetius or Eurycleia), male and female, human and divine – or monstrous; genuinely and falsely heroic.

These grades and locales are brought into dramatic contact, are made to overlap, by the central characters: Odysseus above all, but also Telemachus, Nausicaa, Eumaeus, Athene. Transitions from place to place and from human to divine are managed with extreme simplicity, amounting at times to abruptness. The audience is simply switched, sometimes in mid-verse, from one environment to the other. There is no need for ponderous temporal explanation, because the epic singers treated all events as successive; the chronology is strictly linear, broken only by explicit reminiscences or generalised statements like similes. It is a convention that grew, presumably, out of the necessary economies and simplifications of oral singers and narrators, but has been exploited for special ends by the master composer of the *Odyssey*. Finally there are stylistic complexities. Oral poetry had developed, by Homer's time, an impressive variety of styles within the limits of hexameter verse: from bald and strongly conventionalised narrative, in which each verse tends to contain a separate statement (as in the simple oral poetry of Yugoslavia in recent times), to elaborate and recherché passages with long, subordinated sentences and strong enjambment; from formal, rhetorical speeches (commoner in *Iliad* than in *Odyssey*) to relaxed conversations; from brief, serviceable descriptions of scene and setting to luxuriant set-pieces on particular places (Calypso's cave, Laertes' orchard, the island off the Cyclops' shore) that range in tone from the geometrical to the numinous; from the cryptic style of prophecy, as by Theoclymenus, to the tantalising omissions of condensed reminiscence and anecdote, especially in Nestor's tales and the reported songs of Demodocus and Phemius. There is an enormous wealth of such stylistic varieties and resources, despite which the *Odyssey* can sometimes seem monotonous to the modern reader – especially, perhaps, in the long conversations and the repeated journeys to and from town that occupy books XIV to XVII or XVIII. But the more closely one notices the nuances of these books the more intriguing they become, and the more valid as a necessary preparation for action and dénouement later; and the more one becomes conscious of inconspicuous changes of pace, style, theme and character which must have appealed to the listening audience and kept it enthralled.

Beneath these integuments the narrative skeleton of the poem stands out strongly. After a conventional but thought-provoking invocation to the Muse and a brief mention of Odysseus' present sojourn in Calypso's island, the singer takes his listeners straight to Olympus, where the gods debate Odysseus' fate and decide that he should be allowed to return home, as all other survivors of the Trojan expedition had long since done. Hermes is to instruct Calypso; Athene descends in disguise to prepare Telemachus, Odysseus' and Penelope's young son, in Ithaca. She makes him grow in maturity and experience by urging him to stand up to the suitors who have camped in Odysseus' palace and are devouring his substance and ogling his wife, then to slip off to Pylos and Lacedaemon, down south, for news of his father. Little in the way of hard information will result and the suitors are half-alerted to danger, but the excursion (in books III and IV) is fascinating in itself, it fills in much of the background of the aftermath of Troy and it builds the young prince into a credible ally for Odysseus.

The divine decision is briefly repeated in the fifth book, after the Peloponnesian interlude, to remind us (or the listening audience more particularly) that Hermes must still instruct Calypso – this is how the oral poet deals with events that are more obviously seen as simultaneous. The goddess is slightly disgruntled, and Odysseus leaves on his home-made raft with a certain apprehension but no regrets; he is longing to return home to his possessions, his household and his wife, and no minor deity, no promises of equivocal immortality, can divert him. Poseidon rages at him because he had blinded his son, the Cyclops Polyphemus: that tale is to be told by reminiscence in the ninth book. So the god makes a fierce storm blow up and smash the raft; Odysseus eventually struggles ashore, not in Ithaca but in Phaeacia, half-way between fantasy and real life, where Nausicaa discovers him (book VI), that delightful creature who elicits Odysseus' most unexpected kind of resourcefulness in the form of gallantry and tact. In the palace of her father King Alcinous he recounts all his adventures – Lotus-eaters, Cyclops, descent to the underworld and the rest (books VIII–XII): and after this almost sacred interval of re-creation, of incipient aggregation into the world of men, he is carried in a death-like sleep back to Ithaca on a magical Phaeacian ship – to the remote harbour of Phorcys, where Athene, at first disguised, meets him, warns him of the crisis with the suitors (who are laying siege to Penelope, a handsome prize, claiming that Odysseus must be dead), and sends him across country to the hut of Eumaeus. We are in the real world again, and will remain there; there is even an exact point of transition, at XIII 86–95, which contains a sort of formal coda to the whole of the first half of the poem.

After a protracted conversation between the still unrecognised Odysseus (whom Athene had made like an old man) and Eumaeus the faithful swineherd, the scene shifts rapidly back to Lacedaemon; for Telemachus has to be brought home with all speed now that his father is there. Farewells are said to Helen and Menelaus and then, in Pylos, to the aged Nestor – these Iliadic characters come through more blandly and less powerfully than in the earlier poem. A mysterious stranger called Theoclymenus, a seer, takes refuge with Telemachus for the passage back to Ithaca. The action reverts for a time to Odysseus and the swineherd, who still continue their talk, including now the long tale of Eumaeus' noble birth and abduction; then Telemachus, evading an ambush set offshore by the perturbed suitors, lands in his native island. He too makes for Eumaeus' hut, where his father eventually reveals himself to him. In book XVII the young man proceeds to the palace to tell his mother he is safe; Odysseus and Eumaeus follow, and there is the famous scene with the old dog Argos, who alone recognises his master and then dies. Playing the role of a beggar, Odysseus undergoes a long series of degradations; three of the chief suitors throw things at him, he has to fight the beggar Irus (but in so doing gives a sinister demonstration of his real strength), and the disloyal herdsman Melanthius, Eumaeus' polar opposite, insults him. All this underlines his almost unnatural patience and strengthens the case for total revenge. Penelope displays herself to the suitors – to arouse their passion, it seems, although Odysseus rejoices secretly that her real intentions are quite different (XVIII 283): was there a different version, hinted at here by the monumental composer, in which husband and wife were already in collusion? However that may be, in our version Odysseus keeps up his false identity, for, after he and Telemachus have secretly removed the armour and weapons that were normally kept in the great hall, he meets Penelope as night falls and

tries to persuade her that the 'real' Odysseus is close at hand. She
persists in her scepticism but treats the beggar kindly and tells
Eurycleia to wash his feet; the old woman recognises her master
by a scar on his leg (and a long digression tells how he had got it
as a young man), but he still prevents her from telling the good
news to her mistress.

Still disguised and still insulted, Odysseus is seated by the door
into the great hall; the suitors become crazed, burst into hysterical
laughter, and Theoclymenus prophesies their doom. Telemachus
is there too, waiting for his father's signal to attack (book XX);
but it is Athene who shows, as always, the way ahead by putting
it into Penelope's mind to set up the trial of the axes; ostensibly
whoever succeeds in it is to win her hand. There are two stages to
the trial, first the difficult stringing of Odysseus' powerful old
bow, then shooting through a line of axes set up along the floor
of the hall. The chief suitors fail to string the bow, even; it is
dramatic and humiliating for them, especially when Telemachus
passes it to the despised beggar and encourages him to try. Still
seated, and as easily as fitting a fresh string to a lyre, Odysseus
draws the bow and shoots right through the axes, and at the end
of book XXI Telemachus springs up and stands at his side. All
this is intensely exciting after the long preparations, and so is the
systematic destruction of the suitors in the book that follows.

Antinous, their leader and easily the most horrible of them, is
pierced through the throat by an arrow as he raises a wine-cup
to his lips; the rest think it is an accident – but only for a moment,
for Odysseus reveals his identity and tells them what he intends.
Eurymachus rallies them, tells them to draw swords and use the
tables as shields, but then he is struck down by Odysseus' second
shot. Telemachus spears Amphinomus, then runs to a store-room
to bring armour and spears for the four of them (for the loyal cow-
herd Philoetius, as well as Eumaeus, is fighting at their side). But
he leaves the door unlocked and Melanthius brings arms for the
suitors; Odysseus' heart sinks but Athene rallies him, and Tele-
machus catches Melanthius and ties him up, and so the slaughter
proceeds on its way; only Phemius the singer and Medon the
herald, who had been forced to work for the suitors, are spared.
Eurycleia is summoned, and Odysseus forbids her to utter the
ritual shriek of triumph as he stands, covered in blood and gore,
among the corpses of his enemies; for, he says, 'Vaunting over men

slain is a monstrous thing. These men have perished because the gods willed it so and because their own deeds were evil. They had no regard for any man, good or bad (XXII 412–14): a remarkably un-Iliadic sentiment, and one that stresses the underlying moral force of Odysseus' revenge. The disloyal maidservants are hanged (a little hard, this; they were silly girls who had slept with the suitors); Melanthius suffers a crueller death after torture and mutilation; then the violence is over. The remainder of the poem is spent in describing how Odysseus is at last recognised by those closest to him: by Penelope above all, who is sceptical to the last but is then reunited in a wonderful scene of sympathy and mature understanding. In the final book (which was almost certainly subjected to a degree of later elaboration), after a view of the dead suitors in the underworld and then of Odysseus' reunion with his pathetic old father Laertes, he prepares with his helpers to meet the inevitable threat from the relatives of the dead men. Athene sees to that, too, and brings the poem to a surprisingly abrupt end.

It stands out that there has been a marked change of tempo between the first half of the poem and most of the second. Once in Ithaca the concentration on detail – of preparation and planning, of insult, of slaughter, of recognition – is far more intense. It is my own opinion (and needless to say I may be wrong) that, compared with the Iliad, there is some falling off in power and concentration in those long preparatory scenes in Ithaca, roughly between books XIV and XXI. To see why that might be so, or indeed to rebut the suggestion, requires a closer consideration of Homer's compositional technique and general aims – one of which, at least, must have been to produce a poem of comparable length to the Iliad. It requires us, even, to tangle peripherally with the old 'Homeric Question'. Down to the time of the First World War scholars tried to explain anomalies and inconsistencies in both epics by the assumption of multiple authorship, along the lines of two or three separate and successive authors, the last of them carrying out some sort of conflation or redaction of the products of his predecessors. Growing interest in the repetitive and conventionalised phraseology of both poems, and its probable reasons, culminated in the work of Milman Parry, who in 1928 claimed that such phenomena showed them to be essentially oral in their mode of composition. That is, they were not written compositions but were composed by ear by unlettered singers, who needed those formular phrases and repeated motifs to be able to construct complex heroic poetry at all.

That view of the Homeric epics has been found essentially correct (although scholars disagree over the tightness of the formular 'system' and over whether writing might have played some ancillary part); and it suggests an altogether different and more convincing explanation of anomalies, real or apparent, in their composition. There is no question of constructing a special 'oral poetics', a set of rules broadly distinct from those that might govern literate composition; but at the same time certain probable differences present themselves. Minor inconsistencies are more to be expected, and are less noticed by the recipient, in this kind of poetry. Repetitions of various kinds are not only tolerated but also welcomed, for they help both the poet and his audience. Another important consideration is this: it is a natural characteristic of a narrative poem designed to be heard that its basic unit of length is the 'session'. That may vary a little according to the circumstances in which the poem is given. Several kinds of circumstance have been suggested for the Greek heroic song, with nobleman's banquet and religious festival as the most common. The first has some support from the *Odyssey* itself, where Phemius in Ithaca and Demodocus in Scheria are, to an extent, court poets – although the latter at least is not exclusively so. The second conjecture is based on what we known about festivals like the Delia in later times, or the Panathenaea, at which contests for rhapsodes reciting Homer were certainly held in the sixth century B.C. But other, less formal and more popular, occasions may have been just as important; Demodocus is classed with seers, doctors and carpenters as a *demioergos*, a 'worker for the community', at XXII 383–5, and village gatherings, weddings, horse fairs and the like must be considered as well. But in none of these contexts is the poet likely to have dealt *as normal practice* with a narrative unit that would outlast the capacity of most members of an audience to sit or stand around and take it in. One might guess at between half an hour and a couple of hours as the usual range; a range into which a Homeric 'book' would fit (although the division into twenty-four books as we have them certainly owes something to Alexandrian or Pergamene editors in the Hellenistic age), but which the whole *Odyssey* would vastly exceed.

A significant conclusion follows: that Homer, in making such a huge, monumental structure as the *Odyssey* (not to speak of the somewhat longer *Iliad*), was doing something that completely transcended the ordinary rules and aims of oral composition, and obviously necessitated not only the heavy use and rearrangement of existing materials (from the standard repertoire, that is) but also much original composition, based always, although not exclusively so, on the traditional phraseology of dactylic poetry and on a rich store of standard major themes and minor motifs. Now these are conditions which would be apt to produce at least one kind of unevenness in the epic, at any rate from the modern reader's viewpoint: the apparently unmotivated variations of pace or the clumsy passages here and there, often at points of episodic juncture. Another source of anomaly is more serious, but affects far fewer passages than used to be believed; for it is unlikely that the rhapsodes, professional reciters to whom the text of the epic was at one stage committed and on whom its transmission probably depended for much of the seventh century B.C., would have been content to leave it entirely unembellished. Here and there we can detect their usually unsuccessful attempts at improvement and expansion: in parts of the underworld scene in the eleventh book and early and late in the twenty-fourth book most especially. But generally speaking the *Odyssey* has come down to us much as Homer left it, and the occasional apparent anomalies, whether they be part of the process of monumental composition itself or arise out of subsequent stages of rhapsodic transmission, are unimportant. One can admit that without acceding to the fashionable modern view, based understandably on revulsion at the 'analytical' excesses of the past but less forgivably on a complacent preference for simplistic explanations, that every word in the modern vulgate text is exactly as Homer sang it – or, as this view almost requires, wrote it.

Many of the details of Homeric composition lie entirely beyond our grasp. It is a reasonable conjecture, based on the predominantly Ionic dialect of the poem as well as on a few allusions to Ionian sights and sounds, especially in the *Iliad*, that Homer did indeed come from Chios or Smyrna or one of the other cities of Ionia, the central region of the east-Aegean coast. That was what the ancients believed, and there was even a guild of rhapsodes in early sixth-century Chios that called itself the Homeridae, the 'descendants of Homer', and claimed to have special access to his *ipsissima verba.* The west-Greek information in the *Odyssey* presents no impediment to this idea, since the vagueness about the exact position of Ithaca (for instance) is just what might be expected of an Ionian singer developing a theme about a remote part of Greece. As for the date of composition, it is a strong probability that both epics were composed during the latter part of the eighth century B.C., or at the widest limits between 800 and 680 B.C., with the *Iliad* preceding the *Odyssey* by not more than, and perhaps not as much as, the length of a generation. The evidence is partly linguistic (for the chronology of dialect-changes like the dropping of the w-sound represented by the 'lost' letter digamma, or the coalescing of adjacent short vowels in 'contraction', can be roughly charted) and partly archaeological – either by the description in the poems of objects or practices that can be approximately dated, like probable references to hoplite tactics in the *Iliad* or specific motifs like the gorgon's head, or by the outbreak early in the seventh century of multiple references in cult or on vases to themes (like the heroic stature of Agamemnon or the blinding of Polyphemus) most likely to have been publicised by the epics themselves. None of these kinds of evidence is absolutely watertight, especially for poems that were traditional and archaising in character – that contained references to people, events and practices going back to the time of the Trojan War itself, as well as to Homer's own time some five hundred years later and to many of the centuries in between. Moreover the growth of interest in cults of Agamemnon, Helen and Menelaus, for instance, could be due to other poems or other factors. Yet the creation of the monumental epics is its most probable source, and the different kinds of evidence do all point to the same general period; the period, indeed, during which illiteracy, and with it a creative oral tradition, was gradually coming to an end under the impact of alphabetic writing, which seems to have spread into Greece, perhaps from Cyprus, precisely during the course of the eighth century B.C.

Few can resist wondering whether those later Greeks were right who maintained that the *Odyssey* and the *Iliad* did not come from the same hand (or, as we might say, mouth). Was there one Homer – or were there two? The old jokes have some point, after all, even today; for the truth is that we cannot answer this question with certainty, neither can we say anything about

Homer as a person beyond the bare facts of his date and probable region of activity. He exists as an author, and only as an author – moreover as one who deliberately withheld his own *persona* from his poetry. In a sense he is the *Iliad*, or *Odyssey*, or both; so that the question whether he composed both epics reduces itself to a question about the differences in style and tone between the poems themselves, together with certain guesses that might be made about the possible range of styles in one single composer, especially an oral one. This last qualification is important, because oral singers evidently depended upon a personal store of phrases, themes, motifs and narrative patterns that they had selected and assimilated from the tradition – from their particular teachers, that is, who formed part of a long succession. That store could not be varied at will; it tended to imprint itself as a kind of personal stamp on any poem, even in slightly divergent *genres*, that a particular singer gave as his own. The *Iliad* and *Odyssey* differ a good deal in subject, the one being primarily martial, the other partly domestic and partly picaresque. Obviously their language will vary accordingly, and differences of phraseology, even of formular phraseology, are to be expected. But it remains a little strange that the *Odyssey* has a number of formulas for common ideas, each of which is used at least five times, which are entirely absent from the *Iliad*: 'pondering evils', 'with steadfast spirit', 'to question and ask', 'dear heart was broken'. The *Iliad* has fewer exclusive formulas which are not clearly subject-conditioned, but 'dark night', 'mighty destiny', 'covered (his) eyes' and (four times only, but especially appropriate, as one might think, to Odysseus) 'with subtle mind' seem significant. Certain exclusively Iliadic single words are also striking; some of them are martial, but even so one would expect to find them in martial parts of the *Odyssey*, especially in the killing of the suitors; they include *klonos*, 'rout' (twenty-eight times), *helkos*, 'wound' (twenty-two times), and *loigos*, *loigios*, 'destruction', 'destructive' (twenty-five times).

These differences in vocabulary are compounded by a striking difference in style, which is hard, however, to define as precisely as one would wish. It is that the *Odyssey*, especially in its speeches, is blander, softer and less taut in expression than the *Iliad*. Again, the difference in subject might be held to account for this, at least in part; but another ancient conjecture has its attractions here, namely that the *Odyssey* was the work of Homer's old age

whereas the *Iliad* belonged to his maturity. That kind of judge-
ment can go to excess, as it did in Samuel Butler's conviction that
the *Odyssey* must have been written by a woman. But the idea
that the *Odyssey* might be a work of relative old age cannot be
dismissed so easily, for against the few stylistic differences there
is, of course, an enormous preponderance of similarities. All heroic
poetry, being traditional, had much in common. Even so one is
reluctant to embark on the assumption of two separate geniuses
so close together in time and place unless one absolutely has to.
If, as one reads through the *Odyssey*, one chooses to believe that
its composer had already achieved the *Iliad*, and that time had
moved on, one will not in any event be making a very blame-
worthy mistake.

As one gets deeper into the narrative these external problems
seem less urgent; they have their effect on how one understands
what one reads, and that is important, but the poem itself becomes
the thing – particularly its central figure, Odysseus. For he lies at
the centre of all the action in a way that Achilles in the *Iliad*
does not. The wrath of Achilles is the stated theme of that poem,
and it is true that, even in the long stretches of fighting when
Achilles is nursing his anger in solitude, that wrath is always
there in the background. Yet Achilles is a less diverse figure than
the Odysseus of the *Odyssey*, and the *Iliad* is less a poem about
him than about war itself, what it does to men, and about the
complex heroic values that bring the triumphs and tragedies that
are part of it. The *Odyssey* exists on one level as a story, one with
plenty of action and a more varied plot than that of the *Iliad*;
which is why children enjoy so much of it. Yet Homer was not
just using monumental scale as a means of making a longer and
more complicated plot; it is plain that he sought for depths of
meaning that lay beyond the scope of the shorter poems upon
which he built, as well as for sheer monumental power and
forcefulness in the totality of action and implication. His Odysseus
is not just the figure to whom the events of the *Odyssey* happen,
the connecting link between a series of beautifully varied adven-
tures. He is, rather, the man who can survive everything that
befalls him because of his particular combination of qualities;
qualities that far surpass those of the Iliadic Odysseus, who is a
good fighter as well as being *polymētis*, 'of many wiles'. The
Odyssean hero is that, too, of course – it was his hallmark in

the heroic tradition. But he is also long-suffering, patient, wise, humane, resigned, philosophical, hard-headed, practical, brutal when circumstances demand it, boastful at times – all these things as well. He is a survivor who fights his way home to take up life again where is should be taken up after war: among one's own people, surrounded by the possessions one has fought for, and solaced by the wife who is one's partner and whom one struggled to win. That at least is what the Greeks of the heroic tradition believed in.

To achieve all that, Odysseus has to hold firmly to the past, to what had happened at Troy, to what he knows himself to be. With Calypso, that means above all remembering that he is mortal, a social being, not destined for solitary love with a creature of another kind. As his raft breaks apart beneath him it means determining to stay alive despite everything, and carefully weighing up the position – exactly what to do as one is swept toward a rocky shore – with the decisive practicality of professional soldier or sailor. With Nausicaa it means tempering all that virility with understanding and consideration, as he stands on the seashore naked, hiding his genitals with a branch, like a weather-beaten lion desperate for food, yet capable of gentle words, of prudent flattery, of the thoughtful consideration that the ritual gesture of supplication would, in the circumstances, be offensive to a young girl. With Athene it means reserving his position until the goddess reveals herself completely – it means concocting long and plausible-sounding tales to explain his presence and yet hide his identity, and mild rebuke, when the bluff is called, for his guardian deity's absence for so long. With Eumaeus it means responding to his kindness, searching him out for proof of total loyalty, carefully establishing the facts about the palace and the degree of guilt or innocence of all that live there. With Penelope, who is shown by sporadic allusions to be suffering from the strain of siege and isolation, it means a quite exceptional caution and self-discipline, more false tales about himself compounded with assertions of Odysseus' imminent arrival that are designed to comfort and strengthen her. Finally, when the suitors lie dead and he has revealed himself to her own cautious self (the equivalent in this respect to his own), they recount to each other all that has happened to each of them, as they lie in bed reunited. And since this is in some respects a realistic story, and certainly not a sentimental one, they also plan what needs to be done now to face the threat of reprisals from the suitors' families; and they look without despair into the future as Odysseus insists on telling her of Teiresias' mysterious prophecy of further travels and trials ahead, followed by a gentle death from the sea in old age.

It is the tale of that complex and inspired man, amid the confused aftermath of the Trojan War, in lands remote from the Ionian coasts where Homer sang, or even at times from prosaic reality in any form, in an amalgam that contains much of what the Greeks continued to feel and to believe, that lies before the fortunate reader now.

G. S. KIRK

ACKNOWLEDGEMENTS

LEAVING aside my obvious debt to the published writings of many scholars, I must thank here certain friends who have given me more direct assistance. My translation has been studied, improved and helped on its way: in the first place by my colleague Philip Smiley; then, at the Oxford University Press, by Richard Brain, to whom I submitted early drafts, by Henry Hardy, who became my scrupulous and untiring Editor, and by a notably sympathetic Reader. And I owe a special gratitude to successive abbots and headmasters of Ampleforth for offering me there the leisure and the background which have let me continue work of my own without forsaking my duties in the school.

W. S.

IT was just as when Artemis the huntress ranges the mountain-side – on lofty Taygetus, it may be, or it may be on Erymanthus – taking her pleasure among the boars and the running deer; country nymphs, daughters of Zeus who holds the aegis, are all around her and share her pastime; Leto her mother is glad at heart. With head and forehead Artemis overtops the rest, and though all are lovely, there is no mistaking which is she. So it was now; among her maidens, this unwedded girl was beyond compare.

Odyssey VI 102–9

BOOK I

GODS IN COUNCIL – TELEMACHUS AND ATHENE

GODDESS of song, teach me the story of a hero.

This was the man of wide-ranging spirit who had sacked the sacred town of Troy and who wandered afterwards long and far. Many were those whose cities he viewed and whose minds he came to know, many the troubles that vexed his heart as he sailed the seas, labouring to save himself and to bring his comrades home. But his comrades he could not keep from ruin, strive as he might; they perished instead by their own presumptuousness. Fools, they devoured the cattle of Hyperion, and he, the sun-god, cut off from them the day of their homecoming.

Goddess, daughter of Zeus, to me in turn impart some knowledge of all these things, beginning where you will.

The tale begins when all those others who had escaped the pit of destruction were safe in their own lands, spared by the wars and seas. Only Odysseus was held elsewhere, pining for home and wife; the nymph Calypso, a goddess of strange power and beauty, had kept him captive within her arching caverns, yearning for him to be her husband. And when there came with revolving seasons the year that the gods had set for his journey home to Ithaca, not even then was he past his troubles, not even then was he with his own people. For though all the gods beside had compassion on him, Poseidon's anger was unabated against the hero until he returned to his own land.

But now Poseidon had gone to visit the Ethiopians, those distant Ethiopians whose nation is parted within itself, so that some are near the setting and some near the rising sun, but all alike are at the world's end; to these he had gone to receive a great offering of bulls and rams, and there he was taking his pleasure now, seated at the banquet. But the other gods were gathered together in the palace of Olympian Zeus, and the father of gods and men began to speak to them. His mind was full of Lord Aegisthus, slain by renowned Orestes, the child of Agamemnon; with him in mind

Zeus began to speak to the Deathless Ones.

'O the waywardness of these mortals! They accuse the gods, they say that their troubles come from us, and yet by their own presumptuousness they draw down sorrow upon themselves that outruns their allotted portion. So now; Aegisthus outran his allotted portion by taking in marriage the wedded wife of the son of Atreus and killing her husband when he returned. Yet he knew what pit of destruction was before him, because we ourselves warned him of it. We sent him Hermes, the Keen Watcher, the Radiant One; we forbade him to kill the king or to woo his wife, under pain of the vengeance for Agamemnon that would come upon him from Orestes when the boy grew up and felt a longing for his own country. Thus Hermes warned him, wishing him well, but Aegisthus' heart would not hear reason, and now he has paid all his debts at once.'

Athene, goddess of gleaming eyes, made answer: 'O son of Cronos, father of us and sovereign ruler, that man lies low by a doom well-earned – no question of it; so perish whoever does as he did! It is for Odysseus my heart is wrung – so subtle a man and so ill-starred; he has long been far from everything that he loves, desolate in a wave-washed island, a wooded island, the navel of all the seas. A goddess has made her dwelling there whose father is Atlas the magician; he knows the depths of all the seas, and he, no other, guards the tall pillars that keep the sky and the earth apart.[1] His daughter it is who keeps poor Odysseus pining there, and who seeks continually with her soft and coaxing words to beguile him into forgetting Ithaca;[2] but he – he would be well content to see even the smoke rising up from his own land, and he longs to die. And yet your own heart, Olympian one, remains all unmoved. There in the wide land of Troy, where the Argives had beached their ships, did not Odysseus do as you would have had him do? Did he not offer you constant sacrifice? Father Zeus, why are you at odds with Odysseus?'[3]

1. I accept Professor Stella's view that the mythology here goes back to the ancient Near-Eastern tradition which makes the sky a roof or a pavilion of bronze ('the brazen sky' elsewhere in Homer) held up by pillars at the edge of the world. Atlas is the guardian of these, not a living pillar and not a mountain.

2. 'And ever with smooth speech insidious seeks
   To wean his heart from Ithaca.' COWPER

3. With word-play as on p. 237.

Zeus who masses the clouds made answer: 'My child, what a word is this that has passed your lips! How could I ever forget Odysseus, that hero who more than any mortal has subtle wit and more than any has offered sacrifice to the deathless gods whose home is heaven? No; but Poseidon the Earth-Sustainer is stubborn still in his anger against Odysseus because of his blinding of Polyphemus, the Cyclops whose power is greatest among the Cyclops race and whose ancestry is more than human; his mother was the nymph Thoosa, child of Phorcys the lord of the barren sea, and she lay with Poseidon within her arching caverns. Ever since that blinding, Poseidon has been against Odysseus; he has stopped short of killing him, but keeps him wandering far from his native land. But come, let those of us who are here contrive together a way for his homecoming. Poseidon will throw aside his anger; he cannot defy alone all the immortal gods at once.'

The goddess Athene answered him: 'O son of Cronos, father of us and sovereign ruler, if indeed the blessed gods now wish that shrewd Odysseus should come to his own land again, then let us instruct the radiant Hermes, the Messenger, to go to the island of Ogygia and without delay to tell the nymph of braided tresses our firm decree that staunch Odysseus is to depart and journey home. As for myself, I will go to Ithaca to rouse his son and to put fresh eagerness in his heart to call together the flowing-haired Achaeans and speak his mind to all those suitors who daily slaughter his thronging sheep and the swaying cattle with curving horns. Then I will send him to Sparta and sandy Pylos, to gather by hearsay what news he can of his father's homecoming and to win himself a good name in the world.'

This said, she fastened sandals beneath her feet, the immortal sandals of lovely gold that carried her, swift as airy winds, over ocean and over boundless earth. And she took the great spear, tall, strong, heavy and brazen-tipped, with which she strikes down the ranks of warriors who have aroused her wrath – is she not the child of a mighty father? Then off she set; from the heights of Olympus she darted downwards, then came to rest in the land of Ithaca, at Odysseus' outer door on the threshold of the court-yard. She held in her hand her spear of bronze, and had taken now the form of Mentes, a friend of the house and leader of the Taphians. She saw before her the headstrong suitors, seated out-side the doors on the hides of oxen that they themselves had killed and beguiling the time with a game of draughts. With them were pages and brisk attendants, the pages mixing wine and water in bowls, the attendants washing tables with pory sponges and setting them in place, or dividing out the abundant meat.

Telemachus, young and handsome, espied her first, as he sat despondently with the suitors. His mind was full of his noble father : would he return from wherever he might be to scatter the suitors in these halls, to retrieve his honours, to be lord of his own estate? Thus the boy wondered as he sat there with suitors all around him; and then he saw Athene. He made straight for the outer porch, inwardly vexed that a guest should stand at the door so long; he came up to her, clasped her right hand and took the bronze spear while his words came forth in rapid flight: 'Greeting, friend; you shall be made welcome here; afterwards, when you have had your meal, you shall tell us what service you require.'

With these words he led the way, and Pallas Athene followed him. When they entered the lofty hall, he laid her spear against a tall pillar, inside the polished spear-stand in which stood also a cluster of spears that were Odysseus' own. He escorted Athene to a chair, a noble piece of good workmanship, spread a cloth above it for her to sit on and gave her a stool to rest her feet. For himself he drew up a lower chair and sat beside her away from the suitors, fearing his guest might resent their boisterousness and shrink from a meal in that overbearing company; he wished, besides, to ask her about his absent father. A maid brought water in a fine golden jug and poured it over their hands for washing, holding a silver basin below; then she drew up a polished table by them. The trusted housekeeper came and put bread where they could reach it; she had many kinds of food as well, and gave ungrudgingly from her store. The carver lifted from his board the trenchers filled with all sorts of meat, put them before guest and host, put goblets of gold before them too, and again and again a page came up to pour the wine.

But now in came the overbearing suitors. They began to take their several places on higher and lower seats : pages poured water on their hands, maids heaped up bread in basketfuls, menservants brimmed the bowls with wine, and the suitors stretched out their hands to the dishes there. When they had eaten and drunk their fill, they turned their thoughts elsewhere. to music and to dancing – these are pleasures that crown a feast. A page put a lyre of cunning workmanship into the hands of Phemius, who always sang in the suitors' company, though this was against his will. So the bard now touched the strings and began his lovely song; but Telemachus turned to address Athene, putting his head near hers so that the others should not hear:

'Dear guest, will you take amiss what I am about to say? The suitors yonder are all intent upon lyre and song; and well they may be, while they consume scot-free these goods that are not their own, the goods of a man whose whitening bones are cast up, perhaps, upon some shore, mouldering in rain, or are wave-tossed in the salt sea itself. If once that man – if once he himself stood before their eyes again in Ithaca, they would rather pray for more speed of foot than for more gold and more garments. But no, he has perished miserably as I said, and no consolation is left for us, even if somewhere in the world there are those who prophesy his return; his day of homecoming has been blotted out.

'But come now, tell me and answer truly: Who are you, and from where? What kind of ship did you travel by? (No one journeys on foot to Ithaca!) How did the sailors bring you here, and what name did they give themselves? And say now frankly – I long to know – is this your first visit here, or are you a friend from my father's time? I know that many guests used to come to this house, because he himself had dealings with many men.'

Athene the goddess answered him: 'I will tell you truly all you ask. My name is Mentes; I am proud to be son of wise Antilochus, and I myself am king of the Taphian oarsmen now. I have come here now, as you see, with my own ship and crew, sailing the wine-dark sea to a foreign land and the city of Temese; I am in quest of copper, and have a cargo of glittering iron. My vessel is not far off, but away from the town, near the fields – in Rheithron harbour under the wooded height of Neion.

'I claim guest-friendship with your family from days long past – you have only to go and question old Lord Laertes; they say he never comes to the city now, but lives a hard life on his distant farm with an aged waiting-woman who brings food and drink up to him when weariness fastens on his limbs as he hobbles about his hilltop vineyard. But I came here now because men were saying your father was home again, though I find instead that the gods are thwarting his return. Surely Odysseus is somewhere still, not dead but alive – in some wave-washed island, it may be, with wide ocean all around him, held by brutish unfeeling men whose chafing prisoner he has become. But now I will give you a prophecy – truth to tell, I am not a prophet, and I have no certainty with omens, but the Deathless Ones have put this into my mind, and I am sure it will happen as I say : Not much longer will he be absent from his own land, not even if iron chains should bind him; he is rich in resource; he will contrive some way of return. But now tell me this, and speak without concealment : full-grown as you are, are you the son of Odysseus himself? Your likeness to him sets me wondering – the head might be his, and the fine eyes; I speak as one who had much to do with him before he embarked for Troy like the other leaders of the Argives – all of them in their hollow ships bound for the same goal; but since that time I have never set eyes upon Odysseus, nor he upon me.'

Thoughtful Telemachus answered her : 'Friend, I will speak as frankly as you desire. My mother says that I am his son, though I myself have no knowledge of it – what man can be sure of his parentage? If only I might have been the child of some happier man whose latter years found him at ease in his own possessions! Instead – think of the most unhappy of mortal men – it is his son I am said to be.'

Athene the goddess answered him : 'If the gods let Penelope bear such a son as you, they did not mean your lineage to be inglorious in time to come. But now tell me this; speak freely. What is this feasting, what is this throng of men? Why must you have such things about you? Is it one man's banquet? Is it a wedding? Certainly it is no such meal as men offer one another in turn. These banqueters in your hall have a swaggering, domineering air. Any man of sense who joined the gathering would stand aghast at all this grossness.'

Thoughtful Telemachus answered her : 'Friend – since you ask me and search things out – this house was doubtless rich and well-ordered as long as Odysseus was in Ithaca. But now the gods have willed otherwise; bent on mischief, they have swept him out of our sight like no other man in the whole world. Had he simply died, I should grieve less – had he perished among his friends in the land of Troy; then all the Achaeans would have heaped up a cairn for him, and then for his son as well as himself he would have won great glory through after-times. But no, the storm-spirits have snatched him ingloriously away; he has passed beyond all sight and knowledge, bequeathing to me grief and sorrow. Nor is this mourning for my father my only reason for distress; the gods have contrived other troubles for me. The great island chieftains in Dulichium, in Same, in forested Zacynthus, and those who are princes in craggy Ithaca – they have all of them come to woo my mother, and they are devouring my inheritance. And although the thought of marriage is hateful to her, she dare not refuse outright and make an end of it. Meanwhile with their greed they waste my inheritance away, and before long they will bring destruction on myself.'

In deep indignation Pallas answered: 'Unhappy boy! How bitterly do you feel the need of that absent one to put forth his strength against the shameless suitors! Would to heaven we might see Odysseus now, standing at his own house's threshold, back from his wanderings, helmeted, shielded, poising a pair of spears, looking as when I saw him first in my own home, though then he was drinking and making merry. He had been at Ephyra, with Ilus the son of Mermerus, and now he was on his way home; he had sailed with his rapid ship to Ephyra in search of a deadly poison to smear on his arrows' brazen tips. Ilus would not give him the poison, for he stood in awe of the deathless gods; but my own father in his unbounded friendship gave it to him instead. Would to heaven he were here, unchanged, to confront the suitors! They would find death quickly, all of them, and their hoped-for wedding would have a bitter taste. But will he or will he not return to deal retribution in his own house? That must rest on the knees of the gods. As for yourself – I urge you to think of means to banish the suitors from your house. Listen now, and take heed of what I say. When tomorrow comes, call the Achaean chiefs together; make known to them what you have resolved, and let the gods be witnesses to it. Tell the suitors they must disperse to their own estates; as for your mother, supposing her heart is set on marriage, let her go back to her father's house – he is a powerful prince – and her kinsmen will prepare the wedding and charge themselves with the many gifts that go with a beloved daughter.[1] And then for yourself I have special counsel; I

1. Meaning uncertain because of a change in bridal customs (there is also an ambiguous pronoun). At an early period the suitor offered gifts to the bride's kinsmen; later, kinsmen offered a dowry with the bride. An alternative translation might be: 'The suitors will bring about a wedding and provide the many gifts ...'.

think it wise and I hope you will follow it. All too long has your father been away. Take twenty rowers to man the best ship you have, and go to find news of him. Perhaps some human witness will speak; perhaps you will hear some rumour that comes from Zeus, a great source of tidings for mankind. First go to Pylos and question King Nestor there; then to Sparta and yellow-haired Menelaus, for of all the bronze-clad Achaeans he was the last to return home. If you hear that your father is alive and is on his way, you may hold your ground for a year more despite your troubles; but if you hear he is dead and gone, journey back to your own country and raise a cairn to him; then pay him in full his due of funeral honours, and find a new husband for your mother. Having done all these things from first to last, set your wits to work and find some means to kill the suitors in your own halls, whether openly or by stratagem; you must not cling to the childish ways that you have outgrown. Have you not been told what fame Prince Orestes has won throughout the world after slaying his father's murderer, that treacherous Aegisthus who slew majestic Agamemnon? You too, whom I see so tall and handsome, you too, my friend, must show your courage and win fair fame among future men. I myself will go back now to my rapid ship and my own crew, who doubtless are fretting at my delay. This new adventure must be your own; take my words to heart.'

Thoughtful Telemachus answered her: 'Friend, all you say shows concern for me; a father might speak so to his son, and these are words I shall not forget. But I beg of you, wait a little longer, eager though you may be to depart; stay to bathe and enjoy good cheer and be given a present to take aboard triumphantly, something precious and very beautiful to remember me by, a true affectionate parting gift from host to guest.'

Athene the goddess answered him: 'Do not keep me longer, now that I so much wish to go; and as for the gift that you have in mind for me, take out from your store as beautiful a one as you will, and when I come back again give it to me to take home; you will find it brings you ample return.'

With these words the gleaming-eyed goddess left him and took her flight upwards like a bird; but she put in his heart strength and courage, and more than ever she brought his father before his mind. He had seen what she did and was astonished; it came to him that this was a god.

Then the princely boy walked at once towards the suitors. The famous bard was singing to them, and they were listening quietly; his theme was the homecoming of the Achaeans from Troy, and how Athene had made it sorrowful.

His inspired singing broke in on the thoughts of wise Penelope, daughter of Icarius; she had been in the upper part of the house, but now she passed from her own room down the high staircase, not unescorted but with two waiting-women. When the great queen had reached the suitors, she halted beside the pillar that bore the massy roof, her bright headscarf drawn over her cheeks, while her faithful women stood there on either side.

With sudden tears she spoke to the heaven-taught bard: 'Phemius, you know many other lays to beguile men's hearts, deeds of heroes and deeds of gods that the bards sing of; choose one of those and sing it among the suitors here while they drink their wine in silence, but cease from this melancholy lay that always wrings my heart within me, because I more than any other am pierced by sorrow beyond forgetting; so peerless a man is he I mourn for, he I remember always, a man whose fame has gone through the length and breadth of Hellas and of Argos.'

But thoughtful Telemachus answered her: 'Mother, why grudge this faithful bard the right to please us by any path that his fancy takes? In all such things it is not the bards who are accountable; Zeus, it may be, is accountable, when he allots to toiling men whatever is his pleasure for each. If Phemius sings of the sorrows of the Danaans, that is in no way blameworthy, for men will applaud most eagerly whatever song falls freshest upon the listening ear. On your own side rather, heart and mind must be schooled to listen. Odysseus was not the only hero whose day of return was blotted out in the land of Troy; many another fell there also. No, go up to your room again and look to your own province, distaff and loom, and tell your women to ply their task; public speech shall be men's concern, and my concern most of all; authority in this house is mine.'

At this she withdrew to her room in wonder, laying to heart her son's wise words. She mounted with her waiting-women to the upper quarters of the palace, then began weeping for Odysseus, her darling husband, till Athene sent down welcome slumber upon her eyelids.

Meanwhile, in the shadowy halls below, the suitors clamorously

called out, voicing prayers, every one of them, to share her bed
and lie beside her. But Telemachus broke in upon them: 'Chief-
tains who seek to woo my mother, you pass all bounds in your
arrogance. Come, for today let us take our pleasure at the feast,
and let there be no din of voices; men should be content to listen
to such a bard as this, who is godlike in his utterance. But to-
morrow morning let us gather and take our seats in the meeting-
place; I shall have a forthright message for you. I shall tell you
to leave my halls and to look for your feasts elsewhere, changing
from house to house to consume possessions that are your own.
But if to yourselves it seems a better thing, a more desirable thing,
to waste one man's substance and go scot-free – so be it, waste on!
I for my part will call aloud on the deathless gods, hoping that
Zeus will let requital be made at last; then you will perish in
these same halls and it is I who shall go scot-free.'

So he spoke; they all of them bit their lips and wondered at
him, so fearless had been his words. But Antinous answered (he
was Eupeithes' son): 'Telemachus, it must be the gods themselves
who teach you to speak so fearlessly and disdainfully. I pray that
it may never be you that Zeus makes ruler in Ithaca, heir to the
kingship though you may be.'

Thoughtful Telemachus answered him: 'Antinous, you may
resent my words, but if Zeus allowed I would gladly enough
accept supremacy. Is that, do you think, the worst evil in the
world? Surely kingship is no bad thing; wealth flows into the
palace readily, and the name of king brings a man more honour.
Nevertheless, in this island of Ithaca there are many princes be-
side myself, some young, some old; one of these may well gain the
kingship, now that great Odysseus is dead. But still I shall reign
over my own house and over the slaves that Odysseus once made
his prize and left for me.'

Eurymachus, son of Polybus, answered him: 'Telemachus, if we
ask who among the Achaeans is to be king in Ithaca, the answer
lies on the knees of the gods. But my hope is that you will keep
your inheritance and be lord in your own palace still; heaven
forbid that while Ithaca still stands any man should do you
violence and rob you of your possessions. But now, dear friend,
may I question you on your guest? Where does he come from,
what land does he call his own, where are his kindred, where are
his native fields? Did he bring some news of your father's home-

coming, or had he some errand of his own? It is strange how he suddenly rose and went, before any of us could come to know him, though by his looks he was no ignoble man.'

Thoughtful Telemachus answered him : 'Eurymachus, doubtless my father's homecoming has been blotted out; I no longer trust the news from here or the news from there; I heed no prophetic message such as my mother seeks when she calls some soothsayer here to question him. No, this is a friend of the house from my father's time; he comes from Taphos; his name, he says, is Mentes, son of Anchialus, and he himself is king of the Taphian oarsmen now.'

So said Telemachus, though in his heart he had known the goddess for an immortal. The suitors meanwhile had turned to dancing and heart-rejoicing music, and taking their pleasure thus, they waited for evening to come on. As they took their pleasure the dusky evening came, and every suitor went back to his own house to sleep. Telemachus had his own room high up in the pleasant courtyard, in a spot with a clear space round it; towards this he walked on his way to rest, while thoughts came thronging through his mind. A faithful servant lighted his way with burning torches – Eurycleia, daughter of Ops, Peisenor's son. Laertes had bought her long ago as a girl, giving twenty oxen's worth of goods for her; in the household he paid her no less regard than he did his wife, but he never lay with her in love, lest the queen should be indignant with him. Among all the maids she was always the fondest of Telemachus; in his childhood she had been his nurse. She it was who lighted his way now. He opened the door of his well-built room, sat down on the bed, took off his soft tunic and handed it to the shrewd old woman. She smoothed the tunic, folded it, and hung it up by the bedstead on a peg; then left the room, pulling the door to by its silver handle and drawing home the bolt by its strap. Telemachus, wrapped in softest wool, meditated inwardly all night the journey counselled him by Athene.

BOOK II

TELEMACHUS DEFIES THE SUITORS

DAWN comes early, with rosy fingers. When she appeared, the son that Odysseus loved sat up to put on his clothes and left his bed, then slung the keen sword about his shoulders, fastened his sandals under his glistening feet and went out from his room, like a god to look upon. At once he ordered the clear-voiced heralds to call the flowing-haired Achaeans to the assembly-place. The heralds made their proclamation and the people soon began to gather. When they were ready – when the assembly-place was filled – Telemachus also took his way there. In his hand was a spear of bronze, beside him were two swift-footed hounds, and Athene shed upon the boy a grace of presence more than human, so that as he came nearer to themselves the people all gazed at him in wonder. He took his place in his father's seat, and the elders made way for him.

The first to speak to those assembled was Lord Aegyptius, bent with age and unfathomably wise. When King Odysseus sailed with his hollow ships, bound for Troy of the noble horses, a son of Aegyptius had gone with him, and this was the spearsman Antiphus; but the savage Cyclops had killed him inside his arching cave, making a meal of him after all the rest. The old lord had three other sons; one of them – Eurynomus – was among the suitors, and the other two saw to their father's farms; but still he never forgot the first in his grief and mourning, and with a tear for him he now spoke in council:

'Men of Ithaca, listen to my words. There has been no council and no assembly here from the day when King Odysseus sailed with his hollow ships. Who has thus called us together now? On whom has there come this pressing need, among our younger men or among our elders? Has our summoner heard some news of a host of men approaching, news he would bring before us clearly as being the first to hear of it? Is there some other public matter which he would tell and apprise us of? A worthy man he must be, I think, a heaven-favoured man. May Zeus bring to accomplishment whatever good thing he has at heart!'

So he spoke, and the son of Odysseus accepted the omen joyfully, nor did he stay seated longer; eager to speak, he stood up in mid-assembly. The staff of office was put in his hands by Peisenor, a herald versed in the ways of wisdom; then he spoke thus, addressing Aegyptius first:

'Sir, the man you speak of is not far off, as you will now find. It was I who summoned the people here, because of a thing that bears hard upon me. I have heard no news of a host approaching, news I might bring before you as having myself first learned of it, nor is there any other public matter I wish to tell and apprise you of. The business is my own. Evil has fallen upon my house – a double evil. First I have lost my noble father, who once was king among all you here and ruled you as gently as a father; then something far worse has befallen me, which before long will ruin my house altogether and bring to nothing my means of living. My mother, greatly to her distress, has been beset by suitors, sons of the greatest nobles here. They dare not go to the house of Icarius her father so that he in person might receive bride-gifts for his daughter,[1] giving her to any suitor he pleased who was acceptable to herself. Instead, they haunt my palace day in, day out; they slaughter my sheep and oxen and fatted goats; they make merry here, they selfishly drink the glowing wine, and thus abundance of things is wasted. All this is because there is no man left with the mettle of Odysseus to ward off ruin from the house. I myself am not able to ward it off; I fear I shall always be a weakling, with no skill to resist at all. Had I the strength, I would take my stand gladly enough, because these men's deeds and the havoc they make of my possessions are beyond all justice, beyond endurance. Do you feel no self-reproach yourselves, no shame for the reproach of your neighbours, of those who live all around you here? You should shrink from the anger of the gods; the gods in their indignation may bring your misdoings down on your own heads. I appeal to you by Olympian Zeus himself, I appeal by Themis, who convenes men's councils and dissolves them, cease from these ways, you men of Ithaca, and leave me unmolested to pine away in my bitter grief. Or can it be that Odysseus my noble father once did in malice some harm to the Achaeans for which in counter-malice you take your revenge on me by hounding on these men against me? Better for me that you yourselves should devour my cattle and hoarded

1. As on p. 7 there is some ambiguity because of a change in bridal customs. Perhaps 'might offer a dowry with his daughter'.

goods. If you of Ithaca were the devourers, amends might indeed be made before long, because we of the household could accost you here and there in the town, asking aloud for our goods again till everything had been given back. Instead, you inflict upon my spirit miseries for which there is no redress.'

So he spoke in his indignation, and threw down the staff upon the ground. He had burst into tears, and compassion came upon the people. They all kept silent, not having the heart to answer him unkindly; all but Antinous, who rejoined:

'What words are these, Telemachus? How arrogantly you speak, how ungovernable you are in passion! You endeavour to put us to the blush; you hope to fasten disgrace on us. Listen; it is not the Achaean suitors who are to blame; it is your own mother with her unexampled trickery. Three years have passed – and a fourth will soon be gone – since she began to baffle her suitors' hearts. She gives hope to all, she promises every man in turn, she sends out messages here and there, yet all the while her purpose is far removed. Here is one scheme that she devised. She set up in her hall an ample web, long and delicate, and began to weave. At the same time she spoke to us: "Young men who after Odysseus' death have come here to woo me, you are eager for this marriage with me; nevertheless I ask your patience till I have finished weaving this robe, so that what I have spun may not be wasted and go for nothing; it is King Laertes' burial-robe, for the time when he is overtaken by the grim doom of distressful death. I dread reproach from Achaean women here for allowing one who had gathered great possessions to lie at his death without a shroud." So she spoke, and our wills consented. From that time on she would weave the great web all day, but when night came she would have torches set beside her and would unravel the work. For three years on end this trickery foiled the trusting suitors; but when seasons passed and the fourth year came, one of her maids who was in the secret revealed the truth, and we came upon her undoing the glossy web; so with ill grace she finished the work perforce.

'And now, this is your answer from the suitors; take it to heart yourself, and let all the Achaeans take it to heart as well. Tell your mother to leave this place and take for husband whatever man her father bids her and she approves. Or does she mean to continue plaguing the sons of Achaeans, setting her wits to work in things where Athene has favoured her so richly? Skill in exquisite workmanship, a keen mind, subtlety – these she has, beyond anything we have heard of even in the ladies of older times – the Achaean ladies of braided tresses like Tyro and Alcmene and garlanded Mycene; not one of these had the mastery in devising things that Penelope has, yet her last device went beyond all reason. So the suitors will not cease devouring your substance and possessions as long as she keeps the frame of mind that the gods are fostering in her now. To herself she is bringing great renown, but to you the loss of wealth and substance. We will neither return to our estates nor depart elsewhere till she takes for husband whichever of us Achaeans she may choose.'

Thoughtful Telemachus answered him: 'Antinous, I cannot unhouse against her will the mother who bore me and who bred me. My father, alive or dead, is for certain far away from here, and it is hard that I myself should pay heavy recompense to Icarius if of my own free will I tell my mother to leave this place. I shall suffer evil from him, her father, and dark powers also will do me evil because when my mother quits this house she will call down the grim Furies on me; and with fellow-men I shall be a byword. Never then will I utter the word you ask. If your own hearts reproach you now, leave my halls and look for your feasts elsewhere, changing from house to house to consume possessions that are your own. But if to yourselves it seems a better thing, a more desirable thing, to waste one man's substance and go scot-free – so be it, waste on! I for my part will call aloud on the deathless gods, hoping that Zeus will let requital be made at last; then you will perish in these same halls and it is I who shall go scot-free.'

So spoke Telemachus, and Zeus the Thunderer in response sent forth two eagles to fly down from a mountain height. For a while they flew as the wind wafted them, straining their wings side by side, but when they were right above the assembly-place with its hum of voices, they wheeled about and shook their thick feathers, sweeping low over all those there and boding death; then with their talons they tore at each other's cheeks and necks and sped away to the right, over the town and houses. The astonished people had followed the eagles with their eyes, and their hearts half guessed things that indeed were to come to pass. All this drew words from an aged lord, Halitherses the son of Mastor, who

beyond the rest of his generation was versed in the lore of birds
and wise in expounding it. Wishing well to all, he gave his in-
terpretation: 'Men of Ithaca, heed what I am about to say. My
exposition concerns the suitors first; a great wave of trouble is
rolling towards them. Odysseus will not be away from his kith
and kin much longer; indeed I think he is near already, sowing
seeds of death and destruction for every suitor here. As for the
rest of us in Ithaca, evil will fall on many of us as well. But let
us, while there is still time, consider how best to check these
men, or rather, let the men check themselves – they will gain
most by so doing now. I speak as no novice in prophecy; I am a
master. I see fulfilment now of everything I once said to subtle-
witted Odysseus himself when the Argives were embarking for
Ilium and he like the rest went aboard his vessel. I told him that
after many trials, after the loss of all his comrades, in the twen-
tieth year, known by none, he would come back to Ithaca. All
this is finding fulfilment now.'

Eurymachus, son of Polybus, answered him: 'Enough of this
now, old prophesier; go home and interpret omens there; save
your own children from threats of doom. This morning's omens
I claim to interpret better than you. There are many birds that
cross the sunlight, and not all of them have fateful meaning. No:
Odysseus has perished far from here, and I wish that you had
gone down to destruction with him. Then you would not have
uttered these tedious soothsayings, nor would you be fanning his
son's resentment in hopes of winning some gift for your own
household. I will tell you plainly, and what I tell you will come
to pass; if you with your store of ancient wisdom inveigle this
boy into defiance, he himself will be first to suffer; and as for you,
sir, we shall impose such a fine upon you as it will fret your soul
to pay; you will find it very hard to bear. To Telemachus I will
give this counsel publicly. Let him bid his mother go back to her
father's house; her kinsmen will prepare the wedding and charge
themselves with the many gifts that go with a beloved daughter.
Short of that, I think that the sons of the Achaeans will never
cease from the wooing that so distresses you, since, come what
may, we fear nobody, not even Telemachus with his eloquence;
and as for your prophecies, old babbler, we have no concern over
them either; they come to nothing and only make you the more
detested. And the reckless devouring of possessions will also go on

just as hitherto, and recompense will never be made so long as in this matter of marriage the queen keeps her suitors in suspense. As it is, we are waiting perpetually, each of us in rivalry with his neighbour over this paragon, instead of seeking those other women whom we might well enough choose to wed.'[1]

Thoughtful Telemachus answered him: 'Eurymachus, and you other overbearing suitors – on that matter I have no more to ask or to say; the gods know already where I stand, and all the Achaeans know. But now let me have a rapid ship and a crew of twenty to make the voyage out and back; I mean to go to Sparta and sandy Pylos to seek for news of my father's homecoming: he has been away from us too long. Perhaps some human witness will speak, perhaps I shall hear some rumour that comes from Zeus, a great source of tidings for mankind. If I hear that my father is alive and is on his way, I may hold my ground for a year more, despite my troubles; but if I hear he is dead and gone, then I will journey back to my own country and raise a cairn to him, then pay him in full his due of funeral honours and find a new husband for my mother.'

With these words he sat down, and Mentor in turn rose to speak – a friend of his noble father in other times. When Odysseus sailed, he had left all his household in Mentor's care, bidding him guard everything securely and respect the wishes of old Laertes. His words now were of honest purpose. 'Men of Ithaca, heed what I am about to say. I could wish that henceforward no sceptred king should set himself to be kind and gentle and equitable; I would have every king a tyrant and evil-doer, since King Odysseus goes utterly unremembered among the people that once he ruled with the gentleness of a father. Nor do I make it a reproach that the headstrong suitors should still do their deeds of violence in all the wickedness of their hearts, because they are staking their own lives when they grossly devour the substance of Odysseus, supposing that he will not return. It is the rest of you I am indignant with, to see how you all sit dumbly there instead of rebuking them and restraining them; you are many; the suitors are few.'

1. 'And 'tis her vertue makes us thus to strive
    Amongst ourselves who shall her favour win;
  For many other Ladies we could wive
    And be sufficiently delighted in.' HOBBES

Leocritus son of Euenor answered: 'Mentor, what words are these? Mischief-making fool, you are urging the people to restrain us. You will find it harder than you think to fight men who in truth outnumber you, and all this for the sake of a meal. If Odysseus of Ithaca himself surprised us feasting in his palace and were bent on thrusting us out again, his wife would have little joy at his homecoming, however much she had longed for it; no, there and then he would meet an ignominious end if he took up arms against such odds; your words are folly. But come, let the people here disperse, each to his own home; and Telemachus shall be sped upon his journey by Mentor and Halitherses, who are friends of his father from long ago. But he is more likely, I surmise, to remain here a good while yet; what news he learns he will learn in Ithaca, and he will never make this journey.'

So he spoke, letting the assembly break up at once. The people dispersed to their own houses; the suitors made for the palace of Odysseus.

But Telemachus went apart and down to the sea-shore. He washed his hands in the whitening water, then began to pray to Athene: 'Hear me, divine one, you who yesterday came to my house and bade me sail the misty ocean to seek for news of my father's homecoming after such years away. Alas, my purpose is being thwarted by the Achaeans – by the suitors most of all, in their malice and overweeningness.'

Thus he prayed, and Athene drew near to him; she had taken the form and voice of Mentor, and her words came forth in rapid flight:

'Telemachus, in your life hereafter you will be no coward and no fool, if indeed your father's fearless spirit has been instilled in you, sure as he was in accomplishing all that he said or put his hand to. Then this journey will not be vain or fruitless. But if you are no true son of Odysseus and Penelope, I cannot hope you should reach fulfilment of your desires. Few children are just what their father was; they are mostly worse, seldom better. But since in truth in your life hereafter you are to be no coward and no fool, and the wisdom of Odysseus has not altogether forsaken you, I am in good hopes that you will achieve your purpose. For the present, then, forget the suitors' plans and plotting; they are witless, reckless, lawless men, not discerning that near them there is death, and the black doom that in one day will destroy them all.

And the journey that you have set your heart on shall not elude you long; I am too good a friend for that – to your father first and now to you; I will rig a fast-sailing ship for you and will sail with you myself. But now go back to the house and join the suitors; get provisions ready and store them all in what holds them best, with jars for the wine and stout skins for the barley-meal that makes men's marrow. I myself in the town meanwhile will quickly gather a crew of volunteers. As for ships, there are plenty of them, new and old, in the island of Ithaca; I will choose whichever of them is best; it will not take long to fit her out, and then we will launch her on broad ocean.'

So spoke the daughter of Zeus, Athene. Telemachus did not linger long. He had heard the voice of the divinity, and now with uneasy heart he made his way home and found the bold suitors at the palace, flaying goats and singeing fat hogs in the open court. Antinous went to meet him smilingly, clasped his hand and addressed him thus:

'Telemachus – you of the lofty words and ungovernable passion – do not harbour thoughts of mischief now in deed or in word. I beg you, do as you used to do, eat and drink. All that you want the Achaeans will supply – a ship and well-chosen oarsmen – to speed you to holy Pylos in search of news of your noble father.'

Thoughtful Telemachus answered him: 'Antinous, among all you roisterers I can never eat undistressed or enjoy myself in peace. Is it not enough for you to have wasted so many good things of mine while I was still a child? Now I am full-grown, and with listening to this man's and that man's talk I have learned at last how things are, and all that I feel has gathered strength. So now I will strive as best I may to set the spirits of doom upon you, whether I go as far as Pylos or stay here in my own country. But indeed I shall go – the journey I speak of will not be thwarted – go as passenger, since a ship of my own is not forthcoming, or oarsmen of my own – that being doubtless what you have considered best.'

So speaking, he snatched his hand from Antinous' hand. The others began to mock and jeer, and among these young and scornful suitors one man would say such words as these: 'Beyond all question, Telemachus is plotting our deaths. He will bring back men to fight for him, from sandy Pylos or else from Sparta, so fierce is his appetite for slaughter. Or perhaps he means to make his way to the fruitful soil of Ephyra and bring from there those poisons that will destroy a man; he will drop them into our mixing-bowl, and that will be the end of us all.'

And another man among the scorners: 'Yet who knows if in his hollow ship he in his turn may not lose his way and perish far from his own people, just as Odysseus has? Then he would give us yet more trouble – there would be all his goods to be shared out among ourselves and the buildings once his to be given to his mother and her new husband.'

So they talked; but the boy passed down to his father's wide vaulted treasure-room; gold and bronze lay piled up here; there was clothing in chests and abundance of fragrant oil, with big jars of old sweet wine standing side by side along the wall, filled with their pure celestial liquor against the time when Odysseus perhaps after all his trials should come back home again. All this was shut in with double-doors, folding and fitting close, and day and night a housekeeper was about the place, using her shrewd wits to watch over everything. She was Eurycleia, daughter of Ops, Peisenor's son, and now Telemachus called her into the room and said: 'Dear nurse, draw me off into smaller jars some of this mellow wine, the choicest you have after the store you are saving still with your thoughts on luckless King Odysseus, hoping for his return to Ithaca after escape from death and doom. Fill a dozen jars, fit lids to them all, then take some skins, securely stitched, and pour crushed barley-grain into them, twenty measures of it. Let none but yourself know of this, and let all the stores be put together in readiness. I will take them away this evening when my mother has gone upstairs and begun to think of sleep. I am going to Sparta and sandy Pylos to gather what news I can of my father's homecoming.'

At these words his nurse Eurycleia shrieked aloud, and amid many lamentations uttered these rapid words: 'Dear child, how came such a thought into your heart? Why are you set on wandering over the wide world, you the sole heir and only child? King Odysseus has perished far from his home, in some strange land. And the moment that you depart, these men will be plotting harm against you, plotting how you may be killed by treachery and they themselves may divide your goods. No, stay here, settled upon your own domains; you have no call to go drifting wretchedly here and there over barren ocean.'

Thoughtful Telemachus answered her : 'Take heart, dear nurse; this purpose of mine came from a god. But now you must swear to tell my mother nothing of this until either some dozen days have passed or she herself misses me or hears from another of my going; we must not let tears stain her lovely face.'

So he spoke. The old woman swore by the gods she would not tell, uttering the solemn oath in the appointed words. This done, she went on to draw the wine in jars and pour the grain into skins securely stitched. Telemachus returned to the hall and joined the suitors.

And now the goddess of gleaming eyes turned her mind to another strategem. She walked through every part of the town in the likeness of Telemachus, came up to the oarsmen, each in turn, and bade them meet at the ship by evening. From Noemon son of Phronius she begged the use of the ship itself, and this he gladly promised.

The sun sank, and light thickened on every pathway. Then the goddess drew down the ship to the water, put on board all the tackle a decked vessel carries, and moored her at the harbour's mouth. The trusty oarsmen were gathered there together, and Athene heartened them every one. Then again she turned to another thing. She took her way to the house of King Odysseus, shed a delicious drowsiness on the suitors, clouded their wits as they drank and made them drop the cups from their hands. So instead of sitting longer there they rose and went off to the town to sleep, now that slumber was falling upon their eyelids. As for Telemachus, the goddess summoned him forth from the pleasant-sited palace and spoke to him in the form and voice of Mentor : 'Telemachus, your Achaean comrades are seated already at the oar, awaiting from you the word to start. Let us go now, and not hold back the voyage longer.'

And quickly, upon these words, Pallas Athene led the way while he followed the footsteps of the goddess. When they reached the ship at the sea's edge, there on the shore they found their comrades. Prince Telemachus spoke to them : 'Come, friends, let us fetch the provisions down; they are all laid ready at the palace; my mother knows nothing of all this, or the waiting-women either, apart from one whom I told the secret.'

And with these words he led the way while the men came

after. They brought everything out, then stowed it inside the decked ship as the king's own son directed. Telemachus went aboard the ship, but Athene walked ahead of him, then sat in the stern with Telemachus beside her. His comrades cast off the hawsers, boarded the ship in their turn and sat at the thwarts. Athene sent them a following breeze, a strong west wind that whistled over the wine-dark ocean. And now Telemachus urged his men to put their hands to the vessel's tackle. They heard his bidding; they raised the pinewood mast and stepped it inside the hollow mast-box; they made it fast with forestays, and with twisted hide ropes they hoisted the white sails. The wind bellied out the mid-sail, and the waves surging round the keel loudly lapped as the ship rode forward; over the waves she still sped on, hastening towards her journey's end. The men made the tackling fast all over the dark rapid ship, then set in place brimming bowls of wine and poured libations to the eternal, undying gods – above them all to the daughter of Zeus with her gleaming eyes. All night through and into the dawn the ship cut her pathway still.

BOOK III

TELEMACHUS, ATHENE, NESTOR

LEAVING the lovely lake of Ocean, the sun leapt upwards into the brazen sky,[1] bringing light for the Deathless Ones, bringing it too for mortal men who live on the earth that gives them grain. As the ship reached Pylos, the town of Neleus planted happily in its place, the townsmen, gathered on the sea-strand, were offering sacrifice of black bulls to raven-haired Poseidon. There were nine companies seated there, with five hundred men in each and with nine bulls in front of each. The sacrificers had tasted the inward parts and were burning the thigh-bones for the god; at this moment the crew put in; they brailed up and furled the sails of the steady ship, moored her and stepped ashore. Telemachus likewise stepped ashore, though Athene was before him. Then at once she spoke: 'You have no cause to be backward now, Telemachus, none at all. You have sailed thus far across the seas to question men about your father. ("Where did earth cover him? What was the doom he met?") Come, without more ado go up to Nestor, master of horsemanship; let us find what wisdom he has within him. Beg him yourself to answer you nothing but the truth – though indeed he will not tell you falsehood; he is too wise for that.'

Thoughtful Telemachus answered her: 'But how can I approach him, Mentor, how can I offer him a greeting? I am unpractised in subtle speech; and a young man questioning his elder – ought he not to be backward then?'

Athene answered: 'Some words, Telemachus, you will find in your own heart unaided: others a god will prompt you with; it was not, I think, under heaven's disfavour that you were born and bred.'

And quickly, upon these words, Pallas Athene led the way, while he followed the footsteps of the goddess. They reached the place where the men of Pylos were grouped and gathered, and where Nestor himself sat with his sons, while the rest around them prepared the meal, roasting the meat or planting it on the spits. When the Pylians sighted the newcomers, they all flocked towards them with friendly gestures, bidding them be seated. The

1. According to Professor Stella, an echo from Egyptian mythology.

first to near them was one of Nestor's children, Peisistratus; taking the hand of each in turn, he seated them on soft fleeces above the sea sand, by his father himself and his brother Thrasymedes. He gave them portions of the inwards and poured them wine in a golden cup, then spoke in greeting to Athene, daughter of Zeus who holds the aegis: 'Friend, offer prayer to Lord Poseidon, for it is his feast you have chanced upon at your coming here. And when you have prayed and poured libation in ritual fashion, then give your comrade the cup of honey-sweet wine to pour with; doubtless he too is a worshipper of the Deathless Ones, because all men stand in need of the gods. But he is a younger man – indeed of my own age – so it shall be to you first that I offer this cup of gold.'

With these words he put in her hand the cup of sweet wine, and Athene rejoiced to find him so right in thought and deed, because it was to her first that he had offered the cup of gold. At once she began an earnest prayer to Lord Poseidon: 'Hear me, Poseidon the Earth-Sustainer, and do not begrudge to us your suppliants accomplishment of our present task. To Nestor first grant glory, and to his sons; then give to these other men of Pylos acceptable recompense for this noble offering; lastly, grant to Telemachus and to me a safe journey homewards with accomplishment of the purpose for which we came in our dark and rapid ship.'

Thus she prayed, and all the while was herself bringing the prayer to its fulfilment. Then she gave Telemachus the cup, a noble two-handled one, and the son of Odysseus made his prayer to a like purpose.

When the men of Pylos had roasted the outer flesh and taken it from the spits, they divided the portions out and began the glorious feast. When they had eaten and drunk their fill, the first words came from the honoured master of the chariot, Nestor himself: 'Now that they have enjoyed the meal, we may rightly put questions to these guests. Friends, who are you? What land did you sail from, over the watery paths? Are you bound on some trading errand, or are you random adventurers, roving the seas as pirates do, hazarding life and limb and bringing havoc on men of another stock?'

Thoughtful Telemachus then answered; he had taken heart because Athene herself had emboldened him to question the king on his absent father: 'Nestor son of Neleus, glory of the Achaean race, you ask of what land we are, and I will give you answer in full. We come from Ithaca, with its town lying beneath Mount Neion. The errand I mean to tell you of is not my country's but my own. I am seeking news about my father – perhaps it has spread far enough abroad for me to encounter it. He is King Odysseus the undaunted; men say that he once fought beside you when he sacked the city of the Trojans. Now as for the rest who fought at Troy, we have heard already how each of them perished piteously; but with my father it is not so – even his death has been put by Zeus beyond our knowledge. No one can tell us certainly where he perished, whether killed by enemies on dry land or drowned at sea amid Amphitrite's billows. So I come as a suppliant to your knees, wondering if you can bring yourself to give me news of his piteous death; perhaps you saw it with your own eyes; perhaps you have heard from another man some tale of Odysseus in his wanderings; for his mother bore him to rare unhappiness. And do not soften your words to me in courtliness or compassion. Tell me outright and frankly what you have seen of him, and how. I beg you earnestly; if ever my father, brave Odysseus, made a promise to you and matched his words with deeds, in the Trojan land where you Achaeans were so hard pressed – remember those times and speak the truth.'

King Nestor answered: 'Friend, your words have brought back to me what wretchedness we endured at Troy, indomitable though we were in spirit – what we endured on shipboard also, roving for plunder over the misty sea, wherever Achilles led the way; and then all our fighting round the great city of King Priam. There it was that the bravest of us fell. There lies the warrior Aias, there lies Achilles, there Patroclus, peer of the gods in counsel, there also my own dear son Antilochus, so strong and noble, so swift a runner, so bold a fighter. And beyond their loss we suffered many calamities; what mortal man could recount them all? No; if you stayed five years, or six, searching out the tale of all the troubles the noble Achaeans bore – no, your patience would fail you first and you would make for home. Nine long years, with all our zeal and all our cunning, we plotted disaster for the Trojans, and only after much toil and pain did the son of Cronos bring fulfilment. There at Troy, none was bold enough to challenge Odysseus in strategy; in cunning of every fashion he was supreme – your own

royal father, if indeed you are his son; as I look at you I am filled
with wonder. All you say has a perfect rightness; who would
have thought a man so young could display such rightness in his
speech? Through the years at Troy, Odysseus and I never spoke at
variance in council or assembly; we were like-minded; the two of
us used our wits and watchfulness to plan how best the Argives
might win their purpose. But when we had sacked Priam's lofty
city, then Zeus devised sad homecomings for the Achaeans, since
not all of them were wise or righteous; thus many of them drew
an evil doom upon themselves through the deadly anger of Athene
– is she not the child of a mighty father? She set at odds the two
sons of Atreus, and in rash and unconsidered fashion they sum-
moned together all the Achaeans and made sunset the hour of
meeting. The people came there heavy with wine, and the brothers
told them the reason of this assembling. Menelaus bade them all
put their minds to returning homeward over the sea's broad back,
but in this he fell foul of Agamemnon; Agamemnon wished to
keep all the army there and to offer sacred hecatombs to appease
Athene's heavy anger – fool, unguessing that the goddess was not
to be won over so! The purpose of the immortal gods is not to be
lightly turned aside.

'There, then, the two brothers stood while high words passed
between them; the greaved Achaeans leapt from their seats in
monstrous uproar, with minds divided still. That night we rested,
brooding mischief against each other, for Zeus was devising grief
and misery. When morning came, some of us began to haul down
our ships to the sea and to put on board our chattels and our
low-girdled women. While half of the people still held back, keep-
ing on shore with their shepherd Agamemnon, the other half of
us went aboard and began our voyage; the ships sailed fast,
for the god had now smoothed the sea with its underworld of
waters. We came to Tenedos and offered sacrifice to the gods,
longing to be home; but return so soon was not the design of
Zeus; unpityingly, he brought disastrous dissension on us a second
time. Some of us turned their vessels Troyward again; these were
the comrades of King Odysseus the subtle-witted, and now once
more they fell in with the wishes of Agamemnon.

'I myself fled homewards with all the ships that had come with
me, because I was sure that the god intended evil. Brave Diomedes
likewise fled and urged his comrades to make for home. Then,

somewhat later, King Menelaus came to join us; he overtook our ships at Lesbos as we pondered over the long sea-journey that remained – should we sail north of craggy Chios and close by Psyra, keeping that island on our left, or south of Chios, past gusty Mimas? We were asking the god to show us some sign, and this he did, counselling a mid-ocean passage towards Euboea to escape disaster as soon as might be. Then a fair wind came whistling over us; our vessels raced through the teeming sea-paths, and during the night reached harbour at Geraestus; then we laid on Poseidon's altar the thighbones of many bulls, because we had passed that great stretch of sea. It was the fourth day when the comrades of Diomedes moored their ships off the coast of Argos; but I myself held on for Pylos, and the fair wind never slacked, from the hour when the god sent it forth to blow.

'Such was my own return, dear child; I had heard no news upon the way, and I still know nothing of the others – which among them returned safe home, which among them perished. True, I have heard certain things without stirring from my own house, and these, as is only right, I will tell you now; I will hide nothing. They say that the spearsmen Myrmidons came home safe, with the glorious child of dauntless Achilles at their head;[1] and Philoctetes, the far-famed son of Poias – he too came safe. Idomeneus also brought back to Crete all of his comrades that war had spared; the sea robbed him of none of them. But the son of Atreus – far away though your home may be, you too will have heard how he returned and how Aegisthus contrived his piteous death. Yet Aegisthus has paid a heavy price. How good it is that when a man dies, a son should be left after him! You see how Orestes took revenge on his father's murderer, that treacherous Aegisthus who slew majestic Agamemnon.'

Thoughful Telemachus answered him: 'Nestor son of Neleus, glory of the Achaean race, sharp indeed was the vengeance Orestes took, and the Achaeans will spread the fame of him far and wide for posterity to hear. Would that the gods would armour me also with such strength, to take my vengeance upon the suitors for the slights that cut me to the quick – so shameless they are and so presumptuous in everything that they plan against me. But for

1. 'The expert speare-men, every Myrmidon
   (Led by the brave heir of the mightie-soul'd
   Unpeerd Achilles) safe of home got hold.' CHAPMAN

me, I fear, for my father and for me the gods have allotted no such happiness; I have no choice but to bear what comes.'

King Nestor answered: 'Dear child, your words bring back to me what I have been told before, that your mother's suitors crowd your halls, defying yourself and plotting evil. Tell me then – do you consent to be thus humbled, or have the people throughout your land conceived detestation for you, moved by some more than human message?[1] Yet who knows if he will not return and take revenge for their acts of violence – Odysseus by himself, it may be, or Odysseus and all the Achaeans with him? If Athene of the gleaming eyes chose to befriend you now with the favour she lavished on Odysseus in the Trojan country where we Achaeans were so hard pressed – because never have I seen a god befriending a mortal openly as Pallas Athene in those days stood openly by Odysseus – if she chose to befriend you and care for you as she did for him, then more than one man among the suitors would never again think of marriage.'

Telemachus answered: 'Sir, even now I dare not think that what you speak of will come to pass; it is too hard a saying; it is beyond my grasp. For myself at least such a thing is past hoping for, even if the gods would have it so.'

But the goddess of gleaming eyes rejoined: 'What a word is this that has passed your lips, Telemachus! If a god so chooses, he may easily bring a man safe home, no matter from how far away. I for my part would gladly pass through a sea of troubles and then return to my own country and see the day of home-coming, rather than reach my country early and then be murdered at my own hearth, as Agamemnon was foully murdered by his own wife and by Aegisthus. Nevertheless it is true enough that death comes to all, and the gods themselves cannot ward it off, even from one they love, on the day when he is overtaken by the grim doom of distressful death.'

Telemachus answered: 'Mentor, no more of this, however deep our care may be. For the man we speak of, there can in truth be no homecoming; long before this the Deathless Ones appointed death and black doom for him. But enough; I seek knowledge now of something else. I wish to enquire of Nestor, because he beyond other men is acquainted with wisdom and with the rules of right,

1. Possibly an oracle, possibly some strange impulse of ill-defined origin. See p. 193.

for they say he has been king through three generations of men, and as I view him he seems like an immortal. Nestor son of Neleus, tell me truly of Agamemnon. How came the son of Atreus to die? Where was Menelaus? What manner of doom did cunning Aegisthus plan for the lord of wide domains who was so much mightier than himself? Was Menelaus not in Achaean Argos but wandering over the world elsewhere, that Aegisthus should pluck up heart to murder Agamemnon?'

Nestor the master of chariots answered: 'Child, I will tell you truthfully all you ask. One thing your own thoughts will tell you – what would have come to pass if Menelaus returning from Troy had found Aegisthus alive in those halls. Men would not even have heaped up earth over the slayer slain; dogs and carrion birds would have devoured him as he lay on the plain outside the city, and not one Achaean woman would ever have shed a tear for him, so dire was the deed that he devised. But no; we were still encamped at Troy, still fighting out many a contest, when Aegisthus, sheltered deep in the Argive plain that pastures horses, had begun already with his cajolings to tempt Agamemnon's wife. And at first Queen Clytemnestra would not consent to the deed of shame; she had discretion, and moreover there was a bard in the palace whom the king as he took ship for Troy had earnestly bidden to guard his wife. But when the gods' purpose ordained that she should yield, Aegisthus carried the bard away to a desert island and left him there to become the spoil of birds of prey;[1] the queen he took to his own home, and he and she were of one mind. He burned many thighbones on the hallowed altars of the gods, and he hung up many offerings also, things of gold and woven things, because now beyond all his hopes he had accomplished a perilous enterprise.

'In the meantime, Menelaus and I were sailing back from Troy together, linked in good fellowship. But when we had come as far as Sunium, the sacred promontory of Athens, Apollo with his gentle shafts visited and brought death to the helmsman of Menelaus as he held in his hands the steering-oar of the swiftly

1. 'But when the Gods these objects of their hate
    Dragg'd to destruction, by the links of fate;
    The bard they banish'd from his native soil,
    And left all helpless in a desart Isle:
    There he, the sweetest of the sacred train,
    Sung dying to the rocks, but sung in vain.' POPE

advancing ship; this was Phrontis, son of Onetor; he excelled all
the tribes of men in steering a ship when gales were high. So at
Sunium Menelaus stayed, though he would gladly have gone on;
he wished to bury this comrade of his and accomplish the funeral
rites. But when he in turn had launched his ships again on the
wine-dark sea and came in his rapid course to the sheer headland
of Maleia, then thundering Zeus devised a distressing voyage for
him, loosing upon him the violent breath of whistling winds and
rearing huge swollen waves that were mountains high. Then,
dividing his company, he brought some ships to that part of Crete
where the Cydonians lived by the waters of Iardanus. There is a
smooth cliff in the misty deep at the verge of the territory of
Gortyn; it stands sheer above the sea where the south-west wind
drives a great surge towards the western headland, and the narrow
rock-face checks the great surge on its way to Phaestus. Some of the
fleet reached this spot; the men barely escaped destruction, and as
for the ships, the billows shattered them on the reefs. The other
ships with their dark prows – five of them altogether – were driven
by wind and wave to Egypt. There Menelaus with his vessels went
to and fro among men who spoke an alien tongue, and he gathered
much substance and much gold. Meanwhile in Argos Aegisthus
had worked his shameful purpose; Agamemnon slain, he had ruled
seven years in Mycene rich in gold, and all the people were subject
to him. In the eighth year destruction came to him – Prince
Orestes returned from Athens to slay the man who had slain his
father, and having slain him, he gave a feast to the men of Argos
for the burying of his wicked mother and dastardly Aegisthus.
And on that same day Menelaus reached him, bringing the many
treasures his ships had been freighted with.

'And you, dear child – do not travel long away from home,
leaving behind you your possessions, leaving also those arrogant
men in your own halls; beware; you may find they have parted
your wealth among them and devoured it while you have gone
on a fruitless errand. Nevertheless there is one journey I earnestly
bid you make – I mean to Menelaus, because he has come only
lately from abroad, from a land whence none would hope to re-
turn if a storm had once driven him off his course into the vast
ocean there; so vast it is and so terrible that not even birds can find
their way back within a year. Go to him now with your ship and
crew; or if you would rather go by land, here at your service are

horses and a chariot, and here are my own sons, who will escort you to Lacedaemon, the home of Menelaus. Beg him yourself to answer you nothing but the truth – though indeed he will not tell you falsehood; he is too wise for that.'

As he ended, the sun sank and darkness came. Then Athene the goddess said: 'Sir, all your words are words well chosen. But now let your men cut up all the victims' tongues and mix the wine so that we may make libation to Poseidon and to the other Deathless Ones. After that, let us turn our thoughts to sleep; it is not too soon, for the light has sunk westward now; we ought not to stay seated long, even at a banquet of the gods; we should depart.'

So spoke the daughter of Zeus, nor did her words go unregarded. Pages poured water over the banqueters' hands, menservants brimmed the bowls with wine and poured the first drops into each man's cup; the company threw the tongues on the fire and stood up to pour wine over them. When all had made their libation and then had drunk to their heart's content, Athene and Prince Telemachus made as if to return to their ship. But Nestor checked them and said reproachfully: 'Zeus forbid – and the other deathless gods forbid – that you should go to your ship and away from me, as from some poor unprovided man who had not rugs and blankets enough in his house for his guests and himself to sleep softly in. No, I have blankets and fine rugs. Never shall my friend's own son, never shall the son of Odysseus go to sleep on a ship's deck while I am alive myself or while there are sons left after me in my halls to entertain any guest who comes to my house.'

Athene the goddess answered him: 'Sir, you endear yourself to us by what you have said so courteously. It is right – it is far the better choice – that Telemachus should do as you say. So he shall go back with you to sleep in your halls; but I myself will return to our ship, to hearten our crew and to tell them what their duties are; because only I among them can boast of the dignity of years; the rest are young men who have come with us in friendship, and they and Telemachus are all of one age. Tonight I will sleep by the dark ship, and in the morning I will set off to the country of the bold Cauconians; they owe me a debt, not a recent one nor yet a small one. But as for Telemachus – since in his quest he has come to your house, send him upon his remaining journey with a chariot and with a son of yours, and let the horses that you give him be the best for speed and endurance.'

So spoke the goddess of gleaming eyes, then went from them in the likeness of an osprey. Amazement came upon all who watched it, and aged Nestor was astounded to see such a thing with his own eyes. He took Telemachus by the hand and said : 'Dear child, I think you will prove no coward and no weakling; you are still a boy, yet even now you have gods to go with you and protect you. Of all the dwellers in Olympus, this is none but the daughter of Zeus, the Driver of Spoil, the Trito-born, she who always favoured your noble father among the Argives. O goddess, be gracious to us now; give good renown to myself, my children, the queen my wife; to you in turn I will sacrifice a heifer, a broad-browed un-worked yearling that never was brought beneath the yoke; such a beast will I offer to you, and her horns shall be overlaid with gold.'

Thus he prayed, and Pallas Athene heard him. Then he led the way, this honoured master of the chariot, walking to his own splendid halls before his sons and his sons-in-law. When they reached the king's noble palace, they began to take their places on higher and lower seats; when they were all there, the king himself mixed into the bowl a delicious wine, eleven years old, which only now the housekeeper had unstopped and opened. Such was the wine that Nestor drew on, and as he poured a libation from it he uttered earnest prayer to Athene, daughter of Zeus who holds the aegis.

Having made libation, and having drunk to their heart's content, the others went off to take their rest in their own homes; but as for the son of King Odysseus, the venerable Nestor kept him to sleep in the palace precincts, in an inlaid bed under the echoing portico; and beside him he put Peisistratus, already a spearsman and commander, though the only son still at home unmarried. The king himself slept in an inner room of the lofty palace, and the queen his wife shared his bed.

BOOK VIII

Dawn comes early, with rosy fingers. When she appeared, Nestor the master of the chariot rose from his bed, left his palace and took his seat on the polished stones (white, and glistening as though with oil) which were placed outside the lofty doors. In bygone days, Neleus had sat there and vied with the gods them-selves in counsel. But Neleus had been brought low by fate and had gone his way to Hades' house; it was Nestor who sat in his place now, to guard the rights of the Achaeans; his sceptre was in his hands. Around him his sons came clustering, having left the rooms where they had slept – Echephron and Stratius and Perseus and Aretus and noble Thrasymedes. After these five came Peisistratus, and they showed Telemachus to a seat beside them. Nestor himself was first to speak:

'Dear sons, you must lose no time in bringing my wishes to fulfilment; before any other divinity, I desire to propitiate Athene, because she came in visible presence to the sumptuous banquet of Poseidon. Let one of you go down to the plain to fetch a heifer; make sure that she comes as soon as may be, with a cowherd driving her; let another go to the dark vessel of bold Telemachus and bring all his comrades except for two; let a third order the goldsmith Laerces to come and gild the heifer's horns. The rest of you stay together here, but tell the serving-women inside to prepare a banquet in this great house, and to bring us seats and wood and sparkling water.'

So he spoke, and they all set about their tasks. Up from the plain came the heifer, from the ship came the comrades of bold Telemachus; the smith came likewise, bringing with him the tools of his metalwork, the implements of his craft, the anvil and hammer and shapely tongs that he worked his gold with; and Athene came to receive the sacrifice. The revered king offered the gold, and the smith deftly worked at it, twining the leaf all round the horns, to delight the goddess when she should see a gift so lovely. Stratius and Echephron led the beast forward by the horns, and Aretus came to them from the store-room, bearing a flowery-patterned vessel that held the lustral water; in his left hand he carried a basketful of crushed barley. Nearby stood the warrior Thrasymedes, with a sharp axe in his hand to fell the heifer, and Perseus held the bowl for the blood. Nestor, the aged lord of chariots, began the rite with the lustral water and the barley, and with these first ceremonies he prayed to Athene earnestly and threw in the fire the few hairs cut from the victim's head.

When they had prayed and had sprinkled the crushed barley-grains, the son of Nestor, Thrasymedes, took his stand forthwith beside the beast and struck her; the axe cut the sinews of the neck and stunned the senses of the heifer, and at this the women called out aloud – Nestor's daughters and daughters-in-law and Eurydice his revered wife, eldest of the daughters of Clymenus.

Then the young men raised the victim's head from earth and held it, and Prince Peisistratus cut the throat; the dark blood gushed out, and the life departed from the bones. Then quickly they divided the flesh; at once they cut out the thigh-bones in ritual fashion, covered them with the fat twice folded, and laid the raw meat above. The old king went on to burn these offerings on cloven wood and to pour glowing wine upon them; the young men came to his side holding five-pronged forks. When the thigh-bones were quite consumed and they had tasted the inward parts, they sliced and spitted the rest; they grasped the spits that went through the meat, and in this fashion they roasted it.

Meanwhile Telemachus had been bathed by Nestor's youngest daughter; this was the lovely Polycaste; she bathed him, anointed him well with oil, then dressed him in handsome cloak and tunic. He came from the bath looking like a god, and then passed on to sit by Nestor, the shepherd of the people.

Having roasted the outer flesh and drawn it from off the spits, they sat down and began to feast, and faithful servants attended on them, pouring wine into the golden cups. When they had eaten and drunk their fill, Nestor the lord of chariots was first to speak:

'Come, my sons; bring Telemachus horses with flowing manes and yoke them to his chariot to let him speed forward on his way.'

So he spoke; they heard and obeyed, and quickly yoked the swift horses to the chariot; the housekeeper put in bread and wine, with such other dainties as heaven-protected princes eat. Telemachus mounted the sumptuous chariot; Prince Peisistratus mounted next to him, grasped the reins and plied the whip; the pair of horses left the hill-town of Pylos, sped down eagerly to the plain, and all day long kept the yoke swinging as they held it up this side and that.

The sun sank, and light thickened on every pathway. Now they had reached the town of Pherae and come to the house of Diocles, son of Ortilochus son of Alpheus; that night they slept there, and Diocles gave them hospitality.

Dawn comes early, with rosy fingers. When she appeared, they yoked their horses, mounted the sumptuous chariot, then drove out through gateway and echoing portico. Thence they passed to the level wheat-land, then hastened on to their journey's end with all the speed of their straining horses.

The sun sank, and light thickened on every pathway.

BOOK IV

TELEMACHUS, MENELAUS, HELEN

THE princes came to the caverned vale of Lacedaemon, and drove
to the palace of Menelaus. They found the king in his own halls,
celebrating with many clansmen a wedding feast for his daughter
and his son as well. The girl was now being sent as bride to the
son of Achilles the resistless; even in Troy her father had promised
and pledged himself to give her in marriage thus, and now the
gods were bringing this to accomplishment; he was sending her
with chariot and horses to the famous city of the Myrmidons,
whose king was her bridegroom. For the wife of his son, Megapen-
thes, he had sought from Sparta the daughter of Alector; this son,
courageous and dearly loved, had been begotten upon a slave-
woman, for the gods had given no child to Helen when once she
had borne Hermione, a girl as lovely as golden Aphrodite.

So guests were feasting in the great lofty hall, neighbours and
clansmen of glorious Menelaus; they were making merry, and in
their midst an inspired bard was singing to the lyre, while a pair
of tumblers along the line of guests twisted and twirled to the
rhythms of the singer.[1]

Meanwhile the travellers with their chariot – Prince Telemachus
and the noble son of Nestor – had stopped short at the entrance
to the palace; Lord Eteoneus, a zealous attendant on Menelaus,
came out and saw them and then went back through the hall
again to give the news to the shepherd of the people; standing be-
side him, he swiftly said:

'King Menelaus, here are two strangers; both seem to belong
to the race of great Zeus himself. Tell me, sir; shall we unyoke
their rapid horses, or send them on to some other host who will
entertain them?'

Indignantly, Menelaus answered: 'Etoneus son of Boethus, be-
fore this day you have seemed no fool, but now you speak with
the foolishness of a child. You and I have come back to our home
at last, and hope that Zeus will spare us sorrow in days to come;
but before returning, how often have we not both received the

---

1. 'And now they merry sat that bidden were,
    Making good chear, and hearing Voice and Fiddle,
    And wondring at two Tumblers that were there,
    That moving to the time stood in the middle.' HOBBES

hospitality of others! Quick now, unyoke the horses, and bring the guests inside to enjoy the feast.'

So he spoke; Eteoneus hastened back through the hall, calling on other brisk attendants to come with him. They unyoked the sweating horses and tied them at the mangers, putting wheat in front of them mixed with white barley, and tilting the chariot against the glittering walls. The guests themselves, escorted into the stately palace, were filled with wonder at what they saw in the monarch's house; for a radiance like that of sun or moon filled the high halls of King Menelaus. When they had both gazed their fill, they went to the polished baths to bathe. They were washed by maids, were anointed with oil, and had tunics and woollen cloaks put round them; then they took their seats beside Menelaus the son of Atreus. Another maid brought water in a fine golden jug and poured it over their hands for washing, holding a silver basin below; then she drew up a polished table by them. The trusted housekeeper came and put bread where they could reach it; she had many kinds of food as well, and gave ungrudgingly of her store. Then with courteous gesture King Menelaus said:

'Eat and be merry. When you have had your meal, we will ask you who you are. Surely you two have not shamed your parentage; you belong to the race of heaven-protected and sceptred kings; no lesser parents could have such sons.'

And with these words he took in his hands and set before them the fat chine of a roasted ox that had been reserved as his own portion, and the two stretched out their hands to the dishes there. When they had eaten and drunk their fill, Telemachus said to Peisistratus, leaning close to him so that the others should not hear: 'Son of Nestor, friend that my heart delights in, see how these echoing halls are bright with the glittering of bronze and gold and amber and silver and ivory. The inner courts of Olympian Zeus must surely be like this house, so numberless are the splendours of it; awe comes over me as I look.'

But Menelaus had overheard, and in response he addressed the two: 'With Zeus, dear children, no mortal man may compare himself; the palace of Zeus is everlasting, and so is everything that is his. But among mankind it may well be that few or none can rival me in possessions. I endured much and I wandered far, but in the eighth year after Troy I brought my ships home, and

these things in them. I passed through Cyprus, Phoenicia, Egypt;
I found my way to the Ethiopians and the Sidonians, the Erem-
bians and the Libyans. In Libya the ewes have lambs three times
in the course of the maturing year, and these are already horned
at birth; neither lord nor shepherd in that land runs short of
meat or cheese or of sweet milk, for milk is there for the lambs to
suck continually. But while I was wandering in those lands and
amassing goods in plenty, a stranger caught my brother un-
guarded and killed him treacherously, through the plotting of his
accursed wife. Hence it is not in joy of heart that I am master of
these possessions – your parents, whoever they may be, have
doubtless told you the tale already. I have had many things to
bear; I have had to see this house decline – the house well planted
in its place that once was so full of noble things. Yet I wish to
heaven I had continued here with but a third of my former
wealth, if only those others had lived on with me – the men who
died then in spacious Troy, far from the pasturelands of Argos.
But though as I sit here in my palace I grieve and lament often
enough for all of these – there are times when I ease my heart
with mourning, there are other times when I refrain, because
mourning strikes a chill through a man and after a while he tires
of it – though regret for all of them is sharp, there is none for
whom I grieve so deeply as for one man who when I remember
him makes food and sleep loathsome to me, because among all
Achaeans no other toiled and achieved so much as Odysseus did.
Yet for him there was only to be misery, and for me unforgettable
distress at his absence from us through all these years. Is he
alive? Is he dead? Not even that do we know at all. In his own
home they must surely make lamentation for him – old Laertes,
faithful Penelope, and Telemachus whom he left in his house a
babe in arms.'

So he spoke, and in the heart of Telemachus he stirred the
desire to lament Odysseus; at his father's name the boy let fall a
tear to the ground, but with both hands held his crimson cloak
in front of his eyes. Menelaus saw him, and wondered awhile
within himself if he ought to leave him to utter his father's name
or if he himself should question him and put all his answers to
the test.

While he was inwardly debating, Helen came forth from her
fragrant lofty room; she had the semblance of golden-shafted

Artemis. Adraste drew out a handsome chair for her, Alcippe brought a soft woollen rug, Phylo added the silver work-basket that was Alcandre's gift to Helen. Alcandre was wife of Polybus, a citizen of Egyptian Thebes (and houses there are richest in precious things). To Menelaus, the husband had given two silver baths, two tripods and ten talents of gold; the wife on her part had brought lovely gifts for Helen, bestowing on her a golden distaff and a silver basket with wheels to it and with rims finished off with gold. This it was that the handmaid Phylo brought forward and put beside the queen; it was full of dressed yarn, and over it lay stretched the distaff with violet wool already on it. Helen now sat down in the chair, with a stool beneath her feet; then without more ado she began to ask her husband everything.

'Have we heard already, Menelaus, the names that our guests give themselves? Shall I hide or tell what I am sure of? Yes, my heart urges me to speak. Never, I think, have I seen such likeness in man or woman – amazement seizes me as I look. This boy is far too much like Odysseus to be any other than his son; surely he is Telemachus, the child that the hero left behind him, a babe in arms, when you Achaeans went up to Troy, planning bold war for the sake of shameless me.'[1]

Yellow-haired Menelaus answered her: 'Wife, your thought has become my thought as well. Odysseus had just such feet and hands; his head and his hair were like this boy's; his eyes had the same glance. And a moment ago, when I recalled Odysseus and spoke of his toils and sufferings for me, this guest of ours let his eyes pour down salt tears, though he raised his crimson cloak to hide them.'

Peisistratus, Nestor's son, replied: 'King Menelaus, son of Atreus and leader of the people: this is indeed Odysseus' son, just as you say, but he is bashful; he is a newcomer here and would think it wrong to speak in your presence all unasked when both of us are hanging upon your words as upon a god's. But Nestor, the honoured lord of chariots, sent me out to escort him here, since he longed to see you and hoped you might offer him some helpful counsel or helpful action. A son whose father is far away has a hard life in his own halls if he has no others to befriend him; so with Telemachus; his father is far away, and in his

1.   '. . . with other *Greeks* to *Ilium*
      He went to fetch away this Monky me.' HOBBES

own land he has no others to keep him out of affliction's reach.'

King Menelaus answered him: 'Ah then, this guest of mine is the son of a friend very dear indeed, one who time after time faced hardship because of me, one whose coming I meant to welcome more than that of all other Argives if Zeus the Thunderer of Olympus had granted us both a safe voyage home in our rapid vessels. I would have made some city in Argos his dwelling-place and built him a palace in it; I would have brought him there from Ithaca with his child and chattels and all his people; I would have emptied a city for him, one of those that are near this and are in my own dominions. Then we should often have met each other here, and nothing would have parted us two in the pleasant converse of host and guest, until death's dark cloud overshadowed us. But that, no doubt, was begrudged us by the god himself, who robbed that unhappy man, as he robbed no other, of the hope of homecoming.'

So he spoke, and in all their hearts he stirred the desire of lamentation; Argive Helen began to weep, daughter of Zeus himself; Telemachus wept, and Menelaus the son of Atreus; nor could Nestor's son refrain from tears, because now there came before his mind the great Antilochus whom the son of radiant Dawn had slain. And remembering him, he uttered these rapid words:

'Son of Atreus, in Nestor's house when we spoke of you or asked about you among ourselves, the old king would say that no one on earth was more wise than you. Can you bring yourself to listen to me? These tears at evening over our meal give me no pleasure: another day will be breaking soon. Not that I grudge lamentation for any man who has died and met his fate; this is the only tribute left for beings all born to misery – the shorn hair and the tears running down the cheeks. And among the dead is a brother of my own, not the least brave among the Argives; you yourself may well have known him; as for me, I was never with him and never saw him, but others tell me that few could match Antilochus, a swift runner and fine fighter.'

Yellow-haired Menelaus answered him: 'Friend, those were wise words, and an older man could speak and act no better. You are your father's son; your wisdom in speech comes from him. There is no mistaking the child of a man whom the son of Cronos marked out for happiness both at birth and bridal; witness the favours bestowed on Nestor through all his days – for himself an old age of comfort in his own palace, for his children wisdom, and prowess with the spear.

'Come then, let us put aside the weeping that came upon us just now; let us turn our thoughts to the meal again, and let someone pour water over our hands. As for Telemachus and myself, tomorrow morning there will be time enough to exchange our thoughts.'

So he spoke; his zealous attendant Asphalion poured water over their hands, and they reached again for the dishes set before them.

Then a new thought came to Zeus-born Helen; into the bowl that their wine was drawn from she threw a drug that dispelled all grief and anger and banished remembrance of every trouble. Once it was mingled in the wine-bowl, any man who drank it down would never on that same day let a tear fall down his cheeks, no, not if his father and mother died, or if his brother or his own son were slain with the sword before his eyes. Such were the cunning powerful drugs this daughter of Zeus had in her possession; they had been a gift from a woman of Egypt, Polydamna wife of Thon. In Egypt, more than in other lands, the bounteous earth yields a wealth of drugs, healthful and baneful side by side; and every man there is a physician; the rest of the world has no such skill, for these are all of the family of Paeon.

When Helen had added this elixir and ordered the wine to be poured out, she in her turn spoke again: 'Menelaus, you who are son of Atreus, and you our guests who are sons of great men: we know that Zeus in his sovereignty gives good and evil, now to this man and now to that, since all things are in his power. But here and now I would ask you to rest here seated, enjoying the feast, enjoying the flow of talk. I will tell you something that fits the hour. I cannot tell you, cannot recount, each single exploit of staunch Odysseus; but here is one thing that he dared heroically and achieved in the land of Troy where you Achaeans were so hard pressed. He disfigured himself with ignominious stripes, threw dismal wrappings over his shoulders, and in servile shape passed into the city of the Trojans. They did not heed him; I alone knew him for what he was; I began to probe him, and he to evade me with his cunning; but when I went on to bathe him and anoint him, when I gave him clothes and swore a great oath that I would not tell of his presence in the city before he was back among his own huts and ships, then at last he disclosed to me the whole design of the Achaeans. Before he returned to the Argive camp his long sharp sword had killed many Trojans; moreover he took back ample news. Then the other women in the city made loud lament, but my own heart was filled with joy, because my desire had turned by now to going back home again, and I wept, too, late, for the blindness that Aphrodite sent me when she made me go there, away from my own dear land, and let me forsake my daughter and bridal room and a husband who fell short in nothing, whether in mind or in outward form.'

Menelaus answered: 'Indeed, my wife, all you have said has been said well. It has been my lot to be acquainted with the thoughts and counsels of many exalted men and to range widely over the world, but never anywhere have I seen so fine a man, so indomitable a man as Odysseus was. What mastery, what heroic mettle he showed us inside the wooden horse! There we all sat, we Argive chieftains, bringing death and doom to men in Troy. There came a moment, Helen, when you yourself approached the spot – approached it, doubtless, at the prompting of some divinity who wished to give glory to the Trojans; and Prince Deiphobus had escorted you. Three times you circled that hollow snare and felt all round it, and you called by name all the chieftains of the Danaans, making your voice like the voice of each man's wife in turn. I and the son of Tydeus sat in the midst with great Odysseus and heard your voice ringing clear, and we other two were eager enough to leap up and to issue forth, or else to answer you instantly from within; but Odysseus checked us and thwarted our eagerness. Then all the rest of us kept silent; one Achaean only would gladly have answered you – Anticlus, but Odysseus with his powerful hands held the man's mouth firmly shut, and did not let go till Athene drew you away again; that was the saving of all of us Achaeans.'

But thoughtful Telemachus said in answer: 'Menelaus, leader of your people: what you tell us makes it all the harder. All this did not save him from lamentable destruction, nor could it have done if the heart within him had been of iron. But now give us leave to go to rest, to be lulled by slumber and be content.'

So he spoke, and Argive Helen ordered her maids to put out bedsteads inside the portico, to lay down first fine rugs of crimson, then to spread coverlets over them and fleecy blankets above again. The maids left the hall with torch in hand and prepared the beds. Then a page led the way for the guests, and there they lay down to sleep in the forecourt of the house, Prince Telemachus and the noble son of Nestor. But the son of Atreus slept in an inner part of the lofty house, and beside him lay long-robed Helen, peerless among all womankind.

Dawn comes early, with rosy fingers. When she appeared, Menelaus put on his clothes and sprang from his bed; he slung the keen sword about his shoulders, fastened his sandals under his glistening feet and went out from his room, like a god to look upon. He came and sat by Telemachus and addressed him:

'What errand has brought you here, Telemachus, over the sea's expanse into lovely Lacedaemon? A public or a private matter? Tell me truthfully.'

Thoughtful Telemachus answered him: 'King Menelaus, son of Atreus and leader of your people – I came in the hope that you might give me some tidings of my father. The goods of my house are all being eaten up; my rich farmlands are ruined already; my palace is thronged with enemies who daily slaughter my flocks of sheep and my swaying oxen; they have come as suitors to my mother and their arrogance goes beyond all bounds. And so I come as a suppliant to your knees, wondering if you can bring yourself to give me news of my father's piteous death; perhaps you saw it with your own eyes; perhaps you have heard from another man some tale of Odysseus in his wanderings; for his mother bore him to rare unhappiness. And do not soften your words to me in courtliness or compassion. Tell me, outright and frankly, what you have seen of him, and how. I beg you earnestly: if ever my father, brave Odysseus, made a promise to you and matched his words with deeds, in the Trojan land where you Achaeans were so hard pressed – remember those times and speak the truth.'

In fierce indignation the king answered: 'Accursed cowards, so eager to sleep in a brave man's bed! But listen – as when a fallow deer leaves the twin fawns just born to her in slumber in some great lion's den, while she herself goes roving and browsing over the mountain spurs and the grassy hollows, but then the lion returns to his lair and strikes the two sucklings with hideous death, so will Odysseus strike these suitors with hideous death. O

Father Zeus and Athene and Apollo, grant that Odysseus might come upon them in such a form as when long ago in happy Lesbos he rose at a challenge, wrestled with Philomeleides and gave him a mighty fall, so that all the Achaeans were filled with joy – in such a form might he join in contest with the suitors! They would find death quickly, all of them, and their hoped-for wedding would have a bitter taste. But as for what you ask me so earnestly, I will say nothing beside the mark, slur over nothing, misrepresent nothing. There are certain things revealed to me by the ancient sea-god who is unerring; of these I will not hide or conceal a word.

'I was in Egypt – longing to make for home but still kept lingering by the gods because I had failed to offer them acceptable hecatombs. Now, away from the shore, in the wash of waves, there lies an island that men call Pharos, as far out as a ship can sail in a whole day with a fresh breeze behind her. It has a fine harbour; crews put in there to draw their water from deep places, and then launch their ships from there on to the high seas. In this place the gods kept me for twenty days; there was not a sign of breezes blowing seaward, such as speed a ship over the wide expanse of ocean. And now our food would have failed utterly, and with it the courage of my men, had not a goddess had pity on me and rescued me; this was Eidothea, daughter of mighty Proteus the ancient sea-god. I touched her heart as I had no other's when she came upon me wandering in solitude apart from my companions (they had kept roaming about the island, fishing with bent hooks, because hunger gnawed their bellies). She halted near me and addressed me: "Stranger, have you no sense, no wits at all? Or are you so reckless wilfully? Do you take pleasure in your distress? All this while you have stayed a prisoner in this island, unable to contrive deliverance while your men grow more and more disheartened." So she spoke, and I answered her: "Goddess, whoever you may be, I will tell you all. Not by my own choice do I stay a prisoner here; I must have offended the Deathless Ones whose home is wide heaven itself. Rather it is for you to tell me – because gods know everything – which of the Deathless Ones it is who has thwarted me in my journeying and keeps me pent here. Tell me also of my return – how am I to go forth again over teeming ocean?" So I spoke, and at once the goddess answered: "I will tell you, stranger, without deceit. An ancient

sea-god comes often to this place – he is unerring and he is death-
less – Proteus of Egypt, a vassal of Poseidon who knows the sea
throughout all its depths; they say that he is the father who begot
me. If only you could ambush and capture him ! Then he will tell
you of your return, the means to pass over teeming ocean and all
the long journey home. And beyond all this, he will tell you, if
so you wish (are you not a king?), what good or evil has come to
pass in your own palace while you have been far away on your
long and toilsome journey."

'So she spoke, and I answered her, "You yourself must contrive
some way to entrap this ancient god; if not, he may see me or
sense me all too soon, and then he will elude me. It is hard for a
mortal man to bend an immortal to his will."

'These were my words. The goddess answered: "So be it,
stranger; I will tell you all without deceit. When the sun in its
course has reached mid-sky, the sage old sea-god leaves his ocean
– the west wind blows then, and the ruffled water is dark enough
to hide him. Once ashore, he lies down to sleep under the arching
caves, and around him is a throng of seals, the brood of the lovely
child of Ocean; they too have come up through the grey waters,
and they too lie down to sleep, smelling rankly of the deep brine
below. To this spot I myself will take you as soon as tomorrow
dawns, and will range you all side by side – because you must
carefully choose three comrades, the bravest you have beside your
vessels. I will tell you all the deluding arts of the ancient god. First
he will pass along all the seals and count them; then, having
viewed them and made his reckoning, he will lie down among
them all like a shepherd among his flock of sheep. As soon as you
see him lying down, you must all summon up your strength and
courage and hold him fast there despite his struggles and his en-
deavours to elude you. He will seek to foil you by taking the
shape of every creature that moves on earth, and of water and of
portentous fire; but you must hold him unflinchingly and you
must press the harder. When at length he puts away all disguise
and questions you in the shape he had when you saw him rest-
ing, then cease from your constraint; then, O king, let the ancient
sage go free and ask him which of the gods is thwarting you and
how you are to reach home again over teeming ocean."

'So she spoke, and sank down through the billowy sea. Then I
set out once more to where the ships were beached on the sand,

and as I walked there my heart was thronged with thoughts. I reached my ship at the sea's edge, and we made our supper. And then mysterious night came on, and we sank to rest by the breaking surf.

'Dawn comes early, with rosy fingers. When she appeared, I began to walk along the shore of the wide-wayed ocean, with many a prayer to the gods meanwhile. I had three of my companions with me, those that on any venture I trusted most.

'The goddess, I said, had sunk down through the wide and yielding waters; now she returned, bringing back the skins of four seals, all newly flayed – such was her scheme to deceive her father. She hollowed out hiding-places for us inside the sea-sand, then sat there waiting; when we had come right up to her, she made us lie down side by side and threw a skin over each of us. Our lying there might have been intolerable, for the hideous stench of the briny creatures distressed us monstrously; who would choose a sea-calf for bedfellow? But the goddess found us rescue and remedy. She brought every one of us ambrosia and put it underneath his nostrils; it smelt delectably; and so she countered the bestial stench. All the morning we waited there in patience; then the seals came thronging out of the sea and lay side by side near the breaking billows. At noon the old god came out of the sea as well, and found the sleek seals already there; he began to pass down the whole line of them, counting them, and among his flock he counted ourselves first of all, never guessing that treachery was afoot; after this, he himself lay down. Then with a shout we rushed upon him and locked our arms about him; but the ancient god had not forgotten his craft and cunning. He became in turn a bearded lion, a snake, a panther, a monstrous boar; then running water, then a towering and leafy tree; but we kept our hold, unflinching and undismayed, and in the end this master of dreaded secrets began to tire. So he broke into speech and asked outright:

' "Son of Atreus, which of the gods taught you this strategy, to entrap and overpower me thus? What do you want from me?"

'These were his words. I answered him: "Old seer, you know that already; why seek to lead me astray with questions? You know already how all this while I have stayed a prisoner in this island, unable to contrive deliverance and eating my heart away. Tell me yourself – since the gods know everything – which of the Deathless Ones it is who has thwarted me in my journeying and keeps me pent here. Tell me also of my return – how am I to go forth again over the teeming ocean?"

'So I spoke, and at once he answered: "Plainly, the thing demanded of you was to make choice offerings to Zeus and the other gods before you set sail; that was the way to reach your own country soonest over the wine-dark sea. Fate ordains that you shall not see your kith and kin, shall not reach your land and well-sited house until you have sailed once more into the Nile's rain-fed waters and sacrificed sacred hecatombs to the deathless gods whose home is wide heaven; then, not before, the gods will grant you the homeward journey that you desire."

'These were his words, and my heart sank to hear him bid me return to Egypt over the misty sea, a long voyage and a hard one. Nevertheless I answered him: "Old sage, I will do all this as you instruct me. But tell me this too, in full and truly. Have all the Achaeans returned by ship unharmed, all that Nestor and I left behind when we sailed from Troy, or has one or another of them perished by some unlooked-for fate, perhaps aboard his own ship, perhaps in his kinsmen's arms when his thread of war was spun to its end?"

'So I spoke, and at once he answered: "Son of Atreus, why ask me thus? Better for you not to know these things, not to learn what my mind holds. I tell you, you will not be long dry-eyed when you have heard the whole truth. Of those you ask for, many have died, many are left. Two leaders alone among the mailed Achaeans perished as they were journeying home (as for the war, you yourself were there); one is alive but kept a prisoner by ocean stretching wide around him. Aias came to his doom among his long-oared ships. Poseidon dashed his vessels first against the great rocks of Gyrae, yet granted him escape from the sea; and indeed he would have been saved from doom, loathed by Athene though he was, had he not in sheer mad passion uttered an overweening boast; he said that in the gods' despite he had safely passed the great gulf of ocean. But Poseidon heard his vaunting words, seized his trident forthwith in his powerful hands and struck and shattered one of those rocks; one part remained, the other hurtled into the sea, the block that Aias had rested on when he spoke those wild and whirling words; it carried him down into the vast surge of ocean, and he drank the brine and perished there. As for your own brother – hitherto with his hollow ships he had escaped and been saved from doom, because Lady Hera had protected him. When he was very near to reaching the lofty headland of Maleia, a violent wind snatched him away, deeply groaning, over the teeming sea to the border of that land which in earlier days had housed Thyestes and housed now his son Aegisthus. Yet by that way too there appeared a prospect of safe return, for the gods made the wind fair again, and Agamemnon and all his men reached home. In jubilation he set foot in his own country; stooped down to his native soil, kissed it over and over, and dropped many a scalding tear in joy to see his own land again. But a watcher perched above had spied him – one whom the treacherous Aegisthus had led to the place and posted there, promising in reward two talents of gold. For a year this man had been keeping guard, lest Agamemnon should pass him unseen and brace his heart to a hero's prowess.[1] The watcher ran to the palace to tell his master, and Aegisthus at once laid his foul snare. He chose a score of his strongest townsmen and put them in ambush on one side of the palace; on the other side he ordered a banquet to be prepared. Then he rode forth with chariot and horses to invite Agamemnon to his banquet, but all the while the thoughts of his heart were evil. From shore to city he drove a king who foresaw nothing of his doom; he feasted his guest, then struck him down as a man strikes down an ox at stall. Nor was one left of the comrades of the son of Atreus who had gone with him to Aegisthus' halls;[2] they were all slain there in the palace."

'So he spoke; my spirit was crushed within me; I sank down on the sand and wept, and my heart lost the desire to live, or to look longer upon the sunlight. I wept, I wallowed upon the ground till the bout of bitterness was past. Then the old god began again: "Son of Atreus, cease from this long and stubborn weeping; we shall find no remedy in that. Rather endeavour as soon as may be to return to your land again. Perhaps you will find the murderer living; perhaps Orestes already will have slain him, and you may join in the funeral feast."

'So he spoke, and for all my sorrow I felt my heart and soul and

1. W. B. Stanford rightly points out that a Homeric hero, like traditional heroes elsewhere (e.g. the Celtic Cuchulain), did not summon up his full prowess in a moment; he must brace himself first; the lion must lash himself with his tail.

2. I translate l. 537 as emended by N. E. Crosby.

manhood revive within me; then in rapid flight my words went
out to him: "For these two I now know the truth. But there is a
third; tell me of him – the man still alive but kept a prisoner by
ocean stretching wide around him."

'So I spoke, and at once he answered: "It is Laertes' son, whose
home is in Ithaca. I have seen him on a certain island, weeping
most bitterly: this was in the domains of the nymph Calypso,
who is keeping him with her there perforce and thwarting return
to his own country. He has no ships and oars and crew to take
him over the wide expanse of ocean.

' "As for yourself, King Menelaus, it is not your fate to die in
Argos, to meet your end in the grazing-land of horses. The Death-
less Ones will waft you instead to the world's end, the Elysian
fields where yellow-haired Rhadamanthus is. There indeed men
live unlaborious days. Snow and tempest and thunderstorms never
enter there, but for men's refreshment Ocean sends out continu-
ally the high-singing breezes of the west. All this the gods have
in store for you, remembering how your wife is Helen and how
her father is Zeus himself."

'So he spoke, and sank down through the billowy sea. I and my
comrades made for the ships again, and as I walked there my heart
was thronged with thoughts. I reached my ship at the sea's edge,
and we made our supper. And then mysterious night came on,
and we sank to rest by the breaking surf.

'Dawn comes early, with rosy fingers. When she appeared, we
hauled our vessels down to the radiant sea, and in the vessels we
set the masts and the sails in place. The men went on board, sat at
the thwarts in accustomed order, and dipped their oars in the
whitening sea. Thus I brought my ships once again into the
streams of the rain-fed Nile, and I offered acceptable hecatombs.
Having thus appeased the anger of the immortal gods, I raised a
cairn to Agamemnon, so that his glory should not die out. This
done, I began the voyage back, and the Deathless Ones gave me a
following wind and brought me soon to my own country.

'But come; stay on in my palace here till a dozen days have
passed. Then I will mark your departure handsomely; I will give
you fine gifts, three horses and a glittering chariot; and beyond
these I will give you a noble goblet; you may make libation in it
to the immortal gods and so remember me all your days.'

Thoughtful Telemachus answered him: 'Son of Atreus, do not

ask me to linger here so long. I myself indeed would gladly sit for another year beside you and never fret for my home and kindred, so charmed I am as I drink in your words and tales. But there are my comrades in holy Pylos, chafing already while you detain me here. As for gifts, whatever you think fit to give me, let it be something I may treasure. Horses I cannot take to Ithaca; I will leave them here to bring glory to yourself. You are king of an ample plain with clover in plenty and galingale, with choice wheat and common wheat and white broad-eared barley; but Ithaca has no riding-spaces, no meadows even. Goats, not horses, go grazing there, though I love it all the more for that. These islands of ours that shelve down seawards are all short of good roads for driving, short too of fields for pasture – Ithaca most of all.'

So he spoke. Menelaus smiled and caressed him with his hand; then he replied: 'What you say, dear child, is proof of the good stock you come from. I will change my gift, then; that is easy. Of all the treasures stored in my house I will give you the loveliest and the richest. I will give you a noble mixing-bowl; it is silver all through and rimmed with gold; Hephaestus made it; King Phaedimus, lord of Sidon, gave it me when his house received me during my voyage home; now it will please me to make it yours.'

Such were their words to one another. Meanwhile in front of the palace of Odysseus the suitors were whiling their time away, hurling discus and javelin over the levelled floor, in the same spot and arrogant as ever. Antinous was seated apart, with handsome Eurymachus beside him; these were the foremost of the suitors, because they excelled in manly prowess. Noemon, Phronius' son, approached them, and asked Antinous a question:

'Antinous, can we or cannot we be sure how soon Telemachus will return from sandy Pylos? When he went, he took a ship of mine that I now need to cross to spacious Elis; because yonder I have a dozen mares with sturdy young mules at the teat, unbroken; one of these I wish to drive off and to break him in.'

His words perplexed them; they had no inkling that Telemachus had departed for Neleian Pylos; they thought he was somewhere on his domain – with the flocks, perhaps, or with the swineherd.

So Antinous, son of Eupeithes, answered: 'Tell me truly: when did he leave and what young men went with him? Did he choose them from all over Ithaca, or were they his own servants and slaves – because that too would be in his power? And tell me also without concealment (I must be satisfied): did he wrest the ship from you by force, or did he importune you so earnestly that you gave it him of your own free will?'

Noemon answered: 'I gave it him of my own free will. What could any man do, if a prince like this, in distress like this, should appeal to him? It would be hard to refuse compliance. As for the youths who went with him – after ourselves, they are the city's best. And I saw a leader embarking with them who was either Mentor or else some god who at all points resembled Mentor. But here is a thing that puzzles me; yesterday early I saw Lord Mentor here; yet, days before, he had embarked for Pylos.'

With these words he went back again to his father's house. But the two were much perturbed at heart; they made the suitors give up their games and sit down together. Then Antinous spoke to them all in indignation; his heart was black with angry passion, and his eyes were like flaming fire:

'Curse Telemachus and his voyage, this piece of daring insolently achieved! We were sure such a thing could never be. Ourselves so many! He a young boy! Yet despite us all he has found his way out; he has picked a crew from the city's best and hauled a ship down to the sea. Now he will go from bad to worse. I only pray that Zeus may cut short his recklessness before he can reach man's estate. But come now; give me a rapid ship and a crew of twenty; then I can ambush his return and watch for him in the narrow waters between Ithaca and craggy Samos, and so his voyage to find his father will come to a miserable ending.'

So he spoke; they all thought with him and urged him to do as he had said; then they rose and went to Odysseus' palace.

Penelope was not long left ignorant of the plan the suitors were meditating. Medon the page told her of it, because he had overheard their scheming when he was outside the courtyard and they were inside, weaving their plot. He passed through the hall to tell Penelope, and she spoke to him as he crossed her threshold:

'Page, on what errand have the proud suitors sent you now? Is it to tell Lord Odysseus' maids to prepare a banquet for them and lay their own tasks aside? Would to heaven they had never wooed me, never met in another man's house! And now would to heaven this banquet might be their last on earth, a banquet with no tomorrow! You come together continually to devour the ample livelihood Telemachus has inherited. In childhood days, did none of you hear from your father's lips what Odysseus was to their generation? Never, in either word or deed, did he wrong any man among the people, though that is the way of heaven-protected kings; true, a king will befriend one man, but then he will persecute another. With Odysseus it was never so; he was never a tyrant to any man. But your own hearts, your own shameful actions show themselves plainly for what they are, and past kindness leaves you ungrateful now.'

Prudent Medon replied to her: 'Queen, I could wish that this were the worst. There is something else, more dangerous and more monstrous, that the suitors are meditating now. I hope indeed that Zeus will thwart it; but their purpose is to slay Telemachus with the keen-edged bronze on his journey home. He went away to seek news about his father in holy Pylos and lovely Lacedaemon.'

Such were his words; and as she stood there, her knees and her heart alike failed her; speechlessness came on her and held her; her eyes filled, and the clear flow of her utterance ceased. After a while she found voice to answer:

'But, Medon, what then possessed my boy to leave me? He had no need to go aboard one of those rapid ships that serve as chariots across the sea for men who speed over the wide waters. Does he wish that not even his name should be left on earth?'

Thoughtful Medon replied to her: 'I cannot say if some god impelled him or if his own heart felt the prompting; but to Pylos certainly he went, and to gather news – perhaps of his father's homecoming, perhaps of the fate he may have met.'

With these words he went back once more through Odysseus' hall. As for the queen, heart-withering anguish invaded her. There were chairs in the room, several of them, but she could not now bear to sit in any; she sank on the floor of the sumptuous room, wailing pitiably; and around her all her handmaids whimpered, all those in the palace, young and old. Through her deep sobbing she said to them:

'Friends, hear me speak. To me, above all other women born and bred in my generation, Olympian Zeus has allotted sorrow. Long ago I lost a noble husband, one of lion heart and all perfections among the Danaans. And now the storm-winds have snatched my only son from the house, and this moreover without my knowledge; I heard not a word of his setting out; not even you, you hard-hearted women, thought of rousing me from my bed, though you knew well enough when he went off to his dark and hollow ship. Had I but known he planned this voyage, he would have stayed here, though never so anxious to depart, or else would have left me dead in my own halls. But now let some-one fetch me old Dolius at once – the slave my father allotted me when I first came here as a bride, and the keeper of my great orchard now. Dolius must hasten to Laertes, sit down beside him and tell him everything, point by point. Perhaps Laertes may frame some plan, leave his retreat and come to rebuke the people for their desire to destroy his grandson, the son of King Odysseus.'

But her good nurse Eurycleia said: 'Dear mistress – kill me, if you choose, with the sword, or let me live in the palace still, but I will not hide the truth from you. I knew the whole thing; I gave him all that he asked me for, food and sweet wine; but he made me swear most solemnly not to tell you until either some dozen days had passed or you yourself missed him or heard from another of his going; he could not let tears stain your lovely face. But now you must bathe and put on fresh clothing, return upstairs with your serving-women and make supplication to Athene, daughter of Zeus who holds the aegis; then she may save him from death itself. As for old Laertes, he is distressed already; do not distress him further. Nor do I think that the race of Arceisius is utterly hated by the gods; there will still be some of Laertes' line to be masters of the high-roofed palace and the fertile fields far and wide around it.'

With such words as these she lulled the lamenting of Penelope and made her eyes give over weeping. So the queen bathed and put on fresh clothes and returned upstairs with her serving-women; she put crushed barley into a basket and made supplication to Athene: 'Hear me, daughter of Zeus of the aegis, Un-wearied One; if in this palace subtle Odysseus ever made you rich burnt-offerings of ox or sheep, remember them, I beseech you, now; preserve my darling son, and keep the proud unrighteous suitors far from his path.'

So she spoke, then uttered the loud ritual cry; and the goddess listened to her prayer. In the shadowy halls the suitors broke forth in clamour, and one or another of these young braggarts said: 'Plainly now the much-courted queen is making ready for marriage with us; she has no inkling that death is ordained for her son already.'

So said one or another of them, but had no inkling how things had in truth been ordained. At this, Antinous spoke among them: 'Have a care, my friends; you must banish all such rash words as these, or someone may tell of them inside. No; let us rise without a sound and pursue the plan we all approved.'

This said, he chose out the twenty boldest, and they went their way to the rapid ship on the sea-shore. And first they hauled the vessel down to the deep water, then placed inside it the mast and sails; fixed the oars in the leather straps, everything in due order, and spread the white sails; their servants brought down the tackle for them. They moored the ship well out in the water, then went ashore and had their supper and waited for evening to come on.

But wise Penelope meanwhile lay in her upper room without touching food or tasting drink, asking herself if her blameless son would escape death or would fall a prey to the haughty suitors. As a lion ringed by a band of hunters is filled with bewilderment and fear as they close their cunning circle round him, in such bewilderment lay the queen till welcome sleep came suddenly upon her. She sank back and slumbered, and all her limbs found ease.

And now the goddess of gleaming eyes turned her mind to another thing. She fashioned a wraith in the likeness of a woman, Iphthime, daughter of bold Icarius and wife of Eumelus who lived in Pherae. Athene sent forth this wraith to the house of King Odysseus to rescue stricken sobbing Penelope from tears and mourning and lamentation. It glided past the thong of the door-bolt into the queen's room, stood at her bedside and spoke to her:

'You are sleeping, then, Penelope, despite all the sorrows of your heart? Listen: the gods who live at ease tell you not to weep or be distressed, because after all your son is to come home again; in no way has he offended the gods.'

Wise Penelope answered her from the gates of dream where she slumbered softly: 'Sister, why have you come to me? You have seldom visited me before, for truly your dwelling is very far from mine. And now you would have me put aside all the griefs and sorrows that wring my heart and soul. Long ago I lost a noble husband, one of lion heart and all perfections among the Danaans. And now the only son I had has sailed in his ship away from me, a child with no knowledge of men's adventures or men's debates. I grieve for him more than for his father. I fear and tremble for what may befall him now, whether in the lands he went to visit or whether at sea, because foes in plenty are in a conspiracy against him, eager to kill him before he reaches home.'

But the glimmering wraith answered her: 'Have courage; do not be thus dismayed. While he travels, there travels with him one that many another hero has prayed to have beside him, a wielder of power, Pallas Athene. She has compassion on your distress, and she it is who sent me now to say to you what I just have said.'

Wise Penelope answered her: 'If indeed you are yourself divine and have come at the bidding of a divinity, then tell me plainly about that other unhappy one. Is he still alive? Does he see the sunlight? Or is he already dead and in Hades' house?'

But the glimmering wraith answered her: 'Concerning him – his living or dying – I shall not tell you the truth in fullness, and idle words are best unspoken.'

And with that reply it glided past the door-bolt again and out into the breath of the breeze. Icarius' daughter all of a sudden woke from sleep, and her heart was comforted, so vivid had been this apparition that winged its way to her through the gloom.

The suitors meanwhile had gone aboard and began their voyage over the watery paths, scheming to plunge Telemachus into death. In mid-sea is a rocky island between Ithaca and rugged Samos. Its name is Asteris; it is small, but it has two harbours with good anchorage. Here the Achaeans laid wait for him.

BOOK V

THE goddess Dawn, who had slept beside Lord Tithonus, was rising now to bring light to immortals and to mortals; the gods were assembling to sit in council, and in their midst was Zeus the Thunderer, sovereign above them all. Athene began to recount to them the many distresses of Odysseus that again had come before her mind, for it irked her that he should still be there in the dwelling of Calypso:

'Father Zeus, and you other blessed immortal gods: I could wish that henceforth no sceptred king should set himself to be kind and gentle and equitable; I would have every king a tyrant and evildoer, since King Odysseus goes utterly unremembered among the people that once he ruled with the gentleness of a father. He is pent up in an island now, overwhelmed with misery; he is in the domains of the nymph Calypso, who is keeping him with her there perforce and thwarting return to his own country. He has no ships and oars and crew to take him over the wide expanse of ocean. And now men are plotting to kill his only son as he returns home; the boy went off to seek news about his father in holy Pylos and lovely Lacedaemon.'

Zeus who masses the clouds made answer: 'My child, what a word is this that has passed your lips! Was it not you who framed this plan, so that Odysseus on his return might take his vengeance upon these men? As for Telemachus, use the craft and the power you have for his homeward journey, so that he may reach his own land unscathed and the suitors sail back empty-handed.'

And with this he turned to his dear son Hermes: 'Hermes, you are always our messenger; go then to the nymph of braided tresses and tell her my firm decree for the homecoming of staunch Odysseus, and how he is to begin his journey back, unescorted by gods or men. It will be on a raft firmly put together; on this, in spite of many troubles, he may come in twenty days' time to fertile Scheria; that is the land of the Phaeacians, a people whose lineage is divine; with all their hearts they will honour him like a god and will send him by ship to his own dear land, with bronze and gold and clothing in plenty, more than he would have brought from Troy if he had made his return unharassed and with his full share of spoil. In that fashion it is his destiny to see his dear ones and come once more to his high-roofed palace and his own country.'

So he spoke; and the Keen Watcher, the Radiant One, did not disobey. At once he fastened under his feet the immortal sandals of lovely gold that carried him, swift as airy breezes, over ocean and over boundless earth. And he took the rod that lulls men's eyes for him, at his pleasure, or awakens others when they slumber. With this in hand the strong Radiant One began his flight; over Pieria he passed, then from the upper air dipped down to the sea and sped on over the waves like the seagull that hunts for fishes in the frightening troughs of the barren sea and wets his thick plumage in the brine; like such a bird was Hermes carried over the multitudinous waves. But when he had reached that far-off island he left the violent ocean and took to the land until he came to a great cavern; in this the nymph of braided tresses had made her home, and inside this he found her now. On the hearth a great fire was burning, and far and wide over the island was wafted the smell of burning wood, cloven cedar and juniper.

In the space within was the goddess herself, singing with a lovely voice, moving to and fro at her loom and weaving with a shuttle of gold. Around the entrance a wood rose up in abundant growth – alder and aspen and fragrant cypress. Birds with long wings roosted there, owls and falcons and long-tongued sea-crows that have their business upon the waters. Trailing over the cavern's arch was a garden vine that throve and clustered; and here four springs began near each other, then in due order ran four ways with their crystal waters. Grassy meadows on either side stood thick with violet and wild parsley. Even a Deathless One, if he came there, might gaze in wonder at the sight and might be the happier in heart. So the Keen Watcher, the Radiant One, stood there and gazed there too; and having gazed to his heart's content, he passed quickly into the ample cavern. When queenly Calypso saw him face to face, she was sure at once who he was, for the deathless gods are no strangers to one another, though one may live far apart from the rest. But bold Odysseus was not to be found within; as his custom was, he was sitting on the shore and weeping, breaking his heart with tears and sighs and sorrows.

Queenly Calypso seated Hermes in a gleaming burnished chair. Then she began to question him: 'What is your errand here, I wonder, Hermes, god of the golden wand? You are an honoured and welcome guest, although not a frequent one hitherto. Tell me the thing that is in your mind; my heart consents to it already if it is something I can do and something that has been done before.'

And with these words the goddess drew up a table by him, heaping it with ambrosia and mixing the rosy nectar. So Hermes began to eat and drink; when the meal was over and his spirit refreshed with food, he answered Calypso thus: 'At my entrance you put a question to me, goddess to god; I will tell you the whole matter frankly, as indeed you wish me to. This visit was not of my own choosing; it was Zeus who commanded me to come. Who of his own free will would traverse those endless briny waters, with not one town to be seen where human beings make sacrifice to the gods and offer choice hecatombs?[1] But when once the master of the aegis has fixed his own purpose, no other god can cross or thwart it. He says that you have with you here a man more luckless than all those others who fought around the great town of Priam. This man he bade you let go forthwith, because it is not appointed for him to find his end here, far away from his own people; he is destined to see his own kith and kin again and return to his high-roofed house and his own country.'

So he spoke. The queenly goddess Calypso shuddered, and her words came forth in rapid flight: 'You are merciless, you gods, resentful beyond all other beings; you are jealous if without disguise a goddess makes a man her bedfellow, her beloved husband. So it was when Dawn of the rosy fingers chose out Orion; you gods who live in such ease yourselves were jealous of her until chaste Artemis in her cloth-of-gold visited him with her gentle shafts and slew him in Ortygia. So it was when Demeter of the braided tresses followed her heart and lay in love with Iasion in

1. '... a horrible long Journey 'tis;
   And then no Town to bait at by the way
   For Hecatomb or lesser Sacrifice.' HOBBES

the triple-furrowed field;[1] Zeus was aware of it soon enough and hurled the bright thunderbolt that killed him. And now so it is with me; you resent this mortal man beside me. I saved him when he was all alone and astride his keel, when Zeus with his flashing thunderbolt had shattered and shivered his rapid vessel in the midst of wine-dark ocean. All his brave comrades perished then; he alone was borne on to this place by wind and wave. I welcomed him and I tended him; I offered him immortality and eternal youth. But, as you say, when once the master of the aegis has fixed his own purpose, no other god can cross or thwart it; so let the man go – if such is the word and behest of Zeus – go where he will over the barren sea. I cannot help him to depart; I have no ships or oars or crew to speed him over the sea's expanse; but gladly enough, without concealment, I will counsel him how best to reach his own land unscathed.'

And the Radiant One answered her: 'In that way, then, allow him to go, and have regard to the anger of Zeus; if not, you may feel his displeasure afterwards.'

With these words the strong Radiant One departed. The queenly nymph, with the message of Zeus still in her ears, went off in quest of bold Odysseus, and found him sitting upon the shore. His eyes were never dry of tears while the sweetness of life ebbed away from him in his comfortless longings for return, since the nymph was dear to him no longer. At night-time, true, he slept with her even now in the arching caverns, but this was against his will; she was loving and he unloving. He passed the daytime seated upon the rocky shore, shedding tears and gazing outwards over the barren sea.

Coming up to him, the queenly goddess began to speak: 'Listen, unhappy man; no need to stay here lamenting longer, no need to let your life be wasted; I am willing now, quite willing, to let you go. Come then; take tools of bronze, cut long beams and fashion them into a wide raft; then build half-decks on it, well above, so that the craft may carry you over the misty ocean. I myself will put food in it, with water and with red wine as well,

---

1. The cutting of three furrows was part of the fertility rites inaugurating the agricultural year. Such ritual ploughing was widespread. In the Chinese *Book of Rites* the Emperor himself cuts three furrows, the Three Dukes cut five, and the Ministers and Lords cut nine.

things that will stave off hunger and please the taste. I will give you clothes to wear and will send a fair wind behind you to let you reach your own land unharmed – all this if it please the gods whose home is wide heaven itself, because they are better able than I both to plan and to achieve.'

So she spoke, but the much-tried hero shuddered. His words came forth in rapid flight: 'Goddess, your purpose cannot be as you say; you cannot intend to speed me home. You tell me to make myself a raft to cross the great gulf of ocean – a gulf so baffling and so perilous that not even rapid ships will traverse it, steady though they may be and favoured by a fair wind from Zeus. I will not set foot on such a raft unless I am sure of your good will – unless, goddess, you take on yourself to swear a solemn oath not to plot against me any new mischief to my ruin.'

These were his words. Queenly Calypso smiled; and caressing him with her hand she answered: 'You are all too cunning. No innocent could have mustered such words as those. So be it then – let earth be witness to me in this, and the arching heaven above, and the downward water of the Styx – most solemn and most fearsome of oaths with the blessed gods – that I will plot against you no new mischief to your ruin. No; I have in mind – I will ponder now – the very plans I would shape for myself if ever need pressed as hard on me. My whole bent is to honest dealing; in this breast of mine there is no heart of iron; I have compassion.'

So she spoke, this lovely divinity, and led the way forthwith; Odysseus followed in her footsteps. Goddess and man reached the arching cavern; Odysseus sat down in the chair that Hermes had risen from, and Calypso put in front of him all manner of things such as mortal men eat and drink, then sat down herself facing the king while her handmaids served her with nectar and ambrosia. He and she stretched out their hands to the dishes there; but when they had eaten and drunk their fill, Calypso the goddess thus began:

'Son of Laertes, subtle Odysseus – so then, your mind is firmly set on returning now without delay to your home and country? Go then, and joy go with you, in spite of all. Yet if you knew – if you fully knew – what miseries are fated to fill your cup before you attain your own land, you would choose to stay here, to join with me in calm possession of this domain, to be beyond reach of death – this despite all your zeal to see once more the wife that you yearn for, day by day. And yet I doubt if I fall behind her in form and feature – for indeed it would be unbecoming that mortal women should vie in form and face with immortal goddesses.'

Subtle Odysseus answered her: 'Goddess and queen, do not make this a cause of anger with me. I know the truth of everything that you say; I know that my wise Penelope, when a man looks at her, is far beneath you in form and stature; she is a mortal, you are immortal and unageing. Yet, notwithstanding, my desire and longing day by day is still to reach my own home and to see the day of my return. And if this or that divinity should shatter my craft on the wine-dark ocean, I will bear it and keep a bold heart within me. Often enough before this time have war and wave oppressed and plagued me; let new tribulations join the old.'

So he spoke; and the sun sank and darkness came; then the pair withdrew, and in a recess of the arching cavern they took their pleasure in love, and did not leave one another's side.

Dawn comes early, with rosy fingers. When she appeared, Odysseus put on his cloak and tunic; the nymph put on a long silvery mantle, graceful and delicate; she fastened a lovely gold girdle round her waist and slipped a scarf over her head. Then she turned her mind to helping his departure. She gave him a great axe of bronze, easy to wield, with keen double blade; its haft was of olive, handsome and fitting close; she gave him a polished adze as well. Then she led the way to the far side of the island; tall trees were standing there, alder and aspen and towering silver fir; for some time past, these had been dry and sapless, ready to float easily. When Calypso had shown him where they stood, she returned homeward while he began to cut down the trees; and the work went briskly. He felled twenty trees, all told, and trimmed them with the axe, smoothed them deftly and trued them to the line.[1] Then the goddess brought him augers, and he bored all his pieces through and made them meet exactly, then pinned the craft together with pegs and joints. When a skilful carpenter builds a big merchant-ship, he rounds off the

1. Nautical experts disagree in interpreting what follows. It is disputed whether it was a raft or a boat that was being built, and my translation of details is tentative. Bowra observes that a wattled fence against swamping is still sometimes used in Greek boats.

hull to a decent width, and such was the width that Odysseus gave his craft. He went on working, setting up the half-decks, fitting them to the close-set ribs, and finishing off with the long side-planks. He put a mast in, fitted a yard-arm to it, then added a steering-oar to keep the craft straight. He fenced in the whole with wattled bulwarks, to keep it proof against the water, making the layer of brushwood thick. Meanwhile the goddess brought him pieces of cloth to make a sail of, and he made that too in proper fashion. Braces, reefs, sheets – he made them all fast, and then on rollers dragged the craft down to the sea.

By the fourth day all his work was done. On the fifth day, Lady Calypso made ready to let him leave her island; she had bathed him first and clothed him in sweet-smelling garments. Moreover, the goddess had put aboard one skin of dark wine, and another, a larger one, of water, with provisions in a sack and many dainties to please the taste; last, she had summoned up for him a fair wind that was warm and kindly.

Odysseus was happy to have this wind and he spread his sail to it. He sat with his hands on the steering-oar, and in expert fashion began to guide his course. Sleep never fell upon his eyelids as he watched the Pleiades, watched the Wagoner, slow to set, watched the Bear that some call the Wain, which turns for ever in the same spot with an anxious eye upon Orion, and which alone among constellations has no share in the baths of Ocean. Calypso the goddess had bidden him in his sailing to keep the Bear on his left hand. For seventeen days he sailed onwards across the sea; on the eighteenth day there loomed before him the shadowy hills of the land of the Phaeacians; at the point where it was nearest, it looked like a shield in the misty sea.

But Poseidon, the lord who shakes the earth, was returning from Ethiopia, and from far away, from among the mountains of the Solymi, he spied Odysseus sailing the seas. His spirit was angered exceedingly; he shook his head, and he spoke thus to the heart within him :

'Treachery! While I have been with the Ethiopians, the gods have changed their purpose about Odysseus, and now he is near the Phaeacian land; there he is destined to be delivered from the sum of sorrow that has been his; yet even now I am in high hopes to give him his fill of tribulation.'

So speaking he massed the clouds, clutched his trident and

churned the ocean up; he roused all the blasts of all the winds
and swathed earth and sea alike in cloud; down from the sky
rushed the dark. East and south wind clashed together, the
stormy west and the sky-born billow-driving north. Then Odysseus
felt his knees and his spirit quail; in desperation he spoke to his
own heroic heart: 'Alas for me! What will become of me in the
end? I fear the goddess spoke all too truly when she prophesied
of trouble on trouble to bear at sea before I reached my own land.
All this is now being brought to pass. What monstrous clouds
has Zeus now spread across the expanse of sky! How he has
churned up the ocean! How the blasts of every wind that blows
rage furiously about me! Only destruction yawns before me.
Thrice happy and more were those among the Danaans who
long ago perished in the wide land of Troy to do the will of the
sons of Atreus! If only I too had died and had met my doom on
the day when the thronging Trojans hurled their bronze-pointed
spears against me in the battle round the dead son of Peleus!
Then I should have had my portion of funeral rites; over all
Achaea, men would have published my renown; but it was my
doom instead to perish by this inglorious death.'

As he finished speaking, a monstrous wave crashed over him
from above, driving upon him violently and whirling his raft
round and round. He was thrown out clear of the raft, having let
the steering-oar slip from his hands. A hideous tempest of wrest-
ling winds descended on him, snapping his mast in two while sail
and sailyard were tossed to a distance in the sea. He himself was
forced under water for some while; he could not emerge at once
from the onset of the great wave, being dragged downwards by
the clothes that Calypso the goddess had given to him; but at
length he came up again, and spat out the bitter brine that came
streaming down from his head. But even then, in all his distress,
he did not forget his raft; he darted over the waves towards it,
grasped it and seated himself in the middle of it, keeping at bay
the death that would end everything. This way and that, the
monstrous wave kept sweeping the craft along with it; like the
north wind, late in summer, sweeping thistle-stalks over the plain
while they catch together and form a mass, so did these storm-
winds sweep the raft this way and that way over the sea; some-
times the south wind would toss it towards the north wind as

plaything, sometimes the east would give it up to the west to chase.

Nevertheless one being saw him, Cadmus' daughter, slender-ankled Ino who is also Leucothea; once she had been a mortal and spoken with human voice, but now she lives in the salt seas and the gods give her the honour that is her due. She it was who now felt compassion for Odysseus the persecuted wanderer; she flew up from the waves as a seagull might, sat on the strong-bound raft and spoke:

'Unhappy man, why has Poseidon who shakes the earth become so monstrously angry with you? Why does he sow all these seeds of misery for you? But despite his malice he shall not destroy you utterly. Only you must do as I say – I think you do not lack understanding; strip off these clothes, leave the raft for the winds to toss, strike out with your arms and try to reach land again on the Phaeacian shore; it is there you are fated to find deliverance. And see – this is a scarf of mine, of celestial make; wind it round you above your waist, and you need fear neither death nor harm. But once you have grasped the shore with your hands, undo the scarf and throw it into the wine-dark sea again, far from the shore; and avert your eyes.'

With that, the goddess gave him the scarf; then sank once more, as a seagull might, into the billowy sea, and the dark wave covered her. Odysseus, acquainted with many perils, was distrustful now and spoke in bitterness to his ardent soul: 'Wretch that I am! Can this divinity in her turn be laying a snare for me in her command to forsake the raft? I will not at once do what she said, because the land that she called my refuge seemed still far away when I caught a glimpse of it. No, I will do this instead – it seems the most prudent thing. As long as the planks hold together, I will stay on board and endure whatever evil comes; but when once the waves have shattered the craft piece from piece, I will take to swimming: there is nothing better I can think of.'

While he was inwardly planning thus, Poseidon the Earth-shaker heaved a huge wave against him – overwhelming, hideous, with arching crest; and it struck him full. As a violent wind tosses a heap of dry chaff and scatters it all this way and that, so the wave now scattered the raft's long planks. But Odysseus bestrode a single plank, like a man riding a horse; he stripped off the

clothes Calypso gave him, drew the scarf round him above his
waist at once, then let himself fall face downwards into the sea,
striking out with his arms and striving desperately to swim. Then
Lord Poseidon, spying him so, shook his head and said inwardly:
'Go then, go after all your troubles to wander again over ocean
until you meet with men once more; these will be men whom
Zeus has favoured, yet even so I do not think you will feel your-
self stinted of misfortune.' With that, he lashed his long-maned
horses, and drove on till he came to Aegae, where is his far-famed
dwelling-place.

Then for two nights and two days Odysseus was driven at
random by swollen billows, and time and again his heart fore-
boded death. But when Dawn of the braided tresses had ushered
in the third day, all of a sudden the wind dropped, and everything
became hushed and still; as the ground swell lifted him, he saw in
a quick forward glance that a little ahead there was land. It was
like the sudden joy of children when they see their father out of
danger; the father has suffered from some disease, has been in
torment, has wasted away month after month, victim of some
detested power; but then the gods rescue him from distress, and
so there is sudden joy; such joy came upon Odysseus now with
the sight of land and trees, and he swam on in eager hope that
his feet would tread dry land again. But when he was no further
distant than the voice of a shouting man can reach, he heard the
roar of the sea against the rocks, for the heavy breakers dashed
themselves on the solid coast, thundering in fury, and the salt
spray veiled everything; because here were no harbours for ships
to rest in, no roadsteads either; only jutting headlands and reefs
and crags. Then Odysseus felt his knees and his spirit quail, and
spoke in bitterness to his ardent soul:

'What misery! Now that Zeus has allowed me against all hope
to see land again, now that I have cut my pathway through the
deep ocean and neared my goal, I can discern no way out at all
from whitening sea to shore. In front there are jagged cliffs;
around them the breakers roar and surge; above, a precipice rises
sheer. Inshore, the sea is too deep for me to find firm footholds
and wade to safety; just as I try to leave the water, some great
wave may seize me and dash me against the naked rock, and all
my labour will have been lost. And if I swim further along the
coast to find some stretch of curving beach that takes the waves

slantwise and shelters one from the sea, then I fear that another sudden gust may seize me and bear me off amid my loud lamentations back to the teeming ocean; or again that some god may send out against me, from the brine, one of the swarming strange huge creatures in the breeding-grounds of Amphitrite. I know how deeply I am hated by the great god who shakes the earth.'

But while such thoughts were still passing through his mind, a great billow began to sweep him towards the rocky shore. And there his skin would have been stripped off and his bones dashed all to pieces if Athene the goddess had not warned him. As he swept forward, he seized the rock with both hands and clung there panting till the mass of water had passed him by; but the wave he thus escaped struck him again as it washed back, and hurled him away far into the sea. As an octopus is dragged from its lair with a cluster of pebbles still clinging to the suckers, so Odysseus was swept from the rocks with the skin stripped from his desperate hands. The great wave covered him up, and there he would miserably have perished before his time if Athene had not sharpened his wits. He struggled forth from the line of breakers thundering against the shore, then swam outside it, looking landwards to find some stretch of beach that took the waves aslant and offered a shelter from the sea. And when in his swimming he came abreast of a flowing river, where he thought the ground best to land on, being clear of rocks and sheltered from winds besides, he hailed the outflowing stream as a god and prayed to him in his heart thus: 'Hear me, Lord, whosoever you may be. I find in you an answer to all my prayers, as I seek a refuge from the sea and from the threatenings of Poseidon. Do not even the Deathless Ones owe compassion to a mortal who comes to them as a wanderer and a suppliant? Such a man am I, approaching your stream, approaching your knees, after much distress. Have pity upon me, Lord; a suppliant is what I claim to be.'

So he prayed, and the god forthwith checked his stream and held back his waves; he stilled the waters before Odysseus and brought him safe to the river's mouth. But the hero's knees failed under him, the sturdy hands dropped to his sides, for the sea had broken the spirit in him. His body was swollen now all over, and brine in streams gushed from his mouth and nostrils. With breath and with speech both failing him, he lay half-swooning, with desperate weariness upon him. But when he had got his breath again and rallied the spirit in his breast, he undid the scarf the goddess had given him and threw it into the seaward-flowing river. The swelling water carried it on downstream, and Ino hastened to catch it in her hands. Odysseus limped away from the river, sank down among the rushes and kissed the earth that gives men grain. Then in much distress he spoke to his ardent soul: 'Alas, what will happen to me now? What will become of me after all? If I watch out an anxious night by the riverside, I fear that the piercing frost and the soaking dew together may be too much for me; just now I was near fainting; I am almost at my last gasp. A chilly breeze blows from the river as dawn approaches. But if again I should climb the hillside to the copse and lie down in the thick bushes there, in hope to escape cold and weariness – if welcome sleep should visit me then, I fear to become a helpless victim to beasts of prey.'

To his puzzled mind the second course seemed better. He went on up towards the wood, which he found to be not far from the water, inside a clearing. There he crept under two bushy olives that were growing together from one stem – one of common stock and one of wild. These were never entered by onset of rainy winds, never reached by rays of dazzling sun, never pierced through and through by thunderstorm, so closely were the two intertwined. Under these Odysseus crept. He heaped up at once a wide bed of leaves, because there was a great mass of them, enough to shelter two men or three in the stormy season, be the weather never so wild. Patient Odysseus rejoiced to see it; he lay down in the very middle, and covered himself with the fallen leaves. A neighbourless man in some lonely spot will bury a burning log under grey ash, keeping alive the seed of fire and hoping thus not to need to rekindle it from elsewhere. So Odysseus buried himself in leaves, and Athene poured sleep upon his eyes, sleep to cover his eyelids over, sleep to release him quickly from toil and pains.

BOOK VI

NAUSICAA

THERE then the much-tried hero lay, overcome with toil and
now with sleep. But Athene went to the land and the city of the
Phaeacians; these were a people that in times past had inhabited
spacious Hypereia near the masterful Cyclops race, who were
stronger than they and plundered them continually. So King
Nausithous the Phaeacian transplanted his people from Hypereia
and settled them in Scheria, far removed from toiling mankind;
he ringed the city with a wall, built houses, gave the gods
temples, apportioned land for tillage. But he by this time had
fallen to fate and gone down to the house of Hades; the king
now was Alcinous, possessing wisdom by grace from heaven, and
to his palace Athene went, planning return for bold Odysseus.
She made her way to the sumptuous bedroom where slept a girl
who in form and feature was like the immortal goddesses –
Nausicaa, daughter of Alcinous; near her, on either side of the
double doors, there slept two handmaids whose loveliness was the
Graces' gift, and the gleaming doors were shut. Athene, like a
breath of wind, glided over swiftly to where the girl lay, stood
at her bedside and spoke to her, taking the form of Dymas'
daughter (the father was famed for his sea-prowess, the child was
of Nausicaa's age and a special favourite with her). In this dis-
guise, then, Athene stood there. 'Nausicaa,' (so she now began)
'how came your mother to have so thoughtless a child as you?
Here are your glossy clothes lying all uncared for, though your
wedding-day is near at hand, and for that you need to be hand-
somely dressed yourself and to have handsome dresses ready also
for those who escort you to your new home. Such things as these
make a bride well spoken of with the people and bring her father
and mother joy. Come then; when morning breaks let us go and
wash these clothes; I will come with you myself to help, and then
the task will be done the sooner. You cannot remain unwedded
long; you are being sought for already here by the noblest suitors
in the Phaeacian land, the land that by birth is yours as well.
So tomorrow early you must urge the king your father to let you
have a wagon and mules. They will carry all the dresses for you,
and the sashes and the brilliant rugs; besides, for yourself, it is

far better to ride than walk; the washing-places lie well beyond the town.'

And with these words the goddess of gleaming eyes departed to Olympus. There, men say, the home of the gods is secretly set for ever, unrocked by tempest, undrenched with rain, unassailed by snow; a cloudless sky stretches out above and a white radiance is everywhere. It is in this place that the blessed gods take their pleasure through all their days; and to it the goddess of gleaming eyes departed after giving her message to the princess.

Forthwith came Dawn in her flowery garment and awakened the lovely-robed Nausicaa. At once the girl remembered her dream with wonder and went her way through the palace halls to tell her tale to her dear parents, her father and her mother. She found them both inside the palace. Her mother was seated at the hearth with her waiting-women, spinning yarn of sea-purple hue; her father she overtook on his way out to meet the Phaeacian lords at a council for which they asked his presence. She came right up to him and began : 'Father dear, could you let me have, I wonder, a tall wagon with easy wheels to take our clothes to the river and wash them there? They are handsome clothes, but I see them in front of me lying soiled. For you yourself it is only fitting to wear garments without a spot when you take your seat in the council-place among all the princes of this land. And then, remember, there are five sons of yours living here; two are married, but three are bachelors in their prime who always like to have fresh garments when they go out to dance. And care for all this falls on my shoulders.'

So the princess appealed to him, too shy in the presence of her father to speak of her own happy bridal day. But her father understood it all, and answered : 'Darling child, I begrudge you neither my mules nor anything else. The servants will get the tall wagon ready for you, with its easy wheels and fitted awning.'

So he spoke, then called to the servants, and they obeyed. Outside the house they brought up the smoothly-running mule-wagon, backed the mules towards it and harnessed them. Nausicaa fetched the bright clothing from her room and laid it inside the polished wagon. Her mother meanwhile had been putting in a basket all kinds of delicious food and dainties and had poured wine into a goatskin; then, when her daughter mounted the wagon, she gave her a golden flask of soft olive-oil, with which both she and her attendants would anoint themselves after bathing. Nausicaa grasped the whip and the glittering reins and whipped on the pair of mules. Away they clattered and on they trotted unflaggingly, carrying their mistress and the clothes; she was not alone, for her handmaids followed her as well.

They came at length to the lovely waters of the river; there were washing-places there, always full, because the clear water kept flowing up and through, copious enough to purge the deepest of stains away. Here the girls unloosed the mules from the wagon-yoke and let them run off alongside the eddying river to crop the sweet dog's-tooth grass. Next they took down the clothes in armfuls from the wagon, carried them to the deep dark water, and briskly began to tread them in the troughs, each of the girls vying with the rest. When they had washed the clothes and scoured all the dirt away, they spread them out on the sea beach, side by side, just where the waves beat on the shore and washed the line of pebbles. Then they bathed and anointed themselves well with oil; after that, they took their meal on the river-bank, waiting until the clothes should dry in the brilliant sun. Having eaten to their heart's content, maids and mistress alike threw aside their head-scarves and began a game of ball; white-armed Nausicaa with her singing set up the rhythm for the rest. It was just as when Artemis the huntress ranges the mountain-side – on lofty Taygetus, it may be, or it may be on Erymanthus – taking her pleasure among the boars and the running deer; country nymphs, daughters of Zeus who holds the aegis, are all around her and share her pastime; Leto her mother is glad at heart. With head and forehead Artemis overtops the rest, and though all are lovely, there is no mistaking which is she. So it was now; among her maidens, this unwedded girl was beyond compare.

But as she began to think it time to fold the clothes and to yoke the mules and to journey home again, the goddess gleaming-eyed Athene had a fresh artifice; she desired Odysseus to awake, to see the lovely Nausicaa and have her guidance into the city of the Phaeacians. At this moment, then, the princess tossed the ball towards one of her waiting-maidens, but missed the girl and sent the ball into the deep and eddying waters; and at this they all shrieked out. King Odysseus woke. He sat up and asked himself in wonder: 'Wretch that I am, whose land have I come to now? Are the people barbarous, arrogant and lawless? Are they hos-

pitable and godfearing? A shriek rang in my ears just then –
womanish, it seemed. Did it come from girls – did it come from
nymphs who live on high mountain-tops or in river-springs or in
grassy meadows? Or have I at hand, beside me now, beings of
human race and of human speech? Come, let me make the ven-
ture and see for myself.'

And with these words King Odysseus crept out from the under-
wood; but first with his powerful arm he tore a leafy bough from
the tangled growth to go across his body and hide his nakedness
as a man. Then he advanced like a mountain lion, sure of his
strength, who goes his way with blazing eyes through wind and
through rain, hunting the wild deer or ranging among sheep or
cattle; if flocks are penned in a strong-built fold, his hungry
belly makes him go after them even there. And Odysseus, naked
as he was, made bold to approach these girls with their braided
hair because necessity was upon him. Frightening he looked as
he stood before them, befouled with brine. The other girls fled
away dismayed, hither and thither over the jutting spits of shore.
The princess alone kept where she was, for Athene put courage in
her heart and took away trembling from her limbs; so she stood
her ground and faced him there. Odysseus pondered, framing a
prayer that would move this lovely girl but unsure if in his utter-
ance of it he should clasp her knees or stand apart. Having con-
sidered, he thought it best to stand apart as he uttered that moving
prayer, because the girl might feel displeasure if he should clasp
her knees. He began at once with words that would touch her
heart and gain his purpose:

'In supplication I come to you, my lady – lady of heaven shall
I call you, or of earth? If you are one of those divinities whose
home is the arching heaven itself, then I think you are most like
Artemis, daughter of sovereign Zeus; you are tall as she is, lovely
as she is, you have her air. But if you are mortal, one of those
who have earth for dwelling-place, then happy thrice over is your
father, happy your lady mother, happy your brothers. How often
their hearts must glow with gladness because of you, as they see
entering the ranks of dancers this matchless flowering of their
race! But happier still, happy in all his being must be the man
whose gifts will prevail with you, the man who will bring you
home as bride. I have seen no mortal creature like you, no man,
no woman; astonishment holds me as I gaze. And yet – I have had

one vision not unlike, at Delos, beside Apollo's altar – a tender palm-shoot rising in air. Delos too was a place I came to, with many warriors escorting me, on that same journey where grief on grief was to overtake me. That vision also was one that I wondered at for long, because no living shaft like that had ever before sprung up from ground. So now, my lady; I am all wonder and astonishment, and deepest reverence forbids me to touch your knees, though grief has come on me past all measure. Only last night did I escape from wine-dark ocean, and this was the last of twenty days through which the waves and the violent winds had borne me on from the island of Ogygia; and now some god has cast me upon this land, doubtless to bear new afflictions here. Not yet, I think, are my troubles over; before that can be, the gods will bring many things to pass.

'But you, my lady, must have compassion; to you first of all I make my plea after all the calamities I have borne; I know no other among your townsmen and countrymen. Instruct me how I may reach the city, and give me some trifle of cloth to cover me, some wrapping perhaps from the garments you carried here.

'As for yourself, may the gods enrich you with everything that your heart desires – may they bring you a husband and a home and the oneness of mind that means content. There is nothing nobler, nothing lovelier than when man and wife keep house together with like heart and with like will. Their foes repine, their friends rejoice, but the truth of it all is with her and him.'

White-armed Nausicaa answered him: 'Stranger, you seem no evil man and no foolish one. It is Zeus himself who from Olympus allots prosperity among men – gives it to the good or the bad, to every one of them as he pleases. To you he has given your present fortune, and despite your wishes you must bear it. But seeing it is our land and city that you have come to, you shall not go short of anything – of clothes or whatever other thing may fill the needs of a toil-worn suppliant crossing one's path. I will show you how to reach the town and will tell you who our people are. Those who live in this land and city are the Phaeacians, and I myself am daughter of bold Alcinous, on whom depends all Phaeacian power and prowess.'

So she answered, then called out to the maids attending her: 'Girls, stand still; where are you running at sight of a man? Do you think he comes of some hostile race? There is no man living

– there never will be – who could come in enmity to the Phaea-
cian land; we are loved too well by the immortals. We live apart,
with the billowing sea all round us; we live at the world's edge,
unvisited by all other mortals. The man you see is a luckless
wanderer cast on our shores, and now it falls to ourselves to tend
him, because Zeus is patron of every stranger and every beggar,
and to such as these, even a humble gift means much. So come,
girls, offer the stranger food and drink, and bathe him in the
river-water at a spot that is sheltered from the wind.'

So spoke the princess. Every girl stood still and called to her
friends to do the same; then they took Odysseus down to a shel-
tered spot where he could sit, as the king's daughter had com-
manded them. They put beside him a tunic and cloak to wear,
gave him soft oil in a golden flask and 'Now,' they said, 'wash
yourself in the running river.'

King Odysseus answered: 'You who wait upon the princess,
stand over yonder till I myself have washed the sea-scurf from
my shoulders and used the anointing oil – how long it is since any
such thing has come near my skin! I will not wash here before
your eyes; I feel ashamed to bare my body in the presence of girls
with braided hair.'

These were his words. The girls withdrew and told their mis-
tress. In the river-water King Odysseus washed from his skin the
brine that clung to his back and his broad shoulders, and wiped
from his head the scurf of the barren sea. But when he had washed
all over and lavishly anointed himself, when he had dressed in
the clothes that Nausicaa had given him, Athene the child of
Zeus gave him ampler stature and ampler presence, and over his
head she made the hair curl and cluster like hyacinth.[1] It was as
when a man adds gold to a silver vessel, a craftsman taught by
Hephaestus and Athene to master his art through all its range,
so that everything that he makes is beautiful; just so the goddess
gave added beauty to the head and shoulders of Odysseus. Then
he walked to the water's edge and sat down apart, radiant with
handsomeness and grace. The princess looked at him in wonder,
then turned to the girls with their braided hair:

'You white-armed girls, listen,' she said, 'to what I tell you. It
can only be by favour of all the Olympian gods that yonder man

1. '*Minerva* renders him more tall and fair,
   Curling in rings like Daffadills his Hair.' OGILBY

has come to our noble nation. Just now he seemed a pitiful sight
to me, but now he looks like the divinities whose home is wide
heaven itself. If only such a man as this might come to be called
my husband, to live in Scheria and be content to be one of us!
But enough! Take food and drink to the stranger, girls.'

So she spoke, and they readily obeyed her. They put food and
drink before Odysseus, and the hero drank and ate eagerly, having
tasted nothing for many days.

Then the princess turned her thoughts to other matters. She
saw to it that the clothes were folded, the handsome wagon loaded
with them and the firm-hooved mules put under the yoke again.
Then she mounted the wagon and hailed Odysseus: 'Stranger,
now you must rouse yourself and begin your journey towards our
city; I will help you to reach my father's house, and there, I
promise you, you will meet the noblest of the Phaeacians. You
must do as I tell you – I think your understanding is quick
enough. While we are passing through fields and farmlands, stay
with my girls and walk on quickly after the mule-wagon, while I
myself lead the way. Then we shall reach the city; a high wall
with towers encircles it, and on either side is a fine harbour; the
roadway leading in is narrow, and at its sides there are curving
ships drawn up, because every citizen has his own landing-place.
The men hold their assembly there, in a space that lies round the
noble precinct of Poseidon, a space set with huge blocks of stone
that are bedded deep. There too they see to the tackling of their
dark vessels – the cables and the sails – and there also they shape
the oars; because the Phaeacians have no regard for bow and
quiver, only for masts and the oars of ships and the balanced ships
themselves in which so proudly they traverse the whitening sea.

'Such are my people; and now I am on my guard against harsh
judgements from them; I fear I may be found fault with later.
There are bigoted minds among us here, and some ill-bred man
might say at the sight of us: "Who is this that we see beside
Nausicaa – who is this tall and handsome stranger? How did she
light on him? Doubtless he is to be her husband. Perhaps she has
rescued some shipwrecked traveller from far away, since no human
being lives near our land. Or perhaps some god has come down
from heaven in answer to her continued prayers, one who will
make her his wife for ever. Better so – better if the girl has gone
roving and found a husband from elsewhere, for plainly she sets

no store by any of our Phaeacians here, though her suitors are plentiful enough and come from the best of us."

'So they will speak, and this would be a reproach to me. And indeed I too should take it ill if another girl acted so – if with father and mother still alive she accepted the company of men before she married in sight of all.

'No, stranger. Listen instead to what I say, so that through my father you may be helped homeward as soon as may be and reach your own land. Near the road you will find a stately grove of poplars; it is dedicated to Athene; inside it there is a running stream, and there is a meadow stretching round it. My father's demesne with its fruitful orchard begins just there, within hailing distance of the city. At this spot you must sit and wait till the rest of us are clear of the town and have reached my father's house. When you think we are at the palace, then you are to walk on again into the city of the Phaeacians and ask for the house of my father Alcinous. It is easy to tell from the rest, and the smallest child could take you to it; among all the buildings of our people there is none to compare with the king's palace. When courtyard and house have closed around you, walk without pausing down the great hall until you find yourself by my mother; she sits in the firelight by the hearth, spinning the wool whose ocean-purple astonishes the beholder; she has her back to the great pillar, and her waiting-women sit behind her. Near her chair is my father's chair; he sits in it while he drinks his wine as a god might do. But pass by him and put your hands on my mother's knees; then you may hope to see in gladness the day of your homecoming – speedily too, from however far away you come.'

So spoke the princess, then touched the mules with her shining whip. Soon the river was left behind, and with flickering feet the mules sped on. Nausicaa drove in such a way that those on foot, the handmaids and Odysseus, might keep the same pace; she plied the lash, but with discretion.

It was just at sunset that they came to the stately grove that was dedicated to Athene. There King Odysseus stopped and sat, and began at once a prayer to the daughter of sovereign Zeus:

'Hear me, child of Zeus of the aegis, Unwearied One. Listen to me at last, since you did not listen in my need when the mighty Earthshaker shattered my craft. Grant that now among the Phaeacians I may find welcome and compassion.'

So he spoke in prayer, and Pallas Athene listened to him; yet she would not as yet come to his sight plainly and undisguised. She shrank from offending her father's brother, who kept unquenched his anger against the hero until he returned to his own country.

BOOK VII

ODYSSEUS AS GUEST OF ALCINOUS

WHILE patient Odysseus was praying thus, the sturdy mules went on to the town with the princess. Having reached her father's noble palace, she halted the wagon at the forecourt, and her brothers, looking like immortals, gathered around her, unyoked the mules and carried the clothes indoors. She herself went up to her own room, and Eurymedusa lighted a fire for her. This was an old waiting-woman who long ago had come from Apeire, brought as a captive here by ship. She had then been chosen as prize for Alcinous because he was king of all the Phaeacians and the people gave their service to him as to a god. She had been Nausicaa's nurse in the palace halls, and now it was she who kindled a fire and made supper ready for the princess in her own room.

Odysseus meanwhile was setting out on his walk to the town. Athene poured a thick mist around him;[1] this was in kindness to Odysseus, so that no presumptuous townsman who crossed his path should accost him with discourteous words and ask him who he might be. Moreover, when he had all but entered this lovely town, the goddess herself came to meet him; she had taken the form of a young girl carrying a pitcher, and in this disguise she halted in front of him. Odysseus asked her: 'Child, could you be my guide to the house of Lord Alcinous, who is ruler of your people here? I am travel-worn, a stranger from far away, and so not acquainted with anyone in your city or your countryside.'

Athene the goddess answered him: 'Sir, I will do as you request; I will show you that house – it is near my own good father's. But you must walk quite silently while I lead the way; do not look at anyone, do not question anyone. Men here do not take to strangers kindly; they do not welcome or befriend someone who comes to them from elsewhere. They put their pride in their rapid ships, which quickly traverse the gulf of ocean; that is a privilege from Poseidon, and the ships are swift as a bird's wing or a man's thought.'

With these words Pallas Athene led the way quickly, and he

1. The magic mist, like a 'cap of darkness', is thought of as being itself invisible as well as making the favoured person so.

followed the footsteps of the goddess. The Phaeacian seamen never saw him as he passed through their midst along the streets; the goddess of braided hair forbade it, august Athene who in protection had shed the enchanted mist all round him. Odysseus looked wonderingly at the landing-places, the trim ships, the assembly-place of the noble townsmen and the long high palisaded walls that astonished all beholders. When they reached the king's noble palace, Athene the goddess thus began: 'Sir, here is the house you desired me to guide you to. You will find inside it our heaven-protected princes banqueting; enter nevertheless and be undismayed; here and everywhere, boldest is best. The first person your eye will rest on should be the queen; she is called Arete, and rightly so.[1] She is from the same stock as King Alcinous. First came Nausithous, son of Poseidon and lovely Periboea, the youngest daughter of bold Eurymedon, who once was king of the overbearing Giants, but then brought doom on his reckless people and on himself. Poseidon lay with Periboea, and she bore him this son, Nausithous, who became king of the Phaeacians and had two sons, Rhexenor and Alcinous. Rhexenor had not been married long when he met his death from Apollo of the silver bow; he was sonless, but left one daughter in his place; this was Arete, whom Alcinous made his wife and has honoured ever since as no other wife in the world is honoured, of all wives who rule a household under their husband's eye. Such has always been, and such still is, the honour paid to Arete by Alcinous and by her children and by the people here, who gaze at her as at a divinity and greet her with loyal words whenever she walks about the town, because she is full of unprompted wisdom. If she takes kindly to anyone – to a man no less than to a woman – she will be a peacemaker in his feuds. You too, then, if she looks kindly on you, may hope to set eyes again on your kith and kin and to reach your own lofty roof and your own country.'

And with these words Athene departed over the barren sea; she left lovely Scheria behind her; she came to Marathon and to wide-wayed Athens and entered Erectheus' mighty house. Meanwhile Odysseus went on his way to the noble palace of Alcinous, and thoughts came thronging through his mind as he halted here

1. i.e. Arete is a 'significant name'; perhaps 'she who is prayed for', but here more likely 'she who is prayed to' by a suppliant like Odysseus.

and again there before he arrived at the brazen threshold. A
radiance like that of sun or moon played over the king's high
palace. Walls of bronze ran this way and that, from the entrance
to the further end, and these were topped with a frieze of cyanus.[1]
Golden doors closed the palace in, and silver posts rose above the
threshold; the lintel was of silver, the door-handle was of gold.
Each side of the door were gold and silver watchdogs, deathless
for ever and unageing, which Hephaestus with his wit and cun-
ning had fashioned as guardians for the great house.[2] Inside, to
the left and right, from the entrance down to the very end, there
were chairs ranged along the wall, and over these hung coverings
of cloth on which women had spent their skill, finely spun and
closely woven. Here the leaders of the Phaeacians would often sit
as they ate and drank, for they always had abundance. Standing
upon shapely pedestals were statues of boys made of gold; they
had flaming torches in their hands and gave their light, all the
evening through, to the banqueters in the hall. Moreover, the
king has in his palace as many as fifty serving-women, some at
their hand-mills grinding the yellow corn, some weaving their
webs or else sitting down to spin their wool – their moving hands
are like quivering leaves on a tall aspen; soft olive-oil drops off
from the closely-woven fabric.[3] Just as the Phaeacian men are the
world's ablest in seamanship, so the women are deftest in weaving;
to them above others Athene has given keen wits and the skill to
make very lovely things.

Outside the courtyard, near the entrance, is a great garden of
four acres, with a fence running round, this way and that. Here
are planted tall thriving trees – pears, pomegranates, apples with
glistening fruit, sweet figs, rich olives. The fruit of all these never
fails or flags all the year round, winter or summer; here the west

1. Cyanus: dark-blue enamel or glass paste, a substitute sometimes
for lapis lazuli.

2. These figures may have been sphinxes or griffins serving magic-
ally as watchdogs (A. Shewan, *Homeric Essays* (1935), pp. 287–8).

3. Perhaps the weaving was so close that oil did not penetrate the
fabric; perhaps oil was actually poured on the wool during the process
of preparation. A passage from Alexandrian comedy (Machon, 3rd
century B.C.) mentions oil as used for cleansing garments. In Verga's
Sicilian novel *I Malavoglia* (1881) there is reference to the use of
bozzima – a mixture of grease and bran – for softening the web on
the loom.

wind is always breathing – some fruits it brings to birth, some to ripeness. Pear upon pear matures to fullness, apple on apple, grape-cluster on grape-cluster, fig on fig. There too the king has his fruitful vineyard planted; behind is a warm and level spot, dried by the sun, where some grapes are being gathered and others trodden; in front there are unripe grapes that have scarcely shed their blossom, and others already faintly darkening. There too, bordering the last row of vines, are trim plots of all kinds of herbs that keep fresh all the year round. Lastly there are two springs of water, and one of these is channelled out over the whole space of garden; the other, facing it, flows under the entrance of the courtyard to issue in front of the lofty palace; and from this the townspeople drew their water.

Such were the god's sumptuous gifts in the demesne of King Alcinous. Much-tried Odysseus stood there and gazed; then, having gazed his fill, stepped quickly over the threshold into the house. He found the Phaeacian lords and rulers pouring libations from their cups to the Radiant One, keen-sighted Hermes, to whom by custom they poured libation last when they turned their thoughts to the night's rest. Then Odysseus strode down the hall, with the mist from Athene covering him, till he reached Arete and King Alcinous; then he put his hands round Arete's knees. The enchanted mist rolled back at once to disclose the hero, and silence fell on the banqueters as they saw this man in the hall beside them. They gazed at him in bewilderment, but meanwhile Odysseus began his plea:

'Arete, daughter of great Rhexenor; after much affliction I come as a suppliant to your knees; I come to your husband and your guests; I pray that the gods may grant them happiness all their lives and that each of them may bequeath his children the wealth that he has in his own halls and whatever rights his people have granted him. As for myself – give me means to return quickly to my own land, because for this long time past I have suffered misery far from my kith and kin.'

So he spoke, and sat down at the hearth in the ashes by the fire. The others were all hushed and dumb, but after a while old Echenaus began to speak, a Phaeacian chieftain of age and eloquence, versed in the wisdom of the past. Wishing well to all, he spoke his mind thus:

'It is not seemly, Alcinous, it is not decent, that a guest should

stay sitting upon the ground, in the ashes by the fire, while all
your people wait there uneasily, expecting a clear word from you.
Come now, ask your guest to stand up; give him a seat on a silver-
studded chair, and tell the pages to mix more wine; then we may
make libation to Zeus the Thunderer, the patron of venerable
suppliants; and let the housekeeper offer the guest a meal from
such things as she has in store.'

The king heard Echenaus out, then took his shrewd and subtle
guest by the hand, raised him from the hearth and seated him in
a glittering chair which he asked his favourite son to leave (this
was manly Laodamas, who had been sitting there next to the
king). A maid brought water in a fine golden jug and poured it
over Odysseus' hands for washing, holding a silver basin below;
then she drew up a polished table for him. The trusted house-
keeper came and put bread where he could reach it; there were
many kinds of food as well, and she gave ungrudgingly of all that
she had; so much-tried Odysseus began to eat and drink. Then
King Alcinous spoke to his page: 'Pontonous, mix wine in the
bowl and serve it to everyone in the hall; then we will make
libation to Zeus the Thunderer, who is patron of venerable sup-
pliants.' And at this command the page began mixing the fragrant
wine, then poured the first drops into every cup in turn. And
when they had made libation and had drunk wine to their heart's
content, Alcinous spoke among them all:

'Listen, Phaeacian chiefs and princes, and let me say what is in
my mind. Tonight, at the ending of this meal, return to your
own homes and sleep. But tomorrow morning we will proclaim a
full assembly of our elders; we will entertain this guest in our
halls and make noble offerings to the gods; then we will think
how to send him home, so that under our convoy he may return
without toil or trouble to his own country – may return both
confidently and swiftly, even if he comes from far away, unharmed
and unthwarted until he sets foot on his own soil; after that,
he must look to meet whatever events his own fate and the stern
Spinners twisted into his thread of destiny when he entered the
world and his mother bore him.

'But if he is one of the Deathless Ones, here and now come
down from the sky, then the gods are contriving something new,
because in the past they have always appeared undisguised among
us at our offering of noble hecatombs; they have feasted beside us,

they have sat at the same table. And if one of us comes upon
them as he travels alone, then too they have never as yet made
concealment, because we are close of kin to themselves, just like
those of the Cyclops race or the savage peoples of the Giants.'

Subtle Odysseus answered him : 'Alcinous, let any such thought
be far from your mind. In no way am I like the immortals whose
home is the arching heaven itself. My frame and aspect are not
like theirs, they are those of men whose end is death. Whatever
mortals you and your people know to be sunk in wretchedness
more than others, it is with them I would rank myself in my
miseries. I could tell you now of tribulation on tribulation that
I have borne because the gods willed it so. But whatever my dis-
tress may be, I would ask you now to let me eat. There is nothing
more devoid of shame than the accursed belly; it thrusts itself
upon a man's mind in spite of his afflictions, in spite of his in-
ward grief. That is true of me; my heart is sad, but my belly keeps
urging me to have food and drink, tries to blot out all the past
from me; it says imperiously : "Eat and be filled." As for you, my
hosts, I would ask you as soon as daylight comes to take swift
measures to set me on my own soil again. I am a luckless man, I
have suffered much; I should be content to let life leave me when
once I had had sight again of my own possessions, my own
servants and the tall roof of my own great house.'

These were his words; the banqueters all applauded; this guest
had spoken as a man should, and they thought it right to send
him in safety home.

When they had made libation and had drunk wine to their
heart's content, they went away to lie down and sleep, each in
his own house. King Odysseus was left in the hall, with Arete
and Alcinous near him. As the maids began to clear the used
things away, white-armed Arete was first to speak. She had spied
the fine clothes Odysseus wore, the cloak and tunic that she her-
self had made with her waiting-women; so her words came forth
in rapid flight :

'My guest, I will take it upon me to question you. Who are
you, and where have you travelled from? Who gave you the
clothes you are wearing now? Did you not say you had reached
us here in the course of wanderings over the seas?'

Subtle Odysseus answered : 'Queen, it would be too hard a task
to tell my troubles from beginning to end, in such abundance

have they been sent on me by the gods in heaven. Thus much I
will answer to your questioning. Far from here there lies in the
sea an island called Ogygia. The daughter of Atlas has her home
there, Calypso, a goddess of awesome power and of many wiles.
She is seldom visited, whether by mortals or by immortals; but I,
alas, was brought by ill fortune to her hearth, a sole survivor
when Zeus with his flashing thunderbolt shattered and shivered
my rapid ship in the midst of wine-dark ocean. There and then
my good comrades perished; for myself, I threw my arms round
the vessel's keel and was carried on for nine whole days; in the
murkiness of the tenth night the gods brought me to Ogygia.
The goddess welcomed me lovingly, tended me, offered me im-
mortality and eternal youth; yet she never won the heart within
me. I remained with her for seven full years, and watered with
continual weeping the celestial garments that she gave me. But
when the eighth year came circling round, she told me and urged
me to return, perhaps because Zeus had sent her warning, per-
haps because her own mind had changed. So she sent me away on
a firm raft, giving me many gifts, food and sweet wine, and
clothing me in celestial garments; moreover she sent a fair wind
for me, warm and kindly. For seventeen days I sailed on across
the ocean, and on the eighteenth there loomed before me the
shadowy hills of this land of yours. My heart leapt up, but fate
was against me, and trouble and I were to be companions a long
while still – trouble launched on me by Poseidon, who stirred his
tempests up against me, balked my passage, and heaved up the
sea to monstrous heights; I groaned aloud, but the waves would
not let me keep to my raft; it was dashed to pieces by the gale,
and only by swimming could I still cut my way through the
sea-gulf yonder. At length I was carried by wind and wave near
to your shore; but there, as I tried to land, the waves would have
seized me and driven me hurtling against the great rocks of that
grim coast; instead, I swam back and changed my course until I
arrived at a river's mouth where the safest landing-place seemed
to be, clear of rocks, and with shelter from the wind. With a last
effort I threw myself out upon the shore and, with that, mys-
terious night came on. I walked away from the rain-fed river and
lay down among the bushes, heaping leaves all over me; then a
god shed care-charming sleep upon me. There in the leaves, des-
pite all the sorrows of my heart, I slept all night and till dawn

and noon; day was declining before sweet sleep released me. Then I looked out, and there on the beach were your daughter's handmaids playing, and there, like a goddess from heaven, was she. So to her I made my supplication, and at no point did she fail in thoughtfulness. One would hardly hope, at a chance meeting, to find such discretion in one so young, so often do youth and thoughtlessness go together. But your daughter offered me food in plenty, with glowing wine; she saw to it that I bathed in the river; she gave me the garments that you see. Thus much I have told you, despite my sorrows; the tale is true.'

Alcinous said to him in turn: 'My guest, there was after all one thing in which this daughter of mine fell short. She did not bring you into my house when she brought her maids; yet it was to her first of all that you came in supplication.'

Subtle Odysseus answered him: 'Sir, let no such thought as that make you blame a daughter beyond reproach. She herself had desired me to join her maids and to come with her; it was I who would not; I was bashful; I feared you might look askance at me if you saw me with her, because all the world over we human beings are quick to take offence.'

Alcinous answered: 'No, my guest; the heart within me is never tempted to groundless anger; right measure in everything is best. I call Father Zeus to be my witness, and Athene and Apollo, how well contented I should be if you as I see you now, a man who thinks as I think myself, should wed my daughter, should be acclaimed as my son-in-law and should stay here. I would give you a house and riches also if you would stay of your own free will – against your will no Phaeacian shall keep you here – may the mind of Zeus never so decree! As for your journey home – let me leave you in no doubt on this – I hereby choose tomorrow for it. Through that journey you can be soundly sleeping while the crew are traversing the calm sea, till you reach your own land and home or whatever place you may desire, even should it be far beyond Euboea. That is the further point of all – so say those of our people who once set eyes on it when they carried yellow-haired Rhadamanthus to visit Tityus son of Gaia. Our men reached there, and then with no hardship returned the same day and finished the voyage home. But you will learn for yourself how much better than others anywhere are my ships and crews as they toss the salt waters with their oars.'

So he spoke. Patient Odysseus rejoiced at heart and uttered a prayer in these words: 'Father Zeus, grant that Alcinous may perform his promise to the full; then his good name will spread the world over and never die, and I myself shall reach my own country.'

Such were the words that passed between them. The white-armed queen ordered her maids meanwhile to put out a bedstead under the portico, to lay down first fine rugs of crimson, then to spread coverlets over them and fleecy blankets above again. The maids left the hall, torch in hand, and having briskly prepared the bed they returned to Odysseus' side and addressed him cheeringly: 'You may rise now, stranger, and take your rest; your bed is made.' So they spoke, and sleep to him was a welcome thought. There, then, patient Odysseus lay down to rest in the morticed bedstead inside the echoing portico, while Alcinous slept in an inner room of the lofty palace, and the queen his wife shared his bed.

DAWN comes early, with rosy fingers. When she appeared, King Alcinous rose from his bed and royal Odysseus the city-sacker rose from his. Alcinous led the way to the Phaeacians' assembly-place by the ships. Having reached it, they sat down together on the smooth stones. Athene meanwhile began to walk up and down the streets; she had made herself like one of the king's pages, and her purpose was to help the homecoming of Odysseus. She stood by the citizens, each in turn, and she said to them:

'Come, you Phaeacian chiefs and princes, hasten to the assembly-place and learn the news about the stranger who came to our wise king's palace yesterday; he has wandered the ocean far and wide, and he looks like an immortal.'

With these words she roused the minds of them all to eagerness. The seats in the assembly-place were soon filled with the flocking people, and many were those who gazed in wonder at Laertes' subtle-minded son. Moreover, Athene shed more than human grace on his head and shoulders, and gave him ampler stature and ampler presence, so that all the Phaeacians should welcome and honour and revere him and that he himself should pass victoriously through the trials they later put before him. When all were gathered there in assembly, Alcinous spoke among them thus:

'Listen, Phaeacian chiefs and princes, and let me speak what is in my mind. This stranger, whoever he may be – setting forth from the East, it may be, or from the West – has come in his wanderings to my house. He asks for help to return home and implores us to ensure him this. Let us hasten, then, to prepare his voyage, just as in times past, for no one who once has come to my house lingers here long, fretting for convoy home. Come, let us drew down to the sea a dark ship that has never sailed before. Let the people choose fifty-two young men of proven vigour; let these all make fast the oars to the thwarts, then come ashore and on to my house, then quickly take their share in the meal; I will make it plentiful for all. These are my orders for the young men; but let those of you who are sceptred princes come to my house without delay to join in feasting our guest in the palace hall; let no one say no. And summon also the sacred bard Demo-

docus, because on him more than on any other the god has
bestowed the gift of song, to delight men on whatever theme he
may be inspirited to sing.'

With these words he led the way, and the sceptred princes
followed. A page went to fetch the sacred bard. The fifty-two
chosen young men went down as they had been commanded to
the shore of the barren ocean, and reaching the ship at the sea's
edge they hauled it down and into deep water, stowed mast and
sails in the dark vessel, secured the oars in the leather thongs,
everything in due order, and spread the white sails. They anchored
their ships well out from shore, then went their way to the palace
of wise Alcinous, and the porticoes and courts and rooms were
filled with the multitude. For all these guests, Alcinous slaugh-
tered a dozen sheep, eight boars, two oxen; these were flayed and
made ready, and a meal was prepared that all would welcome.

Then, led by the page, the faithful bard came in. The Muse had
favoured him above others, yet had given him good and evil
mingled; his eyes she took from him, but she gave him entrancing
song. Pontonous found him a silver-studded chair, placed it amid
the banqueters against a tall pillar, hung up the clear-sounding
lyre on a peg above his head and showed him how he could put his
hands on it; by his side he placed a table, with a basket of bread
and a goblet of wine, to drink from whenever he desired. The
banqueters stretched out their hands to the food before them, and
when they had eaten and drunk their fill the goddess of song
moved the bard to sing the deeds of heroes. He chose the lay
whose fame then reached to broad heaven itself, the quarrel be-
tween Odysseus and Achilles, how once at a sumptuous feast of
the gods these two begun to wrangle with violent words, and
Agamemnon rejoiced in secret that the noblest of the Achaeans
had fallen out; because this was the sign that Phoebus Apollo
had spoken of at his oracle in holy Pytho when the king crossed
the stone threshold to ask his counsel; for then the first billow of
calamity was rolling towards both Trojans and Danaans because
of the will of sovereign Zeus.

It was of this that the famous bard now sang; but Odysseus
firmly seized the big crimson cloak that he was wearing, drew a
piece of it down over his head and covered his countenance,
ashamed that the Phaeacians should spy the tears that streamed
from his eyes. Whenever the sacred bard paused in his song,

Odysseus would wipe his tears, draw back the cloak from over his head, take his two-handled goblet and pour a libation to the gods; but when the bard began once more at the wish of the Phaeacian nobles (for indeed his lay enchanted them), then Odysseus would cover his head again and would groan and weep. This went unnoticed by all the rest; only Alcinous, sitting beside him, both saw the tears and heard the deep groans. So without more ado he said to these lovers of seamanship :

'Listen, Phaeacians chiefs and princes; by now we have had our heart's content of the sumptuous well-apportioned banquet and of the music that goes with it. Now let us leave the house again and try our skill in varied contest, so that when our guest is home once more he may tell his people how much we outstrip other men in boxing and in wrestling, in jumping and in running.'

With these words he led the way and the others followed. The page hung up the lyre on its peg, then took Demodocus by the hand, led him away out of the hall and guided him down the same path that the nobles were following already as they prepared to watch the games. So they walked to the assembly-place, and with them went a great multitude, very great indeed. Many young nobles stood up in challenge; Acronaus did, and Ocyalus and Elatreus; Nauteus, Prymneus, Anchialus and Eretmeus; Ponteus, Proreus, Thoon, Anabesinaus; Amphialus son of Polynaus son of Tecton; then Euryalus, looking like Ares, men's destroyer; he was son to Naubolus, and of all Phaeacian men was noblest in form and figure after peerless Laodamas. Laodamas also now stood up, and with him two other sons of the king, Halius and noble Clytonaus.

The first of the contests was a footrace. From the very start the race was fierce; swiftly they all sped over the course while the dust went up, but of all these runners Prince Clytonaus was far the best. A pair of mules ploughing a fallow go a furrow's length before they turn; by that length he ran ahead, and came back to the watching people while the other runners were left behind. Then others took their turn at wrestling – no sport for cowards; and here Euryalus worsted the others of his rank. In jumping, Amphialus came first. In discus-throwing Elatreus was by far the best; and in boxing, Prince Laodamas.

But when all of them had tried their skill to their heart's con-

tent, Prince Laodamas said to them: 'Come, friends, let us ask
the stranger if there is some sport he is well versed in. There is
nothing amiss with the looks of him – those thighs and legs and
that pair of arms, the firm-set neck, all the massive strength. He
is in his prime, even if much battered by misfortune – and to my
thinking there is nothing worse than the sea to unstring a man,
be he as vigorous as he may.'

Euryalus answered: 'That was well thought of, Laodamas. Go
to him yourself, put the matter to him and make the challenge.'

At this reply the prince stepped forward. 'Come, sir,' he said to
Odysseus now, 'will not you in turn take part in some sport that
you are versed in? It is only right that you should be master of
some sport. Through all a man's lifetime, there is nothing that
brings him greater glory than what he achieves by speed of foot
and by strength of arm. Make the venture, sir; put your cares
aside. Your journey home is not far in front of you; the ship has
been hauled down into the water; the crew are ready.'

But wise Odysseus answered him: 'Laodamas, why this mock-
ing challenge? What fills my thoughts is my own plight, not
sports like these. How long I have suffered, how much I have
borne already! Yet here I am still, sitting in your assembly-place,
aching for home and begging help from the king and all your
people.'

Euryalus answered, insulting him to his face: 'Yes truly,
stranger; there are sports in the world of more kinds than one,
but I take it you have no bent for them. More likely, I think, you
are one who plies here and there in some big ship, a master of
trading sailors; anxious over the cargo out, watchful over the
cargo home and his greedy gains; nothing about you speaks the
athlete.'

Grimly frowning, Odysseus answered: 'Sir, that speech was un-
becoming; you seem like an arrogant young man. The gods, I
find, do not give their favours all together, form and wisdom and
eloquence. A man may seem in outward aspect unworthy of much
regard, yet heaven hangs beauty about his words, and those who
hear him gaze at him in delight while he speaks unfalteringly
and with winning modesty; he stands out among those assembled
there, and as he goes his way through the city, men look at him
as if at a god. Another man is in aspect like the Deathless Ones,
but then no grace attends on his words at all. So it is with you;

features and form are noble; not even a god could better that mould; yet your mind is all nothingness. Those ill-judged words have left me resentful. Say what you will, I am not a stranger to manly sports; in all such things I would claim that I was among the foremost until my mettle and strength of arm came to play me false. As you see me now, I am ground down by distress and misery; I have had many trials to endure, fighting my way through hostile warriors and battering waves. Yet nevertheless, despite all sufferings, I will try my fortune in your contests. Your insult rankles, and you have roused me.'

And upon these words, without throwing off his cloak, he started up and seized a discus; it was big and thick, by far more massive than those the Phaeacians used for throwing among themselves. He whirled it, hurled it forth from his powerful hand; the stone sped whizzing past them all,[1] and down went the heads of the Phaeacians, masters of ships and wielders of oars, but cowering earthwards now as this thing rushed by. The stone that sped so easily from his hand outshot all the marks of other throwers, and Athene herself, in the likeness of a man, measured the distances and declared: 'Sir, even a blind man, groping round it, could tell your mark from the rest; it is not one discus in a crowd, it is far ahead of all the others. For this contest at least you need fear nothing; no Phaeacian will reach this mark, much less will any of them outshoot it.'

So spoke Athene, and staunch Odysseus was glad and comforted to see his kind comrade there in the lists. Then with lighter heart he cried out to the Phaeacians: 'Now, you young men, reach that; though I think that a little later I may throw a second as far or further. And let any of you whom his heart and spirit so inclines come here and make trial with me – the truth is you have much provoked me – in boxing or wrestling or even running – even that I do not refuse. I speak to all the Phaeacians except Laodamas himself. He is my host, and what man would challenge his entertainer? Foolish and worthless the man must be who should ask his host in a strange land to enter some contest with himself; he would cut the ground from beneath his own feet. Of all the rest there is no one I set aside or think beneath me; I am ready to meet any man and to try his mettle. In what-

1.   'The heavy Flint
    With violence went, as *Pluto* had been in't.' OGILBY

ever contests men practise anywhere, I can play my part without disgrace. I know well enough how to wield the bow. My arrow would be the first to find its mark in a throng of foemen, even though the friends at my side were many and each of them took aim at his man. In the land of Troy, when we Achaeans were shooting there, Philoctetes alone excelled me in archery. As for all others, I think myself much their better – I speak of men still alive and eating their bread on earth. The men of old I will not presume to challenge – Heracles or Oechalian Eurytus. These in their archery challenged the gods themselves, and hence it was that great Eurytus died before his time, and age never stole upon him in his own halls; Apollo slew him in indignation because he had challenged him with the bow.

'Then, besides, I can send a spear further than others can send an arrow.[1] Only in running I fear some Phaeacian may outstrip me. I was sadly battered by thronging waves, and my stores on shipboard did not last; so my limbs have lost their suppleness.'

Such were his words. The rest of them all remained in silence; only Alcinous answered thus: 'Sir, what you say in no way transgresses courtesy. You are eager to put beyond all question the prowess that belongs to you, and you were outraged when this young man strode up to you in the lists to taunt you. He mocked your prowess as no man would if his wit had taught him words of prudence. But now you must listen to me in turn, so that later you may tell these things to some other chieftain as you sit and feast in your own halls with your own wife and your own children and recall what prowess is ours also, and what forms of excellence Zeus has bestowed on us ever since the days of our forefathers. We are neither boxers nor wrestlers of renown, but our feet are swift to run the race, and in seamanship there are none to equal us. Feasting we love, and the music of strings, and dancing; change of garments, and warm baths, and the pleasures of the bed.

'So come, you finest of the Phaeacian dancers, and play your parts before the stranger, so that when he has come home again he may tell his kinsfolk how much we excel other men in sailing

---

1. It may perhaps be not arrow-shooting but arrow-throwing that is in question. A modern observer, S. O. R. Robertson-Luxford, claims to have seen American Indians throw an arrow sixty or seventy yards (*Classical Review* xxiii 151).

and running and dance and song. And let one of you at once fetch Demodocus his clear-sounding lyre from where it hangs in our halls.'

So spoke Alcinous. A page sprang to his feet at once to fetch the hollow lyre from the palace, and nine umpires stood up, chosen to serve the people thus, and accustomed to ordering things aright in such sports as these; they smoothed out a floor for the dance, making a fine spacious ring. Then the page came back with the clear-sounding lyre for Demodocus. The bard stepped into the middle of the ring, and round him stood the young boys who were skilled in dancing and began to tread out a rhythmic measure. Odysseus gazed at the flashing feet and his heart was filled with wonder.[1]

Demodocus struck his lyre and began a beguiling song about the loves of Ares and Aphrodite, how first they lay together secretly in the dwelling of Hephaestus. Ares had offered many gifts to the garlanded divinity and covered with shame the marriage bed of Lord Hephaestus. But the sun-god had seen them in their dalliance and hastened away to tell Hephaestus; to him the news was bitter as gall, and he made his way towards his smithy, brooding revenge. He laid the great anvil on its base and set himself to forge chains that could not be broken or torn asunder, being fashioned to bind the lovers fast. Such was the device that he made in his indignation against Ares, and having made it he went to the room where his bed lay; all round the bed-posts he dropped the chains, while others in plenty hung from the roof-beam, gossamer-light and invisible to the blessed gods themselves, so cunning had been the workmanship. When the snare round the bed was all complete, he made as if to depart to Lemnos, the pleasant-sited town, which he loved more than any place on earth. Ares, god of the golden reins, was no blind watcher. Once he had seen Hephaestus go, he himself approached the great craftsman's dwelling, pining for love of Cytherea. As for her, she had just returned from the palace of mighty Zeus her father, and was sitting down in the house as Ares entered it. He took her hand and spoke thus to her: 'Come, my darling; let us go to bed and take our delight together. Hephaestus is no longer here; by now, I think, he has made his way to Lemnos, to visit the uncouth-spoken Sintians.'

1. 'Such sparkling feet *Ulysses* ne'er had seen.' HOBBES

So he spoke, and sleep with him was a welcome thought to her. So they went to the bed and there lay down, but the cunning chains of crafty Hephaestus enveloped them, and they could neither raise their limbs nor shift them at all; so they saw the truth when there was no escaping. Meanwhile the lame crafts-man god approached; he had turned back short of the land of Lemnos, since the watching sun-god had told him everything. Cut to the heart, he neared his house and halted inside the porch; savage anger had hold of him, and he roared out hideously, cry-ing to all the gods:

'Come, Father Zeus; come, all you blessed immortals with him; see what has happened here – no matter for laughter nor yet for-bearance. Aphrodite had Zeus for father; because I am lame she never ceases to do me outrage and give her love to destructive Ares, since he is handsome and sound-footed and I am a cripple from my birth; yet for that my two parents are to blame, no one else at all, and I wish they had never begotten me. You will see the pair of lovers now as they lie embracing in my bed; the sight of them makes me sick at heart. Yet I doubt their desire to rest there longer, even a moment longer, fond as they are.[1] They will soon unwish their posture there; but my cunning chains shall hold them both fast till her father Zeus has given me back all the betrothal gifts I bestowed on him for his wanton daughter; beauty she has, but no sense of shame.'

Thus he spoke, and the gods came thronging there in front of the house with its brazen floor. Poseidon the Earth-Sustainer came, and Hermes the Mighty Runner, and Lord Apollo who shoots from afar; but the goddesses, every one of them, kept within doors for very shame. Thus then the bounteous gods stood at the en-trance. Laughter they could not quench rose on the lips of these happy beings as they fixed their eyes on the stratagem of Hephaes-tus, and glancing each at his neighbour said some such words as these: 'Ill deeds never prosper; swift after all is outrun by slow; here is Hephaestus the slow and crippled, yet by his cunning he has defeated the swiftest of all Olympian gods, and Ares must pay an adulterer's penalty.'

Such were the words that passed between them. Then Lord Apollo the son of Zeus spoke thus to Hermes: 'Hermes, giver of blessings, messenger, son of Zeus, would you be content to be

1. 'How keen soever on their love they be.' HOBBES

chained as fast, if then you could lie abed with golden Aphrodite?'
And the Radiant One answered him: 'O Lord Apollo of darting
arrows – would that it might be so! Though desperate chains in
thrice that number were to enclose me round – though all you
gods were to have full sight of me, and all the goddesses too – I
would even then choose to lie with golden Aphrodite.'

So said Hermes, and laughter arose among the immortal gods.
But for Poseidon there was no laughing; he kept imploring the
master smith Hephaestus in hopes that he would let Ares go. He
spoke in words of urgent utterance: 'Let him go; I promise that
he shall pay in full such rightful penalty as you ask for – pay in
the presence of all the gods.' But the great lame craftsman an-
swered him: 'Poseidon, Sustainer of the Earth, do not ask this of
me. Pledges for trustless folk are trustless pledges. If Ares should
go his way, free of his chains and his debt alike, what then?
Could I fetter yourself in the presence of all the gods?'

Poseidon who shakes the earth replied: 'Hephaestus, if Ares
indeed denies his debt and escapes elsewhere, I myself will pay
what you ask.' Then the great lame craftsman answered him: 'I
must not and cannot refuse you now', and with that he undid the
chains, powerful though they had proved. Unshackled thus, the
lovers were up and off at once; Ares went on his way to Thrace,
and Aphrodite the laughter-lover to Paphos in Cyprus, where she
has her precinct and fragrant altar. In this home of hers the
Graces washed her, anointed her with the celestial oil that gleams
on the limbs of the immortals,[1] and clad her in lovely garments
that ravished the gazing eye.

Such was the lay of the famous bard. With contented heart
Odysseus listened, and with him the Phaeacians, masters of ship
and oar.

Then Alcinous gave the word for Halius and Laodamas to
dance – these two apart, because no one could rival them. So they
took in their hands a lovely crimson ball that the craftsman
Polybus had made them; one of them would lean back and toss
it up towards the shadowy clouds, and the other leap upwards
from the ground and deftly catch it before his feet touched earth
again. Having had their turn at throwing the ball straight up-
wards, they continued dancing and tossing the ball to and fro
between them, but now they remained close to the ground, while

1. 'And with immortall Balms besmooth her skin.' CHAPMAN

the other youths standing round the ring beat out the rhythm and let the sound rise in air.

Then noble Odysseus spoke to the king: 'Alcinous, most illustrious lord, you boasted a little while ago that your dancers were supreme, and now the boast is no more than truth. I am all astonishment as I look.'

So he spoke. The great king was overjoyed, and called at once to his court of seamen: 'Listen, Phaeacian chiefs and rulers. Our guest, I think, is exceedingly discerning. Let us offer him the parting gifts he deserves. There are in this land twelve princes of mark who rule the people; add myself, and there are thirteen. Let each of us bring him a clean cloak and tunic, and a talent of precious gold; and let us assemble the presents speedily, so that with these displayed before him he may come into supper well content. And let Euryalus make amends to him, man to man, with both words and gift, after those unseemly words of his.'

So said the king, and all the chiefs accepted his word and gave approval; each of them sent his own messenger to bring in the gifts. And Euryalus made this response:

'Alcinous, most illustrious lord, I will do your bidding and make our guest amends. I will give him this sword of bronze with its silver hilt and encircling sheath of freshly sawn ivory; he will find it a treasure of great price.' So speaking he put the silvered sword into Odysseus' hands and addressed him in ready utterance: 'Good luck go with you, honoured guest. May any word that has been ill spoken be snatched and whirled away by the winds forthwith. And may the gods grant you to see your wife and reach home again; you have been a sufferer all too long, far from your kith and kin.' And subtle Odysseus answered him: 'Friend, good luck go with you also; may the gods give you all their blessings, and may you never feel need for the sword you have given me now with words that make full amends.' And with this response he passed round his shoulders the silver-studded sword.

It was sunset now; the precious gifts stood ready before Odysseus, and the messengers carried them forward inside the palace; there the king's sons took them over and laid them down by the queen their mother; and splendid gifts they were. King Alcinous led the way for the rest and they followed him and then sat down in their high seats. Thereupon the king turned to Arete: 'Come, wife, have a handsome chest brought here, whichever is the finest, and put a clean cloak and tunic in it as your own gift. And have a cauldron warmed for our guest over the fire, and the water heated; then he can bathe, can see our chieftains' presents all neatly stowed and then can enjoy the feast and whatever lay he listens to. And here is a goblet of mine that I myself will give him; it is of gold, it is very beautiful, and all his days he will think of me as he pours from it in his own halls to Zeus and the other gods.'

Thus he spoke, and Arete told her maids to set the great cauldron over the fire at once. So they set it there – the fire was already burning; they poured in the water that was to fill the bath, and put logs beneath and kindled them. The flames licked the belly of the tripod, and the heat began to reach the water. Meanwhile the queen had a fine chest brought out from an inner room and began to lay the gifts in it, the gold and garments from the Phaeacians; she put in also her own fine gift of cloak and tunic; then rapidly she advised her guest: 'Now look to the lid of this yourself, and tie a knot upon it at once, so that no one may rifle it on your journey, when later on you find sweet sleep as the dark ship bears you homewards.'

Heeding her words, staunch Odysseus made the lid fast at once, and hastened to tie the cunning knot which Lady Circe had brought to his knowledge in other days. Forthwith the housekeeper called to him to enter the bath and bathe; and a welcome sight the warm water was to one who had been unused to comfort ever since he left the palace of lovely-haired Calypso, though all the time that he was with her he had had the comforts a god might have.

When the maids had washed and anointed him and wrapped a tunic and handsome cloak round him, he left the bath and began to walk on to join the chieftains at their wine. But Nausicaa in her heavenly beauty had paused by the pillar that bore the massy roof, and now with Odysseus before her eyes she was gazing at him wonderingly. She said, and the words were not unheeded: 'Friend from far off, all good go with you, so that when hereafter you are in your own land you may remember me, and how to me before any other you owe the ransoming of your life.' And subtle Odysseus answered her: 'Nausicaa, daughter of great Alcinous, may Zeus the Thunderer, Hera's husband, bring all to pass that you wish me thus; may he grant me return to my own land, grant me sight of the day of homecoming; and then there also, through all my days, your name on my lips will be like a god's, because you gave me my life, Nausicaa.'

So he spoke; then he took his seat next to King Alcinous. There already the portions were being served and the wine mixed. A page approached, leading in Demodocus, the faithful bard whom the people reverenced; the page now gave him a place to sit in, with banqueters on each side of him and a tall pillar behind his back. Then Odysseus called the young man, having just cut a portion, rich in fat, from the chine of a white-tusked boar (even so, there was plenty left). 'Here, young man; let Demodocus have this dish to eat; I must do him this courtesy, sad though my mood is. For in all men's eyes all over the world bards deserve honour and veneration, because the goddess of song has taught them lays and has shown her favour to all their brotherhood.'

So he spoke; the page carried off the gift and placed it in the hands of Demodocus, and he on his part received it joyfully. The guests stretched out their hands to the good things that lay before them. But when they had eaten and drunk their fill, Odysseus himself addressed the bard :

'Demodocus, I admire you beyond any man; either it was the Muse who taught you, daughter of Zeus himself, or else it was Apollo. With what utter rightness you sing of the fortunes of the Achaeans – all they achieved and suffered and toiled over – as though you yourself were there or had talked with one who was ! Come, change now to a later theme – the wooden horse and its fashioning; Epeius made it, Athene helped him, noble Odysseus planned its cunning climb to the citadel; inside the horse he had housed his warriors, and the warriors achieved the sack of Troy. If you recount all this for me in the fashion it deserves, then I will tell the world forthwith how the god has blessed you ungrudgingly with the gift of inspired song.'

So spoke Odysseus. The bard felt the prompting of the god and began his utterance of the lay, taking it up where the Argives had set their huts aflame, had boarded their ships and were under sail already, while the few left behind with great Odysseus were crouched inside the sheltering horse in the Trojans' own assembly-place, because the people of the town had themselves dragged it up to the citadel. There the horse rested, while the Trojans sitting round it debated confusedly. There were three plans then that one or another party welcomed: to pierce the hollow wood right through with relentless bronze; to haul it up to the topmost ridge and hurl it down over the rocks; or to let it stand untouched as a solemn offering to please the gods. It was this last plan that was to prevail, for fate had decreed that calamity should come when once the town had received inside it the great wooden horse in which lay the boldest of the Argives, bearing down on Troy with death and doom. Then the bard sang how the sons of the Achaeans forsook their cavernous hiding-place, slid from the horse and sacked the town. He sang how they went this way and that to ravage the lofty city, but Odysseus strode like Ares himself to the palace of Deiphobus, and with him was kingly Menelaus. And this, so the lay declared, was the grimmest feat of arms that ever Odysseus ventured on, but in this too he won the day through the help of indomitable Athene.

These were the things the great bard sang of. Odysseus meanwhile was greatly moved, and down from his eyes the tears came coursing over his cheeks. It was as when a woman weeps with her arms around her darling husband, one who has been defending his country and countrymen, striving to keep the day of mercilessness far from his city and his children, but now has fallen and is dying and gasping out his life. She gazes at him, she clings to him and she shrieks aloud, but the victors behind her, with their spears, beat her on back and shoulders and lead her away into captivity to suffer lamentable oppression; her cheeks are wasted with piteous sorrow. So from Odysseus' eyes the tears fell piteously. This went unheeded by the rest; only Alcinous, sitting beside him, both saw the tears and heard the deep groans. So without more ado he said to those lovers of seamanship:

'Listen, Phaeacian chiefs and princes, and now let Demodocus hush his ringing lyre, for in what he sings he is far from pleasing all of us. Ever since the divinely guided bard entered upon the lay as our meal began, ever since then our guest has not ceased from mourning and lamenting; sorrow has filled his heart indeed. Let Demodocus therefore make an end, so that hosts and guests may be content together; surely that is the better way. We revere our guest; it is for his pleasure that all these things have been set in train – the means for his journey home, the gifts of friendship that show how dear we hold him; a man needs no great grasp of things to understand that a guest and suppliant is no less precious than a brother. But then for that very reason, friend, I beg you not to withhold in craftiness the answer to what I ask you now; frank speaking is surely better. Tell us what was your name at home – what your father and your mother called you, and the townsmen and those in the countryside. No human being is left unnamed; whether his birth be high or low, once he is born his parents always give him a name. And tell me the place you come from also, the country and the city, so that our ships may take you there, using their wisdom to find the goal; because we Phaeacians have no steersmen or steering-oars like those of vessels elsewhere; our ships themselves understand men's thoughts and wills; they are well acquainted with towns and farmlands everywhere. Swiftly they pass over depths of ocean, enveloped in mist and cloud, with no risk of harm or shipwreck. True, there is a certain tradition which I once heard from Nausithous my father. He said that Poseidon was angry with us because we took home all manner of men without coming to any harm; and hence, one day, when some nobly built ship of ours was returning from such an errand over the misty sea, Poseidon would shatter it and would block our town with a massy mountain. So my old father prophesied; as for fulfilment, the god may bring it or may withhold it, as pleases him.

'But come now, tell me fully and faithfully : what lands have you wandered through, what countries of men have you visited? What of the men themselves, what of their pleasant-sited cities? Who among them were harsh and lawless and barbarous? Who were hospitable and godfearing? And tell me too why you weep and lament thus bitterly when you hear told what things befell the Argives and Ilium. These things were the doing of the gods; they spun for mortals this thread of doom to become a theme for generations hereafter. Did some kinsman of yours die before Ilium, some man of courage, your daughter's husband, your wife's father? Such ties as these come nearest to men after their own flesh and blood. Or was it a friend, perhaps, one who was brave and whose thoughts were one with yours? Not less than we cherish our own brother do we cherish a wise-hearted friend.'

BOOK IX

ODYSSEUS BEGINS HIS TALE — THE CYCLOPS

SUBTLE Odysseus answered him: 'Alcinous, most illustrious lord, truly it is a happy thing to listen to such a bard as this, whose utterance is like a god's. Indeed I think life is at its best when a whole people is in festivity and banqueters in the hall sit next to each other listening to the bard, while the tables by them are laden with bread and meat, and the cupbearer draws wine from the mixing-bowl and pours it into the cups. That, I think, is the happiest thing there is. But your mind is set on questioning me on the bitter sufferings I have borne, and for me this means more lamentation and more unhappiness. Be it so; what shall I tell you first, what shall I leave for last? My griefs have been many – so heaven ordained.

'But first at least you shall have my name – then you will know it henceforth, and if I escape the day of evil I shall remain your guest-friend, although my own home is far from here.

'I am Odysseus, son of Laertes; among all mankind I am known for subtleties,[1] and the fame of me goes up to heaven. The place I live in is far-seen Ithaca; on it stands out Mount Neriton, quivering with leafy coppices; round it are clustered other islands – Dulichium, Same, forested Zacynthus. Ithaca itself is low-lying, farthest out in the sea westwards, and the other islands lie away from it, towards the rising sun. My land is rugged, but knows how to breed brave sons. A man can see no country more lovable than his own, and so it is with myself and Ithaca. There was a time when divine Calypso kept me within her arching caverns and would have had me to be her husband, and another time when subtle Aeaean Circe confined me in her palace and would have had me for husband also. Yet neither of them could win the heart within me; so true it is that nothing is sweeter to a man than his own country and his own parents, even though he were given a sumptuous dwelling-place elsewhere, in a strange land and far from his parents.

'Enough; I must speak now of the fearful journeying that Zeus enforced on me when I left Troy and made for home.

1. 'I am Ulysses Laertiades,
   The feare of all the world for policies.' CHAPMAN

'The wind behind me brought me from Ilium to Ismarus, the town of the Cicones. I sacked the town and I killed the men. As for the women and all the chattels that we took, we divided them amongst us, so that none of my men, if I could help it, should depart without his fair share. Then I told the crews we must escape as fast as we could, but they in their folly would not listen. Instead there was much drinking of wine and much slaying of sheep and oxen down on the beach; and meanwhile such townsmen as had escaped made their way out and called to the other Cicones inland, who were more in number and stronger too, able to fight either from chariots or else on foot when that was needed. And these came upon us in the morning, countless as leaves and flowers in spring, and evil fortune, sent from Zeus to afflict us all, overtook both me and my doomed comrades. In the first hours, while the sacred sun was climbing towards the zenith, we held our ground and stood firm against them although they outnumbered us; but when day sank down towards unyoking-time, the Cicones broke the Achaeans and drove them back. From each of my ships, six of the crew were killed; the rest of us fled from death and doom.

'Thence we sailed on, glad enough to be snatched from death, yet sick at heart to have lost those others, the comrades that we had known; nor had I let the ships go from there till the ritual call had thrice been made for each of these luckless men whom the Cicones had killed on the plain. But Zeus who masses the clouds now sent a north wind upon our vessels in hideous tempest, veiling earth and sea alike with cloud; and blackness rushed down from heaven. The ships plunged head-foremost. The sails were ripped into three strips, four strips by the great hurricane, so in fear of death we lowered them into the hold and with might and main rowed for land. On land, for two nights and two days together, we lay eating out our hearts with weariness and misery. But when Dawn at length brought the third day, we stepped the masts, hoisted the sails and sat down to our oars, and wind and steersmen carried our ships forward. After that, I might have reached my own land unscathed; but no, as I was doubling Cape Maleia I was caught by wave and current and wind from the North and was driven off course and past Cythera.

'Then for nine days I was carried by ruthless winds over teeming ocean. On the tenth day we reached the land of the Lotus-

Eaters, whose only fare is that fragrant fruit. We stepped ashore there and drew water, and without delay my men and I took our meal by the ships. When we had had our portions of food and drink, I sent away some of my comrades to find what manner of human beings were those who lived here. They went at once, and soon were among the Lotus-Eaters, who had no thoughts of making away with my companions, but gave them lotus to taste instead. Those of my men who ate the honey-sweet lotus fruit had no desire to retrace their steps and come back with news; their only wish was to linger there with the Lotus-Eaters, to feed on the fruit and put aside all thought of a voyage home. These men I then forced back to the ships; they were shedding tears but I made them go. I dragged them down under the thwarts and left them bound there. The rest of my crews I despatched aboard with all speed, so that none of them should taste the lotus and then forget the voyage home. They embarked quickly, sat at the thwarts in due order and dipped their oars in the whitening sea.

'Thence we sailed on with downcast hearts. We came to the land of the Cyclops race, arrogant lawless beings who leave their livelihood to the deathless gods and never use their own hands to sow or plough; yet with no sowing and no ploughing, the crops all grow for them – wheat and barley and grapes that yield wine from ample clusters, swelled by the showers of Zeus. They have no assemblies to debate in, they have no ancestral ordinances; they live in arching caves on the tops of high hills, and the head of each family heeds no other, but makes his own ordinances for wife and children.

'Outside the harbour of this country, neither very near it nor very far from it, there is a small well-wooded island; in it, wild goats breed beyond counting, unstartled by any stranger's tread; hunters elsewhere may toil through woods and may range the hill-tops, but to this island they never come. No flocks are found there, no ploughland either; it remains unploughed and unsown perpetually, empty of men, only a home for bleating goats. For the Cyclops nation possess no red-prowed ships; they have no ship-wrights in their country to build sound vessels to serve their needs, to visit foreign towns and townsfolk as men elsewhere do in their voyages. Craftsmen like these might have made this is-land good to live in; the land is by no means to be despised; it might bring everything forth in season. Beside the shore of the whitening sea it has soft moist meadows where vines might flourish and never cease. Its soil would make for easy ploughing; they might reap tall harvests there in season, for beneath the surface the loam is rich. Moreover there is a good harbour there; inside it you need no mooring-tackle, no stones to be thrown down for anchors, no cables to be stretched from the stern; seamen have only to run ashore and then wait till their own heart moves them or till the winds blow fair. At the harbour's head, from beneath a cave, there comes gushing out the bright water of a spring, and on either side there grow black poplars.

'Such was the spot where we sailed in. Some god must have guided us through the deep dark; there was not enough light for us to see by, because heavy mist lay round the ships, and the clouded moon could not reach us with its rays from above. So to none of us was this island visible, nor did we see the long breakers rolling towards the beach until our ships ran ashore; when they did, we hauled down the sails and stepped out upon the strand. There we fell fast asleep, awaiting ethereal Dawn.

'Dawn comes early, with rosy fingers; when she appeared, we began in wonder to view the island and roam about it.[1] The nymphs, the daughters of sovereign Zeus, started some hillside goats to give a meal to my companions. Quickly we fetched out from the ships our curved bows and our long spears. We divided ourselves into three parties; we began the hunt, and it was not long before the god gave us game in plenty. The crews of twelve ships were with me, and for each crew there were nine goats; to my ship alone they assigned ten. So there all day, until sunset, we sat and banqueted with the lavish meat and the good drink, because the red wine that our ships carried had not yet failed us; there was still enough, since each of these crews had drawn it in plenty in their jars when we sacked the sacred Ciconian citadel. Then we began to turn our glances to the land of the Cyclops tribe nearby; we could see smoke and hear voices and the bleating of sheep and goats. When the sun set and darkness came, we lay down to sleep by the breaking waves.

> 1. '... straight we our Sails unfurl'd,
>   Then landing, on the Ocean's margents lay,
>   In sweet repose, expecting blessed Day.
>   No sooner had the Daughter of the Dawn
>   With rosie Fingers Day's Portcullice drawn,
>   But we admiring walk along the Shore.' OGILBY

'Dawn comes early, with rosy fingers. When she appeared, I called my men together and spoke to them all: "My friends, let the rest of you stay here. I myself with my own ship's crew will go and find what manner of men live yonder. Are they barbarous, arrogant and lawless? Are they hospitable and godfearing?"

'With these words I boarded my ship and told my comrades to board also and cast off; they came up quickly, sat at the thwarts in due order and dipped their oars in the whitening sea. When we reached the stretch of land I spoke of – it was not far away – there on the shore beside the sea we saw a high cave overarched with bay-trees; in this flocks of sheep and goats were housed at night, and round its mouth had been made a courtyard with high walls of quarried stone and with tall pines and towering oaks. Here was the sleeping-place of a giant who used to pasture his flocks far afield, alone; it was not his way to visit the others of his tribe; he kept aloof, and his mind was set on unrighteousness. A monstrous ogre, unlike any man who had ever tasted bread, he resembled rather some shaggy peak in a mountain-range, standing out clear, away from the rest.[1]

'Most of my men I ordered to stay by the ship and guard it, but I chose out twelve, the bravest, and sallied forth. With me I had a goatskin full of dark fragrant wine, given me by Maron, Euanthes' son; he was priest of Apollo, the guardian of Ismarus, and he lived in the god's leafy grove; because in reverence we protected him and his wife and child, he gave me both this and other gifts. They were all noble: seven talents of wrought gold, a mixing-bowl all in silver, and then this wine – he drew twelve jars of it altogether – unmixed and fragrant, a drink for the gods. In his own house, neither manservants nor maidservants knew of it; it was a secret he shared with his wife and with one housekeeper. When they drank this red delicious wine, he would pour just one cupful of it into twenty measures of spring-water; from the mixing-bowl there would be wafted a fragrance beyond all words, and no one could find it in his heart to refrain. Of this wine I now carried a great goatskin with me, and food as well in a leather wallet, because from the first I had forebodings that the

---

1. 'It was a huge and ugly Monster, and
    Look'd not unlike a rocky Mountains head
   That does 'mongst other hills asunder stand
    With a great Perriwig of Trees o'rspread.' HOBBES

stranger who might face us now would wear brute strength like
a garment round him, a savage whose heart had little knowledge
of just laws or of ordinances.

'We came to the cavern soon enough, but we did not find him
there himself; he was out on his pasture-land, tending his fat
sheep and goats. We went in and looked round at everything.
There were flat baskets laden with cheeses; there were pens filled
with lambs and kids, though these were divided among them-
selves – here the firstlings, there the later-born, and the youngest
of all apart again. Then, too, there were well-made dairy-vessels,
large and small pails, swimming with whey. My men's first
thought was to ask my leave to take away some of these cheeses
and depart, driving kids and lambs out of their pens and on to
our rapid ship and then setting off again at once over the salt
seas. I would not agree (better, much better, if I had!); but no, I
was eager to see the cavern's master and hoped he would offer me
the gifts of a guest, though as things fell out, it was no kind host
that my comrades were to meet.

'Then we lit a fire, and laying hands on some of the cheeses we
first offered the gods their portion, then ate our own and sat in
the cavern waiting for the owner. At length he returned, guiding
his flocks and carrying with him a stout bundle of dry firewood to
burn at supper. This, with a crash, he threw down inside, and we
in dismay shrank hastily back into a corner. Next, he drove part
of his flocks inside – the milking ewes and milking goats – but
left the rams and he-goats outside in the fenced yard. Then to fill
the doorway he heaved up a huge heavy stone; two-and-twenty
good four-wheeled wagons could not shift such a boulder from
the ground, but the Cyclops did, and fitted it in its place – a
massive towering piece of rock. Then he sat down and began to
milk the ewes and the bleating goats, all in due order, and he put
the young ones to their mothers. Half the milk he now curdled,
gathered the curd and laid it in plaited baskets. The other half
he left standing in the vessels, meaning to take and drink it at his
supper. Having quickly despatched these tasks of his, he re-
kindled the fire and spied ourselves.

'He asked us: "Strangers, who are you? What land did you
sail from, over the watery paths? Are you bound on some trading
errand, or are you random adventurers, roving the seas as pirates

do, hazarding life and limb and bringing havoc on men of another stock?"[1]

'So he spoke, and our hearts all sank; his thundering voice and his monstrous presence cowed us. But I plucked up courage enough to answer. "We are Achaeans; we sailed from Troy and were bound for home, but path and course were not of our choosing. We were driven astray by this wind and that over the great gulf of ocean, and now we are here; such, it seems, is the plan Zeus framed for us. It is our claim that we are men of Agamemnon, that son of Atreus whose fame is paramount under heaven because of the mighty town he sacked and the multitudes of men he slew. We have reached your presence, have come to your knees in supplication, to receive, we hope, your friendly favour, to receive perhaps some such present as custom expects from host to guest. Sir, I beg you to reverence the gods. We are suppliants, and Zeus himself is the champion of suppliants and of guests; 'god of guests' is a name of his; guests are august, and Zeus goes with them."[2]

'So I spoke. He answered at once and ruthlessly: "Stranger, you must be a fool or have come from far afield if you tell me to fear the gods or beware of them. We of the Cyclops race care nothing for Zeus and for his aegis; we care for none of the gods in heaven, being much stronger ourselves than they are. Dread of the enmity of Zeus would never move me to spare either you or the comrades with you, if I had no mind to it myself.[3] But tell me a thing I wish to know. When you came here, where did you moor your ship? Was it at some far point of the shore or was it near here?"

'So he spoke to me, feeling his way, but I knew the world and guessed what he was about. So I countered him with crafty words.

1. 'Merchants are you, or have you lost your Way?
   Or Piccaroons, who wander through the Floods
   To make a prey of Honest People's Goods?' OGILBY

2. 'Illustrious lord! respect the Gods, and us
   Thy suitors; suppliants are the care of Jove
   The hospitable: he their wrongs resents,
   And where the stranger sojourns, there is he.' COWPER

3. 'Know then we *Cyclops* are a race above
   These air-bred people, and their goat-nurs'd Jove:
   And learn, our pow'r proceeds with thee and thine,
   Not as He wills, but as our selves incline.' POPE

"My ship was shattered by Poseidon, who drove it upon the rocks at the edge of this land of yours; a wind had carried it in from the open sea, and the Earthshaker dashed it against a headland. I myself and my comrades here escaped the precipice of destruction."

'To these words of mine the savage creature made no response; he only sprang up, and stretching his hands towards my companions clutched two at once and battered them on the floor like puppies; their brains gushed out and soaked the ground. Then tearing them limb from limb he made his supper of them. He began to eat like a mountain lion, leaving nothing, devouring flesh and entrails and bones and marrow, while we in our tears and helplessness looked on at these monstrous doings and held up imploring hands to Zeus.

'But when the Cyclops had filled his great belly with the human flesh that he devoured and the raw milk he washed it down with, he laid himself on the cavern floor with his limbs stretched out among his beasts. Then with courage rising I thought at first to go up to him, to draw the keen sword from my side and to stab him in the chest, feeling with my hand for the spot where the midriff enfolds the liver; but second thoughts held me back, because we too should have perished irremediably; never could we with all our hands have pushed away from the lofty doorway the massy stone he had planted there. So with sighs and groans we awaited ethereal Dawn.

'Dawn comes early, with rosy fingers. When she appeared, the Cyclops rekindled the fire, milked his beasts in accustomed order and put the young ones to their mothers. Having quickly despatched these tasks of his, he clutched another two of my comrades and made his breakfast of them. This over, he drove his flocks out of the cave again, easily moving the massy stone and then putting it back once more as one might put the lid back on a quiver. Whistling loud, he led off his flock to the mountainside; so I was left there to brood mischief, wondering if I might take vengeance on him and if Athene might grant me glory.

'After all my thinking, the plan that seemed best was this. Next to the sheep-pen the Cyclops had left a great cudgel of undried olive-wood, wrenched from the tree to carry with him when it was seasoned. As we looked at it, it seemed huge enough to be the mast of some great dark merchant-ship with its twenty oars, well-used to traversing ocean's depths, so long and so thick it loomed before us. I stood over this, and myself cut off six feet of it; then I laid it in front of my companions and told them to make it smooth; smooth they made it, and again I stood over it and sharpened it to a point, then took it at once and put it in the fierce fire to harden. Then I laid it in ·a place of safety; there was dung in layers all down the great cave, and I hid the stake under this. I asked the men to cast lots for joining me – who would help me to lift the stake and plunge it into the giant's eye as soon as slumber stole upon him? The men that the lots fell upon were the very ones I should have chosen – four of them, and I made a fifth.

'Towards nightfall the Cyclops came home again, bringing his fleecy flocks with him. He drove all the beasts into the cave forthwith, leaving none outside in the fenced courtyard – had he some foreboding, or was it a god who directed him? He lifted the massy door-stone and put it in place again; he sat down and began to milk the sheep and the bleating goats, all in accustomed order, and he put the young ones to their mothers. Having quickly despatched these tasks of his, he clutched another two of my comrades and made his meal of them. And at that I came close to the Cyclops and spoke to him, while in my hands I held up an ivy-bowl[1] brimmed with dark wine: "Cyclops, look! You have had your fill of man's flesh. Now drain this bowl and judge what wine our ship had in it. I was bringing it for yourself as a libation, hoping you would take pity on me and would help to send me home. But your wild folly is past all bounds. Merciless one, who of all men in all the world will choose to visit you after this? In what you have done you defy whatever is good and right.'

'Such were my words. He took my present and drank it off and was mightily pleased with wine so fragrant. Then he asked for a second bowlful of it: "Give me more in your courtesy, and tell me your name here and now – I wish to offer you as my guest a special favour that will delight you. Earth is bounteous, and for my people too it brings forth grapes that thrive on the rain of Zeus and that make good wine, but this is distilled from nectar and ambrosia."

'So he spoke, and again I offered the glowing wine; three times I walked up to him with it; three times he witlessly drank it off. When the wine had coiled its way round his understanding, I

1. Made of ivy wood, or perhaps with an ivy pattern.

spoke to him in meek-sounding words: "Cyclops, you ask what name I boast of. I will tell you, and then you must grant me as your guest the favour that you have promised me. My name is Noman;[1] Noman is what my mother and father call me; so likewise do all my friends."

'To these words of mine the savage creature made quick response: "Noman then shall come last among those I eat; his friends I will eat first; this is to be my favour to you."

'With these words he sank down on the floor, then lay on his back with his heavy neck drooping sideways, till sleep the all-conquering overcame him; wine and goblets of human flesh gushed from his throat as he belched them forth in drunken stupor. Then I drove our stake down into the heap of embers to get red-hot; meanwhile I spoke words of courage to all my comrades, so that none of them should lose heart and shrink from the task. But when the stake, green though it was, was about to catch fire and glowed frighteningly, I drew it towards me out of the fire, while the others took their stand around me. Some god breathed high courage into us. My men took over the keen-pointed olive stake and thrust it into the giant's eye;[2] I myself leaned heavily over from above and twirled the stake round, like a ship's carpenter boring through timber with a drill, while his mates below ply a strap between them to keep the drill spinning and running without a pause. In the same way we grasped the stake with its fiery tip and whirled it round in the giant's eye. The blood came gushing out round the red-hot wood; the heat singed eyebrow and eyelid, the eyeball was burned out and the roots of the eye hissed in the fire. It was as when a smith plunges an axe or adze into cold water, and it hisses loudly at the tempering, though this is what makes the strength of iron; so his eye hissed now with the olive-stake penetrating it. He gave a great hideous roar; the cave re-echoed, and in terror we rushed away. He pulled the blood-stained stake from his eye and with frantic arms tossed it away from him. Then he shouted loud to the Cyclops kinsmen who lived around him in their caverns among the windy hill-tops.

1. 'My name is *Nemo*.' OGILBY

2. 'Then forth the vengeful instrument I bring;
   With beating hearts my fellows form a ring.
   Urg'd by some present God, they swift let fall
   The pointed torment on the visual ball.' POPE

Hearing his cries they hastened towards him from every quarter, stood round his cavern and asked him what ailed him: "Polyphemus, what dire affliction has come upon you to make you profane the night with clamour and rob us of our slumbers? Is some human creature driving away your flocks in defiance of you? Is someone threatening death to yourself by craft or by violence?"

'From inside the cave the giant answered: "Friends, it is Noman's craft and no violence that is threatening death to me."

'Swiftly their words were borne back to him: "If no man is doing you violence – if you are alone – then this is a malady sent by almighty Zeus from which there is no escape; you had best say a prayer to your father, Lord Poseidon."

'With these words they left him again, while my own heart laughed within me to think how the name I gave and my ready wit had snared him. Racked with anguish, lamenting loudly, the Cyclops groped for the great stone and pushed it from the doorway, then in the doorway he seated himself with outstretched hands, hoping to seize on some of us passing into the open among the sheep – so witless did he take me to be. Meanwhile I was pondering the likeliest means to find some way out from death for my comrades and myself; I set to work all my wits and cunning, for our lives were at hazard, doom was near us. The best device I could find was this. There were big handsome rams there, well-fed, thick-fleeced and with dark wool. Making no noise, I began fastening them together with plaited withies, the same that the lawless monstrous ogre slept on. I took the rams three by three; each middle one carried a man, while the other two walked either side and safeguarded my companions; so there were three beasts to each man. As for myself – there was one ram that was finest of all the flock; I seized his back, I curled myself up under his shaggy belly, and there I clung in the rich soft wool, face upwards, desperately holding on and on. In this dismal fashion we waited now for ethereal Dawn.

'Dawn comes early, with rosy fingers. When she appeared, the rams began running out to pasture, while the unmilked ewes around the pens kept bleating with udders full to bursting. Their master, consumed with hideous pains, felt along the backs of all the rams as they stood still in front of him. The witless giant never found out that men were tied under the fleecy creatures' bellies. Last of them all came my own ram on his way out, burdened both with his own thick wool and with me the schemer. Polyphemus felt him over too and began to talk to him: "You that I love best, why are you last of all the flock to come out through the cavern's mouth? Never till now have you come behind the rest; before them all you have marched with stately strides ahead to crop the delicate meadow-flowers, before them all you have reached the rippling streams, before them all you have shown your will to return homewards in the evening; yet now you come last. You are grieving, surely, over your master's eye, which malicious Noman quite put out, with his evil friends, after overmastering my wits with wine; but I swear he has still not escaped destruction. If only your thoughts were like my own, if only you had the gift of words to tell me where he is hiding from my fury! Then he would be hurled to the ground and his brains dashed hither and thither across the cave; then my heart would find some relief from the tribulations he has brought me, unmanly Noman!"

'So speaking, he let the ram go free outside. As for ourselves, once we had passed a little way beyond cave and courtyard, I first loosed my own hold beneath the ram, then I untied my comrades also. We herded the many sheep in haste – fat plump creatures with long shanks – and drove them on till we reached our vessel; and a welcome sight we were to our friends, those of us who had been snatched from death. For the others, my men began to pour out their tears and groans, but I would not have this; with nods and frowns to each one of them I checked this lamentation, and signified that without delay they were to put the sheep aboard and return to sail the salt seas. My comrades went aboard at once, sat at the thwarts and in due order began to dip their oars in the whitening sea.

'But when we were no further away than a man's voice carries easily, I called to the Cyclops and taunted him: "Cyclops, your prisoner after all was to prove not quite defenceless – the man whose friends you devoured so brutally in your cave. No, your sins were to find you out. You felt no shame to devour your guests in your own home; hence this requital from Zeus and the other gods."

'Rage rose up in him at my words. He wrenched away the top of a towering crag and hurled it in front of our dark-prowed ship. The sea surged up as the rock fell into it; the swell from beyond

came washing back at once and the wave carried the ship land-
wards and drove it towards the strand. But I myself seized a long
pole and pushed the ship out and away again, moving my head
and signing to my companions urgently to pull at their oars and
escape destruction; so they threw themselves forward and rowed
hard. But when we were twice as far out on the water as before,
I made ready to hail the Cyclops again, though my friends around
me, this side and that, used all persuasion to restrain me: "Head-
strong man, why need you provoke this savage further? The
stone he threw out to sea just now dashed the ship back to the
shore again, and we thought we were dead men already. Had he
heard any sound, any words from us, he would have hurled yet
another jagged rock and shattered our heads and the boat's
timbers, so vast his reach is."

'So they spoke, but my heart was proud and would not be gain-
said; I called out again with rage still rankling: "Cyclops, if
anyone among mortal men should ask who put out your eye in
this ugly fashion, say that the one who blinded you was Odysseus
the city-sacker, son of Laertes and dweller in Ithaca."

'So I spoke. He groaned aloud as he answered me: "Ah, it comes
home to me at last, that oracle uttered long ago. We once had a
prophet in our country, a truly great man called Telemus son of
Eurymus, skilled in divining, living among the Cyclops race as an
aged seer. He told me all this as a thing that would later come to
pass – that I was to lose my sight at the hands of one Odysseus.
But I always thought that the man who came would be tall and
handsome, visibly clothed with heroic strength; instead, it has
been a puny and strengthless and despicable man who has taken
my sight away from me after overpowering me with wine. But
come, Odysseus, return to me; let me set before you the presents
that befit a guest, and appeal to the mighty Earthshaker to speed
you upon your way, because I am his son, and he declares himself
my father. And he alone will heal me, if so he pleases – no other
will, of the blessed gods or of mortal men."

'So he spoke, but I answered thus: "Would that I were assured
as firmly that I could rob you of life and being and send you down
to Hades' house as I am assured that no one shall heal that eye of
yours, not the Earthshaker himself."

'So I spoke, and forthwith he prayed to Lord Poseidon, stretch-
ing out his hands to the starry sky: "Poseidon the raven-haired,

Earth-Enfolder: if indeed I am your son, if indeed you declare yourself my father, grant that Odysseus the city-sacker may never return home again; or if he is fated to see his kith and kin and to reach his high-roofed house and his own country, let him come late and come in misery, after the loss of all his comrades, and carried upon an alien ship; and in his own house let him find mischief."

'This was his prayer, and the raven-haired god heeded it. Then the Cyclops lifted up a stone (it was much larger than the first); he whirled it and flung it, putting vast strength into the throw; the stone came down a little astern of the dark-prowed vessel, just short of the tip of the steering-oar. The sea surged up as the stone fell into it, but the wave carried the ship forward and drove it on to the shore beyond. In this fashion we reached the island where the other vessels all remained, while the crews sat disconsolately there, waiting and waiting for our return. Then we beached our vessel on the sand and stepped out on the shore ourselves. The giant's sheep we took from the hold and divided them out so that not one man, if I could help it, should depart without his fair share. Only to me did my comrades allot a special share when the beasts were portioned out, and this was my own ram. I sacrificed him upon the shore to Zeus of the thunderclouds, the all-ruler, and in his honour I burnt the thigh-bones. But the son of Cronos disregarded my offering there, pondering only how my decked ships and loyal comrades might be destroyed together.

'So all that day, till the sun set, we sat and feasted on meat in abundance and pleasant wine. When the sun went and darkness came, we lay down to sleep on the sea shore.

'Dawn comes early, with rosy fingers. When she appeared, I bade my men go aboard again and cast off. They embarked at once, sat at the thwarts in due order and dipped their oars in the whitening sea.

'Thence we sailed on, glad enough to be snatched from death, yet sick at heart to have lost those others, the comrades that we had known.

BOOK X

CIRCE

'WE came to the Aeolian island; here lived Aeolus, son of Hippotas; the deathless gods counted him their friend. His island is a floating one; all round it there is a wall of bronze, unbreakable, and rock rises sheer above it. Twelve children of his live in the palace with him; six are daughters, six are sons in the prime of youth; moreover the king has given his daughters as wives to his sons. These all hold a continual feast with their dear father and much-loved mother; countless dainties are there before them, and through the daytime the hall is rich with savoury smells and murmurous with the sound of music. At night they sleep, each with his own chaste wife, on inlaid bedsteads with coverlets over them.

'To their city and noble palace we now came, and for a whole month Aeolus gave me hospitality and questioned me on all manner of things, Ilium and the Argive ships and how the Achaeans sailed for home. I duly told him all he desired; then in my turn I asked his leave to depart and begged him to help me on my way. Nor was he unwilling; he set about speeding my return. He gave me a bag made from the hide of a full-grown ox of his, and in the bag he had penned up every wind that blows, whatever its course might be; because Zeus had made him warden of all the winds, to bid each of them rise or fall at his own pleasure. He placed the bag in my own ship's hold, tied with a glittering silver cord so that through that fastening not even a breath could stray; to the west wind only he gave commission to blow for me, to carry onwards my ships and men. Yet he was not after all to accomplish his design, because our own folly ruined us.

'For nine days and through nine nights we sailed on steadily; on the tenth day our own country began to heave in sight; we were near enough to see men tending their fires on shore. It was then that beguiling sleep surprised me; I was tired out, because all this time I had kept for myself all handling of the sheet, never entrusting it to one of the crew, for I wished to speed our journey home. Meanwhile the crew began murmuring among themselves; they were sure that I was taking home new presents of gold and

silver from Aeolus. One of them would say as he eyed his neigh-
bour: "What injustice! In whatever city or land he comes to, this
man wins everyone's friendship and regard. He is taking back a
mass of fine things from the spoils of Troy, while we who have
journeyed with him from first to last are returning home all
empty-handed. And now come these latest gifts that Aeolus in his
hospitality had indulged him with. Come, let us look without
wasting time. What are these gifts? How much gold and silver is
there inside the bag?"

'Thus the men talked among themselves, and the counsels of
folly were what prevailed. They undid the bag, the winds rushed
out all together, and in a moment a tempest had seized my crew
and was driving them – now all in tears – back to the open sea
and away from home. I myself awoke, and wondered if now I
should throw myself overboard and be drowned in ocean or if I
should bear it all in silence and stay among the living. I did bear
it and did remain, but covered my face as I lay on deck. My own
ship and the others with it were carried back by the raging storm
to the island of Aeolus, amid the groaning of all my company.

'There we set foot ashore and drew water, and without delay
my crews and I took our meal by the rapid ships. When we had
had our portion of food and drink, I chose to come with me one
man as my own attendant and one besides; then I went up to the
palace of Aeolus, and found him feasting there with his wife and
children. We went in and we sat down at the threshold by the
doorposts, while the household asked in deep amazement:
"Odysseus, how is it that you are here again? What malicious
god has set upon you? Surely we did our best before to speed
you upon your way, meaning you to reach your own land and
home or whatever place you might desire?"

'So they spoke, and I said despondently: "Faithless comrades
were my undoing, they and the slumber that betrayed me. But
you are my friends; you have the remedy; grant it me."

'With these humble words I made my appeal to them. They re-
mained in silence, except the father, who answered me: "Away
from this island, away at once, most despicable of creatures! I am
forbidden to welcome here or to help to send elsewhere a man
whom the blessed gods abhor. This return reveals you as god-
forsaken; go!"

'And with these words he drove me forth despite my pitiful

lamentations. Then we sailed onwards, sick at heart; the heavy rowing broke the men's spirit, though our own folly was to blame; no easy passage was offered us now.

'For six days and through six nights we sailed on steadily; on the seventh day we came to Telepylus, the lofty town of the Laestrygonians[1] whose king is Lamus. There one herdsman as he drives in his beasts will hail another driving his out and the second answers the first. In those parts a man who never slept could have earned wages twice over, one wage for herding cattle and another for pasturing white sheep, because the pathways of day and night come close together there.

'We entered the harbour; on either side there stretches a long sheer wall of cliff; at the mouth are promontories facing each other, and the entrance is narrow. The other crews all steered their ships in, mooring them near each other inside the enclosing harbour, for within this no wave swelled up, whether great or small; there was limpid calm all around. I alone kept my ship outside, where the harbour ended, and made the cable fast to a rock. From where we were no trace could be seen of men's or oxen's labours; we only discerned some smoke going up from the land below. Then I sent out some of my comrades to find what manner of human beings were those who lived here; I chose two men, and a spokesman to go with them. Having left the ship, they took to a made road that was used by wagons for bringing timber into the town from the hills above. Just short of the town, they came on a girl drawing water; she was tall and powerful, the daughter of King Antiphates.[2] She had come down to the clear stream of the spring Artacia, from which the townsmen fetched up their water. They approached her and spoke to her, asking who was king of this land and who his subjects were; and she pointed at once to her father's lofty house. They entered the palace and found his wife there, but she stood mountain-high and they were aghast at the sight of her. She sent out forthwith to fetch King Antiphates her husband from the assembly-place, and his only

1. The place here described is not known otherwise, and it is not certain if two unfamiliar words are nouns or adjectives. Denys Page may well be right in taking the town's name to be Laestrygonia and replacing 'Telepylus' as a proper noun by the compound adjective 'strong-gated'.
2. A second name for King Lamus.

thought was to kill them miserably. He clutched one of my men at once and made a meal of him, but the other two rushed away and ran till they reached the ships. The king raised a hue and cry through the town, and the other great Laestrygonians heard him; they came thronging up in multitudes, looking not like men but like the lawless Giants,[1] and from the cliffs began to hurl down great rocks that were each of them one man's burden. A hideous din rose amid my fleet as men were killed and vessels shattered. The Laestrygonians speared men like fish and then carried home their monstrous meal. But while they thus made havoc among my crews inside the deep harbour, I snatched the keen sword from my thigh, severed the hawsers of my ship and urgently called to my own crew to lean to their oars and escape destruction; and so, with the fear of death before them, they pulled together, one and all. What joy it was when our ship escaped from under the beetling cliffs into open sea! But the other ships all perished there together.

'Thence we sailed on, glad enough to be snatched from death but sick at heart to have lost those others, the comrades that we had known. Then we came to the island of Aeaea; here Circe dwelt, a goddess with braided hair, with human speech and with strange powers; the magician Aeetes was her brother, and both were the radiant sun-god's children; their mother was Perse, Ocean's daughter. We brought the ship noiselessly to shore, and with some divinity for guide we put in at the sheltering harbour. We disembarked, and for two days and two nights we lay there, eating out our hearts with sorrow and weariness.

'But when Dawn of the braided hair brought the third day at last, I took my spear and my sharp sword and hastened up to a vantage-point, hoping to see some human handiwork or to catch the sound of some human speech. I climbed a commanding crag, and from where I stood had a glimpse of smoke rising from the ground. There were gleams of fire through the smoke, and at sight of this I wondered inwardly whether to go and look. But as I pondered, it seemed a wiser thing to return first to my vessel on the beach, give my men a meal and then send them out to spy. I was on my way back and near the ship when some divinity

1. Not merely of giant stature, but lawless and impious like the race of Giants who challenged the gods themselves.

pitied me in my loneliness and sent a great antlered stag right across my path; it was going down from its feeding-ground in the wood to drink the river-water, for it found the sun's heat hard to bear. As it left the wood I struck it upon the spine, half-way down the back. The spear of bronze went right through, and with one cry the stag fell in the dust and its breath departed. Setting foot on it, I pulled the spear from the wound, then left the weapon to lie on the ground while I broke off brushwood and willow-twigs to twine a rope of about a fathom long; I plaited it well, across and across, and tied the great creature by the feet. Then, carrying it slung round my neck, I went on down to the dark ship, leaning upon my spear; with one hand on one shoulder I could never have held so huge a beast. I threw it down in front of the ship, went up to the men one by one and enlivened them with cheerful words:

' "Friends, whatever our plight may be, we shall not go down to Hades' house before the appointed day is on us. Come then; while there is meat and drink in our ship, let us turn our thoughts to food and not starve to death."

'So I spoke. They heeded my words at once, and there on the beach of the barren sea they uncovered the heads that they had muffled and wonderingly gazed at the stag, so huge a beast it was. Having satisfied their eyes with the sight, they washed their hands and prepared a noble meal. So all that day, till the sun set, we sat and feasted on plenteous meat and delicious wine. When the sun went and darkness came, we lay down to sleep on the sea-shore.

'Dawn comes early, with rosy fingers. When she appeared, I assembled all my men together and thus addressed them: "Comrades, as things now are, we do not know where the region of dawn or of darkness lies, in what quarter the radiant sun sinks below the earth or in what quarter he rises up. Let us ask ourselves quickly if some good plan may yet be found, though I fear there is none. When I climbed that commanding crag, I could see that we were in an island encircled by boundless ocean. The main part of the land lies low, and in the mid-point of it I saw smoke rising across thick undergrowth and woodland."

'So I spoke, and their hearts quailed within them as they thought again of the deeds of Antiphates the Laestrygonian and the fierce and fearless and man-devouring Cyclops. They wept aloud, and the great tears rolled down their cheeks, though lamentation availed them nothing.

'I divided my crew into two companies, and gave each its own leader; I myself captained one, Eurylochus the other. Then we shook the lots in a bronze helmet, and the lot that leapt out was that of bold Eurylochus. So he went his way, and twenty-two comrades with him; themselves in tears, they left the rest of us weeping too. In the glades they found the palace of Circe, built of smooth stones on open ground. Outside, there were lions and mountain wolves that she had herself bewitched by giving them magic drugs. The beasts did not set upon my men; they reared up, instead, and fawned on them with their long tails. As dogs will fawn around their master when he comes home from some banquet, because he never fails to bring back for them a morsel or two to appease their craving, so did these lions, these wolves with their powerful claws, circle fawningly round my comrades. The sight of the strange huge creatures dismayed my men, but they went on and paused at the outer doors of the goddess of braided hair. And now they could hear Circe within, singing with her beautiful voice as she moved to and fro at the wide web that was more than earthly – delicate, gleaming, delectable, as a goddess's handiwork needs must be.[1] Then Polites spoke to the rest there – a commanding man, and of all my comrades the trustiest and the closest to me: "Friends, there is someone inside the house, a goddess or a woman, moving to and fro at her wide web and singing a lovely song that the whole floor re-echoes with. Come, let us make ourselves heard at once."

'So he spoke. The men called out and made themselves heard; she came forth at once, she opened the shining doors, she called them to her, and in their heedlessness they all entered, all but Eurylochus; he stayed outside, foreboding mischief. The goddess ushered them in, gave them all seats, high or low, and blended for them a dish of cheese and of barley-meal, of yellow honey and Pramnian wine, all together; but with these good things she mingled pernicious drugs as well, to make them forget their own country utterly. Having given them this and waited for them to have their fill, she struck them suddenly with her wand, then

1.   '... as at her web she wrought,
    Subtle, and glorious, and past earthly thought,
    As all the housewiferies of Deities are.' CHAPMAN

drove them into the sties where she kept her swine. And now the men had the form of swine – the snout and grunt and bristles; only their minds were left unchanged.[1] They shed tears as they were shut in, while Circe threw down in front of them some acorns and mast and cornel – daily fare for swine whose lodging is on the ground.

'Eurylochus hastened back to the ship to tell the news of his comrades' dismal fate. But for all his zeal he could not bring out one word, so wrung was his heart with its great sorrow; the tears were standing in his eyes, and his thoughts were all of lamentation. We questioned him, all of us, in bewilderment, and at last he found plain words to tell how our other friends had been lost to us:

' "Noble Odysseus, we went, as you bade us, through the thickets, and in the glades we found before us a stately palace. Someone inside it, a goddess or a woman, was singing in high pure notes as she moved to and fro at her wide web. The men called out and made themselves heard; she came out at once, she opened the shining doors and she called them to her. They in their heedlessness all entered; only I myself foreboded mischief and stayed outside. They vanished utterly, all of them; not one among them appeared again, though I sat a long while there, keeping watch."

'So he spoke. I slung across my shoulders my great silver-studded sword of bronze; I slung on my bow as well, then told him to guide me back by the same path. But he clutched my knees with both his hands and made supplication: "Heaven-favoured king, do not force me back that way again; leave me here. I know you will neither return yourself nor yet bring back any of your comrades. Instead, let us flee from this place at once, taking these others with us; we may still escape the day of evil."

1. 'But venom'd was the bread, and mix'd the bowl,
   With drugs of force to darken all the soul:
   Soon in the luscious feast themselves they lost
   And drank oblivion of their native coast.
   Instant her circling wand the Goddess waves,
   To hogs transforms 'em, and the Sty receives.
   No more was seen the human form divine,
   Head, face and members bristle into swine:
   Still curst with sense, their mind remains alone,
   And their own voice affrights them when they groan.'   POPE

'Such were his words. I answered thus: "So be it, Eurylochus; keep your own place here, eating and drinking beside the ship; I must go yonder; stern necessity is upon me."

'And with that I left the ship and shore and took the path upward; but as I traversed those haunted glades, as I came close to Circe's house and neared the palace of the enchantress, I was met by golden-wanded Hermes; he seemed a youth in the lovely spring of life, with the first down upon his lip. He seized my hand and spoke thus to me: "Luckless man, why are you walking thus alone over these hills, in country you do not know? Your comrades are yonder in Circe's grounds; they are turned to swine, lodged and safely penned in the sties.[1] Is your errand here to rescue them? I warn you, you will never return yourself, you will only be left with the others there. Yet no – I am ready to save you from all hazards, ready to keep you unscathed. Look. Here is a herb of magic virtue; take it and enter Circe's house with it; then the day of evil never will touch your head. I will tell you of all her witch's arts. She will brew a potion for you, but with good things she will mingle drugs as well: Yet even so, she will not be able to enchant you; my gift of the magic herb will thwart her. I will tell you the rest, point by point. When Circe strikes you with the long wand she has, draw the keen sword from beside your thigh, rush upon her and make as if to kill her. She will shrink back, and then ask you to lie with her. At this you must let her have her way; she is a goddess; accept her bed, so that she may release your comrades and make you her cherished guest. But first, make her swear the great oath of the Blessed Ones to plot no mischief to you thenceforward – if not, while you lie naked there, she may rob you of courage and of manhood."

'So spoke the Radiant One; then gave me the magic herb, pulling it from the ground and showing me in what form it grew; its root was black, its flower milk-white. Its name among the gods is *moly*.[2] For mortal men it is perilous to pluck up, but for the gods all things are possible.

  1. 'O blind to fate! what led thy steps to rove
     The horrid mazes of this magic grove?
     Each friend you seek in yon enclosure lies,
     All lost their form, and habitants of Styes.' POPE
  2. For the lore of moly and mandragora, see Hugo Rahner, *Greek Myths and Christian Mystery* (1963), ch. 5.

'Then Hermes departed over the wooded island and went his way to the mountain of Olympus. I myself passed on to Circe's palace, with my thoughts in turmoil as I walked. I paused at the doorway of the goddess, and standing there I gave a great cry; she heard my voice and came out quickly, opening the shining doors and calling me in. I went up to her though my heart sank. She ushered me in and gave me a tall silver-studded chair to sit in – handsome and cunningly made it was – with a stool beneath it for the feet. In a golden goblet she brewed a potion for me to drink, and treacherously mingled her drug with it. When I had taken and drunk it up and was unenchanted still,[1] she struck at me with her wand, and "Now" she said "be off to the sty, to wallow with your companions there."[2]

'So she spoke, but I drew the keen sword from beside my thigh, rushed at her and made as if to kill her. She shrieked, she slipped underneath my weapon, she clasped my knees and spoke in rapid appealing words: "Who are you, and from where? Where are your city and your parents? It bewilders me that you drank this drug and were not bewitched. Never has any other man resisted this drug, once he has drunk it and let it pass his lips. But you have an inner will that is proof against sorcery. You must surely be that man of wide-ranging spirit, Odysseus himself; the Radiant One of the golden wand has told me of you; he always said that Odysseus would come to me on his way from Troy in his dark and rapid vessel. But enough of this; sheathe your sword; then let us go to bed together, and embracing there, let us learn to trust in one another."

'So she spoke, but I answered her: "Circe, how can you ask me to show you gentleness? In this very house you have turned my comrades into swine, and now that you have me also here you ask me in your treacherousness to enter your room and lie with you, only that when I lie naked there you may rob me of courage

1. 'I ebb'd the bowl, but no effect it had.' OGILBY (This vigorous use of 'ebb' for 'drain' seems unrecorded in dictionaries.)

2. 'She mixt the potion, fraudulent of soul;
   The poison mantled in the golden bowl.
   I took, and quaff'd it, confident in heav'n:
   Then wav'd the wand, and then the word was giv'n.
   Hence, to thy fellows! (dreadful she began)
   Go, be a beast! – I heard, and yet was man.' POPE

and of manhood. Never, goddess, could I bring myself to lie with you unless you consented first to swear a great oath to plot no mischief to me henceforward."

'So I spoke, and she swore at once the thing I asked for. When Circe had uttered the due appointed words, I lay down at last in her sumptuous bed.

'All this while, four handmaids of hers were busying themselves about the palace. She has them for household tasks, and they come from springs, they come from groves, they come from the sacred rivers flowing seawards. One spread the chairs with fine crimson covers above and with linen cloths beneath; in front of the chairs, a second drew up silver tables on which she laid gold baskets for bread; a third mixed honey-sweet lovely wine in a silver bowl and set the golden goblets out; the fourth brought water and lit a great fire under a massive cauldron. The water warmed; and when it boiled in the bright bronze vessel, the goddess made me sit in a bath and bathed me with water from the cauldron, tempering hot and cold to my mind and pouring it over my head and shoulders until she had banished from my limbs the weariness that sapped my spirit. And having washed me and richly anointed me with oil, she dressed me in a fine cloak and tunic, led me forward and gave me a tall silver-studded chair to sit on – handsome and cunningly made – with a stool beneath it for the feet. She bade me eat, but my heart was not on eating, and I sat with my thoughts elsewhere and my mind unquiet.

'When Circe saw me sitting thus, not reaching for food but sunk in despondency, she came and stood near me, quickly questioning: "Odysseus, why do you sit there tongue-tied eating your heart out, not touching food or drink? Can it be that you fear some further treachery? You should have no doubts; I have sworn the great oath already."

'So she spoke, but I answered her: "Circe, what man of right-eous thoughts could bring himself to taste food or drink before winning liberty for his friends and seeing the men before his eyes? If it is in earnest that you tell me to eat and drink, release them now, and let me see my trusty companions face to face."

'So I spoke, and Circe went through the hall and out, wand in hand; she flung open the doors of the sty and set the men running out in the shape of fat and full-grown swine. Then they stood facing her, and she went to and fro among them, anointing them one by one with another charm. Their limbs began to shed the bristles that Circe's poison had planted on them, and they became men again, but younger than they had been before, and taller and handsomer to the eye. They knew me at once, and man after man they clasped my hand. A melting mood stole upon them all, and they sobbed aloud till the house re-echoed dolefully. Circe herself felt compassion; then she came up and said to me: "Son of Laertes, subtle Odysseus, now go back to your rapid vessel by the beach. First, with your men, haul the ship ashore; then fetch out all your gear and goods and stow them inside the caves; then return yourself and bring your trusty companions with you."

'Such were her words, and my own heart desired nothing better. I went my way to the rapid vessel by the beach, and there I found my comrades aboard; they were shedding big tears and lamenting piteously. Just as on a farm, when the cows have had their fill of grass and the herd of them comes back to the yard, the calves all push their way out of their pens and run with much lowing to meet their mothers and frisk around them[1] so, when they saw me with their own eyes, my weeping comrades crowded round me, and in their hearts it was as if they had reached their own land again, and the very town of rocky Ithaca where they were born and bred. Lamenting still, they spoke to me in words that went home: "Heaven-favoured king, we are as happy at your return as if we had reached our own native land again, Ithaca itself. But now you must tell from first to last how our other friends were lost to us."

'So they spoke; I answered them with consoling words: "First let us haul the ship ashore, then take out all our gear and goods and stow them inside the caves; after that, make haste to come with me, all of you, and to see your friends in the goddess Circe's palace, eating and drinking; they have enough and to spare."

'So I spoke, and the men were quick to do my bidding; only

1. 'As well-fed Heifers play at Prison-Base
   About their Mothers coming home from Grass;
   Lowing they frisk, their Stals the Wantons shun . . .'
                                              OGILBY

Eurylochus endeavoured to keep them back: "Wretched men, where are we going? Why do you court disaster thus, why venture down to Circe's dwelling? She will turn us all into swine or wolves or lions, to guard her palace whether we will or no; just as the Cyclops penned our companions in when they reached his steading – foolhardy Odysseus went in with them, and his presumption was their undoing."[1]

'So he spoke; I was half minded to draw the long keen sword from my sturdy thigh, strike off his head and send it to meet the ground, although he was close of kin to me; but my men all round me restrained me with pacifying words: "Heaven-born one, let us leave this man, if you consent, to stay by the ship and guard it. As for the rest of us, we ask you to guide us on the way to the palace of the goddess Circe."

'And with these words they began the upward walk, leaving the vessel and the sea. Nor did Eurylochus linger there; he came with the rest, dreading my powerful indignation.

'In the meantime inside her palace Circe had bathed the others hospitably, had richly anointed them with oil and had clothed them in tunics and fleecy cloaks; we found them dining in the hall, every man of them. When the two groups espied each other – when the men looked each other in the face – they began to weep and make lamentation till the house around them echoed with it. But the goddess came up and said to me:

' "Son of Laertes, subtle Odysseus, you must all give over these loud laments that you are making. I myself well know what tribulations you have endured on the teeming sea and what injustices you have borne from barbarous men on land. But enough! Eat your food and drink your wine till you have regained the same spirit that you had when you first set sail from your own country, rocky Ithaca. You are listless now, you are spiritless, brooding for ever and for ever on the calamities of your wander-

1. 'Whither (he cry'd) ah whither will ye run?
    Seek ye to meet those evils ye shou'd shun?
    Will you the terrors of the dome explore,
    In swine to grovel, or in lions roar,
    Or wolf-like howl away the midnight hour
    In dreadful watch around the magic bow'r?
    Remember *Cyclops*, and his bloody deed;
    The leader's rashness made the soldiers bleed.' POPE

ings. Your hearts are never disposed to mirth, because you have suffered all too much."[1]

'Such were her words, and our hearts accepted them. So every day, till the year's end, we sat there feasting on plenteous meat and delicious wine. When the year was out and the seasons had circled round, then my comrades called me apart and said:

' "Forgetful man, it is time now to call your own land to mind once more, if indeed heaven means you to come safe home to your lofty house and the country of your fathers."

'Such were their words, and my heart accepted them. So all that day, till the sun set, we sat and feasted on plenteous meat and delicious wine. When the sun went and darkness came, the men lay down to sleep in the shadowy halls, but I, returning to Circe's sumptuous bed, clasped her knees and made supplication to her, and the goddess heard my plea: "Circe, you gave me once your promise to help me homewards, and the time has come to make it good; my own desire is set that way, and the desire of my comrades also – they are there around me, vexing my heart with their lamentations when once you yourself are out of sight."

'The goddess answered my words forthwith: "Son of Laertes, subtle Odysseus, if it is in spite of yourselves that you all stay in my palace still, then you must stay here no longer. But another path must be travelled first: you must visit the house of dread Persephone and of Hades, and there seek counsel from the spirit of Theban Teiresias. The blind seer's thought is wakeful still, for to him alone, even after death, Persephone has accorded wisdom; the other dead are but flitting shadows."

'So she spoke; my spirit was crushed within me. I sank down on the bed and wept, and my heart lost the desire to live or to look longer upon the sunlight. I wept, I writhed till the bout of bitterness was past. At length I answered and said to her: "But Circe, who will pilot me on that voyage? Never since time began

1. 'Forget whatever was in Fortune's pow'r,
   And share the pleasures of this genial hour.
   Such be your minds as ere ye left your coast,
   Or learn'd to sorrow for a country lost.
   Exiles and wand'rers now, where-e're ye go,
   Too faithful memory renews your woe;
   The cause remov'd, habitual griefs remain,
   And the soul saddens by the use of pain.' POPE

has the dark ship of any traveller brought him to Hades' house."

'And at once the goddess answered me: "Son of Laertes, subtle Odysseus, when you reach your ship, no lack of a pilot need trouble you. Raise the mast, spread the white sail and seat yourself: the north wind's breathing will waft the vessel on. When you have sailed through the river Ocean, you will see before you a narrow strand and the groves that are Persephone's – the tall black poplars, the willows with their self-wasted fruit;[1] then beach the vessel beside deep-eddying Ocean and pass on foot to the dank domains of Hades. At the entrance there, the stream of Acheron is joined by the waters of Pyriphlegethon and of a branch of Styx, Cocytus, and there is a rock where the two loud-roaring rivers meet. Then, Lord Odysseus, you must do as I enjoin you; go forward, and dig a trench a cubit long and a cubit broad; go round this trench, pouring libation for all the dead, first with milk and honey, then with sweet wine, then with water; and sprinkle white barley-meal above. Then with earnest prayers to the strengthless presences of the dead you must promise that when you have come to Ithaca you will sacrifice in your palace a calfless heifer, the best you have, and will load a pyre with precious things; and that for Teiresias and no other you will slay, apart, a ram that is black all over, the choicest in all the flocks of Ithaca.

' "When with these prayers you have made appeal to the noble nations of the dead, then you must sacrifice a ram and a black ewe; bend the victims' heads down towards Erebus, but turn your own head away and look towards the waters of the river. At this, the souls of the dead and gone will come flocking there. With commanding voice you must call your comrades to flay and burn the two sheep that now lie before them, killed by your own ruthless blade, and over them to pray to the gods, to resistless Hades and dread Persephone. As for yourself, draw the keen sword from beside your thigh; then, sitting down, hold back the strengthless presences of the dead from drawing nearer to the blood until you have questioned Teiresias. Then, King Odysseus, the seer will come to you very quickly, to prophesy the path before you, the long stages of your travel, and how you will reach home at last over the teeming sea."

'Scarcely had she ended her words when Dawn appeared in her

1. For the symbolism of these willows, see Hugo Rahner, *Greek Myths and Christian Mystery* (1963), ch. 6.

flowery cloth of gold. Circe gave me my tunic and cloak to wear; she herself put on a big silvery mantle, graceful and delicate; she fastened a lovely gold girdle round her waist and slipped a scarf over her head. Then I went through the halls and roused my comrades, standing near each in turn and uttering persuasive words: "You have slept enough; give over that drowsy pleasure now. It is time to go – Lady Circe has shown me how and where."

'So I spoke; and the men agreed gladly enough. Yet not even from this adventure could I bring my comrades away unscathed. There was one of them called Elpenor, the youngest of all, neither brave in battle nor firm in mind; he had left the rest of my company and had lain down on the top of Circe's house, heavy with wine and seeking the cool. When my comrades began to stir and he heard the sound of their feet and voices, he leapt up in haste and quite forgot to take the long ladder downwards and so return. Instead, he fell headlong from the roof; his neck was wrenched away from the spine, and his soul went down to the house of Hades.

'As the rest came out I had words to say to them: "Doubtless you think you are on your way to your own homes, to your own country. But no; Circe has said we must sail elsewhere, to the house of Hades and dread Persephone; we are to ask counsel there of Theban Teiresias."

'So I spoke, and their hearts were crushed within them. They sank down on the ground where they were and began to groan and tear their hair; but no good could come of this lamentation.

'While we made our melancholy way to the ship at the sea's edge, weeping without restraint, Circe already had passed before us and tethered a ram and a black ewe beside the vessel. She had slipped past us unperceived; what eyes could discern a god in his comings and his goings if the god himself should wish it otherwise?

BOOK XI

ODYSSEUS AMONG THE GHOSTS

'W E reached our ship at the sea's edge and hauled it down to the bright water, then stowed the mast and the sails inside; we took the sheep and put them aboard; last of all, we ourselves embarked, still despondent, weeping still unrestrainedly. But Circe of the braided tresses, the goddess of awesome powers and of human speech, sent the best of comrades after our dark-prowed vessel, a following breeze to fill our sails. We made fast the tackling everywhere, then seated ourselves while wind and helmsman bore the ship forward on her course. The sails were taut as she sped all day across the sea till the sun sank and light thickened on every pathway.

'The vessel came to the bounds of eddying Ocean, where lie the land and the city of the Cimmerians, covered with mist and cloud. Never does the resplendent sun look on this people with his beams, neither when he climbs towards the stars of heaven nor when once more he comes earthwards from the sky; dismal night overhangs these wretches always. Arriving there, we beached the vessel, took out the sheep and then walked onwards beside the stream of Ocean until we came to the place that Circe had told us of.

'There, Perimedes and Eurylochus seized the victims and held them fast, while I myself drew the keen sword from beside my thigh and cut a trench a cubit long and a cubit broad. Round it I poured a libation for all the dead, first with milk and honey, then with sweet wine, then with water; over this I sprinkled white barley-meal. Then with earnest prayers to the strengthless presences of the dead I promised that when I came to Ithaca I would sacrifice in my palace a calfless heifer, the best I had, and would load a pyre with precious things; and that for Teiresias and no other I would slay, apart, a ram that was black all over, the choicest in all the flocks of Ithaca.

'When with my prayers and invocations I had called on the peoples of the dead, I seized the victims and cut their throats over the trench. The dark blood flowed, and the souls of the dead and gone came flocking upwards from Erebus – brides and unmarried youths, old men who had suffered much, tender girls with the heart's distress still keen, troops of warriors wounded with brazen-pointed spears, men slain in battle with blood-stained armour still upon them. With unearthly cries, from every quarter, they came crowding about the trench until pale terror began to master me.

'Then with urgent voice I called my comrades to flay and burn the two sheep that now lay before them, killed by my own ruthless blade, and over them to pray to the gods, to resistless Hades and dread Persephone. As for myself, I drew the keen sword from beside my thigh, seated myself and held back the strengthless presences of the dead from drawing nearer to the blood before I had questioned Teiresias.

'First came my comrade Elpenor's soul. He had not been buried yet under the wide-wayed earth; we had left his body in Circe's palace unburied and unlamented because we were urged by other tasks. I wept to see him, pitying him from my heart, and my words came forth in rapid flight: "Elpenor, how did you journey down to this murk and mist? I in my vessel have been outstripped by you on foot."

'So I spoke; he groaned as he answered me: "Son of Laertes, subtle Odysseus, I was led astray by the cruel sentence of some divinity and by excess of wine. I had lain down on the top of Circe's house and had not the wits to take the long ladder downwards and so return. Instead, I fell headlong from the roof; my neck was wrenched away from the spine, and my soul came down to the house of Hades. But now I make appeal to you in the name of those who are not here – your household in Ithaca, your wife, the father who cared for you in childhood and Telemachus whom you left behind in your house alone. I know that when you depart from this house of Hades your ship will put in once more at the island of Aeaea; when you are there, my lord, I beseech you to take thought for me; do not turn your back and leave me unburied and unlamented at your going – I should haunt you with the wrath of heaven. No, burn me with what armour I have, and build me a mound on the shore of the whitening sea, so that men hereafter may learn my luckless story. Accomplish these rites for me, and plant on my tomb the oar I rowed with, beside my comrades, while I was still among living men."

'So he spoke, and I answered him: "Luckless friend, I will see all this accomplished duly."

'As we exchanged these words of sorrow, we stayed sitting

opposite each other, I apart, with my sword drawn over the blood, and my comrade's ghost on the other side, telling his long-drawn tale.

'Then the soul of my dead mother came, Anticleia, daughter of bold Autolycus; I had left her alive when I went to sacred Ilium, and I wept to see her and pitied her from my heart; yet even so, despite all my sorrow, I would not let her draw near the blood till I had questioned Teiresias.

'Then came the soul of Theban Teiresias, holding a golden staff. He knew me and spoke to me: "Son of Laertes, subtle Odysseus: unhappy man, why did you thus forsake the sunlight and travel here to visit the dead in this joyless place? No matter; draw back from the trench, put your keen sword aside; then I will taste the blood and give you true prophecy."

'So he spoke, and I drew back, sheathing the silver-studded blade. The holy prophet drank the dark blood, then uttered these words: "Noble Odysseus, you are seeking return home, and return is very sweet, but there is a god who will make it hard for you. I mean the Earthshaker; I am sure you will not escape him unseen, because he has laid up resentment in his heart against you, and is angry still for your blinding of his son. Yet even so, you and your men may perhaps reach home, though with much misery, if only you have the strength of will to curb your own and your comrades' appetites when you leave dark ocean and bring your vessel near the Thrinacian island. You will find sheep and cattle grazing there; they belong to a god, the all-seeing, all-hearing sun. If you leave these unharmed – if you set your mind only on return – you may all of you still reach Ithaca, though with much misery. But if you harm them, then I foretell destruction alike for your ship and for your comrades; and if you yourself escape that end, you will return late and in evil plight, having lost for ever all your comrades, a passenger in an alien ship. And in your own house you will find mischief, I mean the presumptuous men who are devouring your substance now, wooing your noble wife and offering her suitors' gifts; yet for these men's outrages you will take due vengeance at your return. When you have killed the suitors in your own palace – whether by guile or whether openly with the keen bronze – then go forth, carrying with you a balanced oar, till you come to men who know nothing of the sea and eat food unseasoned with salt, men unacquainted with ships and their crimson cheeks or with balanced oars that are to ships as are wings to birds. I will give you a plain token you cannot miss. When another traveller falls in with you and takes the thing upon your shoulder to be a winnowing-fan, then plant that balanced oar in the ground and offer to Lord Poseidon the noble sacrifice of a ram and a bull and a boar that mates with sows. Then return home and make offering of sacred hecatombs to the deathless gods whose home is wide heaven itself, to each one of them in turn. And death will come to you far from sea,[1] a gentle death that will end your days when the years of ease have left you frail and your people round you enjoy all happiness. This is my prophecy; it is true."

'So he spoke, and I answered him: "Doubtless, Teiresias, these fateful threads have been spun by the gods themselves. But now tell me this and answer truly. Yonder I see my dead mother's soul, but she sits there speechless near the blood, without giving a word or glance to her own son. Tell me, my lord Teiresias – how can she be brought to know me for what I am?"

'So I spoke, and he answered me forthwith: "The thing is easy, and I will make it plain to you. Whichever among these ghostly dead you allow to approach the blood, that one will speak to you truthfully; whichever you thwart, that one will go back again."

'When the shade of Lord Teiresias had ended its prophecies, it ceased its utterance and went its way back to Hades' house. I myself waited there unmoving till my mother came and drank the dark blood; straightway she knew me, and her words of sorrow reached me in rapid flight: "My child, how have you come, still living, down to this murk and mist? These realms are perilous for a living man to see. Have you come from Ilium only now, after straying long with your ship and comrades? Have you still not returned to Ithaca, still not seen your wife in your halls?"

'So she spoke, and I answered her: "Mother, necessity has constrained me to travel down to the house of Hades in search of counsel from Theban Teiresias. No, I have still not neared Achaea, nor have I set foot on my own country ever since among Agamem-

---

1. The death so described has often been thought of as coming 'out of' the sea, and later Greek legend amplified this in various ways. The interpretation I follow takes the same Greek preposition to mean 'away from' – 'home from sea' or as Hopkins has it 'out of the swing of the sea.'

non's followers I went to Ilium to fight against the Trojans; I have only wandered in endless misery. But now tell me this and answer truly. What doom of distressful death subdued you? Was it some long-continued sickness, or did the archeress Artemis visit you with her gentle shafts and slay you? And tell me of my father also, and of the son I left behind. Is my domain still in their hands, or does some other hold it already because men think I shall not return? And tell me of the mood and mind of my wedded wife. Has she remained beside our child, has she kept all my possessions safe, or has she become wife already to some Achaean more noble than the rest?"

'So I spoke, and my lady mother answered: "Indeed she remains in your halls most patiently; each night, each day wears to its ending for her only amid her grief and tears. No other holds your noble domain. Telemachus possesses your lands in peace and takes his part in the shared banquets as any giver of justice should, for everyone invites him. Your father stays on his own farm and never comes down to the city now. He has no bed to lie on, no blankets or shining rugs; in wintertime, he sleeps in the house just where his servants do, in the ashes by the fire, and the clothes on his back are wretched ones. When summer and mellow autumn come, his sleeping-places are on the ground, anywhere on the vineyard slope with its thick-strewn leaves. There he lies dismally, with grief in his heart ever more intense as he longs for your homecoming, and old age is hard for him besides. It was in such grief that I myself came to my end and met my fate. No, it was not the unerring Archeress who slew me with gentle shafts, nor did such sickness fall upon me as most often severs soul and body with painful wasting; it was longing for you, my pride, Odysseus – for you with your wisdom and gentle ways – that parted me from a life still sweet."

'Such was her tale; my mind was full, and I longed to embrace my dead mother's ghost; three times did I spring forward to her, for the will to clasp her was strong in me; three times she vanished between my arms, like a fleeting shadow, a fleeting dream. Each time keen anguish went through my heart, and my words came forth in rapid flight:

"Mother, why will you not wait for me? I long to clasp you, so that even in this house of Hades we may throw loving arms about each other and have our fill of bitter weeping. Or is this some wraith that august Persephone has sent me to increase my sorrowing and my tears?"

'So I spoke, and the queen my mother answered me: "Alas, my child, ill-fated beyond all other mortals, this is no mockery of Persephone's; it is all men's fortune when they die. The sinews no longer hold flesh and bones together; these are all a prey to the resistless power of fire when once the life has left the white bones; the soul takes wing as a dream takes wing, and thereafter hovers to and fro. And now hasten back to the light of day, but hold in memory all you have heard from me, and tell it afterwards to your wife."

'Such were the words that passed between us; meanwhile there appeared a whole company of women, sent by Persephone the august; and these were the wives or the daughters of great men. They gathered flocking round the dark blood. I wondered how best to question each one of them, and I thought the best device was this. I drew the long sharp sword from beside my thigh, and would not let them drink the dark blood all together. So they came forward one after another, and each in turn told me her lineage, for I left none of them unquestioned.

'The first that I saw was high-born Tyro, daughter of great Salmoneus and wife of Cretheus the son of Aeolus – such was her twofold boast. She fell in love with the river-god Enipeus, whose waters are the most beautiful of any that flow on earth; and she haunted his beguiling streams. But in place of Enipeus, and in his likeness, there came the god who sustains and who shakes the earth. He lay with her at the mouth of the eddying river, and a surging wave, mountain-high, curled over them and concealed the god and the mortal girl. And when the god had finished the work of love, he uttered these words with her hand in his: "Girl, be happy in this our love. When the year comes round you will be the mother of glorious children (an immortal's embrace is not in vain); tend them and care for them. Now return home; be wary, and say no word of me; nevertheless I would have you know that I am the Shaker of Earth, Poseidon."

'With these words he sank beneath billowing ocean. She conceived and brought forth Pelias and Neleus, and both became powerful liegemen of mighty Zeus. Pelias, possessor of many flocks, had spacious Iolcus for his dwelling; the domain of Neleus was sandy Pylos. Queen Tyro bore other sons to Cretheus – Aeson and Pheres and the chariot-warrior Amythaon.

'After Tyro, I saw Antiope, daughter of Asopus; it was her pride to have slept in the arms of Zeus himself. She bore two sons, Amphion and Zethus, primal founders of Thebes of the seven gates; they added walls to the spacious city because without them they could not hold it as their dwelling, strong though they were.

'After her I saw Alcmene, wife of Amphitryon, who lay in the arms of mighty Zeus and brought forth Heracles of the dauntless spirit and lion heart. And I saw bold Creon's daughter Megara, who became wife to indomitable Heracles.

'I saw the mother of Oedipus, lovely Epicaste, who did a most evil thing in the ignorance of her heart and wedded her own son, and he, before he wedded her, had slain his own father; but a time came when the gods revealed all these things to men. Then, since the gods were bent on ruin, while Oedipus in lovely Thebes continued despite his misery to rule the sons of Cadmus, his mother went down to the house whose gates mighty Hades guards; in the passion of her grief she made fast a noose for herself from the lofty roof-beam; and for Oedipus she left behind such endless woes as a mother's avenging spirits bring.

'I saw likewise most lovely Chloris, whom for her beauty's sake Neleus long ago wooed and won with a thousand gifts, the youngest daughter of Amphion. Amphion was child of Iasus and mighty ruler of Minyan Orchomenus. She was queen in Pylos, and bore her husband noble sons, Nestor and Chromius and princely Periclymenus. After the sons she had one daughter, Pero, a marvel whom all her neighbours wooed; but Neleus would not give her to any man who could not drive off from Phylace the broad-browed cattle with curving horns that were in the hands of powerful Iphiclus. They were hard to take; one man alone, a noble prophet,[1] made bold to say he would drive them off, but a god's hard sentence entangled him; he was caught by herdsmen and galled with chains. But when, with the turning year, the days and the months reached their end and the seasons came onwards in their course, he revealed all the counsels of the gods and powerful Iphiclus let him go; thus the will of Zeus found accomplishment.

'Next I saw Leda; she was wife of Tyndareos and bore him

1. Melampus. See p. 183.

two stalwart sons, the charioteer Castor, the boxer Polydeuces; grain-giving earth now holds them both, yet both are alive, because even underground they have this favour given them by Zeus that each of them lives one day and dies one day, this and that in turn; and the honour given them equals them with the gods.

'After her I saw Aloeus' wife; she was Iphimedeia, whose boast it was to have lain beside Poseidon. She bore him two sons, though their life was short – Otus the peer of gods and far-famed Ephialtes; these were the tallest men, and the handsomest, that ever the fertile earth has fostered, save only incomparable Orion; at nine years of age their breadth was nine cubits, their height nine fathoms. They threatened the Deathless Ones themselves – to embroil Olympus in all the fury and din of war. And so indeed they might have done had they reached the full measure of their years, but the god that Zeus begot and lovely-haired Leto bore destroyed them both before the first down could show underneath their brows and overspread and adorn their cheeks.

'I saw Phaedra and Procris too, and lovely Ariadne, that daughter of subtle Minos whom Theseus bore off from Crete towards the hill of sacred Athens; yet he had no joy of her, since, before that could be, she was slain by Artemis in the isle of Dia because of the witness of Dionysus.

'I saw Maera too, and Clymene, and loathsome Eriphyle, who took a great bribe of gold to lure her own husband to his doom.

'But I cannot name and tell of them every one – those princes' wives and princes' daughters that then I saw; the night heaven gives us would end too soon. And indeed it is now time to sleep, whether I join my crew in the rapid vessel or whether I stay here instead; my departure rests with the gods and you.'

So spoke Odysseus. They all kept silence, rapt and hushed in the shadows of the hall. Then white-armed Arete began to speak: 'Phaeacians, what do you say of this man now – his air and presence and poise of mind? He is my own guest especially, but each of you is of princely rank. So be in no haste to send him from us, and do not be sparing with your gifts; his need, as you see, is great, and – heaven be thanked – the possessions housed in your halls are plentiful.'

Old Lord Echenaus added his counsel (he was eldest among the men of Scheria): 'Friends, the words of our thoughtful queen are not ill-aimed or unlike our expectations. Do as she says – though it is on Alcinous here that speech and action alike depend.'

Alcinous answered: 'The thing she speaks of shall be done, as sure as I am a living man and king of the Phaeacians. But this guest of ours, much as he longs for his return, must have patience to wait until tomorrow, until I make up the full measure of the gift. To send him home shall be the concern of all men here, and in the first place of myself, since mine is the supremacy in this land.'

Shrewd Odysseus replied to him: 'Alcinous, most exalted lord, if you bade me wait a whole year with you and then granted me my return and offered me noble gifts, even to that I would consent, since indeed I should gain much by returning to my own country with fuller hands, and should win more friendship and respect among all who witnessed my homecoming to Ithaca.'

Alcinous answered: 'Odysseus, as we look at you we cannot think you to be a deceiver and a cheat, though the dark earth breeds a great crop of such, forgers of lies drawn from places beyond our ken. But with you the spoken words are eloquent and the mind they come from is a wise one. You have told your tale as skilfully as a bard – the toils and trials of all the Achaeans and yourself. But now tell me this also truly – did you see in the halls of Hades any of those heroic comrades who went in your company to Troy but met their fate then and there? The night still stretches far before us – who knows how far? – and in this hall the hour for sleeping has not yet come. Tell me more of these strange adventures. Indeed I would wait here in this hall even till the ethereal dawn if you would only take up again the theme of your tribulations.'

Subtle Odysseus answered him: 'Alcinous, most exalted lord, there is a time for many words and there is a time for sleep. Yet if you desire to hear me further, I will not begrudge you the tale of things more pitiful still than these, disasters that fell upon those comrades who met their fate when the wars were over – who escaped the turmoil of Trojan battles only to perish on their return because of the will of a wicked woman.

'So then – when chaste Persephone had dispersed this way and that the souls of those many women, there came before me in bitter sorrow the soul of Agamemnon; round the son of Atreus were gathered those other dead who, no less than he, had met their doom in the palace of Aegisthus. He drank the dark blood and at once knew me. He continued making loud lamentation with tears unchecked, stretching out his hands to me, eager to touch; but he had no such vigour or strength left in him as once had dwelt in his lithe limbs. I wept to see him, my heart went out to him, and I uttered these words in rapid flight: 'Renowned Atreides, Agamemnon the lord of men, what doom of distressful death overmastered you? Did Poseidon rouse some hideous blast of contrary winds and destroy you among the ships that went with you? Or did hostile men strike you down on land as you drove off their flocks and herds or battled to win their town and women?'

'So I asked, and at once he answered: "Son of Laertes, subtle Odysseus, Poseidon roused no hideous blast of contrary winds to destroy me among the ships that went with me, nor did hostile men strike me down on land. It was Aegisthus and my accursed wife who plotted death and destruction for me; he invited me to his house and gave me a feast and killed me as a man kills an ox at stall. Thus I died the most pitiful of deaths, and my comrades too were killed around me mercilessly like white-tusked boars in the house of some rich and powerful man, at a wedding or feast or sumptuous banquet. You have seen in your time many men meet death, in single combat or violent battle, but much more then would compassion have pierced your heart, had you seen how we lay there in the hall by the mixing-bowl and the laden tables, while the whole floor seethed with blood. But most pitiful of all was the cry I heard from Priam's daughter Cassandra as treacherous Clytemnestra slaughtered her over me; and as I died with the sword thrust through me I raised my hands and beat them upon the ground; but that shameless one turned away from me and even as I went down to Hades' house would not stretch out her hand to close my eyes and mouth. Truly nothing is deadlier and loathsomer than a woman when she sets her mind on deeds like these. Thus did my wife devise this abomination, contriving murder against her own wedded husband, when I had been thinking all the while how children and household would bid me welcome home. By her utter wickedness of will she has poured dishonour both on herself and on every woman that lives hereafter, even on one whose deeds are virtuous."

'So he spoke, and I answered him: "Alas, too surely has Zeus the Thunderer nourished unbounded hatred from long ago for the seed of Atreus, with woman's wiles for his instrument. How many of us have been killed for Helen's sake, and now there is this betrayal by Clytemnestra, plotted against you while you were far away!"

'So I spoke, and at once he answered: "Yes, and therefore you too must never favour your wife too far; when you have perfected some scheme, do not tell her the whole of it, but reveal part, and part leave hidden. Not that you, Odysseus, need ever fear murder by your wife; the child of Icarius, wise Penelope, has true judgement, and all her thoughts are thoughts of virtue. When we set out to war we left her as a still youthful bride with a baby at her breast, a son who doubtless now sits among grown men. Happy he! The father he loves will see him when he comes home again, and the boy, as is right and due, will embrace his father. But my own son – my wife would not let me feast my eyes on him; she killed me first. But tell me this plainly and truly; have you news of my son as still alive, whether in Orchomenus or in sandy Pylos, or perhaps in the plains of Sparta with Menelaus? In whatever region of the world, it cannot be that Prince Orestes has died already."

'So he spoke, and I answered him: "Son of Atreus, why ask me this? I have no knowledge of either his living or his dying, and if words are but wind they are best unspoken."

'As these sad words passed between us we stood in sorrow, and with both of us the tears flowed fast. Then there came before me the souls of Achilles and Patroclus, of noble Antilochus and of Aias, who in form and feature was best among all the Danaans after the matchless son of Peleus. The soul of fleet-foot Achilles knew me, and in mournful tones he uttered these words in rapid flight: "Son of Laertes, subtle and overbold Odysseus, what venture will ever tempt your mind more reckless than this? What daring has led you down to the house of Hades, the dwelling-place of the dead who have no understanding, of the wraiths of mortals who have perished?"

'So he spoke, and I answered him: "Achilles, son of Peleus, mightiest of the Achaeans, I came on an errand to Teiresias, in hope of counsel about my return to Ithaca, because as yet I have not approached the Achaean land or set foot in my own country; distress has dogged me. But you, Achilles – no man has been more

blest than you in days past, or will be in days to come; for before
you died we Achaeans honoured you like a god, and now in this
place you lord it among the dead. No, do not repine in death,
Achilles."

'So I spoke, but at once he answereed: "Odysseus, do not gloss
over death to me. I would rather be above ground still and labour-
ing for some poor portionless man, than be lord over all the life-
less dead. But tell me now all that you know of my princely son.
Did he follow me to the wars to become a chieftain, or did he
not? And tell me also what news you have of noble Peleus. Is he
honoured still among the thronging Myrmidons, or do they des-
pise him in Hellas and in Phthia because old age has fettered his
hands and feet? If only I might return to help him, return to the
sunlight as once I was when in the wide land of Troy I cham-
pioned the Argives and slew the bravest of the foe! If in that
likeness I could return to my father's house, were it but for one
brief moment, then I would make my strength and resistless
hands a thing to be loathed by any who do him violence now and
who thrust him out from his place of honour."

'So he spoke, and I answered him: "Of noble Peleus I have no
news, but concerning your dear son Neoptolemus I will tell the
whole truth as you desire, since I myself in my own trim vessel
brought him from Scyros to join the greaved Achaeans. When we
sat in council outside Troy town, he was always the earliest to
speak, and he never spoke amiss; only great Nestor and myself
were his betters there. And when we Achaeans were battling
upon the Trojan plain, he never stayed in the throng and press of
fighters; he ran far forward; he yielded to none in warlike spirit.
Many were those he killed in the grim encounter, nor can I now
recount by name all the host of those who fell to him as he
championed the Achaeans. But one above all was a worthy foe –
Eurypylus son of Telephus. Of all men that ever I saw – after
Memnon, whose mother was a goddess – this man was the hand-
somest. He was slain by the sword of Neoptolemus, and round
him his band of Ceteian comrades – all dead through the bribing
of a woman.[1] Again, as we entered the horse that Epeius made,
we foremost of the Danaans, with myself in chief command, the
other Achaean lords and leaders were wiping tears away from

1. Astyoche, mother of Eurypylus, had refused to send her son to
Troy until Priam bribed her with a golden vine.

their faces, and their limbs were trembling under them. But when I looked at your son's face, I could see no blanching there, no wiping away of tears from cheeks; no, he kept begging me to let him climb out of the horse, kept clutching his sword-hilt and great bronze spear, kept brooding mischief against the Trojans. And when we had sacked the high town of Priam, he boarded his ship with a fine share of booty, yet quite unscathed – not pierced by the hurling of keen bronze nor wounded by sword hand to hand, though that is the common way of war, since it is at random that Ares rages."

'So I spoke, and the soul of the fleet-foot son of Peleus went pacing forth over the field of asphodel, happy thus to hear from my lips the tale of the glory of his son.[1]

'Other souls of the dead and gone still stood there sorrowfully, each of them questioning me on whatever touched him most. Only the soul of Aias the son of Telamon kept aloof, nursing anger still at my victory in the contest when beside the ships I made my claim for the armour of Achilles, whose goddess-mother offered the prize. Would I had never won that prize! Because of it, the earth closed over heroic Aias, who alike in presence and in prowess surpassed all other Danaans after the matchless son of Peleus. To him I now spoke appeasing words:

' "Aias, son of the noble Telamon, is it then a thing beyond all hope that in death at least you should set aside your wrath against me for the winning of those hateful arms? The prize that the gods there offered us was to bring distress on all the Argives when the tower of strength that you had been was forever lost to them. Ever since you perished, our grief for you has been like the grief for the son of Peleus, Achilles himself; and no other was cause of all this but Zeus; he it was who bore hate unbounded against the host of Achaean spearsmen, and because of that decreed your doom. Come to me now, Lord Aias, and hear the words that I wish to speak; conquer your spirit and pride of heart."

'So I spoke, but he made no answer to me, only followed to Erebus the other souls of men dead and gone.

'Then, despite his anger, he still might have spoken to me, or I to him, but that my heart was eager to see the souls of the other dead.

1. 'This made the soule of swift Achilles tred
   A March of glorie through the herbie meade.' CHAPMAN

'Then I saw Minos the son of Zeus holding a golden sceptre and delivering judgements among the dead. There he sat, and around him the others sat or stood in the ample-gated house of Hades, seeking from this master of justice the firm sentences of law.

'Next I discerned huge Orion, driving wild beasts together over the field of asphodel, the very ones that he once had killed on lonely mountains; he grasped in his hands a mace of bronze, never to be broken.

'I saw Tityus also, son of the mighty goddess Earth; he lay on the ground, his bulk stretched out over nine roods. Two vultures, one on each side of him, sat and kept plucking at his liver, reaching down to the very bowels; he could not beat them off with his hands. And this was because he had once assaulted a mistress of Zeus himself, the far-famed Leto, as she walked towards Pytho through the lovely spaces of Panopeus.

'And I saw Tantalus in great torment. He stood in a pool that touched his chin; he was parched and he was eager to drink, but powerless to reach the water, for as often as the old man bent forward thirstily, so often it would be sucked down and vanish, and the ground show dark at his feet instead, because a god dried up the source. There were leafy trees, morever, dangling their fruit overhead from high above – pears and pomegranates, apple-trees with bright fruit, sweet figs and luscious olives; but when the old man made to clutch them, the wind would toss them all up again towards the overshadowing clouds.

'Sisyphus too I saw tormented, heaving with both his hands at a massy stone. Straining with hands and feet together, he kept pushing the stone uphill, but just as he should have cleared the top with it, some force would thrust the thing back again; the unregarding boulder would tumble afresh down to the level and the straining man renew the struggle while sweat poured down from his limbs and the dust rose from round his head.

'After him I saw heroic Heracles. Round him rose, like the clamour of birds, a clamour of dead men scattering in fear hither and thither; he himself looked like sable night, with bow uncased and with shaft on string, glaring about him horribly, like one for ever about to shoot. Grim was the baldric that crossed his breast and carried his sword; it was of gold, and wonderful things were worked upon it, bears and wild boars and lions with gleaming eyes, struggles and battles, men slain and men murdered. May the man whose mind housed the image of that baldric, having once made that, never make such a thing again !

'When Heracles saw me, he knew me forthwith, and in mournful mood he uttered these words in rapid flight: "Son of Laertes, subtle Odysseus – you too, then, it seems, are trailing with you some such evil fortune as I endured while I saw the sunlight. My father was Zeus the son of Cronos, yet I suffered measureless misery. I was made to serve a man much beneath me who forced upon me some fearsome tasks. Indeed he once sent me even here to fetch away the hound of Hades, for he thought no task could be more fearsome for me than that. But I brought the hound out of Hades' house and up to earth, because Hermes helped me on my way, and gleaming-eyed Athene."

'With these words he went back again into Hades' house. I myself remained where I was, hoping some other one might come from among the heroes who perished long ago. And indeed I might then have seen those men of past days I wished to see, but before I could, there came before me with hideous clamour the thronging multitudes of the dead, and ashy terror seized hold of me. I feared that august Persephone might send against me from Hades' house the gorgon head of some grisly monster. I made for my ship at once, telling my comrades to step aboard and to loose the cables. Swiftly they went aboard and sat at the thwarts, and the ship moved out over the river Ocean above the billowing waters; there was rowing for us at first, then a fair wind.

BOOK XII

'THE ship in due course left the waters of the river Ocean and reached the waves of the spacious sea and the island of Aeaea; it is there that Dawn the early comer has her dwelling-place and her dancing-grounds, and the sun himself has his risings. We came in; we beached our vessel upon the sands and disembarked upon the sea-shore; there we fell fast asleep, awaiting ethereal Dawn.

'Dawn comes early, with rosy fingers. When she appeared I sent my comrades to Circe's palace to fetch the body of dead Elpenor. We cut logs in haste, and then where the shore ran furthest out we celebrated his funeral rites in sorrow and with abundant tears. When the fire had burned the dead man and the dead man's armour, we heaped a mound, dragged up a gravestone to stand above, and on the very top of the mound we planted his balanced oar.

'Thus we performed these rites in order. Nor did our coming back from Hades escape the watchfulness of Circe. She attired herself and hastened towards us, while the handmaidens with her brought bread and meat in plenty, and glowing red wine. Then, coming forward to stand among us, the queenly goddess began to speak: "Undaunted men who went down alive to Hades' dwelling, men fated to taste of death twice over, while other men taste of it but once, – come now, eat food and drink wine here all day. At break of morning you must set sail, and I myself will tell you the way and make each thing clear, so that no ill scheming on sea or land may bring you to misery and mischief."

'Such were her words, and our own hearts accepted them. So all that day, till the sun set, we sat and feasted on plenteous meat and delicious wine. When the sun went and darkness came, my men lay down to sleep by the vessel's hawsers, but as for myself, the goddess took me by the hand and made me sit down apart; she lay down near me and questioned me about everything, and I told her all from first to last. Then Lady Circe began again:

'"The things you speak of are all fulfilled, then; but listen now to my further words – later, without your seeking it, some god will recall them to your mind. You will come to the Sirens first of all;

they bewitch any mortal who approaches them. If a man in ignorance draws too close and catches their music, he will never return to find wife and little children near him and to see their joy at his homecoming; the high clear tones of the Sirens will bewitch him. They sit in a meadow; men's corpses lie heaped up all round them, mouldering upon the bones as the skin decays. You must row past there; you must stop the ears of all your crew with sweet wax that you have kneaded, so that none of the rest may hear the song. But if you yourself are bent on hearing, then give them orders to bind you both hand and foot as you stand upright against the mast-stay, with the rope-ends tied to the mast itself; thus you may hear the two Sirens' voices and be enraptured. If you implore your crew and beg them to release you, then they must bind you fast with more bonds again.

' "When your crew have rowed past the Sirens, I will not expressly say to you which of two ways you ought to take; you must follow your own counsel there; I will only give you knowledge of both. On the one side are overshadowing rocks against which dash the mighty billows of the goddess of blue-glancing seas. The blessed gods call these rocks the Wanderers; even things that fly cannot pass them safely, not even the trembling doves that carry ambrosia to Father Zeus; even of those the smooth rock always seizes one, and the Father sends another in to restore the number. Nor has any ship carrying men ever come there and gone its way in safety; the ship's timbers, the crew's dead bodies are carried away by the sea waves and by blasts of deadly fire. One alone among seagoing ships did indeed sail past on her way home from Aeetes' kingdom – this was Argo, whose name is on all men's tongues; and even she would soon have been dashed against the great rocks had not Hera herself, in her love for Jason, sped the ship past.

' "On the other side are a pair of cliffs. One of them with its jagged peak reaches up to the spreading sky, wreathed in dark cloud that never parts. There is no clear sky above this peak even in summer or harvest-time, nor could any mortal man climb up it or get a foothold on it, not if he had twenty hands and feet; so smooth is the stone, as if it were all burnished over. Half-way up the cliff is a murky cave, facing north-west to Erebus, and doubtless it is past this, Odysseus, that you and your men will steer your vessel. A strong man's arrow shot from a ship below would not reach the recesses of that cave. Inside lives Scylla, yelping hideously; her voice is no deeper than a young puppy's, but she herself is a fearsome monster; no one could see her and still be happy, not even a god if he went that way. She has twelve feet all dangling down, six long necks with a grisly head on each of them, and in each head a triple row of crowded and close-set teeth, fraught with black death. Sunk waist-deep in the cave's recesses, she still darts out her head from that frightening hollow, and there, groping greedily round the rock, she fishes for dolphins and for sharks and whatever beast more huge than these she can seize upon from all the thousands that have their pasture from the queen of the loud-moaning seas. No seaman ever, in any vessel, has boasted of sailing that way unharmed, for with every single head of hers she snatches and carries off a man from the dark-prowed ship.

' "You will see that the other cliff lies lower, no more than an arrow's flight away. On this there grows a great leafy fig-tree; under it, awesome Charybdis sucks the dark water down. Three times a day she belches it forth, three times in hideous fashion she swallows it down again. Pray not to be caught there when she swallows down; Poseidon himself could not save you from destruction then. No, keep closer to Scylla's cliff, and row past that as quickly as may be; far better to lose six men and keep your ship than to lose your men one and all."

'So she spoke, and I answered her: "Yes, goddess, but tell me truly – could I somehow escape this dire Charybdis and yet make a stand against the other when she sought to make my men her prey?"

'So I spoke, and at once the queenly goddess answered: "Self-willed man, is your mind then set on further perils, fresh feats of war? Will you not bow to the deathless gods themselves? Scylla is not of mortal kind; she is a deathless monster, grim and baleful, savage, not to be wrestled with. Against her there is no defence, and the best path is the path of flight. If you pause to arm beside that rock, I fear that she may dart out again, seize again with as many heads and snatch as many men as before. No, row hard and invoke Crataeis; she is Scylla's mother; it is she who bore her to plague mankind; Crataeis will hold her from darting twice.

' "Then you will reach the isle of Thrinacia. In this there are grazing many cows and many fat flocks of sheep; they are the sungod's – seven herds of cows and as many fine flocks of sheep. In each herd and each flock there are fifty beasts; no births increase them, no deaths diminish them. They are pastured by goddesses, lovely-haired nymphs named Phaethusa and Lampetie, whose father is the sun-god Hyperion and whose mother is bright Neaera; having borne and bred them, she took them away to remote Thrinacia to live there and tend their father's sheep and the herds with curling horns. If you leave these unharmed – if you set your mind only on return – you may all of you still reach Ithaca, though with much misery. But if you harm them, then I foretell destruction alike for your ship and for your comrades, and if you yourself escape that end, you will return late and in evil plight, having lost for ever all your comrades."

'Scarcely had she ended her words when Dawn appeared in her flowery cloth of gold. Then queenly Circe took her way back across the island; I went to my ship and told my comrades to go aboard and loose the hawsers. They embarked forthwith, sat at the thwarts and, grouped in order, dipped their oars in the whitening sea. And Circe of the braided tresses, the goddess of awesome powers and of human speech, sent the best of comrades after our dark-prowed vessel, a following breeze to fill our sails. We made fast the tackling everwhere, then seated ourselves while wind and helmsman bore the ship forward on her course.

'Then with heavy heart I spoke to my comrades thus : "Friends, it is not right that only one man, or only two, should know the divine decrees that Lady Circe has uttered to me. I will tell you of them, so that in full knowledge we may die or in full knowledge escape, it may be, from death and doom. Her first command was to shun the Sirens – their enchanting notes, their flowery meadow. I alone was to hear their song, she said. You for your part must bind me with galling ropes as I stand upright against the mast-stay, with the rope-ends tied to the mast itself; then I shall stay there immovably. And if I beg and beseech you to set me free, you must bind me hard with more ropes again."

'Thus I told my comrades and made things plain, point by point. Meanwhile the trim ship sped swiftly on to the island of the Sirens, wafted still by the favouring breeze. Then of a sudden the wind dropped and everything became hushed and still, because some divinity lulled the waters. My men stood up, furled the sails and stowed them in the ship's hold, then sat at the thwarts and made the sea white with their polished oars of fir. I myself, with my sharp sword, cut a great round of wax into little pieces and set about kneading them with all the strength I had. Under my mighty hands, and under the beams of the lordly sun-god whose father is Hyperion, the wax quickly began to melt, and with it I sealed all my comrades' ears in turn. Then they bound me fast, hand and foot, with the rope-ends tied to the mast itself, then again sat down and dipped their oars in the whitening sea. But when with our swift advance we came within hailing distance of them, the Sirens saw the quick vessel near them and raised their voices in high clear notes: "Come hither, renowned Odysseus, hither, you pride and glory of all Achaea! Pause with your ship; listen to our song. Never has any man passed this way in his dark vessel and left unheard the honey-sweet music from our lips; first he has taken his delight, then gone on his way a wiser man. We know of all the sorrows in the wide land of Troy that Argives and Trojans bore because the gods would needs have it so; we know of all things that come to pass on the fruitful earth."

'So they sang with their lovely voices, and my heart was eager to listen still. I twitched my brows to sign to the crew to let me go, but they leaned to their oars and rowed on; Eurylochus and Perimedes quickly stood up and bound me with yet more ropes and with firmer hold. But when they had rowed well past the Sirens – when music and words could be heard no more – my trusty comrades were quick to take out the wax that had sealed their ears, and to rescue and unbind myself.

'But the island was hardly left behind when I saw smoke above heavy breakers and heard a great noise. The men took fright, the tapered oars all flew from their hands to drop with a crash into the sea, and with not a man using his oar the vessel came to rest where she was. I began to walk up and down the vessel, halting beside each of my men and offering them words to soothe and hearten:

' "Friends, we are not unschooled in troubles, and the trouble that is upon us now is no worse than when the Cyclops penned us by might and main in his arching cave. Yet even from there my courage and wit and strategy rescued us, and I make no doubt we shall live to look back on this ordeal also. Come, let us all agree to do as I say. Let the rest of you sit there at the thwarts and dash your oars into the heaving sea, trusting that Zeus will enable us to shun and escape destruction here. And to you, steersman, I speak especially – take good heed, because it is you who hold the rudder: Keep the craft away from the smoke and breakers, and rather make for the rock yonder, lest unawares you should let the ship drive the other way and should bring us all to ruin."

'So I spoke, and at once they obeyed my words. I had stopped short of mentioning Scylla, an inexorable horror; the crew in fear might have left their oars and have huddled down inside the hold. And here I let myself forget that irksome command of Circe's; she had told me not to arm at all, but I put my glorious armour on, took a long spear in either hand and strode up to the half-deck forward, since it was from there that I thought to catch the first glimpse of Scylla, that monster of the rock who was bringing doom to my companions. I could not as yet spy her anywhere, and my eyes grew tired as I peered this way and that toward the misty rock.

'So with much lamenting we rowed on and into the strait; this side lay Scylla; that side, in hideous fashion, fiendish Charybdis sucked the salt water in. When she spewed it forth, she seethed and swirled throughout all her depths like a cauldron set on a great fire, and overhead the spray fell down on the tops of the two rocks. But when she sucked the sea-water in, one might look right down through the swirling eddy while the rock roared hideously around her and the sea-floor came to view, dark and sandy. Ashy terror seized on the crew. We had looked her way with the fear of death upon us; and at that moment Scylla snatched up from inside my ship the six of my crew who were strongest of arm and sturdiest. When I turned back my gaze to the ship in search of my companions, I saw only their feet and hands as they were lifted up; they were calling to me in their heart's anguish, crying out my name for the last time. As when a fisherman on a promontory takes a long rod to snare little fishes with his bait and casts his ox-hair line down into the sea below, then seizes the creatures one by one and throws them ashore still writhing; so Scylla swung my writhing companions up to the rocks, and there at the entrance began devouring them as they shrieked and held out their hands to me in their extreme of agony. Many pitiful things have met my eyes in my toilings and searchings through the sea-paths, but this was most pitiful of all.

'When we had left the rocks behind us, with Scylla and terrible Charybdis, we came soon enough to the lovely island of the sun-god. Here were the fine broad-browed herds, here were the plentiful fat flocks of Hyperion. While the dark ship was still out at sea, I heard sheep bleating and cows lowing as they entered their quarters for the night; and into my heart came back the blind prophet's words and Aeaean Circe's also; both of them had enjoined me earnestly to shun this island of the all-gladdening sun-god. Troubled at heart, I spoke to my comrades thus:

' "Comrades, listen to what I say, sad though your plight is; I must tell you of the prophetic words of Theban Teiresias and of Circe. They urged me solemnly, both of them, to shun this island of the all-gladdening sun-god, because there, they said, the direst of perils awaited us. Take heed then; row the dark vessel past this island."

'So I spoke, and the men's hearts sank within them. Eurylochus answered me at once, and in hostile fashion:

' "Odysseus, you have no sense of pity. You have strangth and to spare; your body is never tired; you must be of iron in every limb. We your comrades are overmastered with toil and drowsiness, yet you say we must not set foot on shore, though there we might have a pleasant meal again, in that ocean-circled island. Instead, you bid us go wandering on unrested, all through the night that comes so soon, far from this island and over the misty sea. Yet it is at nightfall that contrary winds spring up and wreck vessels. How can a man escape the precipice of destruction if a blast of wind comes upon him suddenly, from the south, perhaps, or the stormy west, the two that most work a ship's destruction beyond the will of the gods our masters? No, let us give way now to night and darkness; let us make supper and still keep close to our rapid ship; then at dawn tomorrow we will embark and launch into wide ocean."

'So spoke Eurylochus, and the rest of the crew applauded him. Then I was sure that some god was indeed contriving mischief for us. The words of answer sped from my lips: "Eurylochus, I am one man against you all, and you overpower me. But at least do this; swear a solemn oath, all of you, that if we come on a herd of cows or a great flock of sheep, not one among you in fatal folly will slay either cow or sheep. No, take your ease and eat the food that immortal Circe gave us."

'So I spoke, and they swore at once as I desired them. When

they had uttered the due appointed words, we moored our ship in the curving bay beside the fresh water of a stream. Disembarking then, my comrades deftly prepared a meal. When they had eaten and drunk their fill, they thought again of the dear companions that Scylla had snatched from our ship and had devoured; they wept for these, and were still weeping when welcome slumber came upon them.

'But when the third watch of the night had come and the stars had shifted towards their setting, Zeus who masses the clouds called forth a great wind with violent tempest and overshadowed both land and sea. Darkness rushed down from heaven.

'Yet Dawn comes early, with rosy fingers. When she appeared, we beached the ship and dragged it up to a certain cave within whose hollows the nymphs could sit or weave their lovely dances. Then I called an assembly of my men and spoke thus among them:

' "Friends, in our ship we have food and drink enough. Let us keep our hands from the cattle, then, lest evil should overtake us; these beasts, the cows and fat sheep, belong to a dread divinity, the sun-god, who sees all things and hears all things."

'So I spoke, and their own strong wills gave consent. Then for a whole month the south wind blew without ceasing; there was no wind but south or east. As long as the men had corn and red wine they let the cattle be, because they were anxious to save their lives. But when all the food in the ship was gone – when they were forced instead to go roaming in search of prey, using bent hooks to catch fish and birds, anything that might come to hand, because hunger gnawed their bellies – then I myself went away from them across the island, meaning to make my prayer to the gods in hopes that one of them would reveal to me some way of returning home. Over the island, then, I walked till I was out of my comrades' way; then, washing my hands in a place that was sheltered from the wind, I began to pray to all the gods whose home is in Olympus, and they poured sweet sleep upon my eyelids.

'But in the meanwhile among my comrades Eurylochus put forth evil counsel: "Comrades, in this sad plight of ours, hear what I have to say. Every form of death is loathsome to wretched mortals, but to perish of hunger, to starve to death – that is the most pitiful thing of all. Enough! Let us carry off the best of the sun-god's cattle and give them in sacrifice to the Deathless Ones whose home is wide heaven. And if ever we should return again to our own land, Ithaca, we will hasten to build a sumptuous temple to Hyperion the sun-god, and there we may place fine offerings in plenty. But if in anger over his long-horned cattle he resolves to wreck our ship and the other gods second him – why, then, I would rather drink the brine and lose life at one gulp than waste away by inches in this forsaken island."

'So spoke Eurylochus, and the rest of the crew applauded him. They drove off at once the best of the sun-god's cattle – it was near at hand, not far from the ship, that they were grazing, these handsome beasts with their broad brows and curling horns. The men surrounded them and began their prayer to the gods, and because they had no barley-meal in the ship, they plucked instead the fresh tender leaves of a tall oak. Prayer over, they slaughtered and flayed the cows, cut out the thigh-bones and covered them with a double fold of fat, then laid the raw meat above. They had no wine to make libation over the burning sacrifice, but instead poured water as they set to roasting the inward parts. When the thigh-bones were quite consumed and the entrails tasted, they sliced and spitted the rest.

'At that moment the sleep that had soothed me passed of a sudden from my eyelids, and I took my way to the shore and ship again. Then, as I neared the curving vessel, the rich savour of roasting meat was wafted all about me. I groaned aloud, I cried out to the deathless gods:

' "Oh Father Zeus, oh blessed and ever-living gods, surely it was for my destruction that you lulled me with that fatal slumber, while the comrades that I left behind me devised this deed of unrighteousness."

'But without delay Lampetie of the trailing robe sped off to Hyperion the sun-god to tell him that we had slain his cattle, and he with his heart inflamed with anger spoke out at once to the Deathless Ones:

' "O Father Zeus, O blessed and ever-living gods, take vengeance on the crew of Laertes' son Odysseus; in their lawlessness they have slain the cattle in which I always took delight, both as I climbed the starry sky and as I took my path again back from the sky and down towards earth. Unless these men pay a just atonement for my cattle, I will descend to Hades' kingdom and shine among the dead."

'Zeus who masses the clouds made answer: "Sun-god, shine on in the sight of the Deathless One and of mortals over the fertile earth. As for those you speak of, soon enough I will strike their ship with my white-hot thunderbolt and shatter and shiver it in mid-ocean."

'All this I heard from Calypso of the lovely hair, who herself had heard it, so she told me, from Hermes, messenger of the gods.

'When I reached the sea where the ship lay, I went round to the men one by one and upbraided them, but as for a remedy, there was none to be found; the cattle were killed already. Then the gods began to show signs and wonders to my crew. The beasts' hides began to move; the flesh on the spits, raw or roasted, began to bellow, and there was a noise like the noise of cattle.

'For six days more the crew still banqueted on the choice cattle that they had seized; but when Zeus brought us the seventh day, the wind and raging tempest ceased. So without delay we went aboard, stepped the mast, hauled up the white sails and launched into wide ocean.

'We had left the island in our wake and now no other land was in sight — nothing but sky and sea – when the son of Cronos stretched a black cloud above our ship and the sea grew dark beneath it. The ship ran on for a little while; then suddenly came a whistling west wind, raging and tempestuous. Under this gale the two forestays snapped, the mast fell backward and all the cordage tumbled into the hold. At the ship's stern the mast struck the steersman's head and shattered every bone in his skull; from the half-deck he fell like a tumbler, and his bold spirit left his bones. And with that, Zeus thundered and hurled his bolt into the ship; struck by the bolt, she whirled round and was filled with sulphur; my comrades were flung overboard. Round the vessel they floated like sea-crows on the waves; the god forbade their returning home.

'As for myself, I strode up and down the ship till the heaving sea pulled away the sides from the keel and the wave carried her on without them and snapped off the mast by the keel; but over the mast had been flung a backstay made of oxhide; with this I lashed the keel and the mast together and, seated on them, was swept along by the ruthless winds.

'Then the raging west wind abated, but the south instead came at once to plague me, forcing me to retrace my track towards pitiless Charybdis. All night I was carried backward thus; then at sunrise I reached Scylla's rock and murderous Charybdis. Just then she swallowed the salt sea-water; I threw myself up to the lofty fig-tree and clung close against it like a bat, because there was no firm foothold there, and no chance of climbing either; the roots were far below, and the big long branches hung out of reach overhead, overshadowing Charybdis. I held on grimly till she should vomit out mast and keel again. That time seemed long to my anxious hopes, but about the hour when a judge in court will hear no more claims from brisk young plaintiffs – when he stands up and goes home to dine – about that hour the timbers swam up again from Charybdis. I let myself drop, hands and feet together, and fell with a crash into mid-strait just by the timbers, then clambered on to them and rowed with my hands. The father of gods and men would not allow Scylla to spy me, else I should never have escaped the precipice of destruction.

'Then for nine days I drifted; on the tenth night the gods let me reach the island of Ogygia; there dwells Calypso, the goddess of braided hair and of strange powers and of human speech; she welcomed and tended me. Why prolong the tale? Yesterday in this very place I recounted the rest to you and your noble queen, and it irks me to tell a second time a story already plainly told.'

BOOK XIII

ODYSSEUS RETURNS TO ITHACA

So spoke Odysseus. They all kept silence, rapt and hushed in the shadows of the hall. Then Alcinous found his voice and answered: 'Odysseus, the trials you have endured have indeed been many, but yet you have come at last to this house of mine with its bronze threshold, and from that I augur that you will go unthwarted the rest of the way till you reach home. And now I turn to you others here. I have a command for you, one and all, who daily in this palace of mine sit listening to the bard as you drink the glowing wine of chieftains. Garments our guest has been given already – they are lying now in his polished coffer, and with them the wrought gold and the other presents brought by our nation's counsellors. But now let us give him also, each man of us, a massive tripod and a cauldron; later we will repay ourselves by gathering from among the people, because all giving and no receiving would bear very hard on us man by man.'

So spoke the king, and his words seemed good to them. Then they departed to take their rest, every man to his own house. But Dawn comes early, with rosy fingers. When she appeared, they hastened down to the ship, taking with them the bronze that men delight in. The great king himself walked up and down the ship and saw that the gifts were safely stowed under the thwarts, well out of the way of the straining oarsmen.

Then they returned to the king's palace and set about preparing a meal. Lord Alcinous slew an ox for them in sacrifice to Zeus of the thundercloud, ruler of all the world. They burned the thighbones and fell to the noble feast in joy. In their midst was the heaven-taught bard Demodocus, he whom the people honoured; he sang to them, but Odysseus all the while kept turning his head towards the glowing sun, impatient for it to set, because he yearned to be on his way home again. He was like a man who longs for his evening meal when all day long his two dark red oxen have drawn his jointed plough over the fallow; thankful he is when sunlight goes; he can limp home to his meal at last. So was Odysseus thankful when sunlight went. Without waiting longer he spoke among the Phaeacian oarsmen, and to Alcinous above all he made his mind clear:

'Alcinous, most exalted lord, now let all of you make libation and send me in safety on my way; and with that I bid you all farewell. Everything that my heart had wished for is now secure – the escort home, the welcome gifts that I pray the gods of Olympus to bless for me; I pray too that when I reach home I may find unharmed my virtuous wife and my close kindred. And you that I leave behind me here – may you long gladden your wives and children; may the gods grant you all manner of prosperity, and may no evil visit your people !'

These were his words; the banqueters all applauded; this guest had spoken as a man should, and they thought it right to send him in safety home. Then King Alcinous spoke to his page: 'Pontonous, mix wine in the bowl and serve it to everyone in the hall, so that first we may pray to Father Zeus and then send forth our guest on his way to his own country.'

And at this command the page began mixing the fragrant wine, then stood by them all in turn to pour it; and they in their places made libation to the blessed gods whose home is wide heaven itself. Then great Odysseus rose to his feet; he placed the two-handled cup in Arete's hand, and this farewell issued from his lips:

'Queen, may all good be yours continually till age and death, which come to all men, come to you also. Now I depart; I wish you joy in this house of yours with your children and people and King Alcinous.'

And with these words great Odysseus passed the threshold. King Alcinous sent a page with him to take him down to the rapid ship on the sea-beach. Arete sent serving-women too; one had the clean cloak and tunic,[1] one was given the strong chest to carry, one was laden with bread and red wine.

When they reached the shore where the ship lay, the noble Phaeacians of the escort took over the food and drink and the rest and stowed them inside the hollow ship; for Odysseus himself they laid both linen and blanket down on the half-deck at the ship's stern so that he could sleep without awakening. Then he in turn stepped aboard and laid himself down quietly. The others sat at the thwarts in order, untied the cable from the hole in the stone, then swung back and began to throw up the water with their oars, while on him fell sleep irresistibly, delicious unbroken

1. 'One bore an Out and In-weede, faire and sweete.' CHAPMAN

sleep that looked like death. As for the ship – it was as when four stallions yoked together feel the whipstrokes and rush away over the plain, lifting their feet high in air and quickly accomplishing their course – so the ship's stern was lifted high, and in the wake surged and seethed the great waves of the sounding sea. Steady, unswerving, the ship coursed onwards; not even the falcon, fleetest of things that fly, could have kept pace with her. Thus then she sped lightly on, parting the waves of ocean and carrying with her a man who was godlike in his counsels, one who had borne much grief of spirit, who had cut his path through embattled foes and wearying waves, but now was sleeping in quietude, with all his troubles put out of mind.

When that brightest of stars appeared that most often heralds the light of early-rising Dawn, then this craft which had crossed the sea drew near the island.

On the coast of Ithaca is a certain haven, sacred to the old sea-god Phorcys; it has two headlands, sheer to seaward but sloping towards the harbour; they break the big waves raised by the high winds outside, and within this space decked vessels can ride un-anchored when they reach the spot where commonly they would make their moorings. At the harbour-head is a long-leaved olive-tree; near this lies a twilit cave, a most lovely one, sacred to those nymphs who are called Naiads; in it are bowls of stone and pitchers of stone; bees also store honey there; and then there are long looms of stone on which the nymphs weave tissues of ocean-purple that ravish the gazing eye. There are streams there too that flow perpetually; and there are two entrances into it, a northern entrance that mortals may descend by and a southern one that belongs to the gods; by this no human being may enter; it is the pathway of the immortals.

To this haven the crew put in, knowing it from of old. The ship ran ashore for half her length, so briskly was she urged on by the rowers' arms. The men disembarked from the benched vessel, and first of all lifted Odysseus, linen and bright blanket and all, out of the hollow ship; then laid him, still fast asleep, on the sandy shore, then took out the treasures which at Athene's prompting the Phaeacian lords had given him as he set out for home; and these they set down all together at the root of an olive tree away from the road, so that no passer-by should come and steal them before Odysseus woke.

Then they themselves made for home; but the Earthshaker had not forgotten the threats once uttered against the hero. So now he sought out the will of Zeus: 'Father Zeus, I shall lose my honour among the immortal gods, since now there are mortals who give me no reverence at all – the Phaeacians, I mean, although you know they are sprung from me. I had said Odysseus must bear much trouble yet, before he returned to his own country, though I did not purpose to thwart his homecoming utterly when once you yourself had promised and given assurance of it. But now these Phaeacians with their swift ship have conveyed him slumbering over the sea and have landed him in Ithaca; besides, they have given him countless gifts, bronze and gold and woven garments, more than he would have brought back from Troy had he returned unscathed with his share of battle-spoils.'

Zeus who masses the clouds made answer: 'For shame, you shaker of the earth and sovereign of wide dominions! What words are these? In no way do the gods fail to honour you. It would be a grievous thing indeed if the eldest and noblest of them all were assailed with contumely. As for mankind, if any among them lets his own strength and power beguile him and pays no honour to yourself, you may always follow the sin with punishment. Do as you will, as your heart desires.'

Poseidon the Earthshaker answered him: 'God of the sable clouds, I am ready enough to do as you bid me do; but now as always I fear and shun your anger. My desire now is to strike that sumptuous Phaeacian ship as she returns from her errand over the misty sea, so that henceforth that nation may change their ways and never again give strangers convoy; and I purpose also to close their city in with a mighty mountain.'

Zeus who masses the clouds made answer: 'Dear brother, what seems to my own mind best is this: at the moment when watchers from the city catch sight together of the approaching ship, turn the craft as she nears the land into a shiplike rock; every beholder will be astonished, nor need you then close the city in with a mighty mountain.'

Having heard this answer, Poseidon set off to Scheria, the land of the Phaeacians, and waited there till the travelling vessel came close to land in her rapid course; then, drawing near her, with one downward stroke of his hand the Earthshaker turned her into stone and rooted her on the ocean-bed; then he departed.

Among the Phaeacians, those oarsmen and seamen of renown, words began to pass to and fro as a man spoke to his neighbour thus: 'Ah, what is this? Who was it that stopped the speeding vessel before she could reach home and harbour? A moment ago she was in full view.'

Such were the words that passed between them, but the truth of things was beyond their ken. Then Alcinous spoke and expounded thus: 'Alas, now I see all fulfilled those ancient oracles that my father spoke of. He said that Poseidon was angry with us because we took home all manner of men without coming to any harm; and hence one day, when some nobly-built ship of ours was on her way back from such an errand, Poseidon would strike her down on the misty sea and block our town with a massy mountain. Such was the tale the old king told me, and now it proves utterly true. But now let us all do as I say. Let us cease to give a homeward voyage to any man who comes to our city; and as for Poseidon, let us sacrifice twelve chosen bulls to him and hope that he will have pity on us and never close our city in with a lofty mountain.' So he spoke; they were seized with awe, and made ready the bulls for sacrifice.

Thus then the chiefs and leaders of the Phaeacians stood round the altars and made their prayers to Lord Poseidon. Meanwhile Odysseus woke from his sleep in the land he had long been absent from; he did not know it for his own because the goddess Pallas Athene had poured a mist all about him, desiring first to tell him herself all things necessary and to shroud his likeness from all eyes, lest wife and kinsmen and townsfolk should know him for what he was before the suitors had paid the price for all their transgressions. Hence it was that all seemed strange to the king himself – the outstretching paths, the hospitable harbours, the sheer cliffs and the leafy trees. He leapt up and stood upright and cast his eyes on his own country, then gave a groan and struck his thighs with the flat of his hands as he cried out in his distress: 'Wretch that I am, whose land have I come to now? Are the people barbarous, arrogant and lawless, or are they hospitable and godfearing? Where can I take this mass of treasure? Where am I myself to turn my steps? Better for all this wealth to have stayed where it was, with the Phaeacians; then I might have gone to some other monarch of wide sway, and he would have welcomed me instead and sent me upon my journey home. As it is, I neither know where to hide these things, nor dare I leave them here to be snatched by some chance comer. After all, alas, those chiefs and rulers of the Phaeacians were not over-thoughtful or over-scrupulous; they promised to bring me to far-seen Ithaca, but they have not kept their word; they have brought me somewhere else instead. May Zeus the protector of suppliants punish them, since he keeps watch over all mankind and takes vengeance on the transgressor! But now let me look my treasure over and count it up; did they sail away with some part of it?' And with these words he began to count the handsome tripods and the cauldrons, the gold and the lovely woven garments. Nothing, he found, was lacking there, but still he sighed for his own land as he paced forlornly the edge of the boisterous sea.

But then Athene drew near to him; she wore the guise of a young shepherd, with the gentle air of a king's son;[1] a lovely mantle fell in two folds about her shoulders; there were sandals on her glistening feet, and she held a javelin in her hand. Odysseus was overjoyed to see her; he walked towards her, and the words sped swiftly from his lips: 'Friend, since you are the first to cross my pathway in this place, I give you greeting and beg you to deal with me not unkindly. Save this treasure and save me also; I implore you as I would a god, and approach your knees in supplication. And tell me besides, because I am eager to be assured: What country, what land is this? Who are the people that dwell in it? Is it one of the far-seen islands, or is it the shelving shore of the loamy mainland?'

The goddess of gleaming eyes made answer: 'Stranger, either you must be simple or you must come from far indeed if this, of all lands, provokes that question. It is not inglorious, far from that; it is known to dwellers in many regions, those who face towards the rising sun and those who look back towards the dusky west. It is rugged; it is no land for horses; it is not ample,

1.   'So saying, he number'd carefully the gold,
    The vases, tripods bright, and tissued robes,
    But nothing miss'd of all. Then he bewail'd
    His native isle, with pensive steps and slow
    Pacing the border of the billowy flood,
    Forlorn; but while he wept, Pallas approach'd,
    In form a shepherd stripling, girlish fair
    In feature, such as are the sons of kings.' COWPER

yet not poor either; it has corn in plenty and wine as well; it is blessed with constant rain and with copious dew; it is good for goats and cattle; it has varied woodlands, and water-sources that never fail. And therefore, stranger, the name of Ithaca has reached even to Troy itself; and Troy, they tell me, is far from the lands of the Achaeans.'

So she spoke, and staunch Odysseus was glad to hear what the goddess Pallas told him; he rejoiced to be in his own country. His words came fast as he answered her, not telling the truth but keeping back what he might have told, and now as always turning this way and that the thoughts of his cunning mind:

'I had heard of Ithaca even in the broad lands of Crete, far overseas, and now I have come to it myself with the goods you see here; I left behind me as much again for my children there, but I myself am a fugitive, having killed the son of Idomeneus; this was Orsilochus, a fine runner who once with his speed of foot outstripped every man in the length and breadth of Crete. I killed him because he tried to rob me of all my Trojan spoils, spoils I had suffered much hardship for, cutting my path through embattled foes and wearying waves. His reason was that there at Troy I would not fall in with his father's wish and serve under him, but captained men of my own instead. So with a friend I lay in wait for him by the roadside as he was journeying home from the fields, and I struck him with my bronze-tipped spear. Murky night was over the sky; not a soul could see us; no one was there when I took his life away. Having so slain him with the spearpoint, I made for a ship at once and begged the Phoenician crew to help me – from my Trojan spoils I gave them enough to satisfy them. I asked them to let me land at Pylos, to see me ashore there – or else at Elis, where the Epeians rule. But violent winds beat them off their course -- much to their distress, for they had no wish to cheat me. Thus we were thwarted of our goal, and reached here in the hours of darkness. With much ado we rowed on and into harbour, giving no thought at all to food, though we needed it badly enough; once off the ship, we all lay down just as we were. On my own tired body the welcome sleep descended quickly, but the others fetched my goods from the hold and put them down on the sand beside me. After this they embarked once more and went their way to Sidon, set in its pleasant seat; thus I found myself left behind and in much distress.'

Such was his tale; Athene smiled and caressed him with her hand; her semblance now was of a woman – one tall and lovely, with skill to make works of beauty. Then from her lips these words sped forth:

'Any man who met you – any god who met you – must indeed be crafty, indeed be cunning to go beyond you in varied stratagem. Shameless and all too subtle man, never surfeited with your trickeries – not even here, in your own land, will you lay aside the deceitfulness and the wily words that you love in every fibre of you. But come now, no more of this; both of us are subtle enough – you excel all mankind in stratagem and well-chosen words, I am renowned among all the gods for wiles and wisdom. Nor did you yourself descry in me the daughter of Zeus, Pallas Athene, one always beside you to keep you safe in whatever adventure it may be. It was I who endeared you to the Phaeacians; it is I again who have come here now to weave a plan together with you, to hide the Phaeacians' parting gifts (though that giving too was by my design and purpose), and to tell you also what affronts you are destined to bear in your own palace. There is no choice; you must hold fast, and to no one at all –no man, no woman – must you reveal that the wanderer has returned. You must suffer silently much humiliation; you must accept men's acts of violence.'

Subtle Odysseus answered her: 'For a mortal man who meets you, goddess – be the man never so wise – it is hard to know you as yourself; there is no semblance you may not take. But of this I am sure, that though in earlier days you were kind to me, while we Achaeans were still waging war at Troy, yet when once we had sacked Priam's tall city, when we had embarked and the god had scattered us far and wide, from then onwards, daughter of Zeus, I never saw you. I caught no glimpse of you boarding my ship to keep off trouble from me there. Only when I had reached the rich land of the Phaeacians did you comfort me with your words and guide me into the town yourself. And now I implore you in your own father's name. I do not believe I have come to far-seen Ithaca; it is some other country I am ranging, and all that you say you say in mockery to puzzle my wits. Tell me then if it is indeed my own dear country that I have come to.'

Athene answered: 'The thoughts in your heart are as they always were; that is why I cannot forsake you in your misfortunes – you are so far-sighted and shrewd and wary. Another man returned from such wanderings would have been happy enough and anxious enough to set eyes again on wife and children in his own halls, but you do not choose to ask and learn from others; before all else, you must make your own judgement on your wife. She is seated there in the hall as ever, and the nights and days come and go for her in misery and in tears. I myself had never a doubt; my heart knew well that you would return, though after the loss of all your comrades, but I had no mind to challenge Poseidon, my father's brother, who had stored up rancour of heart against you because of the blinding of his son. But come, I will show you the shape of Ithaca and make you believe. Here is the harbour sacred to the old sea-god Phorcys; here at the harbour-head is the long-leaved olive tree; here is the vaulted cave where many a time you offered the nymphs due sacrifice; and the slopes above you, forest-clad, are the slopes of Neriton.'

So saying, the goddess dispelled the mist, and the land appeared. At this, King Odysseus was filled with happiness, filled with joy that this land was his. He kissed the grain-giving soil of it, then prayed to the nymphs with uplifted hands: 'Nymphs of the springs, daughters of Zeus, I had never thought to see you again. Receive forthwith my greeting, my loving prayers; afterwards I will offer gifts as well, just as of old, if the daughter of Zeus who is goddess of the foray so favours me as to let me live and to bring my son to man's estate.'

The goddess of gleaming eyes made answer: 'Take courage and put away misgivings. And now at once let us store away your treasures in some recess of the sacred cave where they may be left untouched; then let us plan how things may be ordered best.'

And with these words she entered the twilit cave, looking for hiding-places there, while Odysseus brought all his gifts inside – the gold, the enduring bronze, the well-made garments that came from the Phaeacians. And when they had all been cunningly stowed away, Pallas Athene sealed up the entrance with a stone.

Then the two sat down by the roots of the sacred olive and began devising death for the overbearing suitors. Athene spoke first: 'Subtle Odysseus, Laertes' son, consider how you may lay your hands on the shameless suitors. For three years now they have been lording it in your house, wooing your noble wife and offering bridal gifts for her; and she, though her heart is always pining to have you home, gives hope to them all, promises every man in turn, sends out messages here and there; yet all the while her purpose is far from this.'

Subtle Odysseus replied to her: 'This is evil news. I see I might well have perished in my own halls by the same ill doom as Agamemnon, had not you, goddess, told me the truth point by point. But come now, weave me a strategem for revenge, stand by my side yourself to aid me, implanting in me such strength and daring as when we tore down from Troy the diadem of her glittering pinnacles. Would you but stand once more beside me, fierce for fight as you were at Ilium, then, my goddess of gleaming eyes, I would battle against three hundred foemen with you as my helper and my friend.'

The goddess Athene answered him: 'Indeed I will be close beside you, indeed you shall not be forgotten when the two of us take this work in hand; and then I think that among the suitors who are devouring your substance now there are those who will spatter your ample floor with their blood and brains. But first I must contrive that not a soul here shall know you. I will wrinkle the smooth skin over your lissom body, I will take the yellow hair from your head and dress you in rags one would loathe to see upon any human being, I will dim the brightness of your eyes, till you seem hideous to all the suitors, to your wife herself and to the son you left in your halls. Your own first task is to journey to the swineherd who has in charge your sows and boars; he is as loyal to you as ever; he loves your son and he loves Penelope. You will find him sitting near the swine as they feed beside the Raven's Rock at the spring of Arethusa, drinking from the deep dark water there and battening upon acorns – good wholesome fattening fare for swine. Stay with him, and, while you are there, ask him whatever you wish to know. Meantime I myself must go to Sparta, the land of lovely women, to recall Telemachus, your own son, Odysseus; he went to that spacious country to become the guest of Menelaus and to find out from what he heard there if you were still alive.'

Odysseus answered: 'And why did you yourself not tell him, you who have knowledge of everything? Was it that he as well as I should stray in misery over the barren sea while others devoured his substance?'

Athene answered: 'Care for him need not overburden you. I

myself was his escort there, and meant his journey to win him a noble name. He is in no distress; he is seated at ease in Menelaus' palace, and he lacks for nothing there. True, there are youths with their dark vessel in ambush for him even now, eager to murder him before he sets foot in his own country. But that, I think, will not come to pass; before it does, earth will have closed on more than one of the suitors who devour your substance.'

So said Athene, then touched Odysseus with her wand. She wrinkled the smooth skin over his lissom body, took the yellow hair from his head, gave all his limbs the flesh of an aged man and dimmed the brightness of his eyes. She gave him dismal rags to wear and a dismal tunic, tattered and foul and besmirched with filthy smoke; over this she laid the big bald skin of a bounding deer. She made him take a staff and a wretched wallet, full of holes, with a cord to hang it by.

Having planned things thus, the two now parted. Athene went off toward sacred Lacedaemon, and her task was to fetch Odysseus' son.

BOOK XIV

ODYSSEUS WITH THE SWINEHERD

ODYSSEUS meanwhile left the harbour and took to the rough woodland track, crossing the hilltops to where the good swineherd was; Athene had told him the way already. Of all the servants Odysseus had ever had, this was the man who cared for his lord's possessions most.

He was sitting, when Odysseus found him, in the forepart of his homestead. He had a high-walled courtyard there, large and fine, with a clear space and clear view round it. He himself, un-helped by his mistress or old Laertes, had walled in the yard to enclose the swine while his master was away; the stones he had used were quarried ones, and he had topped the whole with wild pear. For the outside he had split an oak and kept the dark heart of it to make a long line of solid stakes. Inside the yard he had made twelve sties, one next to another, to bed the swine. In each of these, fifty brood sows were penned and slept on the ground. The hogs lay outside, but of them there were far fewer – the princely suitors with constant eating had thinned their numbers, for the swineheard sent them every day the very best of the fat-tened hogs, and these now were three hundred and sixty all told. Near these again lay always four savage-looking dogs, bred by the master swineherd. He himself was making a pair of sandals to fit his feet, cutting out a piece of handsome-coloured oxhide. As for his men, three of them had herded their swine and gone out this way and that; the fourth he had grudgingly sent to town to take a hog to the overbearing suitors for them to slaughter and have their fill of meat.

The yelping dogs suddenly saw Odysseus and made for him with a great noise. Warily he dropped to the ground and let the stick fall from his grasp. Then and there he came near to suffering ignoble hurt at his own steading, but the swineherd dropped his piece of hide and in hot pursuit rushed up to the gate, stormed at the brutes and scattered them with a shower of stones. Then he addressed his master: 'Old friend, my dogs all but tore you to pieces in a moment, and your mishap would have meant my dis-grace – though apart from that the gods have given me sorrows and tribulations enough. Here I sit, in distress and grief for my kingly master, tending his fattened swine for others to eat while he, it may be, is wandering foodless about some town or region of foreign speech, if indeed he still lives to see the sunlight. But now come in to my cottage, friend, so that you also may have your fill of both food and wine, and then may tell me what place you come from and all the troubles you have endured.'

And with these words he led the way to the cottage door and ushered his guest in; to seat him he put some thick brushwood down, then laid on top the soft wide skin of a shaggy wild goat that had been a coverlet for himself. Odysseus rejoiced at such a welcome and uttered his thoughts aloud: 'My host, may Zeus and the other deathless gods reward your generous welcome to me by granting you what you most desire!'

Eumaeus the swineherd answered him: 'My guest, I should think it a monstrous thing not to honour any guest who came to me, even one more miserable than you, because Zeus is patron of every stranger and every beggar, and to such as these, even so humble a gift as mine means much. More than this is beyond the reach of servants, who always need to walk warily when the masters over them are young. As for my own true master, the gods must have barred his journey home, because he would have shown me generous favour and given me possessions for my own – a farm, a farmhouse, a wife any man would be glad to wed – such gifts as a kindly master does give a servant who has worked for him hard and has had his work prospered by heaven. The work I myself am at is being thus prospered, and hence my master would have done much for me had he lived here into old age. But he has perished – would that the whole of Helen's race had been brought to its knees and perished so, just as she has loosened the knees of many a man! For he too went away to Ilium – Ilium of the noble horses – to fight the Trojans and help to wreak Agamemnon's vengeance.'

With these words the swineherd buckled the belt round his tunic and made his way out towards the sties where all the young hogs were penned. Two of these he took and brought out and slaughtered, then singed and sliced and spitted them; when they were roasted he came and put them before Odysseus, smoking hot with the spits still through them, and sprinkled white barley-groats on top. Lastly he mixed sweet wine in an ivywood bowl, sat down facing his guest and bade him set to:

'And now, friend, eat – such fare as a serf may be allowed. These are young hogs; the full-grown fat ones are eaten by the suitors, who have no compassion in their hearts, and no fear either of punishment from the gods. Yet the blessed gods are no friends of wickedness; they honour justice and righteous action in men. Even men of violence and ill-will who land on a foreign coast and under sufferance from Zeus carry off spoil and load their ships and sail home again – even these find penetrating their hearts a powerful fear of the retribution of the gods. But the suitors here have doubtless heard some rumour that comes from heaven assuring them of my master's dismal death, and that is why they will neither woo in decent fashion nor yet return to their own homes; instead, they devour another's goods – wanton, untroubled, sparing nothing. Every night, every day that Zeus sends us, it is never one beast alone, never two alone they slaughter; and the wine too – they draw it recklessly and drain the store dry. I tell you, my master's wealth was huge; no other lord had as much as he, either on the dark mainland or here in Ithaca; not twenty together could equal such abundance. I will reckon it up for you. On the mainland twelve herds of cattle and as many of swine, twelve flocks of sheep and as many of wide-ranging goats, tended by either his own herdsmen or others from outside his household. And in this island, at its edge, eleven other flocks of goats find scattered pasture with trusty men to watch over them; each of these men takes the suitors a beast a day, whichever seems best of the fatted goats. And I myself keep and tend these swine and choose every day the best among them and send it to the suitors.'

Such were his words. Hastily and ravenously, Odysseus began to eat the flesh and to drink the wine, uttering no word but sowing seeds of doom for the suitors. When he had eaten his fill and was satisfied, he filled to the brim the cup that he had been drinking from and offered it to his host. Gladly Eumaeus accepted it, and Odysseus broke into rapid speech : 'Friend, who was it then that once purchased you with his wealth, a man of such riches and power as you tell me of? You say he perished in helping to wreak Agamemnon's vengeance. Tell me his name, for I may have knowledge of such a man. Zeus and the other deathless gods know if I have seen him and might offer news of him, because my travels have taken me far.'

The swineherd answered: 'Old friend, no roving man bringing news of my master here is likely to be believed by his wife and son. One vagrant and then another comes here with lies, just for the sake of bed and board and with no desire to speak the truth. Yet when any such wanderer visits the land of Ithaca and sees my mistress and tells his trustless tale, she receives him hospitably and kindly and questions him on every particular, indulging her grief till the tears flow from her eyes – such is a woman's way when her husband has died in a far country. You too, old friend, might quickly enough forge such another tale in hope of a gift of tunic and cloak to wear. But no – by now the dogs and the darting birds have doubtless stripped the skin from his bones after life has left him, or else the fish have devoured him in the sea and his bones lie on some shore, covered deep in sand. He himself has perished in some such place, and for those who loved him nothing is left henceforth but grief – for me more than anyone, because never now shall I meet with a master as kind as he was, go where I may – no, not if I returned to my own father's and mother's house, to the birthplace where they brought me up; not even for them do I grieve so much, happy though I should be to set eyes on them in my home again. But for lost Odysseus my longing is overpowering. Even though now he is not here, friend, I am chary of uttering his name, for he loved me and cherished me exceedingly; and although he is far away from here, I speak of him as my lord and brother.'[1]

Odysseus answered: 'Friend, since you stand by your denial, since you think he will never come again, since your heart is set in unbelief – so be it; I for my part will not give my bare word, I will take my oath that Odysseus will return. And as for reward for that good news, I look to receive it only when he is in his own house again; before that moment I will accept no gift, needy though I may be. I loathe, as I loathe the gates of hell, one who tells lies under stress of poverty. I call to witness Zeus among gods, and after him this table of hospitality – in sober truth these things are all of them near fulfilment, as I tell you. Within this same year Odysseus will return; as the old moon wanes and the

1. 'Ah stranger, absent as he is, his name
   Fills me with rev'rence, for he lov'd me much,
   Cared for me much, and, though we meet no more,
   Holds still an elder brother's part in me.' COWPER

new moon rises, he will achieve his homecoming and be revenged on whoever in Ithaca affronts his wife and his noble son.'

Eumaeus answered: 'Old friend, that reward is one I shall never have to give; Odysseus will never return home. No; drink on in peace while we turn to other themes, and do not bring that to my mind again, for indeed my heart is wrung within me when any man speaks of my dear master. Let no more be said of taking oaths – yet would that Odysseus might return in such fashion as I myself desire, and with me Penelope and old Laertes yonder, and Prince Telemachus. For him, for this boy that Odysseus fathered, I lament inconsolably. The gods made him thrive like some young sapling, and I was sure that among grown men he would be the match of his own dear father, noble in frame and form; but now the rightmindedness that he had has been somehow warped, whether by a god or by a man. He has gone off to holy Pylos in quest of news about his father, and the suitors are in wait for him on his homeward journey, hoping that all the race of royal Arceisius may pass from Ithaca into namelessness. But of him too let no more be said, whether he is to be caught in that snare or whether sheltered and saved by the hand of Zeus. Instead, old friend, let me hear the tale of your own troubles. Tell me and answer truly. Who are you and from where are you? Where are your city and your parents? What kind of ship did you travel by? (No one journeys on foot to Ithaca!) How did the sailors bring you here, and what name did they give themselves? These are all things I long to know.'

Wily Odysseus answered him: 'Good; I will tell you everything faithfully. If only we two had food and sweet wine enough to linger on here inside this cottage and feast undisturbed while other men went about their tasks! Then I might well enough spend a twelvemonth recounting the sorrows of my spirit and still not come to an end of them – all the sorrows that I have toiled through because the gods willed it so. Wide Crete is the home I boast of, and I was a rich man's son. He had many other sons as well, bred in his house and born in wedlock. My own mother was a concubine, bought as a slave; yet I, no less than the true-born sons, was given regard by Castor son of Hylax. It is Castor that I claim for father, a man who throughout all Crete was honoured just as a god might be because of his riches and his prosperity and his noble sons. But the death-spirits carried him

down to Hades' house, and his haughty sons divided his sub-
stance up, casting lots for it. To me they gave a house and very
little besides, but by my own merits I won for wife a daughter of
very wealthy parents, because I was no fool and no coward. I no
longer am what I was then – I have had more than my share of
miseries – yet even today, I think, if you look close you can see
from the stubble what the grain was. Athene and Ares gave me
courage, and strength to shatter the ranks of men when I chose
out champions for ambuscade, sowing seeds of destruction for my
foes. My heart was fearless, it never foreboded death; I was fore-
most always to leap forward and slay with my spear whoever
among the enemy was less quick-footed than I myself was. Such I
was in war. Work on the land I was never fond of, or such care of
the household as brings up children in prosperity. The things that
I loved were ships and oars and battles and arrows and gleaming
spears, the things of mischief that others shudder at. Doubtless all
that delighted me was what the god planted in my breast, because
one man finds his bent here and another there. For before the
sons of the Achaeans ever set foot on the land of Troy, I had nine
times had under my command men and swift ships to sail against
foreign shores, and hence much booty reached my hands; I chose
for myself all I wished, and much besides came to me by lot. Thus
my riches increased apace, and henceforth I found myself hon-
oured and reverenced among the Cretans.

'But when Zeus the Thunderer planned that distressful enter-
prise that loosened the knees of so many warriors, then the people
began to urge myself and Idomeneus to lead an expedition of
ships to Ilium. To deny what they asked was not possible, the
people's voice was too compelling. At Ilium, then, we sons of the
Achaeans warred on for nine years, and in the tenth, having
sacked the town of Priam, we began the voyage home, but the
god scattered us far and wide. For myself, alas, Zeus the all-wise
planned new sorrows. For a month, no more, I stayed at home and
cheered myself there with my children and my wedded wife and
my possessions; then impulse urged me to fit out vessels and sail
to Egypt with my heroic comrades.

'Nine vessels I fitted out, and the crews gathered fast enough.
Then for six days my comrades feasted, while I for my part
brought many beasts to sacrifice to the gods and furnish the tables
of the feasters. On the seventh day we went aboard, and leaving

the plains of Crete we began to sail with a fine strong north wind behind us. It was easy sailing, as if downstream; none of my ships came to grief. With no harm from without, no sickness among ourselves, we sat on board while wind and steersmen carried us forward on our course; on the fifth day we came to the Nile's majestic waters, and in the Nile I anchored the curving ships. Then I gave orders to my comrades; most, I said, were to stay by the ships and guard them; a few were to climb to higher ground and look out from there.

'But the crews yielded to recklessness; giving way to impulse, they began to plunder the rich farmlands of the Egyptians, to carry away the women and little children and kill the men. The clamour reached the city at once, and the townsmen when they heard this uproar came out at dawn and filled the whole plain with men on foot and chariot-fighters and flashing bronze. Zeus the Thunderer hurled vile panic among my comrades, and none of them dared to stand his ground, since on every side peril hedged them in. Many of us the Egyptians killed with the keen bronze, others they took inland alive to labour for them in slavery. As for me, Zeus himself sent a thought into my mind – though I wish now I had died then and met my fate there in Egypt, such misery still awaited me. I dashed the wrought helmet from my head, I threw down the shield from my shoulder, the spear from my hand; I ran to meet the king's chariot and I touched and kissed his knees. He had compassion and rescued me, gave me a place in his own chariot and took me in tears back to his palace. There were many who rushed at me with their spears, eager in their hot indignation to slaughter me; but the king kept them away from me, fearing the wrath of Zeus who protects strangers and who more than all other gods shows his displeasure at deeds of wickedness.

'In that place I stayed for seven years, and I gathered much wealth among the men of Egypt, because they all made me gifts. But when the eighth year came in its course, there came with it a cunning-witted Phoenician, a rogue who had done harm enough in the world already. He won me over with his craftiness and took me away with him to Phoenicia, where his house and his possessions lay. There I stayed with him till the year was out. But when the due days and months were past, when the year had travelled its full circle and the seasons had come round again, he put me aboard a ship that would sail the sea to Libya. His plan in this was a treacherous one; I was to help him to take the cargo there, but then he hoped to sell me myself and get a huge price for me. Though my heart misgave me, I had no choice but to go aboard with him. On the high seas, beyond Crete, the ship sped on with a fine strong north wind behind, but Zeus meanwhile was planning destruction for the crew. Crete was behind us; there was no land in sight ahead, nothing but sky and sea, when the son of Cronos poised a black cloud above our ship, and the sea went dark beneath it. At the same moment he thundered and hurled his bolt into the ship; as the bolt struck, her whole frame rocked, and she was filled with the stench of sulphur. All the crew were swept overboard, and the waves tossed them up and down round the ship like cormorants, for the god denied them their home-coming. As for me – Zeus himself in this hour of my distress thrust into my arms the massive mast of the dark-prowed vessel, to let me once more escape destruction. I clung to the mast and was carried onward by violent winds. For nine days I was carried so, and on the tenth, as the black night fell, a huge billow rolled me forward and up to the Thesprotian beach.

'There Lord Pheidon, the king of the Thesprotians, received me kindly and sought no recompense. His own son had found me fainting with cold and weariness, had lifted me up by the hand and had taken me to where he lived in his father's palace and had clothed me in cloak and tunic. It was there that I had news of Odysseus, for the king said he had welcomed him and entertained him on his way home. Moreover he showed me in his palace the great store of wealth Odysseus had gathered for himself – bronze and gold and the iron that men had long toiled over – enough to sustain ten whole generations after him; so vast was the treasure left in the king's house. But Odysseus, he said, had gone to Dodona at that time to hear from the tall and leafy oak what Zeus himself counselled him : how after all these years should he make his way back to bounteous Ithaca – openly or in secret? The king swore to me, as he poured libation in his palace, that the ship was hauled down and the crew in readiness to take him to his own native land. But he found a passage for myself before Odysseus returned, since it happened that a Thesprotian ship was sailing then for Dulichium and its cornfields. King Pheidon gave orders to the crew to treat me well and take me to King Acastus, but they chose rather to hatch a scheme for my undoing, to make me sink deeper still into misery and distress. When the ship on its voyage was far from land, they took at once the first step towards enslaving me. They stripped me of my cloak and tunic, and gave me instead the vile rags and tattered tunic you see upon me now. They had come by evening to the tilled fields of clear-seen Ithaca. There with a firmly-twisted rope they bound me fast on the benched ship, went ashore themselves and hastened to eat their meal on the beach. But the gods themselves readily undid the rope that bound me. I wrapped my rags round my head, slid down the smooth lading-plank until my chest touched the sea, then struck out with both arms and swam away. Very soon I was out of the water, beyond the range of my enemies. Then I crept up to a copse of flowering undergrowth, dropped to the ground and lay there. The men meanwhile hunted this way and that, loudly lamenting the loss of me, but when it seemed useless to seek me further, they went back to their hollow vessel. For the gods it was light work to hide me, and they again guided me to this home of a man of understanding, since destiny means me to live on.'

Eumeaus the swineherd answered him : 'My much-tried friend, you have touched my heart with this tale of troubles multiplied, of all your sufferings and all your wanderings; yet some of your words, I think, were wide of truth, and I will not believe what you tell me of Odysseus. What call have you, being what you are, to utter lies so purposelessly? I know well what I ought to think of my master's homecoming – how he has been utterly hated by all the gods, because they did not give him his death either among the Trojans or in his friends' arms after winding up the skein of war. Then all the Achaeans would have heaped up a cairn for him, and for his son as well as himself he would have won great glory through after-times; but no, the storm-spirits have snatched him ingloriously away. And now I must live away from the world, next to my swine, never visiting the city unless Penelope summons me when news has been brought to her from somewhere. Then men sit beside the newsbearer, questioning point by point – both those who mourn for the master so long away and those whose delight it is to devour scot-free all that he has. But I for my part have come to dislike asking and questioning ever since an Aetolian deceived me with his tale; he had killed a man, he had wandered far and wide, and now he came here to my house and was made welcome. He said he had seen Odysseus as guest of Idomeneus in Crete, mending his tempest-battered ships; he said furthermore that he and his noble crew would return in early or late summer and bring great store of treasure with them. So I ask you, now that the god has brought you here, you who are so old and have suffered so much – do not try to humour me or soothe me with lies. Not because of such things as these shall I show you regard and hospitality, but because I reverence the patron of strangers, Zeus, and because for your own sake I have compassion on you.'

Odysseus answered: 'How unbelieving your heart must be, if not even my oath could win you over or make you trust me! Come then, let us make a bargain, and the gods whose dwelling is in Olympus shall be witnesses to us both. If your lord returns to this house of yours, then give me a cloak and tunic to wear and send me on my way to Dulichium, the place where I wish to be; but if your lord does not return as I say he will, then set your servants to hurl me down from some great cliff, so that beggars who follow in my footsteps may think twice before telling lies.'

Eumaeus answered: 'Yes indeed, my friend, what fame and fortune might I not gain among mankind, then and thereafter, if after receiving you in my cottage and giving you hospitality I next went on to kill you and take your life! With what assurance might I not then make my prayers to the son of Cronos! But enough of this – it is time for a meal by now, and I hope my companions may soon be home; then we can make a cottage supper we shall enjoy.'

Before they had finished conversing thus, the other herdsmen approached with their swine and penned the sows in their sties for the night, not without much noise from the creatures thus herded in. Eumaeus called out to his companions: 'Bring me the best hog you have – I mean to slaughter it for this guest from distant parts. We ourselves shall be gainers too, after suffering toil and trouble so long for the sake of these white-tusked hogs, while others devour scot-free the creatures that we have laboured over.'

So saying, he turned to splitting firewood with ruthless bronze while the others brought in a fat five-year hog and held it by the hearth. The swineherd did not forget the Deathless Ones, for he was a right-minded man. To begin the sacrifice he plucked hairs

from the beast's head, and as he threw them into the fire he be-
sought the gods, one and all, that sage Odysseus might return to
his own home. Then he raised himself to his full height, and with
a billet of oak left unsplit he struck the hog, and it fell stunned.
They cut the throat and singed the carcase and quickly divided
it. Eumaeus took strips from all the limbs, covered the thigh-
bones with rich fat and with the strips, then sprinkled them with
barley-meal and threw them into the fire. Then his men cut up
the rest, spitted the pieces, roasted them carefully, took them all
off again, then heaped them on serving-dishes. The swineherd
stood up to portion them out justly and fairly, as was his way.
He divided the whole into seven portions, assigning one, with the
due prayer, to the nymphs and to Hermes child of Maia, and
giving the rest to the diners one by one. He honoured Odysseus
with a whole length of chine from the hog, and with this tribute
he cheered his master's heart. And Odysseus said to him:
'Eumaeus, I pray that Father Zeus may hold you as dear as I do
now, because you have honoured one like me with the best you
have.'

Eumaeus the swineherd answered him: 'My much-tried guest,
eat and enjoy such things as you have before you there. As for
the god, he will give one thing and withhold another, just as
seems good to him; all things are within his reach.'

So he spoke, and burned the parts he had set aside as an offer-
ing to the immortal gods. Then, having made libation, he put the
glowing wine into the city-sacker's hands. Odysseus sat down by
his portion, and bread was served them by Mesaulius, whom the
swineherd in his master's absence had himself purchased from the
Taphians, exchanging his own goods for him, unhelped by the
queen or old Laertes. So they all put out their hands to the food
lying there before them, and when they had eaten and drunk
their fill, Mesaulius took the bread away, and the others, satisfied
with the bread and meat, made ready to go to their sleeping-
places.

The night that now came on was cheerless. There was no
moon; Zeus sent down never-ceasing rain, and the wet west wind
blew strong. Odysseus spoke to the company, meaning to test the
swineherd's feelings; since he showed Odysseus such regard, would
he take off his own cloak then and offer it to his guest, or at least
tell one of his men to do so? 'Listen, Eumaeus and all friends here.

I am now about to voice a wish. It is wine that prompts me, wine that crazes a man's wits and urges even the sage to burst into song and feeble laughter and tempts him to dance and to utter words best left unspoken. But since I have blurted out thus much, I will hide nothing now. I wish I had still the same fresh vigour, the same strength of body unimpaired, as when we planned and set an ambush under the walls of Troy. In command for this were Odysseus and the son of Atreus, Menelaus; and at their desire the third leader was myself. When we neared the town and its lofty walls, we made for the reedy marsh outside it, and sinking down in our armour amid the dense growth, we lay there while the comfortless night came on, a night icy-chill under the north wind's breath; from above came snow, as cold as rime, and ice froze hard over our shields. The others all had their cloaks and tunics, and lay there comfortably enough, with their shoulders covered by their shields, but I in my folly when I departed had left my cloak with my companions, confident that in any case I should not be cold, and had joined the rest with no more protection than shield and bright loin-cloth. But when the third watch of the night had come and the stars had passed the zenith, I jogged Odysseus, who was next me. I said to him, and he listened at once: "Princely Odysseus of many strategems, I shall not be long among the living – I have no cloak, and the cold is killing me. Some god misadvised me; I came with nothing above my tunic, and now there is no escape for me." So I spoke, and he with a veteran's practised wit had his plan at once. With his voice in a whisper, "Hush," he said; "some of our men over there might hear you." Then with head on elbow he spoke aloud: "Listen, friends: I was drowsing then, and a vision came to me from some god. The truth is, we have come a long distance from the ships. I wish that someone would carry word to King Agamemnon – he might send out more men from the ships to join us." In response to this, the son of Andraemon, Thoas, leapt up at once, threw aside his scarlet cloak and ran off to the ships, while I could wrap myself blissfully in the garment he left behind, till Dawn appeared in her flowery cloth of gold. I wish I had that fresh vigour now, that same strength of body undiminished.'

Eumaeus the swineherd answered him: 'Old guest, this tale you have told is excellent; not a word of it was misjudged or went to waste, so you shall not go short either for covering or for anything else a suppliant in distress ought to be given when he comes one's way. This for tonight – but tomorrow early you must fling your old rags round you again, because here there are not many cloaks and tunics to change into; it is one man, one cloak.'

With these words Eumaeus leapt up and made him a sleeping-place by the fire, throwing down sheepskins and goatskins there. Here Odysseus laid himself down, and the swineherd put over him a wide cloak that he kept in store as a spare garment, to wear when some monstrous storm came on.

This then was where Odysseus lay, and the younger men lay near him. Eumaeus himself was not content to lie indoors, away from his swine, and he made ready to go outside, while Odysseus admired his eager care for what belonged to his absent lord. First of all he had slung a keen sword over his sturdy shoulders; next he put on a very thick cloak to keep out the wind, adding the hairy skin of a big well-fed goat; then he picked up a sharpened javelin that would keep either dogs or men at bay; lastly he issued forth, to lie where the white-tusked hogs were sleeping, under a hollow rock and under shelter from the north wind.

BOOK XV

PALLAS Athene in the mean while had travelled to spacious Lacedaemon, to rouse remembrance in bold Odysseus' princely son and urge him to hasten home again. She found Telemachus and Peisistratus in the vestibule of Menelaus' palace; they were both in bed, but while Peisistratus slumbered peacefully, Telemachus was held back from sleep by troubled night-thoughts about his father. The goddess of gleaming eyes stood at his bedside and said to him:

'Telemachus, it is not right for you to be roving still so far from home, leaving your goods unguarded there and leaving in your own palace such conscienceless men as those. What if they parcel out and devour everything you possess, and if all your travelling prove in vain? No, you must waste no time; you must ask Menelaus, that friend in need, to hasten your journey back, to let you find your noble mother still in her own home; because already her father and her brothers are urging her to marry Eurymachus, who outbids all the other suitors with presents to her and has offered her kinsmen richer and richer gifts. So see to it that she carries no treasure away from the house against your will. You know what a woman's instincts are; she longs to swell a new bridegroom's riches and has no remembrance and no thought of her living children and the dead husband she loved before. Go back then; and with your own hands entrust this or that prized possession to whichever maidservant seems to you the trustiest, until the gods grant you the sight of a noble bride.

'One thing besides I have to tell you; take it to heart. The chief men among the suitors have wilfully set an ambush for you in the straits between Ithaca and rugged Samos; they mean to kill you before you can reach home. But what they wish will not come to pass, I think; before that can be, the earth will cover some of these wasters of your wealth. Only keep your ship clear of the islands, and sail by night as well as by day; the Deathless One who protects and guards you will send a fair wind behind you. But when you have reached the nearest shore of Ithaca, let ship and crew sail on to the city; your own first task is to seek out the swineherd who has in his charge your sows and boars; he is as loyal to you as ever. Sleep the night there; then send him to the city to tell Penelope you are safe and are back from Pylos.'

So she spoke, and went off once more to high Olympus. Telemachus with a touch of his foot roused Nestor's son from his pleasant slumbers. 'Wake up, Peisistratus,' he said. 'Harness the horses to the chariot and let us be on our way.'

Peisistratus answered him: 'No matter how eager we are to go, we cannot drive on through pitch-dark night. It will soon be dawn, Telemachus. Wait till the child of Atreus, the warrior Menelaus, has placed his gifts inside our chariot and bidden us kind farewell before speeding us on our way. It is for such things that a guest remembers forever afterwards a host who has entertained him graciously.'

So he spoke; and soon enough came Dawn in her cloth of gold. Then Menelaus, that friend in need, went to join his guests, having left the bed where lovely-haired Helen had been beside him. When Prince Telemachus saw him coming, he hastened to put his glittering tunic on, threw the great cloak over his manly shoulders and went out to meet his host. 'Menelaus,' he said, 'child of Atreus and sovereign of your people, now let me go to my own land; my heart is yearning now to be home.'

Menelaus answered him at once: 'Indeed, Telemachus, I will not keep you here long with me if your heart is set upon return. Too much warmness to guests, and too much coldness, are both things that I blame in others. Measure is best in everything; to press departure on one who is loath to go, to hinder it for one who is loath to stay – either thing is as bad as the other. Cherish a guest while he is with you; when he wishes to go, speed his going. But as for yourself, you must wait at least until I have brought you handsome gifts and placed them inside the chariot for you to see, and until I have told the women to make a meal ready in the hall from the plenteous stores this house possesses. It means not only refreshment for you, it means honour and glory also to have such a meal before setting off on this long journey. If you wish to visit more of Hellas and of Argos and have me with you, then I will harness the horses and guide you to the cities of men; no one will send us on empty-handed; each will give us something at least, a fine bronze tripod or a cauldron, a pair of mules or a golden goblet.'

Thoughtful Telemachus answered him: 'Royal Menelaus, child

of Atreus and sovereign of your people, I wish to return to my
own land now, because when I departed I left behind me no other
man to watch over my possessions, and I fear that while I search
for my father I may be lost myself or that some fine thing treas-
ured in my halls may be lost to me.'

Hearing his answer, Menelaus forthwith told his wife and
maids to make a meal ready in the hall from the plenteous stores
the house possessed. Then Eteoneus son of Boethus advanced to-
wards them; he lived nearby and had only just left his bed.
Menelaus told him to light a fire and roast some meat, and the
man did as he was told. Then the king went down to his fragrant
store-room, and Helen and Megapenthes with him. When he
reached the spot where his treasures lay, he chose out a two-
handled cup and told his son, Megapenthes, to bring out a silver
mixing-bowl. Queen Helen paused by the coffers there that held
the rich robes woven by herself. There was one that lay beneath
the rest, the amplest and the most richly broidered, with sheen
like a star's coming up from it; she lifted it out and took it with
her. Then the three went back through the house again to rejoin
Telemachus. Yellow-haired Menelaus said to him: 'May Zeus
the Thunderer grant you, Telemachus, just the homecoming you
desire. As for gifts – of all the treasures stored in my house I will
give you the finest and most precious; I will give you a wrought
mixing-bowl; it is silver all through, finished with gold around
the rim; the craftsman was Hephaestus himself; Lord Phaedimus,
king of Sidon, gave it me when his palace sheltered me on the
voyage home. Now it will please me to make it yours.'

With these words the king put the two-handled cup into the
young man's hands, while Megapenthes placed before him the
glittering bowl that he had been carrying. Then lovely Helen
came up to him with the robe between her hands. 'Dear boy,' she
said, 'I too have a present for you, a keepsake of Helen's handi-
work; it is meant for the day of blissful marriage. Your bride will
wear it then; meanwhile let it stay in your mother's room. And
may you reach in all happiness your own pleasant-sited house in
your own country.'

With these words she put the robe into his hands and he took
it joyfully. Prince Peisistratus took the gifts, laid them down in
the wagon-basket and eyed them all with heartfelt wonder. Then
Menelaus led his guest back into the hall. A maid brought

water in a fine golden jug and poured it over their hands for washing, above a silver basin; then she drew up a smooth table for them. The trusted housekeeper came and put bread where they could reach it; there were many kinds of food as well, and she gave ungrudgingly of all that she had. The son of Boethus carved the meat and dealt out the portions, and the son of King Menelaus poured the wine. So Telemachus and Peisistratus stretched their hands to the dishes there. But when they had eaten and drunk their fill, they harnessed the horses, mounted the carefully-fashioned chariot and then drove out through the gateway and echoing portico. Menelaus followed them out; in his right hand he held sweet wine in a golden cup, so that before they went they might make libation. He took his stand in front of the horses and said with courteous phrase and gesture: 'Young men, farewell, and take my greeting to good King Nestor, for indeed he was kind to me as any father in the days when we of Achaean stock were making war in the land of Troy.'

Thoughful Telemachus answered him: 'When we reach his house, Lord Menelaus, we will assuredly give your message and tell the old king all that has passed here. Would that I were as sure to tell the same thing again in Ithaca – would that after a safe return, after finding Odysseus himself at home, I could say once more what boundless kindness I had from you before leaving here with these noble and ample gifts !'

As he ceased speaking, a bird flew up to the right of him, an eagle carrying in its talons a great white household goose from the courtyard there; in pursuit of it came men and women, screaming;[1] from left to right the eagle sped, in front of the chariot and close to hosts and guests, who one and all rejoiced at the sight and were cheered at heart. Peisistratus was the first to speak: 'Consider, King Menelaus, whether the god has shown this portent for us or for you.'

Such were his words, and martial Menelaus pondered how he should view the sign to interpret it aright. But long-robed Helen was before him. 'Listen while I expound this thing as the Deathless Ones put it in my heart and as I am sure will come to pass. Just as yonder eagle left the mountain that holds his eyrie and

1.   'As he said this, an Eagle dexter flew
     And seiz'd a great white tame Goose grazing near.
     The standers-by shouted and cri'd, Shue, shue.' HOBBES

his brood, just as he snatched the goose that was fattening in this house, so, after all his trials and travels, Odysseus will come back home and will be avenged; or it may be he is home already, sowing for all the suitors the seeds of doom.'

Thoughtful Telemachus answered her: 'May Zeus the Thunderer, Hera's husband, bring what you prophesy to pass; and then there also your name on my lips shall be like a god's.'

With these words he brought down the lash, and the horses eagerly rushed on, through the city on to the plain, and all day long kept the yoke between them quivering. Then the sun sank, and light thickened on every pathway; and now they had come to Pherae, the home of Diocles. He was the son of Ortilochus, son of Alpheus. In Diocles' house they slept that night, and he gave them hospitality.

Dawn comes early, with rosy fingers. When she appeared, they harnessed the horses, mounted the chariot and drove out through the gateway and echoing portico. Soon they approached the steep citadel of Pylos, and then Telemachus spoke to his friend: 'Son of Nestor, there is something I wish you to undertake for me; can you succeed with is? We two may well call ourselves firm friends; your father and mine were friends before us, you and I are both of one age, and now this journey of ours together will have brought us further into sympathy. Prince Peisistratus, do not drive me beyond my ship; leave me here instead. Your father is old, and I fear that in his delight at being host he may keep me with him beyond my wishes; I must reach home as soon as may be.'

Such were his words. The son of Nestor debated inwardly how he might in honour undertake such a thing and do it. He mused a moment, then found the best answer thus. He turned the chariot towards the ship on the sea shore; he placed in the stern the noble presents of Menelaus, the clothing and the gold, then urged his friend on in rapid words. 'Be quick; go aboard yourself and make your comrades join you before I reach home and tell my father how things are. Of one thing I am quite sure, that with his masterful ways he will not consent to let you go; he will come here himself to bid you become his guest, and I do not think he will go back without you. This much is certain, he will be very angry.'

With these words he whipped the long-maned horses onwards,

back to the city of the Pylians, and very soon he had reached home. Telemachus called to his comrades urgently : 'Put all the ship's gear in place, comrades; then let us embark and be on our way.'

So he spoke; they heard and obeyed, boarded quickly and sat at the thwarts. But while Telemachus was thus busied, and while he stood by the vessel's stern, offering prayer and sacrifice to Athene, a man from a distant land approached him. This was a seer, in flight from Argos because he had killed a man; by race he descended from that Melampus [1] who had earlier lived in Pylos, the land of flocks – a man of wealth with the stateliest house among the Pylians – but later went to a land of strangers, seeking escape from his own country and from bold Neleus, proudest of all men living. For the space of a whole year Neleus had kept by force the ample possessions of Melampus, who all the while was imprisoned in galling bonds in the house of Phylacus, enduring violent ill-usage because of Neleus' daughter and because of the lamentable folly which the grim Erinys had laid upon his mind. Nevertheless he escaped destruction, drove back the loud-bellowing herd from Phylace to Pylos, took vengeance on princely Neleus for his unworthy deed, and brought Pero home as his brother's bride. But he himself went on to another country, to Argos, the pastureland of horses, because there he had been destined to live, ruling the multitude of Argives. There too he married a wife, built a lofty palace and had two strong sons, Antiphates and Mantius. Antiphates begot Oicles the bold, Oicles Amphiaraus the warrior chief, whom Zeus of the aegis and Apollo both befriended with all manner of lovingkindness. Yet he never set foot on the threshold of old age; he died at Thebes because of a bribe a woman took. His sons were Alcmaeon and Amphilochus. As for Mantius, he begot Polypheides and Cleitus, but Dawn of the golden robe snatched Cleitus away for his beauty's sake to dwell with the Deathless Ones, and Apollo made Polypheides the best of all seers on earth after Amphiaraus' death; Polypheides fell out with Mantius and departed to Hyperesia, lived there and prophesied to all.

It was the son of this Polypheides – Theoclymenus was his

---

1. For the rest of the intricate story of Melampus see page 134.

name – who now came up to Telemachus and found him by his swift dark vessel praying and offering libation. In rapid words he addressed him thus: 'Friend, since I find you offering sacrifice in this place, I implore you by that sacrifice and by the god you are worshipping, and then by your own life and the lives of the comrades with you – answer my question fully and speak without concealement. Who are you, and from where? Where are your city and your parents?'

Thoughtful Telemachus answered him: 'I will tell you it all unswervingly. By birth I belong to Ithaca. My father is Odysseus; as surely as he was ever living, so surely I am his son; yet by now he must have perished miserably. To gather tidings of this long absent one I have travelled here with my ship and comrades.'

Theoclymenus answered: 'I also have left my country, because I killed a man of my own tribe; and in Argos the pastureland of horses there are many brothers and kinsmen of his who hold great sway over the Achaeans. To escape dark doom and death from these, I am now self-banished; I am fated to be a wanderer about the world. I come to you as a fugitive and suppliant; take me aboard then and let them not kill me; I fear they are in pursuit already.'

Thoughtful Telemachus answered him: 'Since such is your wish, I will not refuse my ship to you; come with us; in my own land you shall have such welcome as we can give.'

So speaking, he took the suppliant's spear of bronze and laid it upon the deck; he himself went aboard, sat at the stern, and gave Theoclymenus a place beside him. His comrades now loosed the cables, and Telemachus urgently gave them word to put their hands to the ship's tackling. They obeyed him readily enough; they raised the mast (it was made of pine), stepped it inside the hollow mast-box and lashed it with the forestays; then with their ropes of twisted hide they hoisted the white sails. Athene sent them a friendly wind that raced boisterously through the sky to make the ship, as swiftly as might be, finish its course through the salt sea. They passed Cruni, and Chalcis of the lovely streams.

The sun sank, and light thickened on every pathway. The ship, sped on by a breeze from Zeus, first made for Pheae, then passed by Elis, where the Epeians rule. Then Telemachus steered for the Jagged Islands, wondering if he were likelier now to escape destruction or to meet it.

Meanwhile in their cottage Odysseus and the swineherd were having supper, and with them the other men as well. When they had eaten and drunk their fill, Odysseus spoke to them, wishing to test if the swineherd would still entertain him courteously and ask him to stay there at the farmstead, or if he would send him citywards: 'Listen, Eumaeus, and all you comrades too. To-morrow early I wish to leave for the town and beg, so as not to burden you and your comrades here. But first, Eumaeus, give me your best advice, and let me have a good guide to take me there; then I must go alone up and down the city, hoping that someone will give me a trifle to eat and drink. Indeed I might go to the house of royal Odysseus himself and give a message to wise Penelope; I might even mix with the haughty suitors, in hopes of a meal from men who have food in such abundance. I could do quickly, and deftly too, any task they cared to set me. I must tell you – listen, and mark my words – that by favour of Hermes the Messenger, who gives all men's work what grace it has and what praise it wins, no one alive can match me in common tasks – in laying a fire as it should be laid, in splitting dry logs and carving and cooking and wine-pouring – all the services lesser men perform for the great.'

Much hurt at this, the swineherd answered: 'Alas, my guest, how came such a thought to cross your mind? You must be set on perishing then and there if you think of entering the throng of suitors whose violence and pride tower up to the iron heavens. The servants who wait on those are of another sort – they are young, gaily clothed in cloaks and tunics, with heads anointed and shining handsome faces to match the smooth tables groaning with bread and meat and wine. No, you must stay here. No one grudges your presence here, neither I myself nor any of these comrades with me. And when Odysseus' own son comes back, he will give you a tunic and cloak to wear and find you passage to any place that your heart and thought desire.'

Patient Odysseus answered him: 'Eumaeus, I pray you may be as dear to Father Zeus as you are to me, because you have given me rest from the pains and miseries of wandering. To be driven hither and then thither – nothing mortals endure can be worse than that, yet men will bear with such utter wretchedness, will accept such wandering and grief and sorrow for the sake of their accursed bellies. But since you desire to keep me here and bid me

await the prince's coming, tell me now about the mother of King
Odysseus and the father he left on the threshold of old age when
he went to Troy. Are they still alive and in the sunlight, or dead
now and in Hades' house?'

The swineherd answered: 'My guest, I will tell you faithfully.
Laertes is still alive, but he prays continually to Zeus that his soul
and body may be parted in his own house. He pines exceedingly
for his long absent son and the wedded wife who was so wise; her
death, most of all, has left him wretched and made him old before
his time. She died of grief for her noble son – a melancholy death;
may no such fate come to anyone that I love, any neighbour
whose actions are a friend's! While she still lived – in whatever
sorrow – I liked to inquire for news of her, because she herself
had brought me up side by side with her noble daughter, long-
robed Ctimene, youngest of all her children; the two of us were
brought up together, and the queen regarded me scarcely less than
her own child. But when we came to the blissful prime of youth,
her parents sent the princess to Same to be a bride, receiving rich
wedding-gifts for her; as for myself, Anticleia gave me a fine
cloak and tunic to wear, with sandals for my feet, and sent me
away into the country; she had been exceedingly fond of me, and
I feel the lack of such kindness now. Yet the blessed gods prosper
the work I labour at, and from its fruits I have had enough to eat
and drink and give to those I have duties to. But from Queen
Penelope I have never heard one thing to rejoice my heart since
the plague of overbearing suitors fell on the house; and her ser-
vants now much miss the old ways – talking in presence of the
the mistress, asking what news there is, eating and drinking in
the palace and taking a trifle back to their cottage too – all of them
things to comfort a servant's heart.'

Subtle Odysseus answered him: 'A strange tale, Eumaeus.
What a child then you must have been when you found yourself
carried far away from your own land and parents! Come now,
tell me and answer truly. Was it that your city was sacked – some
peopled and wide-wayed city in which your father and mother
dwelt? Or were you alone, tending sheep or cattle, when hostile
men came there in their ships and seized and sold you?'

The master swineherd answered him: 'Friend, since you ques-
tion me so searchingly – listen quietly and in comfort as you sit

here and drink your wine. Nights in this season are very long, giving time for sleep or time for listening and enjoyment. You need not lie down before the hour; even sleep is wearisome in excess. Let anyone else who is so minded leave us and sleep, and when dawn comes let him make his breakfast and after that go out with our master's swine We two will eat and drink in the cottage here and find comfort in calling to mind one another's griefs and sorrows, for there comes a time when a man takes comfort from old sorrows, a man who has suffered much and has wandered far. So now I will tell you what you ask me.

'There is – perhaps you have heard of it – an island called Syros, above Ortygia, where the sun sets at solstice; not thickly peopled, but a good country, with fine sheep and fine cattle; it is rich in wheat, rich in wine. Famine never enters this land, nor again does any dread disease come upon poor mortals there. No; when these islanders grow old, Apollo of the silver bow visits them with his gentle shafts and brings death upon them, or Artemis visits them instead. There are two townships in this place, and the whole island is shared between them. My father was king over them both; he was Ctesius, son of Ormenus, and he was like one of the Deathless Ones.

'To this island came some Phoenicians – notable seamen but greedy rogues – and in their cargo they brought all manner of pretty things. Now in my father's household was a Phoenician woman, tall and handsome and skilled in fine handiwork. The sly Phoenicians were bent on seducing her, and when one day she had come to wash clothes nearby, one of the seamen lay with her by the ship in those embraces that steal the soft heart of any woman, even an honest one. Then he began to question her – who was she? where was her home? – and she pointed at once to the tall roof of my father's palace. "I am proud to be from Sidon, the land of bronze. My father was Arybas, a man very rich indeed; but Taphian pirates carried me off on my way townwards from the country; they conveyed me here and sold me into the household of yonder lord when he paid the price they asked."

'Then her secret lover said to her: "Are you willing to come back home with us to see your parents' lofty house and to see themselves? They are living still and are known as rich."

'The woman replied: "That might be done if you seamen bound

yourselves by oath to take me back to my home unharmed."

'So she spoke, and they all took the oath she asked of them. When they had sworn solemnly, the woman began again: "And now be secret. Let none of your crew speak to me openly if he comes upon me in the street or beside the well; someone might go to the old king's house and tell him, and then in distrust he would confine me in galling bonds and scheme the destruction of you all. No; keep the secret in your own breasts, and be quick with your bargaining for the freight home. When the ship is laden with goods, let a message be sent to me at the house at once. I will bring you what gold I can lay hands on, and there is something besides I will gladly give you for passage – money. I am nurse to my noble master's son, a knowing child enough who trots by my side out of doors. I could bring you him aboard as well, and in foreign parts, wherever you sold him, he would fetch you a fine price."

'With these words she went back to the palace. The men stayed with us a whole year, gaining wealth by barter and storing it in their hollow ship. But when the vessel was laden for departure, they sent a messenger to inform the woman. This cunning rogue brought up to my father's house a necklace of gold with amber beads between, and in the hall the maids and my lady mother kept handling it, gazing at it with all their eyes and proffering the price asked. The man nodded silently to my nurse and, having once made that signal, went back to the ship. She herself took me by the hand and began to lead me out of the house; on the way, in the entrance-hall, she chanced upon some tables and drinking-cups that had been used by my father's guests, his accustomed counsellors; and now the men had gone out together to the place where townsmen meet and sit with each other and debate. My nurse in haste hid three of these goblets in her bosom and went out with them; I in my innocence went with her. Then the sun sank, and light thickened on every pathway. We walked quickly down to the harbour; the Phoenicians' vessel was waiting there. They went aboard, took us aboard ourselves and began to sail the watery ways, while Zeus granted us a fair wind. We sailed for six days, day and night; but when Zeus brought the seventh day also, Artemis with a shaft of hers struck the woman, and sent her – like a sea-swallow diving – to tumble

below into the hold.[1] The sailors threw her overboard to be a prey
for the seals and fishes. I remained alone and heavy-hearted, till
wind and wave carried them onwards to this land, and there
Laertes purchased me with his goods. In that fashion I first set
eyes on Ithaca.'

Royal Odysseus answered him: 'Eumaeus, indeed you have
touched my heart within me with all this tale of the miseries you
have suffered. Yet Zeus after all has brought you good, side by
side with evil. After much distress you came to the house of a
kindly master, and by his care you have food and drink enough;
your way of life is a good way of life. As for myself, I have
wandered from city to city through the world, and now I am
here.'

So these two talked to one another; then they went to sleep,
but not for long, because Dawn in her flowery robe came soon.
Meanwhile Telemachus and his crew had approached the shore;
they struck their sails, quickly took down the mast, and rowed
the ship on into harbour. They threw out the anchor-stones,
made the cables fast, then disembarked on the sea shore and began
to prepare a meal and mix the wine. When they had eaten and
drunk their fill, thoughtful Telemachus addressed them: 'Your
own task now is to row the ship on to the town. I myself shall
make for my farmlands and my herdsmen, and after visiting my
estates I shall come back to the town by nightfall. In the morn-
ing I will reward your labours for me throughout this voyage –
I will set before you a noble banquet of meat and wine.'

Then Theoclymenus spoke to him: 'And I, dear child – what
place am I to make for? Among all the chieftains in craggy
Ithaca, whose is the house I should approach? Or ought I to take
my way forthwith to your own mother, your own house?'

Thoughtful Telemachus replied: 'Had things been otherwise
than they are, I would indeed have invited you to our house, which
has ways enough of welcoming guests; but here and now that
would be no good thing for you, because I myself shall not be
there and my mother would never see you. She seldom shows her-

1.   'She that shafts doth love
Shot dead the woman, who into the pumpe
Like to a Dop-chick div'd, and gave a thumpe
In her sad setling.' CHAPMAN

self publicly to the suitors; she keeps her distance, weaving her web in her upper room. I will tell you of someone else that you might approach – Eurymachus, who is the far-famed son of wise Polybus. The people of Ithaca in these days regard him with reverence like a god; among all the suitors he stands highest, and is most eager to wed my mother and gain the sovereignty of Odysseus. But regarding that, the truth is with Zeus in high Olympus; Zeus knows if before that marriage he will bring the day of doom on Eurymachus and the rest.'

As he ceased speaking, a bird flew up to the right of him, a hawk, the swift messenger of Apollo; in its talons it held a dove, plucking out its feathers and strewing them on the ground between Telemachus and the ship. Theoclymenus called him away from the crew, clasped his hand and addressed him thus: 'Telemachus, it is not without some god's intention that this bird flew up to the right of you; as soon as I saw it there before me, I knew it for a bird of omen. No family in the land of Ithaca is to be kinglier than your own; the supremacy is with you for ever.'

Thoughtful Telemachus answered him: 'If only those words might find fulfilment! Then, my guest, you would soon know what a host's gifts and a host's welcome mean from me; anyone who met you would call you a happy man.' Then, turning towards a trusted comrade: 'Peiraeus,' he said, 'son of Clytius, of all the comrades who went with me to Pylos it is you who fall in most readily with anything I request; I ask you therefore to take this stranger, entertain him hospitably in your house and show him all honour till I come.'

Peiraeus the spearsman answered him: 'Telemachus, even should you wish to remain longer away from town, I will entertain him; he shall lack nothing a guest desires.'

And with this Peiraeus went aboard, telling the crew to follow him and to loose the cables; so they went aboard and sat at the thwarts. Telemachus fastened on his sandals and took from the deck the strong spear of his that was tipped with bronze. The crew loosed the cables, pushed off from shore and began to row citywards as the king's son had commanded them. He himself strode forward on hurrying feet till he reached the steading, the place where his countless swine were housed and where often Eumaeus slept beside them, a loyal and loving servant to his masters.

BOOK XVI

In the cottage, meanwhile, Odysseus and the swineherd were making their breakfast ready. It was now dawn; they had lit the fire and sent off the other men with the herded swine. As Telemachus came nearer, the barking dogs did not bark at him; they whimpered round him instead. Odysseus heard the sound of whimpering and the tread of feet that came as well. So his words sped quickly to Eumaeus: 'Eumaeus, surely some friend of yours is about to enter, someone you know at least; the dogs are not barking, they are fawning, and I hear the tread of feet as well.'

The words had not fully passed his lips when his own dear son stood in the doorway. Up leapt the swineherd in amazement; down from his hands dropped the jar and bowl he was busy with as he mixed the glowing wine. He went straight up to his young master; he kissed his head and both his bright eyes and both his hands, and a big tear rolled down his cheek. As a father embraces lovingly an only and darling son, one for whom he has borne much sorrow, when after nine years away he returns home from a far country, so now did the swineherd put his arms round the radiant prince, covering him everywhere with kisses as one who had just escaped from death. Then the tearful words came hastening out: 'You are here once more then, Telemachus, dear light of my eyes; I never thought to see you again when once you had sailed for Pylos. Come in, dear child; let me gaze at you to my heart's content – you under my own roof in these first moments of your return. It is seldom you visit the country and countryfolk; you linger there in the town instead, doubtless preferring to rest your eyes on that pernicious mob of suitors.'

Thoughtful Telemachus answered him: 'Dear Eumaeus, it shall be as you wish; it is all for you I have come this way, to see you with my own eyes and to hear what you have to tell. Is my mother in the palace still, or has some other married her now, while Odysseus' bed lies tenantless, a dismal mass of cobwebs?'

The swineherd answered: 'She is indeed in your palace still, waiting patiently, but her nights and days come and go in sorrowfulness and tearfulness.'

So saying, he took the spear of bronze from the other's hands;

the prince stepped over the stone threshold and came inside. As he came forward, Odysseus his father made as if to give up his place to him, but the son on his side motioned him back and said: 'Be seated, stranger; in this steading of ours we can find a sitting-place elsewhere, and here is the man to contrive it for us.'

At these words Odysseus went back and sat down again; as for his son, Eumaeus threw him down fresh brushwood, with a fleece on top of it, and here Telemachus took his place. Then Eumaeus set down before them platters of roasted meat left from the meal the day before, quickly heaped up bread in baskets by them, mixed sweet wine in the ivywood bowl and then sat down facing Odysseus. They put out their hands to the food lying there before them, and when they had eaten and drunk their fill, the prince questioned the swineherd thus: 'Dear Eumaeus, whence comes your guest? How did sailors bring him to Ithaca and what name did they give themselves? No one surely comes here on foot?'

Eumaeus answered: 'Child, I will tell you truthfully all you ask. Wide Crete is the home he boasts of; he says that in his rest-less journeying he has roamed through many cities of men; such was the thread spun by his destiny. He has just escaped from the ship of some Thesprotians and so has arrived at my steading here. Now I will put him in your hands, to do with him as seems good to you; he claims the character of a suppliant.'

Thoughtful Telemachus replied: 'Eumaeus, your words are gall to me. What welcome can I give this guest in my house? I myself am young, and if someone suddenly turns to violence I am still not sure enough of myself to meet force with force. And then my mother – her mind still halts between two opinions: shall she stay with me and keep house, respecting her husband's bed and the people's voice, or shall she depart after this long time with whoever among her Achaean suitors is the noblest man and offers the richest bridal gifts? But as for this guest – since indeed he has come to your house, I will clothe him with a good cloak and tunic, give him a two-edged sword and sandals and find him passage to wherever his heart desires. Or if you wish, keep him at your own steading, care for him here; I will send in clothing and food enough to eat – then he need be no burden on you and your companions. But I am against his joining the suitors yonder. They are reckless in their violence; I fear they may make a jest of him, and that would be a great grief to me. And yet it is hard for one man alone to defy so many; whatever his strength, they are far stronger.'

Then patient Odysseus turned to him: 'Friend, since I in turn have no doubt the right to speak – my heart is wrung when I hear you, as I heard Eumaeus, telling of these vile things devised by the suitors in your palace with never a thought of you the prince. Tell me then – do you consent to be thus humbled, or have the people throughout your land conceived detestation for you, moved by some more than human message? Or have you brothers to blame in this? A man puts trust in brothers who fight beside him, however grim the feud once begun may be. Would that I myself, in my present mood, were as young as you or indeed were a son of great Odysseus or, better still, were the king himself; then let any man cut off my head if I did not prove the destruction of them all! Or if I, one man, must fall by the hands of that mass of men, why then, I would rather perish, rather meet death in my own palace, than look on perpetually at things as detestable as these – guests being set upon, serving-maids dragged in shame down the noble halls, wine drawn to waste, food devoured in folly and recklessness, all for a purpose that never shall be achieved.'

Thoughtful Telemachus replied: 'Friend, I will tell you the truth unswervingly. No, the people here have no hatred or bitterness against me. Nor have I brothers to blame in this, though I know that a man puts trust in brothers who fight beside him, however grim the feud once begun may be. Zeus has made us a house of only sons. Laertes was the only son that Arceisius had, Odysseus the only son that Laertes had, and I myself am an only son; Odysseus begot me and left me here in his halls and had no joy of me. Hence it is that this house is thronged with so many foemen now. The great island chieftains in Dulichium, in Same, in forested Zacynthus, and those who are princes in craggy Ithaca – they have all of them come to woo my mother, and they are devouring my inheritance. And although the thought of marriage is hateful to her, she dares not refuse outright and make an end of it. Meanwhile with their greed they waste my inheritance away, and before long they will make an end of myself also. But after all, these things remain in the lap of the gods. Here and now, my old friend Eumaeus, I must ask you to go out at once and tell my mother Penelope that I am safe and am back from Pylos. I shall stay here. Give the message to her alone and then come back again. Let no one else among the Achaeans learn the truth; there are all too many devising my destruction.'

Eumaeus answered: 'I take your meaning, I understand; your orders come to a ready listener. But now tell me plainly one thing more. Am I on this same journey to go with the news to poor Laertes? For a long while, despite all his sorrow for Odysseus, he kept an eye on the farming there and ate and drank in his house with the labourers whenever his heart so inclined him; but in these last weeks, ever since you sailed to Pylos, they say he has neither eaten nor drunk as before nor gone to visit his own farmlands. He sits at home in grief and melancholy and mourning, and the flesh grows thin over his bones.'

Thoughtful Telemachus replied: 'That makes sad hearing; still, we must not go out of our way for him, much though we feel for his distress. If mortal men could be granted any wish they chose, my first wish would be for my father and his return. No, deliver your message and then come back; no wandering afield to find Laertes. Only tell my mother to send her old housekeeper out to him, quickly and secretly; one like her would be the best messenger to my grandfather.'

Thus did he urge the need for haste; and the swineherd seized his sandals, put them on and made for the town. His going did not escape Athene, and now she drew near in likeness of a woman, tall and handsome and skilled in fine handiwork. She stood outside the cottage gateway, making herself visible to Odysseus. Telemachus did not see her before him or sense her coming, because it is not to every man that divinities make themselves manifest. Odysseus saw her; so did the dogs, and they did not bark, but fled away whining across the yard. She made a sign to Odysseus with her eyebrows; he saw it and went out from the room and past the big courtyard wall; there he stood facing her. Athene spoke: 'Royal son of Laertes, Odysseus of many wiles, now is the moment to tell your son the truth. Hide nothing; and then you two can devise the suitors' death and doom before you enter the town again. And I myself shall not be absent from you long; I burn for battle.'

She touched him then with her golden wand. First she put a fresh mantle and tunic over him, then made him more tall and young and lithe; his skin grew bronzed again and his cheeks filled out; the beard on his chin showed dark once more.

Having thus transformed him she went her way, and Odysseus returned into the cottage. His own son gazed at him in wonder, then turned his eyes away, terrified – was not this a god? His words hastened forth in rapid flight: 'Stranger, your likeness is other than what I saw before – the garments on you have changed, and your skin is of a different hue. Surely you are some god, one of those whose home is wide heaven itself. Be gracious to us, and let us offer you acceptable sacrifices and gifts of wrought gold. Only have compassion on us.'

Odysseus answered him: 'I am not a god. Why liken me to the Deathless Ones? I am your own father, the very man for whose sake you have grieved long and borne much and suffered the violences of men.'

With these words he kissed his son and let fall a tear from his cheeks to the ground, though until then he had been firm and tearless. But Telemachus could not yet believe that this was his own father, and therefore answered him thus again: 'You are not Odysseus, not my father; no, some god is beguiling me, only to make me grieve and despair the more. No mortal man could do such a thing by his own devising; it would need a god, no less, to intervene and make a man young or old – a god's wish makes such marvels easy. A moment ago you were old and dressed in rags, but now you look like those divinities whose home is wide heaven itself.'

Subtle Odysseus answered him: 'Telemachus, you need not be much bewildered or much amazed at sight of your father at home again. No other Odysseus will come to this land for you after this; there is only I, such as you see me, after many trials and many wanderings, returning now to my own land in the twentieth year. Athene the goddess has transformed me; it is her way to make me, according to her all-powerful will, now like a beggar, now like a youth in handsome garments. To the gods whose home is heaven itself it is an easy thing to exalt a mortal or to abase him.'

So he spoke, then seated himself; Telemachus embraced his father and sobbed and wept. On both of them there came the desire for tears, and they cried as piercingly and as vehemently as vultures or as crooked-clawed eagles whose nestlings the hunters have snatched away unfledged; so it was with these as their eyes let fall the piteous tears. And indeed the sun might have gone down upon their weeping, had not the boy asked his father suddenly: 'Dear father, what was the ship that brought you to Ithaca? No one surely comes here on foot. What name did the sailors gives themselves?'

Odysseus answered: 'Child, I will tell you the whole truth. I was brought here by the Phaeacians, famous seamen whose custom it is to take back to his own country any stranger who comes to theirs. They conveyed me alseep in their rapid vessel and set me ashore in Ithaca. They had given me moreover precious gifts, bronze and gold in plenty and woven garments, and these things, by the gods' help, are lying safe in a certain cave. After that, at Athene's bidding, I have come to this place to consult with you on the slaughtering of our enemies. So tell me now of the suitors and their numbers; I must be sure how many they are, and how resolute. Then I will bring all my wits to bear and consider if we two unaided can counter them or if we must seek the help of others.'

Thoughtful Telemachus answered him: 'Father, I always have heard high praise of you as bold in battle and deep in stratagem, but what you say now is beyond reason. I am left bewildered; it cannot be that two men alone should challenge a throng of powerful enemies. Make no mistake; there are not just ten or just twenty suitors, there are far more – a moment, and you can reckon them up for yourself. From Dulichium there are fifty-two chosen youths, with six servants waiting on them; from Same there are twenty-four men, from Zacynthus twenty young Achaeans, from Ithaca itself twelve nobles in all; then besides there are Medon the page, the inspired bard, and two attendants who carve the meat. If all these are there and we pit ourselves against them, then vengeance for wrongs at your homecoming may turn, I fear , to bitter sorrow and to our doom. Ask yourself if you can call to mind some helper who might befriend us wholeheartedly.'

But Odysseus said: 'I have an answer. Listen, and take it well to heart. Ask yourself this – will Athene and Father Zeus together be helpers enough for us two, or must I call to mind some other?'

Telemachus answered: 'True; those you speak of are both good helpers, though they sit aloft among the clouds; they have sway over mortal men and over immortal gods as well.'

Staunch Odysseus replied to him: 'Those two will not hold

aloof for long from the din and stress of battle when the martial
mettle both of the suitors and of ourselves is put to the proof in
my own hall. For the present – when dawn appears, you must
return home yourself and join the unruly throng of suitors; as
for me, the swineherd will bring me to town later – I shall look
like a beggar again, old and wretched. And if they insult me in
the house, your heart must be resolute within you, no matter
what outrage comes my way; even if they drag me by the feet
along the hall and out through the doors, even if they hurl mis-
siles at me – look on, be patient. Only protest with mild words;
ask them to cease such acts of folly. They will not heed, for truly
the day of doom is near them. There is this thing too you must
take to heart. When Athene, mistress of stratagem, makes clear
the moment to my mind, I will signal to you with a nod; when
you see that, take down all the armour and arms in the hall and
store them away, every piece, well inside the room upstairs. When
the suitors miss them and question you, lead them astray with a
soft answer: "I put them away out of the smoke, because they
had lost the look they had when Odysseus long ago went to Troy
and left them. They have tarnished over, wherever the fumes of
the fire have reached them. There is this too, a graver matter,
which the son of Cronos has warned me of; I fear that when you
are in your cups and have started some quarrel among yourselves,
you may wound one another and bring disgrace on your banquet-
ing and wooing, because iron of itself lures a man on." Only
leave there for our two selves a pair of swords and a pair of spears
and a pair of oxhide shields to grasp. Then with a rush we can
seize those arms, and after that – Pallas Athene and Zeus the
wise have enchantments to daze our enemies. There is one last
thing you must take to heart. If indeed you are my son and of
my blood, then let no man hear that Odysseus is home again; let
not Laertes hear, nor Eumaeus; no servant of ours, nor Penelope
herself. You and I alone must sound the mood of the women
servants; and we should do well to test the menservants too –
where among them are those who still have regard and heartfelt
reverence for you and me, and who are those who care nothing
for us and disesteem you as you now are.'

His noble son answered him thus: 'Father, what spirit I have
within me you will learn before long, I think; I am not a slave
to idle whims. Yet I doubt if what you spoke of last will serve a

good purpose for us both. I would ask you to consider again. You will waste much time going round your lands and testing the men one by one, while the suitors without let or hindrance devour your wealth recklessly and unsparingly. No; the women you should seek out, I think – learn which of them are disloyal to you and which are innocent; but as for the men, I am against our probing them farm by farm. Let that task be left for later, if indeed you have knowledge of some strong token from Zeus who holds the aegis.'

Such were the words that passed between them. Meanwhile, approaching the port of Ithaca, there came the trim ship that had brought Telemachus back from Pylos with all his comrades. When they reached the deep haven's shelter, they beached the ship and zealous attendants bore off the tackle or quickly took the sumptuous presents up to the house of Clytius. They sent a page to Odysseus' palace to bring the news to Penelope that Telemachus was on his estate but had ordered his crew to sail on townwards; thus the queen would not take alarm and melt in tears. Page and swineherd had the same errand, to give their messages to the lady; and hence they met. When they reached the king's palace, the page spoke out in the circle of maidservants: 'Queen, the son you love has come home again.' The swineherd came closer to Penelope and told her all that her son had bidden him say; when he had given that message in full, he left the palace hall and precincts and went his way back to the swine.

But the suitors were distressed and downcast. They left the house, passed the big courtyard wall and held session beyond the gates. Eurymachus son of Polybus was the first to speak: 'Friends, this is a bold thing that Telemachus has achieved in his pride, this voyage we thought would come to nothing. Well, we must launch our best ship now and get together a crew of seamen to row out to our friends at once and warn them to hasten home again.'

He had not quite ended when Amphinomus, looking round from his seat, caught sight of the ship already inside the harbour with the crew lowering sails and shipping oars. He laughed out blithely and said to his companions: 'No need to send them a message now – they are home and in sight; either some god told them the truth or they themselves saw the other vessel passing but could not come up with it.'

So he spoke. The suitors rose and went down to the shore.

Swiftly the crew beached the ship, and zealous attendants bore off the tackle. The suitors went off together to the assembly-place and would let no one else, young or old, sit there with them. Antinous son of Eupeithes addressed them all: 'Strange how the gods have rescued this man from harm! Through the daytime our watchers were always sitting there, close to each other along the windy heights, and after sunset we never slept through the night on shore – we were out at sea in our rapid vessel, awaiting the dawn and ambushing Telemachus, in high hopes of catching and killing him then and there. But meanwhile, it seems, he was wafted homeward by some god. Well then, we must continue here to devise grim destruction for him; he must not slip through our hands again, because while he lives I am sure we shall never gain our ends. He himself is gifted in mind and counsel, and the people now by no means look kindly on us. We must act, then, before he summons the Achaeans to assembly. He will surely not let this matter pass; he will give his indignation rein, stand up among all the townsmen and tell them how we planned sheer slaughter but could not lay hold of him. When they hear of our wickedness they will take it hard; I fear they will turn to violence, drive us out from our own country and force us to seek some foreign land. Come then – before any such thing, let us kill him somewhere outside the city – on the farmlands or on his road here; then let us keep his possessions and wealth ourselves, sharing them out fairly; and as for the house – that we might well leave for his mother and her husband to be. But if that design displeases you – if you wish Telemachus to live in full enjoyment of his inheritance – then let us cease gathering together in his house and battening on all the good things he has; instead, let each of us come from his own halls and woo and seek to win her with gifts. Then she may marry whichever suitor brings her the richest gifts and comes with good fortune favouring him.'

Such were his words. They all remained hushed and silent till Amphinomus began to speak; he was the son of Nisus and grandson of Aretes; he was moreover chief of the suitors from Dulichium, that island of pasture and of wheat, and he above all the rest of them could please Penelope with his words, for he had sound sense. With their good at heart he now addressed them: 'Friends, I for my part am not for killing Telemachus. To kill a prince of the blood is no light matter. Let us first inquire what the will of the gods may be. If the verdict of great Zeus approves, I myself will join in the killing and bid the rest of you do as much; if the gods disadvise, I say : Refrain.'

So spoke Amphinomus and persuaded them. They left their places and went forthwith to the palace of Odysseus, entered, and sat in the burnished seats.

Then wise Penelope made a new resolve – to face in person these overweening suitors. She had heard how they planned her son's destruction in the palace, for the page Medon had learned of the plot and told her of it. The stately queen entered the hall with her women round her, and reaching the part where the suitors were she halted beside the pillar that bore the massy roof, her gleaming scarf drawn across her cheeks; then she spoke out and rebuked Antinous, 'Presumptuous man, plotter of evil, Antinous – and they even say that among all those of your age in Ithaca it is you who are wisest in words and counsel ! You are not, I find. Besotted man, why do you thus plot death and doom for Telemachus, disregarding those who deserve compassion though Zeus himself has his gaze on such? Receivers of mercy to plot against the givers – such a thing is sacrilege ! Do you not know that your own father fled here for refuge in terror of the people? They were raging violently against him because he had joined the Taphian pirates to harass the Thesprotians, though these were close friends of ours. The people were set on killing him, making an end of him, devouring his patrimony themselves – it was rich and tempting. Yet Odysseus checked their passion and held them back, Odysseus whose wealth you are eating away scot-free, whose wife you are wooing, whose son you are striving now to kill, to my utter misery. Have done, I tell you, and bid your comrades have done likewise !'

Eurymachus son of Polybus answered her : 'Wise Penelope, daughter of Icarius, set your mind at rest; have no misgivings about these things. There is no man born, there never shall be, no child of woman, who will lift his hands against Telemachus your son while I am alive and have eyes to see. I will say plainly, and time shall prove it – such a man's dark blood shall gush in a moment round my spear, because I too have often been taken upon Odysseus' knees; yes, the city-sacker himself has put the roast meat into my hands and held the red wine for me to drink. And therefore Telemachus is the dearest man in the world to me, and

I tell him to fear no death from the suitors' hands; what comes from the gods one cannot escape.'

So he spoke in disarming phrase, but he himself was plotting destruction for Telemachus. The queen went up to the glittering room above and wept for Odysseus her darling husband till Athene of the gleaming eyes shed welcome slumber upon her eyelids.

The swineherd, when he returned at nightfall to join Odysseus and his son, found they had slaughtered a year-old swine and were busy preparing it for supper. But Athene had come near, meanwhile; she had struck Odysseus with her wand, made him old once more and clothed his body with dismal rags, lest the swineherd should know the master facing him and go to give the news to the queen instead of hiding it in his heart.

Telemachus addressed him first: 'Welcome back, Eumaeus, my honoured friend! What news is there in the city now? Are the suitors back from their place of ambush or still awaiting my passage there?'

Eumaeus answered: 'I took no pains to go through the town and search or inquire about such things; my heart urged me to do my errand as soon as might be and then return here. But I did meet a messenger sent in hot haste by your own crew, an attendant who gave your mother the message first. And one other thing I know, because I saw it with my own eyes. I was on the path above the city, where Hermes' Hill is, when I saw a vessel entering our harbour. The crew was large, and the ship laden with shields and with curving-headed spears. I took these men to be those you mean, but I am not sure.'

So he spoke. Prince Telemachus gave a smile, glancing at his father but not meeting the swineherd's eyes.

When their task was over and supper ready, they began to eat and found nothing lacking in the repast they shared. And having eaten and drunk their fill, they turned their thoughts to the night's rest and gladly received the boon of sleep.

BOOK XVII

THE KING AS BEGGAR

DAWN comes early, with rosy fingers. When she appeared, Telemachus tied his fine sandals on[1] and seized the strong spear that fitted his grasp. He was off to the city now, and thus addressed the swineherd: 'Old friend, I am going townwards again, to let my mother see me. I am sure she will not give up her plaintive moaning and dismal tears till she has me there before her eyes. My orders to you are these. Take this luckless stranger to the city and let him beg for a meal there; whoever wishes will give him a trifle to eat and drink. I for my part cannot put myself out for everyone, distressed as I am with so many things. And if the stranger should take this hard, so much the worse for him; I myself am all for plain speaking.'

Subtle Odysseus answered him: 'Friend, my own wish is by no means to linger here, because for a man in beggary it is better to beg in town, not country; whoever desires will give me something. I am not of an age now to be tied to a farm and obey each order the bailiff gives me. So go on your way. Eumaeus will do as you have told him and take me to town as soon as I have enjoyed the fire and got warm again. My clothes now are pitifully thin; I fear the morning hoar-frost would be too much for me, and the town, you tell me, is some way off.'

Such were his words. Telemachus with his rapid strides had gone across the farmyard and on, plotting mischief against the suitors. When he reached the pleasant-sited palace he left his spear outside, against a tall pillar, and himself passed over the stone threshold and into the hall.

The first to see him was Eurycleia his nurse. She had been spreading fleeces over the richly fashioned chairs, and now she burst into tears and rushed across to him. Other maids of her father's too came to gather round; they caressed him and kissed his head and shoulders. Then Penelope came from her room, looking like Artemis or like golden Aphrodite.[2] She wept as she threw

1. 'Soon as in th' East appear'd the blushing Dawn,
   The Prince his curious Sandals did clap on.' OGILBY
2. 'Swift from above descends the royal Fair;
   (Her beauteous cheeks the blush of Venus wear,
   Chasten'd with coy Diana's pensive air).' POPE

her arms round her darling son; she kissed his head and both his
bright eyes. Then the tearful words came hastening out: 'You are
here once more then, Telemachus, dear light of my eyes; I never
thought to see you again when once you had sailed for Pylos,
without my knowledge, against my will, searching for news of
your dear father. Come then, tell me how near you have been to
seeing him.'

Thoughtful Telemachus answered her: 'Mother, do not move
me to tears, do not distress my heart within me, saved as I am
from the precipice of destruction. No; bathe your face and put on
fresh garments; pray, and promise to all the gods the sacrifice of
unblemished hecatombs, in hope that then Zeus will bring about
requital. I myself must go down to the assembly-place to invite a
guest here, one who came with me from abroad on my return. I
sent him ahead of me with my comrades, asking Peiraeus to take
him home and show him all care and kindness and honour till I
returned.'

The words he spoke did not go unheeded. She bathed her face
and put on fresh garments; she prayed, and promised to all the
gods the sacrifice of unblemished hecatombs, in hope that then
Zeus would bring about requital.

Meanwhile Telemachus, spear in hand, had passed through
the hall and out; at his heels there were two swift hounds. Athene
shed more than human grace upon him, and all the people gazed
at him as he neared them. The haughty suitors gathered round
him with words of friendship upon their lips but depths of evil
within their hearts. He turned aside from the crowd of them and
walked instead to where Mentor sat with Antiphus and with
Halitherses – old friends of his father as they were; there he took
his own seat, and they questioned him about everything. Then
the spearsman Peiraeus made his way to them, escorting his guest
across the city to the assembly-place. Telemachus was not back-
ward either. He went to the stranger's side, and Peiraeus said:
'Telemachus, lose no time; send some of your maidservants to my
house to take back the presents that Menelaus made you.'

Thoughtful Telemachus answered him: 'Peiraeus, we do not
know what the end of all this will be. If the headstrong suitors
kill me by treachery in my halls and part all my father's wealth
among them, then my wish is that you yourself rather than one
of them should enjoy these things; but if I contrive death and

doom for them, then have these gifts sent back to the palace, to the happiness of both of us.'

So speaking, he set off homewards, taking the much-tried stranger with him. When they reached the pleasant-sited palace, they laid their cloaks aside in the hall, went to the shining baths and bathed. When the maids had washed them, rubbed them with oil and given them their tunics and fleecy cloaks, the host and the guest left the baths and took their seats. A maid brought water in a fine golden jug and poured it over their hands for washing, above a silver basin; then she drew up a smooth table for them. The trusted housekeeper came and put bread where they could reach it; there were many kinds of food as well, and she gave ungrudgingly of all that she had. Telemachus' mother sat opposite, leaning back on a low chair and spinning fine wool. The two men stretched out their hands to the dishes there before them, and when they had eaten and drunk their fill, Penelope thus began to speak: 'Telemachus, I will go to my room upstairs again and lie down on the cheerless bed that my tears have stained, day in, day out, ever since Odysseus sailed for Troy with the sons of Atreus. Even during this respite from the suitors you have not had the grace to tell me plainly what tidings you may have heard of your own father's return home.'

Thoughtful Telemachus answered her: 'Mother, I will tell you the whole truth. We went to Pylos and saw King Nestor. He welcomed me in his lofty palace and gave me the loving entertainment a father might give a son just home after long absence in foreign lands; such was the care he lavished on me, he and his noble sons. But of staunch Odysseus, living or dead, he said he had heard no news from a single soul. He sent me on with horses and chariot to the house of the son of Atreus, the warrior Menelaus. And there I saw Argive Helen, for whose sake the gods decreed that the men of Troy and the men of Argos should bear so much. Menelaus, that friend in need, asked me at once what errand brought me to noble Lacedaemon. I told him the whole truth, and he answered thus: "Accursed cowards, so eager to sleep in a brave man's bed! But listen – as when a fallow deer leaves the twin fawns just born to her to slumber in some great lion's den, while she herself goes roving and browsing over the mountain spurs and grassy hollows, but then the lion returns to his lair and strikes the two sucklings with hideous death, so will

Odysseus strike these suitors with hideous death. O Father Zeus and Athene and Apollo, grant that Odysseus might come upon them in such a form as when long ago in happy Lesbos he rose at a challenge, wrestled with Philomeleides and gave him a mighty fall, so that all the Achaeans were filled with joy – in such a form might he join in contest with the suitors ! They would find death quickly, all of them, and their hoped-for wedding would have a bitter taste. But as for what you ask me so earnestly, I will say nothing beside the mark, slur over nothing, misrepresent nothing. There are certain things revealed to me by the ancient sea-god who is unerring; of these I will not hide or conceal a word. The old god said he had seen Odysseus in much distress. This was upon a certain island and in the house of the nymph Calypso; she is keeping him with her there perforce and thwarting return to his own country. He has no ships and oars and crew to take him over the wide expanse of ocean." Such were the words of Menelaus. With thus much accomplished, I turned homeward. The gods gave me a following wind and quickly brought me to my own country.'

So spoke the prince, and the queen's heart was moved within her. Then Theoclymenus also spoke : 'Revered wife of Laertes' son : Menelaus has no certain knowledge, but I have a word which I bid you heed. I will give you a truthful prophecy, hiding nothing. I call to witness Zeus among gods, and after him this table of hospitality to which I have come – in solemn truth, Odysseus is in his own land already, sitting or walking as it may be, acquainting himself with these deeds of iniquity and sowing the seeds of evil for all the suitors; so sure was the omen I described as I sat on the benched vessel; I proclaimed it aloud to Telemachus.'

Wise Penelope answered him : 'Ah, my guest, if only your words might be fulfilled ! Then you would learn soon enough what friendship and multiplied gifts from me were worth; anyone then who came your way would call you a happy man.'

Such were the words that passed between them. Meanwhile, on the levelled ground outside the palace, the suitors in all their arrogance were still at their sports, throwing quoits and javelins. But when the time for their meal came on – when the flocks with their accustomed herdsmen returned from their pastures here and there – then Medon spoke; it was he who among all the pages was most favoured by the suitors and used to be present at their meals :

'Young chieftains, now that you all have enjoyed your sport, come into the palace and let us prepare our meal; it is no bad thing to dine betimes.'

So said Medon; they stood up accordingly and walked towards the house. Having entered, they laid their cloaks aside on the seats and chairs, then began to slaughter fat hogs and a cow from the herd in preparation for the meal.

Meanwhile Odysseus and the swineherd were about to make their way from the steading to the town. The master herdsman was first to speak: 'Friend, I know you are bent on going townwards this very day, just as my master wished – but for that, I would rather have left you there to protect the farm. Nevertheless, I reverence him, and have fears of being upbraided later – a master's rebukes are hard to bear. So let us set out now; the best part of the day is over; it will soon be nightfall, and colder still.'

Subtle Odysseus answered him: 'I take your meaning well enough, and need no more telling. Let us be off, then; from now on you must be my leader all the way. And if you have a stick cut ready, let me have it to lean on, since you tell me the road is very slippery.'

And with these words he slung across his shoulders a shabby and very tattered wallet, with a strap to hang it by, and Eumaeus gave him a staff to his liking. So off they set, leaving the herdsmen and dogs behind to protect the steading; and here was Eumaeus, guiding his master towards the town in the shape of an old, wretched beggar, stooping over a stick and with dismal rags about his body. The two walked on over the rugged path till they neared the city and came to the fountain of fashioned stone from whose lovely streamlet those of the town drew their water. Ithacus had built it, with Neritus and Polyctor; encircling it was a group of black poplars that throve on the moist ground; overhead, cool water ran down from the rock; above the fountain the nymphs had an altar built to them, and passers-by always made offerings there.

At this spot the two crossed the path of Melanthius son of Dolius; he was driving goats, the choicest of all the herds, to provide the suitors' meal, and he had two herdsmen with him. When he saw the others he turned upon them with jeering words, and with monstrous arrogance burst out, rousing the anger of Odysseus: ' "A knave in front and a knave behind" – here we have it with a vengeance, and heaven, as always, brings like to like. Miserable swineherd, where are you taking this filthy creature, this loathsome beggar, this scavenger of banquets? He will be a lounger at many men's doors, rubbing his back against the posts, seeking for scraps, not swords or cauldrons. If you gave him to me to guard the farmstead, sweep out the pens and take green fodder to the young goats, then he might drink whey and round out his thighs. But no – he has learned bad ways and will never keep at any work; instead, he means to go cringing and begging about the country to fill his never-sated belly. But there is one thing I can tell you – one thing that will prove true; if he enters the palace of Lord Odysseus, a volley of stools from chieftains' hands will thump him about the head and ribs as he runs the gauntlet through the hall.'

So he taunted the beggar; and as he passed him – such was his folly – he kicked him on the hip, but without thrusting him from the path. Odysseus remained there firm enough; only he wondered whether to leap upon the fellow and dash the life out of him with his cudgel or whether to lift him by the middle and batter his head against the ground. Nevertheless he mastered himself and checked his impulse; but the swineherd looked Melanthius full in the face and called down a curse upon him. Lifting his hands he prayed aloud: 'Nymphs of the fountain, daughters of Zeus, if ever upon your altars Odysseus has made burnt-offerings from his young sheep and goats and covered the thigh-bones with rich fat, I beg you to grant this wish of mine: May that man return, with a god for guide.[1] And then, Melanthius, he would make short work of the airs and graces you flaunt here now as you go strutting about the town while your careless underlings let your beasts go to rack and ruin.'

The goatherd Melanthius said in answer: 'Hear the fellow! What words to come from a vicious cur! One day I will ship him off to some place far away from Ithaca, and there he might fetch me a handsome price. If only I knew that this very day Telemachus would be struck in his hall by one of Apollo's silver arrows, or would be slaughtered by the suitors, as certainly as I know that for Odysseus the day of return has been blotted out in some far country!'

1. 'Ah! grant me my request, that He may come,
   Escorted by his better Angel, Home.' OGILBY

With these words he left the others to follow slowly while he himself strode quickly on to his master's palace. He entered at once and took his seat among the suitors, facing Eurymachus, his great patron. The servants put his portion of meat before him, and the trusted housekeeper brought him his bread.

Odysseus and the swineherd walked on meanwhile, then halted near enough to the house to catch the sound of the hollow lyre, for Phemius was preluding his song. Odysseus seized the swineherd's hand. 'Eumaeus,' he said, 'this noble house is surely Odysseus' own; one could tell it at once among a hundred. Each part of it opens out from another, the courtyard has been made complete with a corniced wall, and then there are double doors for protection; no man alive could hope to storm it. Also I take it that many hands are making ready a banquet there – a savoury smell floats about it and I hear the ringing of the lyre, which the gods have made the companion to a feast.'

Eumaeus the swineherd answered him: 'To guess as much was easy for one as shrewd as you. But now let us plan what is to follow. Either you should go into the palace first and enter the throng of suitors while I stay here; or if you wish, you might remain here yourself while I go first; but in that case do not linger long, or someone may see you there outside and pelt you or assault you: I warn you, have a care.'

Patient Odysseus replied to him: 'I take your meaning well enough; I do understand; I need no more telling. Well, you shall go first and I will stay behind. I am no stranger to blows and peltings. I have a hardy temper; I have suffered much from waves and wars, and now let this trial join the rest. A man cannot put away the cravings of the accursed belly, which brings so much trouble into life and makes us rig ships to cross the seas and harry our enemies.'

While these words were passing between them, a dog that was lying there lifted his head and ears. This was Argos, whom long ago Odysseus himself had brought up at home but had little pleasure in, because all too soon he had departed to sacred Ilium. In days gone by, the younger men had taken him with them to hunt wild goats and deer and hares; but now, with his master gone, he lay unwanted on the deep pile of dung from the mules and cattle that was waiting there in front of the doors till the king's servants should carry it away to fatten the wide estates; on this the dog Argos lay, full of vermin.[1] But now, as he saw Odysseus close by and knew him, he wagged his tail and dropped his ears, though he could not now move nearer to his master. Then Odysseus glanced aside, wiped away a tear unheeded by Eumaeus, and hastened to put a question to him: 'Eumaeus, surely this is a strange thing, a dog like this lying on a dunghill. He is handsome to look at; I wonder if he had speed to match his looks. Or was he only one of those dogs whose masters pamper them at table and keep them for show alone?'

Eumaeus the swineherd answered him: 'The plain truth is that this dog's master was one who has died far from his home. If in looks and power Argos could be again such as Odysseus left him when he set out for Troy, then you would not be slow to wonder when you saw what strength and speed he had. There was no beast in any nook of the bushy woodland that could escape him when he pursued. How sure he was in tracking the prey! But now his plight is pitiable; his master has perished far from his own land, and the women care nothing and will not tend him. When masters are not there to command, serfs lack zeal to do as they should, for Zeus the Thunderer takes half the virtue away from a man when once the day of bondage has come on him.'

So saying, he went through the palace entrance and down the hall to the haughty suitors. As for Argos, the fate of dark death fell on him suddenly when in this twentieth year he had once again set eyes upon Odysseus.

Telemachus was the first to see the swineherd as he came walking down the hall, and at once he beckoned to him invitingly. Eumaeus looked round and took a stool placed by the spot where the carver sat portioning out meat for the suitors eating in the hall. He carried it over and set it down facing Telemachus' own table. Then he sat down himself, and a page put a portion of meat in front of him and took out bread from the basket for him.

Close behind him, Odysseus also entered the palace in the shape

1. 'Till then in ev'ry sylvan chace renown'd,
   With *Argus, Argus,* rung the woods around;
   With him the youth pursu'd the goat or fawn,
   Or trac'd the mazy leveret o'er the lawn.
   Now left to man's ingratitude he lay,
   Un-hous'd, neglected, in the publick way;
   And where on heaps the rich manure was spread,
   Obscene with reptiles, took his sordid bed.' POPE

of an old, wretched beggar, stooping over a stick and with dismal
rags about his body. He sat down on the ashwood threshold inside
the doorway, leaning against the cypress pillar which a master
carpenter long ago had smoothed deftly and trued to the line.
Telemachus called the swineherd over, took a whole loaf from
the handsome basket and as much meat as his hands could hold.
'Take this,' he said, 'to give to the stranger, and tell him to go to
the suitors one by one and beg from them all; bashfulness is no
good companion for one in need.'

Such were his words. When Eumaeus heard them he went and
stood near Odysseus and swiftly gave the message: 'Stranger,
Telemachus sends you this and tells you to go to the suitors one
by one and beg from them all. He says that bashfulness does not
sit well on beggars.'

Subtle Odysseus said in answer: 'Lord Zeus, grant that Tele-
machus may be blest among men; may his heart's desires be all
fulfilled.'

With these words he took the food in both hands, placed it
there in front of him at his feet, on his shabby wallet, and began
his meal to the bard's singing; when his meal was done and the
music in the hall was over, a hubbub of talk arose among the
suitors. Then Athene came and stood near Odysseus, bidding him
gather crusts from the suitors and learn which were righteous
and which unrighteous, though after all it would never be that
she warded off doom from any of them. So he went to beg from
each in turn, moving from left to right, stretching out his hand
here and there and everywhere, as if to the manner born. They
gave him something in compassion; they were puzzled too, and
asked one another who he was and where he came from. Then
Melanthius the goatherd spoke among them: 'You suitors of our
great queen, hear what I have to tell you about this stranger. I
have seen him before – the swineherd was leading him this way;
but as for himself, I have no clear knowledge who he may claim
to be.'

So he spoke, and Antinous turned upon the swineherd;
'Infamous swineherd, why have you brought this man to town?
Have we not vagrants enough besides, loathsome beggars,
scavengers of our banquets? Are you not content to have men
gathering here already to devour your master's substance? Must
you invite this fellow too?'

Eumaeus the swineherd answered him: 'High-born you may be, Antinous, but the words you speak do you no honour. No man of his own accord goes out to bring in a stranger from elsewhere, unless that stranger be master of some craft, a prophet or one who cures diseases, a worker in wood, or again an inspired bard, delighting men with his song. The wide world over, men such as these are welcome guests. But a beggar to eat up what one has – who would invite such a guest as that? But you, Antinous, are always harshest of all the suitors to anyone of Odysseus' household – to me above all. Still, I pay little heed to that, as long as the queen is with us still and is in the palace, and Prince Telemachus is here also.'

Thoughtful Telemachus interposed: 'Enough, Eumaeus! Do not answer him at such length. It is always the way with Antinous to provoke a man with his abuse and urge on others to do likewise.' Then to Antinous he said, and the words came winging from his lips: 'How you take thought for me, Antinous! Father with son could be no kinder. And now you would have me drive this stranger out of the hall with imperious words. Heaven forbid I should do such a thing! Take what you please and give it to him. I do not grudge you the gift, I urge it, and as for that, you need have no scruples about my mother or anyone else. But no – the thoughts in your heart are not thoughts of thrift. It is eating, not giving, you have in mind – it is yourself, not others.'

Antinous answered him in turn: 'Telemachus, passionate and proud-spoken, what words are these? If every suitor gave him as much as I, this house would be quit of him for three months.' And with this he grasped and showed from beneath his table the stool on which he rested his feet in the hours of banqueting.

The other suitors all gave Odysseus something, filling his wallet with bread and meat; and indeed he seemed likely in a moment to be back again at the hall threshold after testing unharmed the mood of the Achaeans. But then he paused in front of Antinous and addressed him: 'Give me something, friend; you seem to me not the meanest of the Achaeans but the noblest – a kinglike man. In the way of food, then, you ought to give me more than the rest – I would sing your praises everywhere. I too had once a sumptuous house of my own; I was rich, and in those days I often made gifts to the wanderer, whatever he and his needs might be. I had servants without number then, and plenty of all those things that make life easy and make men count one as fortunate. But the son of Cronos – such was his will – shattered all this when he tempted me to sail to Egypt with roving pirates; the voyage was long, and it meant my ruin. I anchored my curving ships in the Nile. Then I gave orders to my comrades; most, I said, were to stay by the ships and guard them; a few were to climb to higher ground and look out from there.

'But the crews yielded to recklessness; giving way to impulse, they began to plunder the rich farmlands of the Egyptians, to carry away the women and little children and kill the men. The clamour reached the city at once, and the townsmen when they heard this uproar came out at dawn and filled the whole plain with men on foot and chariot-fighters and flashing bronze. Zeus the Thunderer hurled vile panic upon my comrades, and none of them dared to stand his ground, since on every side peril hedged them in. Many of us the Egyptians killed with the keen bronze, others they took inland alive to labour for them in slavery. As for me, when a certain stranger came their way they gave me to him to take to Cyprus – this was the son of Iasus, Dmetor, then ruling Cyprus imperiously. Thence I have come here, as you see, in much distress.'

Antinous cried out in answer: 'What malicious god has sent this plague here to spoil our feast? Stand away towards the middle yonder, take yourself away from my table, or the Egypt and Cyprus you come to next may be less to your liking than the last. You are simply a bold, brazen beggar; you stand by each one of us in turn, and with no second thoughts they all give something, with no scruple and no remorse at lavishing things that are not their own, because each man has plenty by him.'

Odysseus drew back and said to him: 'So you have no handsome thoughts to go with your handsome looks; a pity! You would grudge a retainer of your own a pinch of salt from your own store – you who sit here at another's table and have not the grace to break one piece of the bread away and give it to me, though there is plenty by you.'

So he spoke. Antinous was beside himself, eyed him grimly and answered swiftly: 'Insults too? Then I fear that when you quit this hall it will be in no enviable fashion.'

And with these words he seized the stool and hurled it at Odysseus; it struck him under the right shoulder, full in the back.

Odysseus did not reel at the blow, he stood there still, firm as a rock; he only shook his head silently as he brooded evil in his heart. He walked back to the threshold, seated himself and put the full wallet down. Then he said for them all to hear: 'Listen, you suitors of the great queen, and let me say what my heart within me bids. There is no distress and no resentment in a man's mind when he gets a blow in a fight for his possessions – for cattle, it may be, or white sheep; but the blow that Antinous gave me then was all because of my wretched belly, the accursed thing that brings so many disasters on mankind. But if there are gods to care for beggars, if there are furies to avenge them, then before Antinous weds a wife may death inescapably come upon him!'

Antinous spoke to him once more: 'Stranger, sit quietly there and eat, or take yourself off elsewhere; otherwise, after such words as those, these youths may drag you by hand or foot the length of the hall till all the skin is stripped off from you.'

So he spoke, but the rest of them took it very ill, and one or other of these young gallants uttered such words as these: 'Antinous, it was an ugly thing to assault this unhappy beggar so; you will rue it if this proves to be some god from heaven. Gods often take upon themselves the likeness of strangers from far countries; they assume this shape and that, wander about our towns and observe both outrage and righteous dealing among mankind.'

Thus did the suitors warn Antinous, but he paid no heed to what they said. As for Telemachus, he left his distress for the sufferer to swell within his breast without letting a tear fall from his eyes; he only shook his head silently as he brooded evil in his heart.

When wise Penelope was told how the stranger had been struck in the hall, she said, with her serving-women round her: 'May you, the striker, yourself be struck by Apollo, master of the bow!' And her housekeeper Eurynome: 'If only all your prayers were granted! Then none of these men would live to see Dawn in her flowered robe tomorrow.'

Penelope answered: 'Nurse, they are hateful, all of them, because all of them are plotters of mischief. But Antinous is the worst – like some black spirit of destruction. An unhappy stranger is going to and fro in the house, asking them for alms because destitution urges him. The others gave him his fill of food, but

Antinous hurled his stool at him and struck him under the right shoulder.'

So she spoke to her serving-women, sitting in her room while Odysseus was finishing his meal. Then she sent for the swineherd and said to him: 'My good Eumaeus, go and ask that stranger to come to me. I wish to give him a word of welcome and ask him if he has gathered tidings of Odysseus or, it may be, has set eyes on him; he looks like one who has wandered far.'

Eumaeus answered: 'Queen, how I wish the Achaeans would be silent! Such are the tales the stranger tells, he would steal your heart away. For three nights and three days I had him as guest in my own cottage because he came first to me after escaping from a ship; but even so he did not finish the story of his sorrows. It was just as when one keeps gazing at a bard whom the gods have taught to give joy to mortals with his song, and whenever he begins to sing, men gladly would listen to him for ever – so did this man enchant my ears as he sat beside me in the steading. He calls Odysseus a guest-friend of his father's and says that he himself had his home in Crete, where the race of Minos is. From there he has journeyed here amid great misfortune, driven on from place to place; and he maintains he has heard of Odysseus not far away, in the fertile land of the Thesprotians – alive, and bringing much treasure home.'

Wise Penelope said in answer: 'Go and call him here and let him speak to me face to face. Let the others sit outside or down in the hall and disport themselves, since they are in merry mood. Their own goods, the food and sweet wine, are stored at home untouched by anyone but their servants. Meanwhile they haunt our palace day in, day out; they slaughter our sheep and oxen and fatted goats; they make merry here, they selfishly drink the glowing wine, and thus abundance of things is wasted. All this is because there is no man left with the mettle of Odysseus to ward off ruin from the house. If Odysseus returned to his own country, he with his son would soon requite the outrages of these men.'

At the queen's last words Telemachus sneezed aloud, and the noise went thundering round the hall. Penelope laughed. With rapid words she addressed Eumaeus: 'Go now, and ask that stranger to speak to me face to face. Did you not see how my son sneezed as I finished then? So death for the suitors may still not be unachieved – for all of them, with not one left to escape death and doom. Now one word more, which I bid you keep in mind. If I see that the man himself speaks nothing but the truth, I will give him a cloak and tunic to clothe him handsomely.'

Such were her words; the swineherd, hearing them, made his way over to Odysseus, stood beside him and swiftly said: 'Aged friend, you are summoned now by the prince's mother, wise Penelope; her spirit bids her, despite her sorrow, to question you on her husband a little. And if she sees you speak nothing but the truth, she will clothe you with a cloak and tunic, gifts that you need more than anything; as for food, by begging for it about the country you will get enough to fill your belly; whoever wishes will give you something.'

Patient Odysseus answered him: 'Eumaeus, I am ready enough to tell the queen nothing but truth about her husband, because I have sure knowledge of him, and he and I have borne the same misery. But I shrink from the ruthless crowd of suitors, whose violence and pride tower up to the iron heavens. Just now, as you know, I was moving through the hall without having done harm to anyone; but when that man threw the stool at me and dealt me that cruel blow, Telemachus did not intervene, nor did any other. And so I would have you ask Penelope, eager though she may be, to wait in the hall till after sunset. Let her question me then on her husband's homecoming and give me a seat near the fire, because the clothes that I have are pitiful – you know that yourself, since you were the first whose help I begged for.'

Such were his words, and the swineherd on hearing them went back. As he crossed her threshold the queen said: 'Have you not brought the beggar, then? What is he at? Is he over-afraid of someone, or does something else make him backward here? Backwardness does not become a beggar.'

Eumaeus the swineherd answered her: 'What the man says is right enough – he thinks as anyone else would think who wished to be unmolested by these swaggerers. He asks you to wait until after sunset. And for yourself it is better, queen, to speak with the stranger then alone and to listen to his words.'

Thoughtful Penelope replied: 'The stranger has his wits about him; what he fears is what might come to pass. I doubt if anywhere in the world there are men so arrogant as these are, and so conscienceless in their designs.'

So she spoke, and the swineherd, having made clear his message, again joined the assembled suitors. Then he whispered rapid words to Telemachus – heads together, so as not to be overheard: 'Dear master, now I must go away; I must see to the swine and everything there – a source of living for both of us. Things here must be your concern. Look to yourself in the first place. Set your wits to work to escape danger, because many of these Achaeans are cherishing thoughts of evil, though I hope that Zeus may destroy them utterly before they are the ruin of us.'

Thoughtful Telemachus answered him: 'Old friend, it shall all be as you say; you have been here a whole afternoon, and now you must go home. Come back early tomorrow morning and bring some fine beasts for slaughter; the rest is with me and the Deathless Ones.'

These were his words. Eumaeus sat down again on his polished stool, had his fill of both meat and drink, then took his way back to tend the swine. He left the palace and its enclosures; the banqueters were still there inside, but finding their pleasure now in dance and in song, because the day had drawn on towards evening.

BOOK XVIII

THE BEGGAR PRAISED AND MOCKED

THEN there appeared a public beggar, one who on that errand haunted the town of Ithaca, known all too well for his greedy belly and his incessant eating and drinking. He had no strength or vigour, though to look at him he was brawny enough. Arnaeus was this man's true name – his mother had given it him at his birth – but all the young men called him Irus because he went on messages to and fro when anyone gave him the commission. This was the man who now appeared, hoping to drive Odysseus from his own house and accosting him roughly with these words: 'Get out from the doorway, you old man there, or soon you will be dragged out by the leg. Can you not see that every man here is winking at me, urging me to haul you away, though I have my scruples too? Up with you now, or in a moment there will be blows, not words, between us.'

With a grim glance Odysseus said to him: 'Misguided man, I am doing no harm and speaking no harm to you. If anyone here picks up and gives you a handsome portion, I shall not resent it. This entrance will be wide enough for the two of us, and you have no call to grudge me what is not yours. You are a vagrant, are you not? I am a vagrant too; and it is the gods, I take it, who give men their portion of good things. But as for challenging me to blows – do not go too far and rouse my anger or – old as I am – I may dabble your chest and lips with blood; that would leave me a quieter life tomorrow, since I do not think you would come again to the house of Laertes' son Odysseus.'

The vagrant Irus replied in anger: 'Hark how glibly the filthy creature talks, like some old hag as she tends the furnace! Well, I can soon find a way to punish him; I will batter him with both my fists and knock every tooth of his out of his jaw on to the ground like a sow's teeth in a wrecked cornfield.[1] Come, tuck your clothes up round you now, and let these lords be witnesses of the

---

1. A law in Cyprus allowed the farmer to pull out the teeth of any swine found wrecking his crops. Ogilby, missing the meaning somewhat, translates:

'I'll on your mouldy Chops your Passport sign,
And drive your Teeth out, as from Corn the Swine.'

battle too. But dare you fight with a younger man?'

Thus fervently did the two of them fan each other's rage on the polished threshold in front of the lofty doors. Lord Antinous heard their wrangling; he laughed out gleefully and said to all the suitors: 'Friends, never before has such good sport come our way as the god has brought to the palace now. That stranger and Irus are challenging each other to fight. Quick, let us make a match between them.'

So he spoke. They all leapt, laughing, up from their seats, and gathered round the two ragged beggars. Then Eupeithes' son went on to say: 'Noble suitors, listen: there is something else I would put to you. Here at the fire we have some goats' paunches roasting; we stuffed them with blood and fat and set them aside to eat at supper. Well then, whichever of these two men gets the better in the fight, let him stand up boldly and take his choice among all these paunches; and afterwards he shall always eat with us, and we will allow no other vagrant to come inside among us and beg.'

The words of Antinous pleased them all. But Odysseus now addressed them craftily. 'Friends, an old man worn down by troubles cannot match himself with a younger man; nevertheless my villainous belly tempts me on to be thumped and mauled. But first you must join in swearing a solemn oath for me, so that no one, wishing to favour Irus, may presume to strike me with heavy hand and by that foul blow make me this fellow's prey.'

At this request they all took the oath he asked of them. When they had done this duly, Prince Telemachus spoke in his turn among them: 'Stranger, if your own heart and courage urge you on to defy this man, then you need fear none of the suitors either, because anyone who strikes you will have many others to contend with. I am your host, and here are two princes to support me, Antinous and Eurymachus, men of good judgement both of them.'

The prince's words were acceptable to them all. Then Odysseus tucked his rags up about his loins and let his fine sturdy thighs be seen; his broad shoulders were seen too, and his chest and stout arms; Athene moreover drew near the king and filled out his limbs. The suitors were utterly astonished, and one would look at another and say: 'Irus will be no Irus soon; he will get the punishment he invited, to judge by the solid thighs this old man brings out from beneath his rags.'

So they spoke, and the heart of Irus was sadly troubled – to no avail, for the servants tucked the clothes up round him and dragged him forward all terrified, with the flesh quivering upon his limbs. Then Antinous uttered biting words: 'Lout that you are, what right have you – what right could you ever have – to be alive at all, if you eye this man with fear and trembling, an old man worn down by all the troubles that have beset him? I will tell you plainly a thing that will certainly come true. If this man masters and overcomes you, I will put you on shipboard and send you off to King Echetus[1] on the mainland. He is savage to any and every man, and as for you, he will shear away your nose and ears with the ruthless bronze, tear out your parts and throw them raw to the dogs to batten on.'

At these words of his a worse fit than ever ran shivering across the limbs of Irus. But others dragged him into the ring, and both of the fighters raised their fists. Then Odysseus wondered whether to give him such a blow that the life would leave him there as he fell, or to give him a more merciful one and only stretch him upon the floor. As he asked himself this, the more merciful thing seemed the better, and then the suitors would not suspect him. And now the pair drew themselves up; Irus struck Odysseus' right shoulder, but Odysseus struck his challenger's neck below the ear, crushing the bones inside; a stream of blood gushed through Irus' mouth, and with a shriek he fell in the dust, grinding his teeth and lashing the ground with his feet. The noble suitors threw up their hands and died of laughter. Odysseus seized the man by the leg and began to drag him through the forecourt till he reached the yard and the doors of the portico; then he propped him against the courtyard fence, put his stick in his hands and briefly said: 'Now sit there to scare dogs and swine away, and do not in your own servile station try to play the master to strangers and to beggars, or worse than this may come to you yet.'

And with these words he again slung across his shoulders the shabby and very tattered wallet with the cord to hang it by, then went back to the entrance and there sat down. The suitors went back as well, laughing gleefully, and hailed him with words of

---

1. Echetus is probably an invented name, with word-play offering the sense 'Hold him!' But some ancient scholars believed in a historical tyrant in Sicily or Epirus. Hobbes has: 'We'll send him to King Takim in Epire.'

commendation: 'Stranger, may Zeus and the other immortal gods grant your wishes and give you your heart's desire. You have rid the land of the comings and goings of that insatiable vagabond; we will soon despatch him to the mainland to face that savage King Echetus.'

So they spoke, and Odysseus rejoiced at these words of omen. Then Antinous brought him a big goat's paunch all stuffed with fat and blood, and Amphinomus took two loaves from the basket and put them in front of him, then drank to him from his golden cup and said: 'Venerable stranger, I wish you well. May happiness come to you hereafter, since here and now you have many sorrows to distress you.'

Odysseus answered: 'Amphinomus, you seem to me to be very wise; such was your father too – I used to hear high praise of him, how Nisus of Dulichium was as virtuous as he was prosperous. You are his son, they tell me, and you have all the marks of courtesy. There is something therefore I wish to say to you; listen, and gather it up in your heart. Of all things that breathe and move on earth, earth mothers nothing more frail than man. As long as the gods grant him prosperity, as long as his limbs are lithe, he thinks he will suffer no misfortune in times to come; but when instead the Blessed Ones send him sorrow, he bears these also with endurance, because he must. The father of gods and men makes one day unlike another day, and earthlings change their thoughts on life in accord with this. Even I myself seemed once marked out as a prosperous man, and I did many reckless deeds to sate my desire for power and mastery, putting great faith in my father and my brothers. And so I would have no man be lawless; rather let each accept unquestioningly whatsoever gifts the gods may grant him. Now here before me I see the suitors plotting their deeds of recklessness, wasting the wealth, affronting the wife of one who now will not remain long away from his kindred and his country; of that I am sure; indeed he is very near already. As for yourself, I hope some god may let you steal home from here; I hope you will never face that man when he comes back to his own country, because I think that once he is under this roof again, the suitors and he will not be parted without the spilling of blood.'

So he spoke, and made his libation, and drank the honey-sweet wine, then put the cup back again into this prince's hands. Amphinomus went back through the hall, heavy-hearted and shaking his head, for indeed his thoughts foreboded evil. Yet even so he did not escape from doom; over this man also Athene had cast her net, designing him to find death by violence from the hands and spear of Telemachus. And now he sat down once again in the seat that he had risen from.[1]

But now the goddess of gleaming eyes put it into the queen's mind to show herself before the suitors and so to open their hearts more widely and win more esteem from son and husband. Penelope therefore forced a laugh and said to her aged nurse: 'Eurynome, I am eager now, though I never was before, to show myself before the suitors whom I detest; moreover I wish to give Telemachus a warning that may be of service to him, not to mix so much with these overweening men; they speak him fair, but are plotting future mischief.'

Eurynome said to her in turn: 'Yes, my child, all that you say is well said. Go then and give your son the message without concealment, but before that you should wash yourself and anoint your cheeks. Do not go down with tear-stained face; there is nothing gained by perpetual mourning. And your son too is to be considered. You used to implore the gods beyond everything to let you live on long enough to see him with a beard; and you see him so now.'

Wise Penelope answered her: 'Eurynome, do not in your affection try to coax me to wash myself and anoint myself with unguents. What beauty I had has departed from me – the gods of Olympus saw to that – ever since the day when Odysseus sailed with his hollow ships. But tell Autonoe and Hippodameia to come and stand by me in the hall; I will not join the suitors alone; I shrink from that.'

So she spoke, and the old woman went through the hall to tell the maids and to bid them come.

And then the goddess of gleaming eyes turned her mind to another stratagem. She poured sweet sleep over the daughter of Icarius. Penelope lay back on the couch she was resting on, and all her limbs were relaxed in slumber. The goddess meanwhile began giving her more than earthly gifts to make the suitors astonished at her. First of all she cleansed the lovely features with the

1. The episode following (ll. 158–303) is rejected by many scholars as an interpolation.

fragrant balm that Cytherea herself puts on when she enters the
bewitching circle of dancing Graces, and with this she made her
skin more white than ivory newly sawn; then she gave her an
ampler stature and ampler presence. This task accomplished, the
goddess left her; and now from the hall the white-armed maids
came chattering in, and the soothing slumber left Penelope. She
passed her hand over her cheeks and said: 'How gentle a sleep
this was that wrapped me round amid all my sorrows! Would
that now, at this very moment, Artemis the chaste would grant
me a death as gentle! Then I need no longer fret life away with
an aching heart, recalling vainly all the great gifts my husband
had, he who was peerless among Achaeans.'

And with these words she began to descend from the glittering
upper room, not unescorted but with the two maids beside her.
When the great queen had reached the suitors, she halted beside
the pillar that bore the massy roof, her bright head-scarf drawn
over her cheeks; her faithful women took their places each side
of her. As for the men, their limbs failed them where they stood;
their hearts were transported with desire, and they voiced a prayer,
every one of them, to share her bed and lie beside her. Then she
spoke to her dear son Telemachus: 'Your wit and discernment are
not what they once were, Telemachus. As a child you were more
shrewd than this. But now when you are a man full-grown – when
a stranger seeing you tall and handsome might think you the son
of some highly-favoured man – now your wit and discernment
seem to fail you. Consider what came to pass in this hall just now
– how you let that stranger be thus insulted. What if such a
guest sitting peaceably in our halls came to grave harm through
brutal handling? It would mean disgrace and dishonour for you
in all men's eyes.'

Thoughtful Telemachus answered her: 'Mother, I do not resent
your indignation, yet I do take note and pay heed to things – the
good and the bad as well; before, I was still a child. But I cannot
contrive everything wisely, because here on each side of me I find
these men with their evil schemes. They dismay me, and I have no
helpers. Yet, after all, the fight between Irus and the stranger did
not go as the suitors wished, and the stranger proved the better
man. In the name of Zeus and Athene and Apollo, I only wish
that at this instant the suitors here, whether out in the courtyard

or in the hall, had such battered bodies and rocking heads and fainting limbs as Irus there at the courtyard gates. He sits over yonder, with head going to and fro like a drunken man's; he can neither stand upright on his feet nor make his way home where he ought to go; his limbs have crumbled.'

Such were the words that passed between them. Then Eurymachus addressed the queen: 'Wise Penelope, daughter of Icarius, if all the suitors who dwell in Iasian Argos could see you thus, more suitors yet would feast in your halls tomorrow, because you surpass all other women in stately stature, in outward beauty, in the steady rightness of your mind.'

Penelope answered: 'Eurymachus, the immortal gods bereft me of beauty and stately presence and everything that was worth praise in me when the Argives went up to Ilium and Odysseus my husband went up with them. If he came back to have the care of this life of mine, then indeed the repute I had would be nobler and more widely spread. As it is, I live in misery – such a multitude of sorrows the god has unleashed against me. When my husband forsook his own country, he caught my right wrist and said to me: "Dear wife, it is too much to hope that the greaved Achaeans, one and all, will return from Troy unscathed. Men say that the Trojans are warriors too, hurling javelins, shooting arrows, mounting the rapid chariots that soonest end the bitter debate of inexorable war; so I am not sure if the god will restore me to my domain or if I shall meet my end at Troy. Everything here must be your concern. Keep in mind my father and mother in this place no less than you do now, or keep them in mind more perhaps when I am far from home. But when you see this son of ours grown to bearded manhood, then leave your own palace and marry whom you will." So he spoke then, and now it is all being brought to pass. There will come a night when a hated marriage will claim a poor wretched woman whom Zeus has robbed of all happiness.

'Meanwhile there is something else that chafes me, something that much offends my spirit. Your ways with me are not the time-honoured ways of suitors when in rivalry with each other they set their minds on courting a lady of noble birth and of wealthy parentage. The custom is that they bring their own oxen, their own fat sheep, to make a banquet for friends and kin of the hoped-for bride. They give her handsome presents as well; they do not devour another's goods without offering anything in return.'

Such were her words, and patient Odysseus saw with glee how she lured them to make presents to her,[1] stealing their souls with persuasive words though her heart meanwhile was set elsewhere.

Eupeithes' son Antinous answered her: 'Wise Penelope, daughter of Icarius – as for presents, whatever suitor may choose to bring them to you, it is right that you should take them, and none but a churl would grudge you a gift. Nevertheless, we will not return to our own estates nor go elsewhere until you have wedded whichever suitor appears the best.'

So spoke Antinous, and the rest approved. Then each of them sent off an attendant to bring back gifts. For Antinous there was brought a big and lovely embroidered robe with twelve gold clasps fitting into curved sheaths; for Eurymachus a chain of gold subtly interspersed with amber beads and flashing like the sunlight; for Eurydamas a pair of ear-rings with triple clusters, glistening daintily. From the house of Lord Peisander, Polyctor's son, a page brought a treasure of a necklace; and among the suitors one offered this lovely gift and another that. Then the great queen went up to her room above, and with her walked her waiting-women, carrying the gorgeous gifts.

Then the suitors turned to dancing and to delightful song, taking their pleasure thus and awaiting the fall of evening. When evening fell on their pleasure and it was dark, they hastened to set three cressets up in the hall, and on these they put dry wood, seasoned long ago but freshly split with the axe; here and there between them they put pinewood slips, and the fires were tended in due order by the serving-maids of King Odysseus. But Odysseus himself said to them: 'Servants of a long-absent lord, go to the room where the queen your mistress is; spin your wool or card it beside her, and cheer her by sitting there. I myself will keep up the blaze for all the suitors. Even if they choose to wait for Dawn in her flowery robe, they shall still not have the better of me; nothing can tire me out.'

At these words of his the serving-maids laughed, and glanced at one another. One of them mocked him insultingly. This was

1. 'Divine Ulysses much rejoyc't to heare
   His Queene thus fish for gifts . . .' CHAPMAN

the lovely-cheeked Melantho. Dolius was her father, but Pene-
lope had brought her up, cherishing her like her own daughter
and giving her toys for her delight. Yet despite all this the girl's
heart was without compassion for Penelope, and she was mistress
and bedfellow to Eurymachus. She it was who insulted Odysseus
now: 'Miserable stranger, you must have had your wits battered
out of you if you will not go to the forge to sleep, or to some other
meeting-place for idlers – if instead of that you stay on to chat-
ter here. Have you quite forgotten yourself because you worsted
that vagrant Irus? Take care, or a better man than Irus may
challenge you, batter your skull with sturdy fists and send you
out from the palace here streaming blood all over.'

With a grim glance Odysseus answered: 'If that is your lan-
guage, shameless hussy, I will go this instant and tell Telemachus;
he will hack you to pieces then and there.'

With these words he scared the women away. They rushed
down the hall, the limbs of each of them quivering with fright,
because they were sure he spoke in earnest. Then he took his
stand by the flaming cressets, tending the lights and keeping his
eyes on them all; but his thoughts were elsewhere, shaping de-
signs that were not to be left unaccomplished.

But Athene would not let the suitors refrain from new and
biting insult; she meant indignation to sink more deeply still
into the heart of Laertes' son. Eurymachus spoke first to the rest,
mocking Odysseus and rousing laughter among his friends:
'Listen, suitors of the great queen; let me say what the mind
within me bids. Surely some god has sent this man to Odysseus'
house; I mean that the torchlight yonder seems to come from his
own head, which has not a wisp of hair upon it.'

Then he turned his speech to the city-sacker: 'Stranger, sup-
pose I were to hire you, would you be willing to work for me at
the border of my farmlands – picking out stones for the dry walls
and planting tall trees? You need have no doubts of the reward;
I would give you food in all abundance, and garments to clothe
you, and sandals for your feet. But no – you have learned bad
ways and will never keep at any work; instead, you mean to go
cringing and begging about the country to fill your never-sated
belly.'

Odysseus answered: 'Eurymachus, I wish we could have a
working contest upon some farm, at the time of year when spring

has come and the days are lengthening. It would be hay-harvest; in my hands would be a curving scythe, and in yours another; then we could try our powers together, both of us fasting till late dusk, with no lack of grass to mow. Or again there might be oxen to plough with – a pair of the best, big and tawny, both having had their fill of fodder, of like age and like strength, not to be easily worn out, with a four-acre field to work upon, and soil that gave beneath the ploughshare; then you would see if I had it in me to plough a straight furrow from start to finish. Or suppose that on this very day the son of Cronos should stir up battle, no matter whence, and I had a shield and a pair of spears and a bronze helmet to fit my temples, then again you would see me ranging among the foremost fighters, and if you spoke, it would not be to mock this belly of mine. The truth is, you are swollen with pride, you are cruel-hearted, and doubtless you think yourself great and powerful because those you meet are few and worthless. But if Odysseus came back once more to his own land, the doors yonder, wide as they are, would be in a moment too narrow for you as you made through the porch to escape outside.'

So he spoke. Eurymachus could not contain his fury, and with scowling face hurled back his answer: 'Wretch, I will make you suffer for this, you who speak so brazenly and boldly in this great gathering of your betters. Either the wine has befuddled you or your mind is already set that way, luring you on to these wild words.' So speaking, he seized a footstool; but Odysseus, to escape the blow, sank down by the knees of Amphinomus of Dulichium. So instead of him Eurymachus hit the right hand of the wine-bearer; the vessel clattered on to the ground, and the wine-bearer, uttering a groan, fell down upon his back in the dust. Through the shadowy hall the suitors were in an uproar, and one with a glance towards his neighbour would say some such words as these: 'If only this newcomer in his wanderings had died elsewhere before he could reach here! Then he would not have raised this turmoil among us all! As it is, we are quarrelling over beggars, and this fine feast can no longer give us pleasure. What is uppermost now is what is basest.'

But then Prince Telemachus spoke to them: 'Deluded men, you have lost your senses. You have eaten and drunk more than enough, and you show it openly; there must be some god enticing you on. Come – you have dined well; now you may go home if you so desire, though I for my part would not chase any guest away.'

These were his words; the suitors all bit their lips, and looked at Telemachus in amazement, with such authority did he speak. And then Amphinomus addressed them: 'Friends, when the word of reason has been spoken, there is no place left for retort and resentment and contradiction. You must do no violence to this stranger, or to any servant in King Odysseus' palace. Come, let the wine-bearer pour the drops; then let us make libation, return home and there sleep. As for the stranger, let us leave him in Odysseus' halls with Telemachus to care for him; the house he has come to is the prince's.'

The words he spoke were acceptable to them all. So Mulius of Dulichium, the noble attendant of Amphinomus, mixed wine for them all, then stood by them each in turn and poured the draught. They made the libation to the Blessed Ones, then drank the delicious wine. Having made libation and drunk to their hearts' content, they went their way back to rest, each of them in his own house.

THUS King Odysseus was left in the hall, pondering how with Athene's aid he should slay the suitors. He began by speaking to Telemachus: 'Telemachus, we must put away out of reach all the arms and armour that there are here, and when the suitors miss them and question you, you must lead them astray with a soft answer: "I put them away out of the smoke, because they had lost the look they had when Odysseus went to Troy and left them. They have tarnished over, wherever the fumes of the fire have reached them. There is this too, a graver matter — some god has brought it before my mind: I fear that when you are in your cups and have started some quarrel among yourselves, you may wound one another and bring disgrace on your banqueting and wooing; because iron of itself lures a man on."'

So he spoke, and the son accepted his father's words. He summoned Eurycleia his nurse and said: 'Nurse, keep the women in their own quarters till I have put inside the storeroom these arms and armour of my father's — fine things, but uncared for in his absence, and smirched with smoke. I was still a child when he went from here, but now I wish to store them away where the fumes of fire will not reach them.'

His nurse Eurycleia answered: 'Indeed, my child, I hope that at last you will take thought to look to the house and protect all the possessions in it. But then, who will fetch a light and carry it for you? The maids, who else could have given you light, you have just forbidden to come out.'

Thoughtful Telemachus replied: 'This stranger will serve my turn. Even if he comes from a distant country, I will not have a man idling here who gets his daily dole from me.'

So he spoke, and without more words she locked the doors that opened into that noble hall. Odysseus and his son sprang up and began to carry to the storeroom the helmets and studded shields and the spears with shafts of beech, and Pallas Athene walked before them, carrying a lamp of gold and shedding a most lovely light. Telemachus instantly exclaimed: 'Father, I see before me now a thing that is very strange indeed, I mean that the sides of

the hall and the fashioned cross-beams, the main-beams of pine
and the soaring pillars seem to my eyes to be lit as it were from a
flaming fire. Surely some god must be present here, one of those
whose home is wide heaven itself.'

Subtle Odysseus answered him: 'Hush, keep your thoughts
in check, ask nothing. This is the way of the Olympians. But
now you ought to lie down and sleep. I will stay here, to stir
more questioning in the minds of your mother and her maids.
She, with her troubled heart, will ask me about all manner of
things.' So he spoke, and torchlight showed the way to Tele-
machus as he passed through the hall to his own bed, in the
same room where so often he had lain before when welcome
slumber visited him. There he lay down this night also, awaiting
ethereal Dawn.

So King Odysseus was left in the hall, pondering how with
Athene's aid he should slay the suitors. But now Penelope began
to descend from her room, looking like Artemis or like golden
Aphrodite. Her women brought close up to the fire her accus-
tomed chair with its curling inlays of ivory and silver; the artist
who long ago had made it, Icmalius, had added under the seat
itself a footstool dovetailed into the chair, and over this a big
fleece was thrown. Here it was that Penelope now sat down.
The white-armed maids who had come with her from upstairs set
themselves to clear away the tables, the many remains of food,
and the cups from which the imperious suitors had been drink-
ing. They raked out on to the floor the old embers from the
cressets and piled up fresh logs for light and warmth.

And now Melantho renewed her insults to Odysseus:
'Stranger, do you mean to plague us here still, roaming about the
house all night and spying on us women? Wretch, get outside,
and be thankful for the food and drink you have had already. If
not, one of these firebrands aimed at you will send you out quickly
enough.'

With a grim glance Odysseus answered: 'What ails you,
woman? Why do you set upon me so spitefully? Because I have
dirt all over me and am dressed in rags and wander about the
country begging? It is fate that forces this on me; such is the lot
of the vagrant and the beggar. Even I had once a sumptuous
house of my own; I was rich, and in those days I often made gifts
to the wanderer, whatever he and his need might be. I had ser-

vants without number then, and plenty of all those things that make life easy and make men count one as fortunate. But the son of Cronos – such was his will – snatched all these things out of my hand. So beware, woman, lest you in turn should lose one day all the glittering gifts that set you now above other handmaids. Your mistress may spurn you in displeasure, or Odysseus may return; there is still room for hoping that. But if he has perished as you suppose and is never to come home again, there is now – Apollo be praised! – Telemachus to fill his place, old enough not to disregard unseemliness among any women in his house.'

Wise Penelope heard his warning and gave her handmaid a sharp rebuke: 'Bold shameless girl, I am far from blind to your iniquities;[1] they shall be upon your own head. You knew well enough – you heard from my own mouth – that in my extreme distress I was to ask this stranger questions, here in my hall, about my husband.'

So she spoke, then turned to an older maid: 'Eurynome, bring a chair with a fleece thrown over it; then the stranger can stay seated there as he talks or listens to me; there are questions I wish to ask him.'

Hastening to obey the command, the maid fetched a polished chair, put it in place and threw a fleece over it; and here Odysseus now sat down. Wise Penelope then spoke first: 'Stranger, I will begin by questioning you. Who are you? Whence have you come? Where are your city and your parents?'

Subtle Odysseus answered her: 'Queen, no mortal upon the boundless earth could find fault with you, for indeed your fame goes up to wide heaven like that of a virtuous king who fears the gods and who rules a strong well-peopled kingdom. He upholds justice, and under him the dark soil yields wheat and barley; trees are weighed down with fruit, sheep never fail to bear young and the sea abounds in fish – all this because of his righteous rule, so that thanks to him his people prosper. I would ask you therefore here in your house to question me on anything else but not to search out my ancestry and the land from which I come, lest you fill my heart with yet more sorrows as I recall the past. I am a melancholy man, and it would not be right for me to

---

1. *Penelope* observing what they said
   Thus in rough Language rattl'd up her Maid;
   "Audacious Drab, how in my Presence dar'st ..." ' OGILBY

sit in another's house in a mood of mourning and lamentation. Grief unrelieved is no good thing, and I fear that one of your women, or you yourself, may become indignant – may think I am in my cups, and maudlin.'

Wise Penelope answered him: 'Stranger, the Deathless Ones took away my form and presence and everything that was worth praise in me, when the Argives went up to Ilium and Odysseus my husband went with them. If he came back to have the care of this life of mine, then indeed my repute would be nobler and more widely spread. As it is, I live in misery – such a multitude of sorrows the god has unleashed against me – because all the nobles who have some sway throughout these islands – those in Dulichium, in Same, in forested Zacynthus and those whose home is here in Ithaca – all these are my suitors against my will and ruiners of my house. So I pay slight heed to strangers and suppliants and messengers going on public service; I only sit longing for Odysseus and fretting my heart away. Meanwhile they seek to hasten the marriage on, but I spin them out a thread of stratagems. First of all the god inspired me to set up an ample web in my hall and weave a long and delicate robe. Then I hastened to address the suitors: "Young men who after Odysseus' death have come to woo me here, you are eager for this marriage with me; nevertheless I ask your patience till I have finished weaving this robe, so that what I have spun may not be wasted and go for nothing; it is a burial-robe for King Laertes, on the day when he is overtaken by the grim doom of distressful death. I dread reproach from Achaean women here for allowing one who had gathered great possessions to lie at his death without a shroud." So I spoke, and their wills consented. From that time on I would weave the great web all day, but when night came I would have torches set beside me and would unravel the work. For three years on end my trickery foiled the trusting suitors; but when seasons passed and the fourth year came, then thanks to my women, shameless and selfish creatures, the suitors came on me and surprised me and bitterly reproached me. So with ill grace I finished the work perforce, and now I cannot escape a marriage; I can think of no other subterfuge. My parents press me to marry again, and my son chafes at this wasting of our wealth. He observes such things now; he is a man, he is of an age to take due care of a great house that Zeus makes glorious.

'But whatever may come of all this, I would still ask you to tell me what race you come from; you have not sprung from the stocks and stones that legends tell of.'

Subtle Odysseus answered her: 'Royal wife of Laertes' son, can you not refrain from asking me of what race I am? So be it! I will tell you plainly, although you will plunge me into more grief than vexes me now. It must be so, when a man has been far away from home as long as I have, wandering over many cities of men and suffering tribulation. Nevertheless I will tell you what you ask me so earnestly. There is a land called Crete, set in the wine-dark sea, lovely and fertile and ocean-rounded. Those who live in this land are many, indeed past counting, and there are ninety cities there. The population speaks many tongues; there are Achaeans, there are the brave True Cretans, the Cydonians, the triply-divided Dorians and the noble Pelasgians. Among the cities is mighty Cnossos; its king was once Minos, who every ninth year took counsel with Zeus himself. Minos was father of my own father, bold-hearted Deucalion. Beside myself, Deucalion had another son, Lord Idomeneus, who went with his beaked ships to Ilium together with the sons of Atreus. My own name is Aethon. I am the younger; he was the older and greater man.

'It was in Crete that I saw Odysseus and gave him gifts of friendship. Violent tempest had driven him there; he was bound for Troy, but at Maleia the storm drove him off his course. He achored in Amnisus, by the cave of Eileithyia. That harbour is not easy to enter, and he was hard put to it to escape the gales. Then he came at once up to the city and asked for Idomeneus, claiming him as a dear and honoured friend; but my brother already had sailed for Ilium, ten or eleven days before this. So I myself brought him into the house and gave him all hospitality, entertaining him unstintingly from the wealth of things the palace offered; and besides this, I drew on the public store to give the comrades sailing with him supplies of barley and glowing wine and cattle for slaughter enough for their desire. For twelve days these noble Achaeans remained with me, penned there by a gale from the north that was doubtless raised by some hostile god; it was so strong that even on land a man could not keep his feet. On the thirteenth day the wind dropped and the men sailed.'

He moulded all these falsehoods of his to resemble truth, and as the queen listened, her tears flowed and her cheeks grew wet. It was as when the snow melts on lofty mountains; the west wind brought it, the east wind melts it, and at its melting the rivers swell up to overflowing. So did her lovely cheeks grow wet as she shed tears and wept for the husband who sat so near her. As for Odysseus, his heart went out to his weeping wife, but beneath his eyelids his eyes kept as firm as horn or iron; he still dissembled, and showed no tears. When she had wept and grieved her fill, she spoke in response to him again: 'Now, stranger, I mean to test you – to find if in your Cretan palace you did indeed entertain my husband and his comrades, just as you say. Tell me what sort of clothes he wore, and how he appeared himself, and who were the comrades with him.'

Subtle Odysseus answered her: 'Queen, it is hard to tell such things after a parting so long ago. It is some twenty years since he left my palace and departed from my country. Nevertheless, I will tell you how my remembrance paints him. King Odysseus wore a thick double mantle; it was crimson, and had a clasp of gold with two sheaths. In front was a cunning piece of work – a hound had a dappled fawn between its forepaws, holding it firm as it struggled. Everyone was amazed to see how the hound and the fawn both were gold, yet the one was gripping and throttling the fawn, and the other striving to break away and writhing with its feet. I noted also the shining tunic Odysseus wore about him; it gleamed like the skin of a dried onion – it had that softness and sunlike sheen. I tell you, this was a thing many women gazed at with admiration. But I must add this for you to consider – I cannot say if Odysseus wore these things at home or if one of his comrades gave him them on shipboard, or again some guest-friend, because Odysseus was dear to many; few of the Achaeans equalled him. Indeed I myself gave him a sword of bronze, a fine red mantle with double folds and a tasselled tunic; with such marks of honour I took my leave of him when he sailed. One other thing; there was an attendant with him, a little older than himself. I will describe him to you. He was round-shouldered, dark-skinned and with curling hair. His name was Eurybates; and Odysseus made more of him than of all his other comrades, because this man's thoughts were most like his own.'

His words inclined her yet more to tears as she saw what powerful proof he offered. When she had wept and grieved her fill, she spoke to him once again: 'Stranger, although till now you have seemed a man to pity, henceforth in these halls you shall count as a friend for me, a revered friend. Hearing what you say, I am sure those garments were those I took from my store myself and folded and gave to him, with the glittering clasp upon the tunic to make his presence the handsomer. But Odysseus himself, returning home to his own country – no, I shall never welcome him here again. In an evil hour did he board his vessel to visit that evil city Ilium whose name is an abomination.'

Subtle Odysseus answered her: 'Royal wife of Laertes' son, put aside this grieving for your husband that wastes your spirit and ravages your fair face. Not that I would decry such mourning; many another wife weeps for the husband she has lost – her wedded bridegroom and her lover, the father of her children – though he was no such man as Odysseus, whom fame compares with the gods themselves. But dry your tears and take to heart what I have to say. I will tell you truly, without concealment. Not long ago and not far from here, in the wealthy country of the Thesprotians, I heard of Odysseus as returning. He is alive, and will bring back with him many choice treasures which he still is questing for in that land. But his trusty comrades and his ship were lost to him on the wine-dark sea as he returned from the Trident-Island. This was because he had against him the anger of Zeus and the anger of the sun-god whose cattle his companions had slaughtered. The crew perished one and all in the stormy sea; he clung himself to his vessel's keel and was washed ashore on the land of the Phaeacians, who claim kinship with the immortals. These men heaped honours on him as on a god, made him great gifts and would gladly have sent him home unscathed. So he might have been here long ago. but he thought how he might make more gain by travelling further afield still and coaxing presents as he went – so much does Odysseus excel all others in cunning wiles; no human being can vie with him. This is what I was told by Pheidon. He is the king of the Thesprotians, and he swore to me as he poured libation in his palace that the ship was hauled down and the crew in readiness to take Odysseus to his own native land. But he found a passage for myself before Odysseus returned, since it happened that a Thesprotian ship was sailing then for Dulichium and its cornfields. Moreover Pheidon displayed to me the store of wealth gathered by

Odysseus – enough to sustain ten whole generations after him –
so vast was the treasure left in the king's house. Odysseus, he
said, had gone to Dodona to hear from the tall and leafy oak what
Zeus himself counselled him: how after all these years was he to
return to his own dear land – openly or in secret? Thus, as I said,
he is alive and quite near at hand; he will not long be parted now
from his kindred and his country. But I will give you an oath as
well. I call to witness Zeus among gods – the noblest and highest
of them all – and after him this hearth of Odysseus that I have
come to – in sober truth these things are all of them near fulfil-
ment, as I tell you. Within this same year Odysseus will return,
as the old moon wanes and the new moon rises.'

Wise Penelope answered him: 'Stranger, if only those words
might find fulfilment! Then you would learn soon enough what
my friendship and bounty mean – anyone who met you would
call you a happy man. But what my own heart bodes is this, and
as it bodes, so will things be. Odysseus will never come home
again, nor will you yourself be given a passage to your own
country, because this house has no masters now to compare with
what Odysseus was; as surely as he was ever living, so surely he
was beyond compare in welcoming here or in speeding homeward
an honoured guest.

'But now, my women, wash the stranger's hands and his feet
and make him a bed – with bedding and blankets and gleaming
rugs; let him sleep warm till he sees before him the golden robes
of Dawn. In the early morning bathe him all over and anoint
him; then he may sit by Telemachus in the hall and enjoy his
meal here. If any suitor disturbs or distresses him, he does so at
his peril, and his suit will certainly come to nothing, let him
rage and bluster as he will. For how can you ever know, my
guest, whether or not I stand high among womankind in thought-
fulness and regard for others if you sit down to a meal in this
hall with skin unsoothed and in wretched garments? Men have
but a short time to live, and if a man is ungentle in thought and
ungentle in deed, then in his lifetime everyone prays that evil
may overtake him, and when he is dead everyone derides him; but
if a man is gracious in thought and gracious in deed, his guests
carry good report of him far and wide over the world, and he
finds many to call him noble.'

Subtle Odysseus answered her: 'Royal wife of Laertes' son, let me tell the truth. Blankets and gleaming rugs have become distasteful to me ever since I boarded that long-oared vessel and left behind me the snow-capped hills of Crete. I will lie down now as I have lain through many a sleepless night before; many a night have I spent on a wretched pallet, awaiting the flowery-robed and ethereal Dawn. And baths for the feet are not a thing that would please me now; of all the women who serve in this house not one shall touch my feet – unless indeed there is some devoted aged one whose heart has borne the same sorrows as my own; to one such as that I would not begrudge the touching of my feet.'

Wise Penelope answered him : 'Dear guest, of all strangers from far away that ever have come into this house, never has one been as welcome as you or as understanding, so right and well-judged is every word you say. I have indeed among my women an old and wise one who reared and cared for my luckless husband – who took him in her arms when his mother bore him; she is frail now, but she shall wash your feet. Come, Eurycleia, you wise old woman, stand up and prepare to wash the feet of someone who is as old as your master is. And perhaps Odysseus himself by now has feet like these and hands like these, because men in distress become old before their time.'

So she spoke. The old woman covered her face with her hands, she shed warm tears and she spoke lamentingly : 'Alas, my child, how helpless I am to serve you now! Surely Zeus is estranged from you as from no other, and yet your spirit was always reverent. Never did any mortal man offer the Thunderer hecatombs and burnt-sacrifices as plentiful and as choice as you did, praying to reach a serene old age and bring up your son to glorious manhood. But no – it is from you alone that Zeus has utterly taken away the day of homecoming. Odysseus himself, as like as not, has been mocked by women in foreign lands when he came to some host's ample palace, just as you, our guest, are mocked by the shameless wenches here; and because you shrink from their gibes and contumely you do not consent to be washed by them. But now the queen's command to me has fallen on willing ears; for her sake then I will wash your feet, and for your sake also, because my heart is stirred with compassion for you. Listen besides to what I say now. Many a stranger in distress has come to this place before, but I tell you, I have never seen one who in voice and build and feet was so much like Odysseus himself.'

Subtle Odysseus answered her: 'Old dame, that is what every-one says who has seen the two of us; all agree we are very like each other, just as you shrewdly say yourself.'

So he replied. The old woman took the burnished basin she used for washing the feet of guests. She poured cold water in lavishly, then added the warm to it. Odysseus was sitting at the hearth, but turned his back to the firelight suddenly as misgiving leapt into his mind that as soon as the woman put her hands on him she would know his scar for what it was, and the truth would be out. She came closer now and began to wash her master, and in a moment she knew the scar.

This was the mark made long ago by a boar's white tusk when Odysseus visited Parnassus in quest of Autolycus and his sons. Autolycus was the noble father of Odysseus' own mother, and excelled all mankind in thieving and subtlety of oaths, having won this mastery from the god Hermes himself, who welcomed his many sacrifices of lambs and young goats and who gladly seconded his actions. When Autolycus once visited the fertile country of Ithaca he had found there his daughter's new-born son. At the feast's end Eurycleia had put the baby upon his knees and said: 'Autolycus, you yourself must think of a name to give your grandson; his birth has come after many prayers.'

And Autolycus responded thus: 'You, my daughter, and you, her husband, must give him the name I utter now. Since I who am here your guest have been at odds with so many people, with men and women over the bounteous earth, let his name by Odysseus to mark those odds. And when he has reached man's estate, let him come to the great house at Parnassus which was his mother's home and where all my possessions lie; from these I will give him gifts enough to send him on his way rejoicing.'

So in due time Odysseus went there to get these gifts from his grandfather. Autolycus and the sons of Autolycus received him with open arms and with words of welcome, and his mother's mother Amphithea embraced him and kissed his head and his two bright eyes. Autolycus told his sons to prepare the meal, and they did not neglect his command. They brought in at once a bull five years old, flayed and prepared it, deftly divided it, cut it up, spitted and roasted it, carefully portioned out the pieces. Then they feasted for all the rest of the day till sunset, and their hearts lacked nothing in the banquet that all shared equally. When the sun sank and darkness came, they went to their rest and gladly received the boon of sleep.

Dawn comes early, with rosy fingers. When she appeared, they set off for the chase – the hounds in front, then the sons of Autolycus and Odysseus who was going with them. They neared Parnassus, the lofty mountain cloaked with forest, and soon drew close to its windy glens. The sun at this hour had risen from ocean's calm deep waters and was just beginning to touch the countryside[1] when the beaters came to a wooded hollow. The hounds ran ahead, tracking the quarry; behind came the sons of Autolycus, and Odysseus came with them, not far from the hounds and brandishing his long-shafted spear. Nearby was couching a huge boar, in a dense copse that was never entered by strong wet winds, never reached by rays of dazzling sun, never pierced through and through by thunderstorms, so thick it was, and under foot was a great mass of leaves. As the men advanced, urging on the hounds, the noise made by the feet of both reached the boar from this side and from that. Leaving his lair he came out to face them, his back bristling all over, his eyes flashing flame, and he stood at bay confronting his enemies. Odysseus rushed forward first, his long spear raised in his sturdy hand, eager to strike; but the boar was quicker, and thrusting sideways with his tusk he gashed Odysseus above the knee and tore away a great strip of flesh, only stopping short of the bone. Then Odysseus' thrust went home, entering the beast's right shoulder and making the point of the gleaming spear pass right through. With a shriek the boar fell straight to earth, and the breath of life fled away from him.

The young men looked to the carcase. In skilful fashion they bound up Odysseus' wound, staunching the dark blood with an incantation, then quickly returned to their father's palace. Autolycus and his sons finished their healing, enriched Odysseus with glorious gifts and soon sent him back rejoicing to his own country Ithaca. His father and lady mother were gladdened at his return and asked about this and that and the whole story of the scar; so Odysseus told them faithfully how the hunted boar with his glistening tusk had wounded him on Mount Parnassus when he went there with the sons of Autolycus.

1. 'When the Sun, rising from the gentle Main,
   Tinsel'd the Meads, and tip'd the blushing Grain...' OGILBY

As old Eurycleia passed her hands down over his thigh she felt the scar, knew what it was, and let the foot fall away from her. Down went his leg into the basin, the vessel of bronze clanged and tilted, and the water spilt over the ground. Joy and sorrow seized on her heart at once, tears welled up in her eyes, and her voice changed from clear to faint. She reached her hand up to his chin, and said: 'My own dear child, you are Odysseus beyond a doubt, yet I did not know you for my master till I passed my hands all over you.'

As she spoke these words she turned her eyes to Penelope, eager to show her that there her own husband was, but the queen failed to meet her glance or pay heed at all, because Athene had turned her thoughts elsewhere. But Odysseus felt for his nurse's throat, clutched it with his right hand while he pulled her towards him with his left, then whispered: 'Nurse, are you bent on my destruction? You reared me once at your own breast, and now after many griefs and trials I have come back in the twentieth year to my own country. Since you have seen the truth and the god has revealed it to your mind – say not a word; make sure that no one else in these halls comes to know. If not, I will tell you what will come to pass. If the god delivers the suitors into my hands, I will not spare you, nurse of mine though you are, when I kill other maidservants in these halls.'

Wise Eurycleia answered him: 'My child, what words are these that have passed your lips? You know my firm and unyielding spirit. I will no more yield than iron or than solid rock. There is this thing too, which I would ask you to lay to heart. If the god delivers the suitors into your hands, I will tell you in full which of the women here are disloyal to you and which are innocent.'

Odysseus answered: 'Nurse, why should you speak of them? It is needless. I myself will observe them carefully and make my judgement on each of them. No, say no more about such things, and leave the issue to the gods.'

So he spoke, and the old woman went back through the hall to fetch fresh water for his feet, because all the first basinful had been spilt. When she had washed and anointed him, he drew his chair nearer the fire again for warmth, and covered up the scar with his rags.

Then wise Penelope spoke again: 'Guest, I have one more thing to ask you – a slight thing too, because it will soon be the hour

for soft repose, I mean for one who in spite of sorrows can give
himself up to soothing sleep. As for myself, the god has assigned
me a grief that has no bounds. My life is one of melancholy
and mourning, though during daytime I take some pleasure in
looking to my own tasks in the house, and my women's tasks; but
when night comes and everyone else is lost in sleep, I lie in my
bed while poignant cares come thronging about my restless heart.
Just as the daughter of Pandareus, the nightingale of the green
woods, warbles her lovely song in the first flush of spring, sitting
among the clustered leaves, pouring out her melody with all its
trills and its shifting notes and lamenting her dear son Itylus
whom long ago she killed in ignorance with the sword, the child
of Lord Zethus – so my own mind shifts hither and thither, won-
dering if I should stay with my son and keep everything un-
changed – my estate, my waiting-women, my lofty-roofed house
itself – respecting my husband's bed and the people's voice; or if I
should now go with whatever Achaean lord seems noblest as he
woos me here and offers my kinsmen countless gifts. And then
my son – when he was a child and unreflecting, he would say that
I must not marry and leave my husband's house, but now, having
grown to early manhood, he even prays heaven that I may depart,
because he frets at the suitors' wasting of his possessions.

'But come, here is a dream that I wish you to listen to and
interpret. I have twenty geese belonging here, and I love to
watch them leaving their pond and eating their wheat; but a
great eagle with crooked beak swooped down from the mountain-
side and broke all their necks and killed them. So there they lay
heaped inside the house while the eagle soared up skywards. Still
in my dream, I wept and moaned, and Achaean ladies with lovely
tresses came and stood round me as I lamented this eagle's slaugh-
tering of my geese. But then he returned; he perched upon a pro-
jecting roof-beam, he spoke with a human voice to check my
grief: "Take heart again, daughter of great Icarius. This was no
dream but a waking vision, a happy one, destined to be fulfilled
for you. The geese were the suitors, and I who was the eagle am
now your own husband, at home again and about to bring a
hideous death upon all the suitors." So he spoke, and the sleep
that had soothed me let me go. I looked about me, and there saw
the geese by their own trough, pecking their grain as they always
did.'

Subtle Odysseus answered her: 'Queen, that interpretation of your dream certainly cannot be wrenched aside, since Odysseus himself has revealed to you how he will fulfil it. For all the suitors, destruction is manifestly foretold; not one of them will escape from death and doom.'

Wise Penelope answered him: 'Dear guest, dreams are beyond our unravelling – who can be sure what tale they tell? Not all that men look for comes to pass. Two gates there are that give passage to fleeting dreams; one is made of horn, one of ivory. The dreams that pass through sawn ivory are deceitful, bearing a message that will not be fulfilled; those that come out through polished horn have truth behind them, to be accomplished for men who see them.[1] But I cannot hope that this dream that bewilders me came from there, welcome though that would be both to me and to Telemachus.

'One thing remains for me to tell and for you to ponder. This approaching day must be loathsome to me because it will sever me from Odysseus' house. I mean to make a trial of skill with the axes he used to set in line in the hall like the blocks for a ship's keel, twelve of them altogether; he used to stand well away from them and shoot an arrow through the whole line. And now I mean to put this ordeal before the suitors; whoever among them strings the bow with his hands most easily and shoots an arrow through all twelve axes, that man I will follow, forsaking then this house that I came to as a bride, a house so beautiful and so filled with treasures, one that sometimes, I think, I shall remember, though it be only in my dreams.'

Subtle Odysseus answered her: 'Royal wife of Laertes' son, do not delay this contest within your palace. Let the suitors handle the bow as they will, Odysseus will reach this house before they can stretch the string and shoot through the iron.'

Wise Penelope answered him: 'Dear guest, if you were willing to sit beside me here in these halls and console me still, sleep would never fall on my eyes. Yet men cannot go without sleep for ever, because for each single thing over this fertile earth the Deathless Ones have assigned a due portion for mortals' use. So I myself will go to my room above and lie on the cheerless bed that my tears have stained continually ever since Odysseus

1. The Greek plays on the similar sounds of the words for 'ivory' and 'deceitful' and again for 'horn' and 'accomplishment'.

boarded his vessel to visit that evil city Ilium whose name is an abomination. It is there that I will seek my rest. Seek your own rest somewhere in this house; lay your own bedding upon the floor or let the women prepare it for you.'

With these words the queen went up to the shimmering room above, not unescorted but with her women; then began to weep for Odysseus her darling husband till Athene of the gleaming eyes sent welcome slumber upon her eyelids.

BOOK XX

ODYSSEUS had gone to rest in the entrance-hall; he had spread on the ground an untanned oxhide and had piled some fleeces over it from the sheep that the suitors daily slaughtered, and when he was settled, Eurynome had given him a blanket above. While he stayed awake there, devising evil against the suitors, women began to come out from the great hall – those who for some time past had been the mistresses of the suitors – laughing and making merry with one another. Anger swelled up in him, and for a while he asked himself if he should leap out then and there and deal death to each of them, or if he should let them lie with the haughty suitors this one last time. His heart within him growled with anger. As a bitch with puppies, mounting guard over the strengthless creatures, spies a stranger and growls at him and prepares to fight him, so Odysseus' heart growled within him as he saw these evil ways and loathed them. But he struck his breast and rebuked his heart: 'Have patience, heart. Once you endured worse than this, on the day when the ruthless Cyclops devoured my hardy comrades; you held firm till your cunning rescued you from the cave in which you thought to die.'

So he spoke, rebuking his own spirit. His heart stayed anchored fast in endurance, yet he himself tossed this way and that. Often in front of a blazing fire you see the spitted paunch of some beast, all filled with blood and fat, and a man keeps turning it to and fro, anxious that it should be roasted as soon as may be; just so did Odysseus twist and turn, wondering how he by himself should make assault on the multitude of shameless suitors.

But now Athene descending from heaven drew near him, wearing the likeness of a woman. She stood at his bedside and said to him: 'Odysseus, more than most men you have been fortune's plaything, yet why should you thus lie sleepless now? This house is your own, and in this house are your wife and child – one that any father would be proud to have for son.'

Subtle Odysseus answered her: 'Yes truly, goddess; all that you say is well said. Yet deep within me I still have thoughts that are disquieting. How by myself shall I make assault on the shameless suitors, who are always together in this hall? And another thought is still more disquieting. I grant that with Zeus and with you to aid me, I might indeed kill these men; but how could I then escape vengeance? These are things I would have you ponder.'

The gleaming-eyed goddess answered him: 'Unbelieving one, most men are ready to trust a comrade, a mortal man without my strength and without my cunning; yet I am a goddess, one who through all your trials has guarded you continually. I will speak plainly. If fifty squadrons of mortal men were to close on the two of us, all of them eager to slaughter us in battle, even then you would carry off the plunder of the herds and fat flocks that once were theirs. Let sleep have its way with you at last. To keep watch all night and never sleep is itself a misery; soon you will rise above all your troubles.' And with these words the goddess poured sleep upon his eyes, and herself passed to Olympus again.

While sleep thus laid its hold upon him, easing his limbs and easing his disquiet, his loyal wife on her soft couch returned to wakefulness and to tears. When she had had her fill of weeping, the queen made especial prayer to Artemis: 'Artemis, high among divinities, daughter of Zeus, how glad should I be if here and now you would plant an arrow in my breast and take my life away all at once - or else if a whirlwind might snatch me up, carry me on through dusky pathways and cast me down at the issuing-place of backward-flowing Ocean.[1] Let it be as when the winds bore off the daughters of Pandareus. The gods long before had slain their parents, and the girls were left orphans in their house. But Lady Aphrodite had nurtured them with cheese and sweet honey and pleasant wine; Hera had given them beauty and wisdom beyond all other women; virgin Artemis made them tall, and Athene taught them the making of lovely things. But when Aphrodite went up to high Olympus to entreat Zeus to let these girls attain the moment of happy marriage - because Zeus knows all things perfectly, what is fated and what not fated for mortal men - meanwhile the storm-spirits snatched them away and delivered them to the ministrations of the detested furies. In selfsame fashion may the Olympians cause me to vanish from the world, or else let Artemis slay me with her arrows, that so I may

[1]. The lines now following, 66-82, are widely considered unauthentic, but are far too interesting to be omitted.

pass beneath cheerless earth with Odysseus himself in my heart's vision. May I never gladden the heart of a man less noble!

'Some grief indeed is endurable – when one whose heart has been pierced with sorrow weeps every day through his waking hours, but then every night sleep enfolds him, sleep that brings a forgetfulness of all things, the good and the evil things alike, when once it has wrapped men's eyelids round. But as for me – even my dreams have been evil ones, sent by some god for my distress.[1] This very night someone lay beside me in the likeness of Odysseus himself when he went from here with the other warriors; and my heart was glad, because I thought that this was no dream, but waking truth.'

As she ended thus, Dawn in her cloth of gold appeared. Odysseus had caught the sound of his wife's lament; he began to muse, and in his fancy it seemed to him that even now she stood at his bedside and knew him for who he was. Taking the blankets and the fleeces that he had been sleeping in, he laid them on a chair in the hall, then carried his ox-hide out of doors, lifted his hands and prayed to Zeus: 'Father Zeus, if indeed you gods, who afflicted me so long, have turned to befriend me and led me over both land and sea to my own country, then let one of those who are now awaking inside the palace utter here some word of good omen for me, and from outside also let there be sent some sign from Zeus.'

So he prayed. Zeus the all-wise heeded him, and at once he thundered from above, from the cloud-country, the radiant heavens; and King Odysseus was filled with joy. Then from inside the palace a woman grinding corn uttered a word of omen. This was from near at hand, where the millstones for the king's corn were set; twelve women laboured at these together, grinding the barley and wheat men thrive on. The other women were sleeping now, having ground their stint of corn already; this one alone – the feeblest among them all – had still not finished. She stopped

---

1. 'When woes the waking sense alone assail,
   Whilst night extends her soft oblivious veil,
   Of other wretches' care the torture ends :
   No truce the warfare of my heart suspends!
   The night renews the day-distracting theme,
   And airy terrors sable ev'ry dream.' POPE

her handmill and uttered words that became an omen for her master: 'Father Zeus, ruler of gods and men alike, loud indeed was your thundering from heaven, and there is not a cloud to be seen; this must be a sign shown by you to someone. Grant to me too, poor wretch that I am, accomplishment of the words I utter. May this very day be the last time, the last of all, that the suitors eat their sumptuous meal in Odysseus' place, those men who have worn my knees away with the wretched drudgery of this grinding; let them feast today and never again!'

So she spoke, and Odysseus rejoiced at the presage of her utterance, and the thunder from Zeus; now he was sure of his revenge upon those workers of wickedness.

The other maids were awake now in the noble halls of King Odysseus, rekindling the hearth's unflagging fire. Prince Telemachus dressed himself; he rose from his bed, slung the keen sword about his shoulders, laced the good sandals under his feet, and took in his hand the powerful spear tipped with keen bronze. He went and stood by the hall's entrance and called to Eurycleia: 'Dear nurse, what care did you women show to the stranger in this house? Did you give him the food and bed he deserved, or has he been left to lie uncared for? That is my mother's way, understanding though she is; she goes by impulse, making much of a man who is unworthy and sending his better away unhonoured.'

Wise Eurycleia answered him: 'Child, you ought not to blame your mother where she is blameless. The stranger sat there and drank his wine as long as he pleased; as for food, the queen asked him that, and he said he was satisfied already. And when thoughts of rest and sleep came upon them both, your mother told the serving-women to lay bedding down for him; but he, feeling himself a luckless outcast, refused to sleep in a made bed between soft blankets. He laid himself down in the entrance-hall, on raw oxhide and sheep's fleeces; and we ourselves threw a blanket over him.'

So she spoke, and Telemachus with his spear went out through the hall; beside him were two swift-footed hounds, and he went his way to the meeting-place of the Achaeans. Meanwhile Eurycleia, daughter of Ops, gave orders thus to the serving-women: 'Come, set to! Sweep out the hall, some of you; sprinkle the floor; put the bright hangings over the chairs; some of you sponge the tables clean and scour the mixing-bowls and the drinking-cups;[1] let the rest of you go and fetch water from the well; quick, no idling. The suitors will not be long away; soon they will be here again, because today is a public feast.'

So she spoke. They listened readily and obeyed. A score of them went off to the well with its deep dark water, while others deftly busied themselves in the hall itself. Then the proud men-servants came in and split the firewood with practised hands. The women now returned from the well, and after them appeared the swineherd, driving three fat hogs, the best he had. These he left to find their food in the ample courtyard while he greeted Odysseus courteously: 'Friend, do the suitors show you more regard now, or do they insult you in these halls as they did before?' Subtle Odysseus answered him: 'Eumaeus, I pray to heaven that the gods will punish the wrongs and the outrages and the schemes these men contrive in another man's house; no thought of shame enters their mind.'

As they talked with each other thus, Melanthius the goatherd came up to them, bringing the finest beasts from his herds to make the suitors' morning meal, and he had two herdsmen with him. He tethered the goats under the echoing portico, then turned once more to revile Odysseus: 'Stranger, are you to plague your betters still with your begging inside this house? Will you never leave us? We shall not part – I am sure of that – without blows between the two of us. You have no decency in your begging; there are other dining-tables among the Achaeans.'

To these words of his Odysseus made no reply; only he shook his head in silence, and brooded evil in his heart.

After these two came a third, Philoetius, bringing the suitors a calfless heifer and fatted goats. He and his beasts had been ferried over by the same boatmen on the mainland who give passage to any comers. He tethered the beasts under the echoing portico, then came towards the swineherd and questioned him: 'Who is the stranger here, Eumaeus, this newcomer to our palace? From what stock does he claim descent? Where are his family and

1. 'What marks of luxury the marble stain !
   Its wonted lustre let the floor regain;
   The seats with purple cloathe in order due;
   And let th' abstersive sponge the board renew:
   Let some refresh the vase's sullied mold;
   Some bid the goblets boast their native gold.' POPE

native soil? Unhappy man! Truly he looks like a lord and king, but when the gods weave sorrow into men's lot – even into the lot of kings – they send them wandering and plunge them into misery.'

So he spoke, then came to Odysseus, gave him his right hand in friendship and let these words wing their way to him: 'Revered stranger, I wish you well; may happiness come to you hereafter, though now you are overwhelmed with sorrows. O Father Zeus, no god is ruthless as you are ruthless. You bring men into the world yourself, yet you have no more compassion for them than to plunge them into suffering and bitter tribulation.

'Stranger, when first I caught sight of you I broke into a sweat, and my eyes are still moist with tears because Odysseus came back to my mind.[1] I feel that he too is wearing such rags and is a wanderer over the world, if indeed he is living still and can see the sunlight. But if he is dead already, already in Hades' house, then alas, I say, for the incomparable Odysseus! When I was still a lad he made me the keeper of his cattle in the country of the Cephallenians. These have grown beyond counting now, nor could any man upon this earth have a richer harvest of broad-browed cattle. But now I must bring them there to Ithaca at the command of strangers; strangers take them for their own feasting, not reverencing the king's son in his halls, not fearing the chastisement of the gods; they can scarcely wait to parcel out the possessions of the long-absent king. And my heart keeps turning one question to and fro. While the king's son is still alive, it would indeed be an evil thing to go from here, cattle and all, to another land and a strange people; but then, is it not worse still to linger on here in misery, helplessly tending herds now alien?

1. 'Stranger! may fate a milder aspect shew
   And spin thy fortune with a whiter clue!
   O *Jove*! for ever deaf to human cries,
   The tyrant, not the father of the skies,
   Unpiteous of the race thy will began!
   The fool of fate, thy manufacture, man,
   With penury, contempt, repulse, and care,
   The gauling load of life is doom'd to bear.
   Ulysses from his state a wanderer still,
   Upbraids thy pow'r, thy wisdom, or thy will.
   O *Monarch* ever dear! – O man of woe! –
   Fresh flow my tears, and shall for ever flow!' POPE

And I might have sought refuge long ago in some other power-ful king's domain, because things now are past endurance; only my thought still goes back to my luckless master – may he come even now from some place unthought of and scatter the suitors in his halls?'

Subtle Odysseus answered him: 'Cowherd, you seem no dis-loyal man and no foolish one. I need no telling that wisdom is at home in your heart. Here then is something I will vouch for – I will swear a great oath upon it. I call to witness Zeus among gods, and after him the table of hospitality and the hearth of Odysseus that I have come to – in sober truth, while you still are here Odysseus will return, and if you so wish you shall see with your own eyes the slaughtering of the suitors who lord it here now.'

The cowherd answered: 'Stranger, would that the son of Cronos might bring to pass all that you say; then you would see what strength I have and how well my hands can play their part.'

And Eumaeus also made prayers to all the gods that wise Odysseus might come once more to his own home.

As they talked thus with one another, the suitors again were plotting death and doom for Telemachus; suddenly on their left there appeared a bird of omen, an eagle of lofty flight, with a cowering dove in its talons. Then Amphinomus spoke among them all: 'Friends, this purpose of ours will never prosper, this plot for the killing of Telemachus. No, let us turn our thoughts to feasting.'

So spoke Amphinomus, and the words he said won their assent. They entered the house of King Odysseus. They laid their cloaks on the chairs and couches, then began to slaughter big sheep and well-fed goats, to slaughter fat hogs and a cow from the herd as well. They roasted the inwards and served them round; they poured wine into the bowls and mixed it. The swineherd gave each man his goblet, Philoetius brought round the bread in baskets, and Melanthius poured the wine. So they stretched out their hands to the good things that lay before them.

Telemachus, for his own purposes, gave Odysseus a seat in the hall close to the stone threshold, setting down a humble stool and a meagre table there. He put beside him a portion of the inwards and poured him wine in a golden cup, saying to him:

'Now sit there, and drink your wine with this company.[1] I my-self will give you protection from the taunts and violence of the suitors, because the wealth of this house is not any and every man's; Odysseus won it, and I am his heir. And as for you suitors – control your passions. No gibes, no blows, or there may be bad blood and contention here.'

Such were his words. The others all bit their lips and looked at Telemachus in amazement, with such authority did he speak. But Antinous son of Eupeithes said: 'Achaeans, these are dis-tasteful words from Telemachus. Nevertheless, we had best accept them, for though he has threatened us openly, the son of Cronos has crossed our purpose; but for that, we should have silenced him here already, eloquent though his speech may be.'

So he spoke, but the prince did not heed his words. Through the streets outside, the public heralds were passing now with the beasts set apart for sacrifice, and under the shady grove of the archer god Apollo the long-haired Achaeans were assembling.

When those in the hall had roasted the outer flesh and drawn it from the spits, they divided the portions and then pursued the sumptuous feast. Beside Odysseus the servants placed as ample a portion as they themselves received, for Telemachus, the king's own son, had commanded this.

As for the overbearing suitors, Athene still would not let them refrain from biting insult; she meant indignation to sink more deeply yet into the soul of Laertes' son. There was among them a lawless-hearted man who was called Ctesippus and lived in Same; confident in his vast possessions, he was wooing the wife of the absent king. This man now spoke to the haughty suitors: 'High-hearted suitors, hear my words. For some while now the stranger has had his portion no less than the rest of us; rightly so – it would not be just or honourable to deny his due to whatever guest of Telemachus comes to this house. And now I also should like to make him a gift in friendship, so that he in turn can offer a present – to the bath-woman, perhaps, or to some other servant of King Odysseus.'

> 1. 'Dispos'd apart, *Ulysses* shares the treat;
> A trivet-table, and ignobler seat,
> The Prince appoints; but to his Sire assigns
> The tasteful inwards, and nectareous wines.
> Partake, my guest, he cry'd, without controul
> The social feast, and drain the cheering bowl.' POPE

With these words he caught up a cow's foot from the basket where it had been left, and with powerful hand hurled it from him. Odysseus, shifting his head just to one side, let the thing pass by him to hit the solid wall, but the smile he gave was grim and angry. Telemachus spoke in rebuke at once: 'So you thought better of it, Ctesippus? After all, you did not hit the stranger; he saw to it that the thing missed its mark. Had he not, I would have sent my sharp spear right through you, and your father would have been busied here with a funeral feast and not a wedding. So now let me see none of you flaunting your shamelessness in this house. I do take note and pay heed to things now, the good and the bad as well; before, I was still a child. Nevertheless there are sights I bear with – there are cattle being slaughtered, wine and corn being consumed; it is hard for one man to curb so many. But I do entreat you – cease from these wicked and spiteful actions, unless you are set on slaying me with the sword; and indeed I would rather have that than this. It would be far better for me to perish than to watch such monstrous things continually – guests maltreated and maidservants dragged in shame down this noble hall.'

At these words of his they were all hushed and silent. After a pause, Agelaus son of Damastor spoke: 'Friends, when the word of reason has been uttered, there is no place left for retort and resentment and contradiction. You must do no violence to this stranger, or to any servant in King Odysseus' palace. But to Telemachus and his mother I would offer a friendly counsel that I hope may satisfy them both. So long as your innermost thoughts still trusted that wise Odysseus would come back home again, none could blame you for waiting still and keeping the suitors here in check; this was the more prudent thing if indeed Odysseus had returned and made his way to his house once more. But as things are – by now it is plain enough that he is not destined to return. Go then, Telemachus, sit down with your mother and tell her plainly – she should marry whichever man is noblest and offers the most generous gifts. Then you may have and hold your father's possessions in ease of mind, eating and drinking, and she may govern another man's house.'

Thoughtful Telemachus answered him: 'Agelaus, I call to witness Zeus himself and all the hard fortunes of my father, who doubtless has died far from Ithaca or else is wandering far from it – I do not delay my mother's marriage, no, not at all. I urge her to marry whom she pleases; I offer her countless gifts as well. But I shrink from driving her from this house with words that would thwart and force her will. God forbid that any such thing should come to pass!'

So spoke Telemachus. Then Pallas Athene roused among the suitors a kind of laughter they could not quench, because she had driven their wits astray. The lips they laughed with seemed as it were not their own, and the flesh they were eating was foul with blood. Their eyes overflowed with tears, and all their thoughts were of desolation.

At this, Theoclymenus broke forth: 'Unhappy men, what is this thing that is come upon you? Your heads and your faces and your knees are wrapped in darkness; the air is alive with lamentation; your cheeks are streaming with tears; the walls and the fashioned tie-beams are dank with blood; the entrance and court beyond are thronged with ghosts speeding down to the murk of Erebus; the sun has been blotted out from heaven, and a ghastly mist hovers over all.'

So he spoke, but the suitors all made merry and laughed at him. Eurymachus son of Polybus was the first to speak to them: 'This newcomer from abroad is out of his wits. Quick, young men, guide him from here out of doors and down to the assembly-place,[1] since here he finds it as black as midnight.'

Theoclymenus answered him again: 'I desire no guides from you, Eurymachus. I have eyes and ears and two feet and a firm-set mind that I need not be ashamed of; led by these I will pass these doors, because I see coming upon you suitors a doom that none of you shall escape or counter, none of you who outrage others and plot unrighteousness in the house of King Odysseus.' And with these words he passed forth from the pleasant-sited palace and on to the dwelling of Peiraeus; Peiraeus received him with rejoicing.

The suitors, looking at one another, began to rally Telemachus and make merry over his guests. One or another of the young swaggerers would utter such words as these: 'Telemachus, was there ever a man so luckless with his guests as you? Here was one vagrant foisted on you, greedy for food and wine, knowing noth-

1. Or if one accepts Wecklein's emendation, 'out of doors and into the blaze of noon'.

ing of honest hard work, a mere cumberer of the ground. And now this other man has stood up among us to prophesy. Do as I say; it would be far better. Let us put both strangers aboard a ship and send them away to the Sicilians; that would bring you a handsome price.'

So spoke the suitors. Telemachus did not heed their words, but looked in silence towards his father, awaiting the moment when he would lay his hands on those shameless men.

Penelope had set her chair opposite, and could hear every word spoken in the hall. Many beasts had been slaughtered, and the suitors in merry mood had prepared a sumptuous meal to gratify their desires; but after this meal there was to come another, prepared by the goddess and the hero. That was to prove as sour a meal as could be,[1] because aggression lay with the suitors, and all their thoughts were of deeds of evil.

1. Cf. Shakespeare, 2 Henry VI, I. iv. 72–3:

'Thither goes these Newes as fast as Horse can carry them,
A sorry Breakfast for my Lord Protector.'

BOOK XXI

THE CONTEST OF THE BOW

AND now the goddess of gleaming eyes put it into the queen's mind to place in the hall before the suitors the bow and the iron that were to be first the means of contest and afterwards the means of slaughter. She climbed the high stair up to her room and with sturdy hand grasped the fine bronze key with its easy curve and ivory handle. Then with her women she made her way to a distant room where her husband had stored certain treasures, bronze and gold and wrought iron. There with the rest was his pliant bow with its ample quiver, packed with arrows that threatened grief.

Bow and quiver had long ago been given him by a friend who looked like the gods themselves, Iphitus son of Eurytus, at a chance encounter in Lacedaemon. It was in Messene the pair had met, in the house of shrewd Ortilochus. Odysseus had come to claim a debt that was owing to him from the whole nation there; Messenians had come to Ithaca with their vessels and sailed away with three hundred sheep and their shepherds also. To press this claim, Odysseus had made the long journey; he was still a lad, but Laertes and his councillors had sent him to speak for them. Iphitus was there in search of animals he had lost – twelve mares with sturdy young mules at the teat. These same mares were afterwards cause of his death and doom when he came to the house of Heracles; that dauntless hero lent himself then to deeds of evil – without remorse the child of Zeus slew his guest in his own house, not heeding the vengeance of the gods, not heeding the rites of hospitality: he welcomed him to his table and then murdered him, keeping the firm-hooved mares in his own palace.

Iphitus was still seeking these when he met Odysseus and gave him the bow; great Eurytus at an earlier time had had it always with him, and when he died in his lofty palace he bequeathed it to his son. Odysseus in turn gave Iphitus a keen sword and a sturdy spear, to be a first token of guest-friendship; yet never were they to know each other as host and guest; before that could be, the child of Zeus murdered Iphitus, the hero of godlike feature who had given this bow to the young prince. King Odysseus never took it with him when he set forth with his dark vessels to make a foray. He would leave it lying there in his palace, a remembrance of his beloved friend; only upon his own domains did he carry it about him.

The queen came to that distant room and set foot on the oaken threshold which a master carpenter long ago had smoothed deftly and trued to the line before he planted the posts in it and added the gleaming doors. At once she undid the thong from the hook, put in the key and with sure aim shot back the bolts. The noise was vast. A bull put to pasture in a meadow would roar no louder than these fine doors at the thrust of the key. They quickly opened before the queen, and she set foot on the raised flooring on which stood the presses that held sweet-smelling garments. She reached out and took down the bow from its peg, still in its bright enclosing case. Then she sat down where she was, and putting the case upon her knees she began to weep aloud as she drew out her husband's bow. When she had wept and moaned her fill, she went down again towards the hall and towards the bold suitors there, clasping the pliant bow with its ample quiver, packed with arrows that threatened grief. Her women came with her, carrying a box with iron and bronze from the master's store, now to become the instruments of contest. When the great queen had reached the suitors, she halted beside the pillar that bore the massy roof, her bright scarf drawn over her cheeks; her faithful women took their places each side of her. Then at once she addressed the suitors:

'Listen to me, you haughty suitors, who all this time have been so ready to eat and drink this house away while my husband has long been far from here. You have found only one excuse for this – the desire to have me as wedded wife. Well, my suitors, the prize at stake is now displayed for you. I will put before you the great bow of King Odysseus. Whoever among you strings the bow with his hands most easily and shoots an arrow through all twelve axes, that man I will follow, forsaking then this house that I came to as a bride, a house so beautiful and so filled with treasures, one that sometimes, I think, I shall remember, though it be only in my dreams.'

So she spoke, and ordered the swineherd, good Eumaeus, to put the bow and the grey iron before the suitors. Eumaeus burst into tears as he took them and laid them down. The cowherd too, at sight of his master's bow, began weeping where he stood. But

Antinous turned on them and reviled them: 'Witless peasants, short-sighted creatures! What do you mean, misguided pair, by shedding tears and troubling the queen's heart further when it is sunk in grief already at the loss of her beloved husband?[1] Either be quiet and sit and eat your meal, or else go outside the house to weep. Leave the bow with its arrows here to plague the contesting suitors – since I think this bow will not easily let itself be strung; among all those here there is no such man as Odysseus was. I myself have seen him, and still remember it, though then I was only a little child.'

Such were his words; but inwardly all his hopes were set on stringing the bow and shooting through the iron. In truth it was he who was first to taste an arrow from that same great Odysseus in whose hall he now sat at ease, himself contemptuous of the king and spurring the others to contempt.

Then Prince Telemachus spoke among them: 'This is a strange thing; surely the son of Cronos has taken my wits away. My own dear mother, for all her wisdom, is saying now she will leave this house in another's company, yet here am I, thoughtlessly laughing and making merry. But come, you suitors; the prize at stake is now displayed for you – a lady who has no peer today in all the Achaean land, not in holy Pylos or Argos or Mycene, nor yet in our own Ithaca or the dark mainland. But that is a thing you know already – what need for me to praise my mother? Let there be no delaying then, no coy excuse, no long evasion of the stringing; let us see the issue. And I myself should be glad to make trial of the bow. Perhaps I may string it and shoot clean through the iron; then I should not grieve to see my mother forsake this house in another's company, if I myself remained behind with prowess enough to take upon me such feats of mastery as my father's.'

With that he leapt up and threw the crimson cloak from his shoulders, lifting off the keen sword that hung there. First of all he planted the axes, digging one long trench for all of them and making the line straight and true; then he heaped up the earth around. Amazement came upon all beholders as they saw the sureness of his movements, because he himself had never watched

---

1. 'Pox on thee, Coxcomb – Rustick, why dost cry,
   Wherefore, forsooth, put finger in thy eye?' OGILBY

this thing being done. Then he walked to the threshold, took his stand and began to make trial of the bow. Three times, as he tried to draw it, he made it tremble; three times he rested from the effort, though his heart still hoped to string the bow and shoot through the iron. Then a fourth time he strained at it, and this time he would indeed have strung it, but Odysseus gave him a warning nod and stopped him short in his eagerness. So the prince spoke once more among them: 'Alas, it seems that for all my days I must be spiritless and a weakling; or it may be I am only too young, still unable to trust my hands for self-defence when a man picks a quarrel with me.[1] Come then, you whose powers are far above mine, make your own trial of the bow; let us bring this contest to an end.'

With these words he put down the bow and leaned it against the smooth clean-fitting doors, resting the arrow against the bow-tip, then sat down again on the seat that he had left. Thereupon Antinous spoke to the rest: 'Now rise, my friends, one after the other from left to right, beginning from where the wine is poured.'

The words of Antinous pleased them all. The first to rise was Leodes son of Oenops; he was their sacrificer, and always sat next to the mixing-bowl. He alone among them was an enemy of unrighteousness, and was indignant with all the suitors. He was now the first to pick up the bow and the swift arrow. He walked to the threshold, took his stand and began to make trial of the bow. But he could not string it; his soft hands were unused to such work, and as he strained they quickly failed him. Then he said to the suitors: 'Friends, this bow will never be strung by me; let some other take it. Many a lord, because of it, will find his courage and spirit leave him. And after all, better surely to die outright than to live on without ever winning the prize we look for as we meet together here day after day. There are still those here who crave and hope to marry Odysseus' wife Penelope; but once such a man has tried the bow and seen the truth, let him seek out and woo with gifts some other long-robed Achaean woman, and let the queen wed whoever brings her the richest gifts and comes to her with good fortune favouring him.'

1. 'Or I am yet too young, and have not strength
   To quell the aggressor's contumely'. COWPER

With these words he put the bow away from him and leaned it against the smooth clean-fitting doors, resting the arrow against the bow-tip, then sat down again on the seat that he had left. But Antinous spoke to him reproachfully: 'Leodes, what words are these that have passed your lips? It is a harsh sentence, a terrible sentence – my anger rises to hear you utter it – if through this bow many a lord is to find his courage and spirit leave him because you yourself lack strength to string it. The son that your honoured mother bore was never meant to draw bows or to shoot arrows, but others among the commanding suitors will string the bow soon enough.' Then he gave an order to the goatherd. 'Come now, kindle a fire in the hall, Melanthius, and beside the fire put a big chair with a fleece over it; and bring out a big cake of fat from the store inside, so that we young men can rub in the grease and supple the bow, then try it again and end the contest.'

So he spoke. Melanthius quickly kindled the fire, put beside it the chair with the fleece and brought the big cake of fat from the store inside; as it melted they warmed the bow with it, then began to try anew, but they could not string the bow and fell far short of the strength it called for. Only Antinous persevered, and Eurymachus of the godlike mien; these were the chief among the suitors and by far the strongest of them all.

Meanwhile the two servants of Odysseus, the cowherd and the swineherd, had left the great hall together, and the king himself had followed them. They were past the doors and past the court-yard when he spoke to them with inviting words: 'Listen, cowherd; listen, swineherd; there is something I would gladly ask you – or shall I keep the thing to myself? No, my heart tells me to speak out. Where would you stand if Odysseus needed helpers – if all of a sudden he came from none knows where, wafted mira-culously to Ithaca? Would you side with the suitors or with Odysseus? Answer me as your heart dictates.'

At this the cowherd uttered a prayer: 'Father Zeus, bring, I beseech, this wish to pass: May that man return with a god for guide. Then' – and here he spoke to the king – 'then you would see what strength I have and how well my hands can play their part.' And Eumaeus too made prayers to all the gods that wise Odysseus might come once more to his own home.

When Odysseus saw that these two at least were loyal-hearted, he spoke in answer to them again: 'I am home already; it is my very self that you see; after much trial and tribulation I have come back in the twentieth year to my own country. I know that of all the men who were in my service you two alone welcome my return; from all the rest I have heard not a single prayer that I should come home again. So to you two I will make solemn promise of the future: if the god subdues the proud suitors beneath my hands, I will find wives for you both and give you possessions and well-built houses near my own; and from henceforward in my eyes you two shall be comrades and brothers of Telemachus. And now there is something else; let me show you plain proof that will let you know me beyond question and will set your hearts at rest – the scar made long ago by the boar's white tusk when the sons of Autolycus and I went to Mount Parnassus.'

And with that he pulled back his rags from over the great scar. The men caught sight of it, looked more closely and burst out weeping; they threw their arms about Odysseus and began in fondness to kiss his head and shoulders, and he in turn kissed their heads and hands. And indeed the sun might have gone down upon their weeping if Odysseus himself had not checked them. 'Cease,' he said, 'from this sobbing tenderness; someone may come out from the hall, may see us here and then take the news to those inside. So let us go back, not all together but one by one – myself first and then you. And let this order of things be agreed upon. When all the rest – I mean the suitors – refuse me the handling of bow and quiver, then you, friend Eumaeus, must carry the bow down the hall and give it into my hands; then tell the women to bar the hall's close-fitting doors; and if any of them in their own quarters hear the din or the groaning of men on our side, then let them not venture out but stay there quietly at their tasks. And for you, friend Philoetius, my orders are to bolt the outer doors of the courtyard and quickly tie a fastening across.' With these words he entered the house, then walked to the stool he had left and sat there; and in their turn the two servants entered.

Just then Eurymachus was handling the bow, passing it now this way, now that, to warm it in front of the bright fire; but even so he could still not string it, and his lofty heart was sadly vexed. In distress of spirit he cried aloud: 'This is hard to bear – a blow to me and to all of us! I am less grieved about the marriage – that rankles too, but there are many Achaean women besides, some of them in this island of Ithaca, some of them in cities else-where. What shames us all is to find our strength no match for the strength of King Odysseus; we are not able to bend his bow, and this will be a disgrace to us that generations to come will hear of.'

Antinous answered: 'Eurymachus, no such thing will hap-pen, nor can you yourself think otherwise. Today is a feast-day throughout this land in honour of the god you know of.[1] Who could bend the bow on such a day? No, set it quietly aside; and as for the axes – what if we let them stand as they are, all of them? No one, I think, will enter Odysseus' hall and carry them off. Come, let the winebearer pour the drops; let us make libation and then put the bow aside. And tomorrow morning tell Melan-thius to bring the best goats from all his herds; thus we may offer thighbones from them to Apollo master of archery, then try the bow and end the contest.'

The words of Antinous pleased them all. Pages poured water on the banqueters' hands, menservants brimmed the bowls with wine, poured the first drops into each man's cup, then filled it. But when they had made libation and drunk to their heart's con-tent, subtle Odysseus spoke among them with cunning purpose: 'Listen, suitors of this great queen. I would ask Eurymachus above all, and with him noble Antinous, who has just uttered such timely counsel – I would ask you indeed to lay aside the bow for today and entrust the issue to the gods; then tomorrow the god will grant victory to whom he pleases. But in the meanwhile let me also take the bow and in your presence put to the proof my strength of hand – have I still the power that once lived in my supple limbs, or has it by now all decayed with my random wanderings and rough living?'

So he spoke. They were all enraged, because they feared he might string the bow, Antinous turned on him and reviled him: 'Miserable stranger, you are out of your wits. Are you not con-tent to dine at ease in our lofty company, never grudged your share in the feast, able to hear all the words that pass between us? No other stranger, no other beggar listens to us discoursing. Wine is crazing you, fragrant wine. Wine is many a man's un-doing, when he gulps his draught and will never drink discreetly.

1. Apollo (the archer).

Wine it was that darkened the wits of Eurytion the centaur in the palace of bold Peirithous. The centaur had come to the Lapiths' country, and now with wine he clouded his understanding and in his frenzy did monstrous things in the very hall of Peirithous. The heroes were seized with indignation; they leapt up, they dragged the centaur across the courtyard and out of doors, they lopped off his ears and nose with the ruthless bronze, and the frenzied creature went his way, taking his retribution with him in his still darkened mind. From this beginning came the long feud between men and centaurs, but it was Eurytion first of all who brought chastisement on himself by his drunkenness. And for you too I predict much tribulation if you should string this bow. You will meet no mild handling hereabouts; we will ship you forthwith to King Echetus, who is savage to any and every man, and from his hands you will never be rescued. No; drink your wine in peace; do not challenge warriors in their prime.'

But wise Penelope countered him: 'Antinous, it is neither honourable nor just to deny his due to any guest of Telemachus who has come to this house. If the stranger here has trust enough in his strength of arm to string the great bow of King Odysseus, do you think he is then to lead me home as bride? He himself – I am sure of it – has no such ambition in his heart. No thought of that need sour the feast of any man here. No, such a thing would be past all reason.'

Eurymachus son of Polybus answered: 'Wise Penelope, daughter of Icarius, we have no fear that this man will wed you – that would indeed be past all reason. But we feel shame at what might be said by Achaean men and women – the common talk of the baser ones: "See these men who are wooing a hero's wife! What feeble creatures they are to him, quite unable to string his bow! Yet a man from nowhere, a roving beggar, has come and strung the bow easily and shot through the iron." So all the gossips' tongues will wag, and that would mean our humiliation.'

Wise Penelope answered him. 'Eurymachus, how can any men expect a good name among the people if they despoil a great lord's house and dishonour it? Why speak of humiliation here? And the stranger that we are speaking of is a powerful man, he is well-built, he claims birth from a noble father. Come, give him the bow and let us see the issue. I will speak plainly, and what I say shall be proved true. If he strings the bow and Apollo grants him triumph, I will clothe him in a fine cloak and tunic; I will give him a cutting javelin to protect him against dogs and men, and a two-edged sword, and sandals for his feet; and I will find him passage to wherever he may choose to go.'

Thoughtful Telemachus said to her: 'Mother, no one among all the Achaeans has a better title than myself to give the bow or to deny it to whomsoever I may decide. Among all the lords in craggy Ithaca and those in the islands that lie towards Elis, not one shall force me against my will, even should I choose to give the stranger this bow outright, to carry away with him.

'And now go up to your room again and look to your own province, distaff and loom, and tell your women to ply their task. The bow shall be the concern of men, and my concern most of all. Authority in this house is mine.'

At this she withdrew to her room in wonder, laying to heart her son's wise words. She mounted with her waiting-women to the upper quarters of the palace, then began weeping for Odysseus, her darling husband, till Athene sent welcome slumber upon her eyelids.

Meanwhile the swineherd had taken the bow and begun to carry it. But the suitors there all made an uproar, and one or another of these young braggarts would throw at him some such words as these: 'Miserable misguided swineherd, where are you bound for with the bow? If Apollo will hear our prayer, he and the other Deathless Ones, it will not be long before the swift hounds that you reared yourself will devour you there among your swine, out of everyone's sight and knowledge.'

At these words he stopped in his course and put down the bow where he stood, dismayed at the outcry from all this multitude in the hall. But then from the other side Telemachus called out threateningly: 'Bring the bow on, all the way, old friend. It will do you no good to serve many masters. Do not make me chase you out from here and stone you back to your own steading. I am younger than you, but I am stronger. I only wish that in hand and sinew I were thus much stronger than all the suitors who fill this palace! Then I would soon send some of them home from this house of mine in a fashion they did not relish – plotters of mischief as they are!'

So he spoke. The suitors burst into merry laughter and forgot the bitterness of their anger towards him. The swineherd now walked on through the hall with bow and arrows, came up to Odysseus and put them in his hands. Then he summoned Eurycleia the nurse and said: 'Wise Eurycleia, Telemachus tells you to bar the hall's close-fitting doors; and if any of you in your quarters should hear the din or the groaning of men on our side, let them not venture out but stay there quietly at their tasks.'

So he spoke. The words were not lost on her, and she barred the doors of the pleasant-sited hall.

Philoetius too went quickly and quietly outside, and shut the outer doors of the fenced courtyard. Under the portico was a fibrous cable from a ship; he made the doors fast with this and came in again, then went and sat on the stool he had left, keeping his eyes upon Odysseus. Odysseus was handling the bow already, turning it to and fro and testing it first this way, then that, in fear that worms had been at the horns when the master of it was far away. And at this, one or another suitor would glance at his neighbour and would say: 'Ah, he must be a knowing fellow, an artist in bows; either he has its twin at home or else he means to make himself one – look at the way he is turning it to and fro, seasoned vagabond as he is!' And another young swaggerer would say: 'May the fellow have as much good fortune as he has a chance of ever stringing the bow!'

So the suitors chattered. As for Odysseus, he finished first his handling and scrutiny of the bow; then, like a master of lyre and song who with utmost ease winds a new string round a peg, fitting the pliant sheepgut at either end, so did Odysseus string the great bow tranquilly. Then he put his right hand to the string to try it, and it sang out beneath his fingers as clear as a swallow's note. Sheer dismay came upon the suitors, and the colour changed on all their cheeks. Then Zeus gave a sign and thundered loud, and King Odysseus was filled with joy that the son of Cronos had sent him such an omen. Then he took the arrow that lay loose on the table by him (the rest were still in the hollow quiver, to be tasted soon by the Achaeans). Next he put it against the bridge and drew the string with the nocks pressed into it – all this without rising from his stool. Then with sure aim he let fly the shaft, not missing the handle-tip of a single one of all the axes; the bronze-pointed arrow went through and out.[1]

With this he spoke to Telemachus: 'Telemachus, the guest who was sitting in your halls has not disgraced you. I did not miss my aim, I had no long labour in stretching the bow. My strength is entire, not sapped as the mocking suitors thought when they taunted me. But the hour has come to get supper too for these Achaeans while daylight lasts, and after that to have the delights of lyre and song, since these are the ornaments of a feast.'

So he spoke, and with his eyebrows he made a sign. At this, King Odysseus' son Telemachus girded on his sword and grasped his spear; then took his stand by the lofty seat close to his father, armed with the glittering bronze.

1. On the ancient problem of how Odysseus shot through the axes I gladly accept the solution offered by Denys Page (*Folktales in Homer's Odyssey* (1973), pp. 95 ff.). These were neither battle-axes nor household axes; they were cult-axes – votive objects of Minoan and Mycenean religion which could be hung upside down on palace walls by bronze or iron rings that were genuine handle-tips. A few such objects actually survive.

Some such explanation was not unknown to antiquity, and Pope seems somehow to have encountered it. In his version of the present book he has for lines 75-7:

'Who first Ulysses' wond'rous bow shall bend
And thro' twelve ringlets the fleet arrow send,
Him will I follow ...'

and for lines 421-3:

'The whizzing arrow vanish'd from the string,
Sung on direct, and thredded ev'ry ring.'

BOOK XXII

VENGEANCE ON THE SUITORS

ODYSSEUS bared his limbs of the rags and leapt up on to the great threshold, grasping the bow and the quiver full of shafts. He poured out the arrows at his feet and spoke thus among the suitors: 'One contest that was to plague contestants[1] is over now. But another mark is left, one that no one hitherto has hit. I mean to find out if I can strike it and if Apollo will grant me glory.'

So he spoke, and aimed the keen arrow at Antinous. The youth had almost raised to his lips a fine two-handled golden goblet, indeed he had it between his hands, ready to taste the wine. No fear of slaughter was in his heart. Who, with his friends feasting round him, would think that one man among so many, let his prowess be what it might, would bring grim death and black doom upon him? But Odysseus took aim and wounded him in the throat, and the arrow-point pierced his delicate neck right through. He swerved to one side, and the cup dropped as the shaft went home. A thick jet of blood gushed from his nostrils; he suddenly kicked the table from him and spilled all the food upon the floor; the bread and the roasted meat were befouled with blood. The suitors filled the house with clamour when they saw Antinous fallen so; they leapt from their seats in huge dismay and their eyes searched up and down the walls, but nowhere was there a shield or spear to lay hands upon. Then with furious words they reviled Odysseus: 'So men are the mark for your arrows, stranger. On your own head be it! Never again shall you make a challenge. You shall not escape the precipice of destruction. The man you have killed was the noblest youth in Ithaca; for that, the vultures shall eat you here.'

Such were their fond imaginings. Every man among them thought it chance that Odysseus had killed his man – fools that they were, unperceiving that the chains of doom were fastened about them one and all!

With a grim frown Odysseus answered: 'Dogs! You thought I should never come home again from Troy, and in that belief you devoured my substance, forced my serving-women to sleep with you, and in cowardly fashion wooed my wife while I still

1. Odysseus echoes the phrase of Antinous, p. 256.

was living. You had no fear of the Deathless Ones whose home
is wide heaven itself, no fear of vengeance from men hereafter.
The chains of doom are upon you now, fastened about you one
and all.'

So he spoke. Ashy terror seized on them all, and every man
looked about him for some escape from the precipice of destruc-
tion. Alone among them, Eurymachus now found words to
answer: 'If you are in truth Odysseus of Ithaca, home again, then
all you have said is just and fair as concerns the doings of the
Achaeans – misdeeds in plenty within these halls, misdeeds in
the countryside as well. But the guilty one lies dead before us;
Antinous was the head and front of all this offending. Nor was
he moved overmuch by any eager desire for marriage. He had
other purposes in view, though Zeus has denied fulfilment to
them – to become himself the king of all this country of Ithaca
and to waylay and kill your son. But now Antinous has his
deserts in death. We ask you then to spare your own people; we
ourselves will go here and there and end by gathering goods
enough to make satisfaction for everything eaten and drunk in
these halls. Every one of us will bring his tribute of twenty
oxen's worth. We will give you bronze and gold till your heart
relents; before that is done we cannot find fault with your indig-
nation.'

With a grim frown Odysseus answered: 'Eurymachus, not if
you all gave me all your patrimony, whatever you have and
whatever more you might come to have, not even then would I
hold back my hands from slaughter till every suitor had paid for
the whole of his transgression. One choice alone lies before you
now – to do battle, or else to take to flight in the hope of shun-
ning death and doom; but I think that many a man among you
will not escape the precipice of destruction.'

So he spoke. Their knees quailed and their heart sank. Eury-
machus spoke again, but this time to them: 'Friends, this man
will never hold back his resistless hands. Now that he has the
bow and the quiver in his grasp he will take aim at us from the
threshold until he has killed us all. Let us at least meet force with
force. Draw your swords and hold up the tables to thwart the
arrows of rapid death. Then let us run at him all together. We
may force him away, perhaps, from the threshold and the door-
way; then let us go up and down the city. We could raise the

hue and cry at once, and soon enough this man would have shot for the last time.'

With these words he drew his keen two-edged sword of bronze and leapt at Odysseus with hideous cries; but at that same moment the king released his shaft, piercing his breast beside the nipple and planting the arrow in his liver. Eurymachus dropped his sword to the ground; he fell down sprawling and writhing over his table, and spilled on the floor his food and his double-handled cup. He struck the ground with his forehead in agony, and with both legs he kicked the tall chair until it rocked; and dimness descended on his eyes.[1]

Amphinomus next rushed upon Odysseus, making at him with keen sword drawn and hoping the king would leave the doorway. But Telemachus was too quick for him, aiming from behind and driving his bronze-tipped spear between his shoulders and out at the chest; he fell heavily and struck the ground full with his forehead. Telemachus darted off, leaving his long-shafted spear in the body, for he much dreaded that if he stayed to pull out the spear, some suitor might dash at him with his sword or stab him as he was stooping down. He ran quickly up to his father and said to him, standing by his side: 'Father, now I will bring you a shield and a pair of spears and a bronze helmet that fits the temples. When I return I will arm myself and give arms to the swineherd too, and the cowherd there; it is better to be armed.'

Odysseus answered: 'Run and get these things while I still have arrows for my defence; I dread to be forced away from the entrance where I am making my stand alone.'

So he spoke, and Telemachus in obedience set off for the room where the good arms were stored. From here he took out four shields and eight spears and four bronze helmets with horsehair plumes. He set out with these and quickly came to his father's side. He himself was first to protect his body with the bronze. The two servants armed themselves likewise and stood beside Odysseus.

As long as the king had arrows enough for his defence, he kept aiming at this or that suitor in his hall; his aim was sure, and down they fell, one upon another. But when the archer's arrows failed him, he let the bow rest against the door-post of the great hall and the gleaming surfaces of the entrance. Round his shoul-

1. 'And endless darkness lay upon his eye.' HOBBES

ders he put a four-layered shield; on his fearless head he set a strong helmet with horsehair crest, while the plume above nodded awesomely; and he seized two powerful spears tipped with gleaming bronze.[1]

Now there was in the wall a certain raised door, and close by the plinth of the hall itself there was a way that led to an open passage; it was commonly shut by close-fitting doors. Odysseus gave the swineherd orders to stand near this and to watch it well. But now Agelaus spoke to the suitors, putting his plan to all of them: 'Friends, could not someone climb to that upper door and give a message to the people? The hue and cry could be raised at once, and soon enough this man would have shot for the last time.'

But the goatherd Melanthius answered him: 'That cannot be, noble Agelaus, the courtyard doors are frighteningly near, and the mouth of the passageway is perilous. One man by himself, if he had but courage, could keep us at bay one and all. But wait! Let me fetch you from the store-room the arms that you need for your defence; it is surely there and nowhere else that Odysseus and his son hid the arms away.'

And with these words the goatherd now went up by the openings[2] in the hall to the store-room of Odysseus. From there he took twelve shields and as many spears and as many plumed helmets of bronze. Then he came out, carrying the arms along with him, and quickly gave them to the suitors. The king's knees quailed and his heart sank as he saw these men putting on the armour and brandishing the long spears, and he felt his task to be hard indeed. To his son he said: 'A new grim fight is upon us now, Telemachus; one of the women must have done this – or perhaps it was Melanthius.'

Telemachus answered: 'Father, the fault lies all with me and with no one else. It was I myself who opened the door of that inner room and then left it open; some enemy must have kept

1. In the long episode following, the vagueness of certain terms in the translation reflects the obscurity of the Greek text. Archaeologists and detectives still vigorously dispute the relative positions and structural nature of doors, passageways, outlets and so forth. In spite of this, the main sequence of events remains clear enough.

2. Probably high up in the hall and serving more or less as loopholes; but the precise meaning is very controversial.

better watch than I. Eumaeus, go and shut the door of that room, and watch to see if one of the women is doing this or if, as I think, it is Melanthius son of Dolius.'

While these words were passing between them, Melanthius went up to the room again to fetch more arms. The swineherd spied him and said to Odysseus, not far away: 'King Odysseus, son of Laertes, look, the same villain that we thought of is going up to the room again. Give me a clear command. Shall I kill him, if I can master him, or shall I bring him here to you to pay for all the iniquities he has plotted in your palace?'

Subtle Odysseus answered him: 'I and Telemachus will hold these headstrong suitors inside the hall, despite their fury. You two must twist back the man's feet and arms and must throw him down inside the room. Then bind his back to a board, fasten a twisted rope to him and hoist him up the tall pillar to near the rafters; then he can live a long time in torment.'

They heard what he told them and obeyed. They approached the room unheeded by the goatherd inside; he was searching for armour in one corner while they took their stand at either door-post and waited there. Then Melanthius made to cross the threshold, in one hand holding a noble helmet and in the other an ample shield, now old and mildewed. It had once been the shield of King Laertes, and he had carried it in his prime; now it was laid aside in the store and the seams of its straps had worn loose. The two men sprang forward and seized the goatherd, dragged him inside by the hair, and threw him fear-stricken on the floor; then, as Odysseus had commanded, they twisted his feet and arms well back, tied them together with galling bonds, fastened a plaited rope to him and hoisted him up the tall pillar to near the rafters. Then Eumaeus mocked at him and said: 'Melanthius, now you can watch the whole night through, reclining upon the easy bed you so well deserve; nor will you miss the sight of Dawn in her broidered robe as she rises from the streams of ocean at that same hour when your custom is to bring in the goats for the suitors' feasting in the halls.'

So Melanthius was left there, racked in those agonising bonds. The others armed themselves again, shut the door and rejoined Odysseus, the man of cunning. Thus then the adversaries stood, facing each other and breathing violence, the four at the threshold and the many warriors down the hall.

But now the daughter of Zeus drew near them; this was no other than Athene, but she had the form and the voice of Mentor. Odysseus rejoiced at sight of her. 'Mentor,' he said, 'keep ruin from us. Do not forget your own dear comrade; I have always been faithful in your service, and you and I have been young together.'

So he spoke, not doubting that this was in truth Athene the gatherer of armies. But the suitors opposite made a great uproar in the hall, and first among them the son of Damastor, Agelaus, spoke to her threateningly: 'Mentor, Odysseus with his pleading must not persuade you to lend him help and to fight the suitors. Our design is this, and I think we shall achieve it: when we have killed these two, father and son, you shall be slain after them because of what you wish to do here; with your own head you shall pay for it. And when our weapons have brought to nothing the violent onslaughts of you all, we will throw together your own possessions, in your house and upon your farmland, with all the possessions of Odysseus. We will neither let your sons live on in your halls nor your wife and daughters go to and fro through the town of Ithaca.'

Such were his threats. Athene's heart was deeply angered, and she turned on the king with harsh indignant words: 'Odysseus, you have not kept unflawed the strength and courage that once you had when for nine years you battled ceaselessly with the Trojans for the sake of white-armed Lady Helen, when you killed so many in deadly fight and by your wisdom contrived the taking of Priam's wide-wayed town. Now that you have returned at last to your own house and your own possessions, how comes it that in face of the suitors you moan for courage as though you had none? Come, dear friend, stand by me and mark my actions.[1] See how well Mentor son of Alcimus will repay your service among these warriors who are your foes.'

So she spoke, but did not as yet give him such advantage as turns the tide; no, she made even further trial of the strength and courage of Odysseus and his noble son. She herself took the semblance of a swallow, and speeding upward she chose a settling-place on the roof-beam of the murky hall.

The suitors were still being urged to battle by the son of Damastor, Agelaus, by Eurynomus and Amphimedon and Demop-

1. 'Come hither Milksop,' says she, 'stand by me.' HOBBES

tolemus, by Peisander son of Polyctor, by subtle Polybus. These were by far the first in prowess of those still left to fight for their lives; the rest of them had been slain already by the bow and the steady stream of arrows. Agelaus spoke his mind to them all: 'Friends, at last this man must let his resistless hands sink down. You see that Mentor has now forsaken him after uttering those empty boasts; the four are left alone at the threshold. So hurl the long spears at them now – not all of you, but the six in front; if Zeus so wills, Odysseus may be struck down and you win glory. Once he has fallen, we need have no care about the rest.'

Thus instructed, the six then threw their spears with a will, but Athene sent every spear astray. One man hit the doorpost of the building, another the close-fitting door itself, and another's spear, heavy with bronze, lodged itself in the wall. Thus the four escaped the suitors' weapons. Then King Odysseus said to them: 'Friends, now is the time, I think, for us in our turn to hurl our spears at the throng of suitors who after all their former misdeeds are now set upon our destruction.'

So he spoke, and they all aimed straight and threw their spears. Odysseus killed Demoptolemus, Telemachus killed Euryades, the swineherd Elatus, the cowherd Peisander. These suitors bit the wide floor together; the rest fell back to a corner of the hall. The four rushed forward and drew their spears from the dead men's bodies.

But now once more in deadly earnest the suitors threw their sharp spears at them. Athene sent most of the weapons wide; one of them struck the doorpost, another the door, and a third spear lodged itself in the wall. Yet Amphimedon with a glancing throw wounded Telemachus on the wrist, though the bronze did not pierce below the skin; Ctesippus too sent his long spear over Eumaeus' shield to graze his shoulder, but the spear flew on and dropped to the ground.

Once more, Odysseus and those around him flung their spears at the thronging suitors, and Odysseus hit Eurydamas, Telemachus hit Amphimedon, the swineherd hit Polybus. The cowherd, aiming at Ctesippus, drove his weapon into his breast and spoke exultingly: 'Son of Polytherses, you who will always have your jest, a man should not yield to folly, should not talk big. He should leave his case to the gods instead, since the gods are stronger far than he. This gift is to match the cow's foot that you once offered to King Odysseus when he walked as a vagrant about his house.'

So spoke the guardian of the cattle. Meanwhile Odysseus with his long spear stabbed Agelaus in close fight. Telemachus stabbed Leocritus in mid-flank, driving the bronze right through; with face forward, the man crashed down, and struck the floor with his full forehead. Then Athene from the roof above lifted up her man-destroying aegis. The suitors were distraught with terror. They fled round the hall like a herd of cattle that the darting gadfly sets upon and drives panic-stricken in the spring season when days are lengthening. Or as when eagles with crooked claws and with hooked beak dart down from the mountains and swoop on lesser birds – the lesser birds scatter in flight over the plain, cowering away from the place of clouds above, but the eagles pounce on them, defenceless and refugeless as they are, while the onlookers enjoy the chase – so did the four rush upon the suitors across the hall and strike them down on this side and that. As the men's heads were dashed on the ground, a hideous groaning rose up from them and all the floor streamed with blood.

But now Leodes threw himself forward and clasped Odysseus' knees. In a rush of words he besought his mercy : 'In supplication I come to you, Odysseus; hold me in reverence, have compassion. I tell you, I spoke no evil and did no evil to the serving-women in your halls; far from it, I strove to check the others when they were guilty of such things, but they would not heed me and keep their hands from unrighteousness. Hence they have met this hideous fate for their own presumptuous deeds. But I who among all these men was only a sacrificer, I who have done nothing – I also am now to fall, since doers of good earn no gratitude.'

With a grim scowl Odysseus answered : 'If indeed you claim to have been their sacrificer, you must have prayed here time and again that the winning of the return I longed for should always be kept far from me while my own dear wife departed with you and bore you children. Therefore you shall not escape bitter death.'

Thereupon he seized in his powerful hand the sword that Agelaus in death had dropped and left lying on the ground. Before Leodes had ended speaking, the sword cut clean across his throat and his head mingled with the dust.

There was one man seeking still to escape black doom – Phemius the bard, son of Terpius, who under duress had made music for the suitors. With the clear-toned lyre still in his hands, he stood not far from the raised door. He was wondering inwardly whether to steal away from the hall and seat himself at the stone altar of Zeus of the Court, the same on which Laertes and then Odysseus had many a time burnt the oxen-bones of sacrifice, or to dart forward to Odysseus and clasp his knees in supplication. As he pondered, it seemed the better thing to clasp the king's knees. So he laid his hollow lyre on the ground between the great bowl and the silver-studded seat, then darted forward to Odysseus and seized hold of his knees and spoke: 'In supplication I come to you, Odysseus; hold me in reverence, have compassion. You yourself will repent it afterwards if you kill a man like me, a bard, singing for gods and men alike. I am self-taught; the god has implanted in my breast all manner of ways of song, and I am worthy to sing before you just as before a god. Do not behead me in thoughtless passion. And besides, your own dear son Telemachus will bear me witness that if I came often to your palace to sing to the suitors after feasting, it was never of my own will or choice; their numbers and strength were too much for me, and they compelled me to come to them.'

When Prince Telemachus heard these words, he spoke at once to his father at his side: 'Stop; do not use the sword on this guiltless man. Then there is also Medon the page, who in my childhood always took care of me in this house. Let us spare him too, unless indeed he was killed just now by Philoetius or Eumaeus, or encountered you as you raged across the hall.'

So he spoke, and the page heard him. A cautious man, he was lying crouched underneath a chair, with a new-flayed oxhide pulled over him as he sought to escape black doom. But now he quickly leapt up from there, threw off the oxhide and darted up to clasp the knees of Telemachus, imploring him in a rush of words: 'Dear friend, I am here. Spare me yourself, and ask your father in his triumph not to destroy me with the sword, inflamed as he is against the suitors who wasted his substance in this hall and who held yourself in no esteem – fools that they were!'

Odysseus smiled as he answered him: 'Take heart; my son's intercession has saved your life. And let this teach you, and fit you to teach others also, how a righteous life triumphs over an unrighteous one. Now leave this hall, this scene of slaughter, you and the bard of many lays. Sit in the courtyard till I have done all that needs doing in this house.'

So he spoke, and the pair of them went out from the hall and sat down at the altar of mighty Zeus, anxiously peering this way and that, and dreading to see at any moment the face of death.

Odysseus too looked searchingly round his hall for any man who still might be lurking there alive and hoping thus to escape black doom. But he saw the suitors, one and all, lying huddled in blood and dust. They were like the fish that fishermen with their close-meshed nets have drawn out from the whitening sea on to the curving beach; they are all heaped upon the sand, longing for the sea waves, but the sun beats down and takes their lives. So did the suitors lie in heaps, one upon another.

Then Odysseus said to Telemachus: 'Now call Eurycleia the nurse for me. I must speak to her about something that is much in my mind.' The son did as his father told him. He rattled the door and called to the nurse: 'Come now, rouse yourself, Eurycleia, you whose long years of service here have made you warden of all our women. Come out now at my father's bidding; he needs to have speech with you.'

The words he spoke were not lost on her. She opened the doors into the hall and stepped out as Telemachus led the way. She found Odysseus among the bodies of the slain, spattered with clotted gore like a lion that has devoured an ox and now paces upon his way with his chest and his jaws each side all over blood and with aspect grim to look upon; such did Odysseus appear now, with hands and feet spattered alike. When she saw the corpses and all the blood, she made as if to shout loud in triumph at the great deed she saw achieved. But Odysseus stopped her and checked her impulse. 'Old nurse,' he said, 'let all rejoicing rest in your heart; do not go too far; utter no cry of exultation. Vaunting over men slain is a monstrous thing. These men have perished because the gods willed it so and because their own deeds were evil. They had no regard for any man, good or bad, who might come their way; and so by their own presumptuous follies they brought on themselves this hideous end. But now you must tell me the whole truth about the women in my palace, which of them are disloyal to me and which are innnocent.'

Eurycleia the nurse answered him: 'My child, I will tell you the plain truth. You have fifty serving-women here whom we have trained in their proper duties – to card wool and to bear servitude. Of these there are twelve in all who have trodden the path of shamelessness, heeding neither me nor the queen herself. As for Telemachus, he had only begun to grow towards manhood, and his mother would not let him assume command over these women. But now let me go up again to the room above and tell your wife about all these things; some god has sent sleep upon her.'

Subtle Odysseus said in answer: 'Do not rouse her yet; speak instead of those of the women whose mind till now has been set on shamelessness; bid them come here.'

So he spoke, and the old nurse went off down the hall to give his message to these women and make them come quickly. Then he called to Telemachus and the cowherd and the swineherd and spoke to them thus: 'Now begin to carry the corpses out, and tell the women to do the same. Then wash and sponge all the seats and tables till they are clean. When you have put the whole house in order, take the servants outside the building, between the round-house and the strong courtyard-wall, and strike them with your long sharp swords till you have taken the life from them and they have forgotten all the delights of secret love that they had once in the suitors' arms.'

So he spoke. And now the women came flocking down together, groaning bitterly, weeping plenteously. First they carried out of the house all the bodies of the dead suitors and laid them under the courtyard portico, propping them one against another; Odysseus directed and urged them on, and under constraint they went on carrying. Then they washed and sponged the seats and tables. Meanwhile Telemachus and the cowherd and the swineherd scraped the floor of the hall with shovels, and the maidservants took the scrapings away outside. When the whole house had been put in order, the men took the women out of doors, between the round-house and the strong courtyard-wall, and penned them inside a narrow space from which there was no way out. Then Telemachus addressed his helpers: 'Never let it be said that sluts like these had a clean death from me. They have heaped up outrage on me and on my mother; they have been the suitors' concubines.'

So he spoke, and stretched a ship's cable between a tall pillar and the round-house, fastening it high up so that no woman's feet could touch the ground. Just as long-winged thrushes or just as doves, on their way to roost, strike against a snare set in a thicket and find their death in what should have been their sleeping-place, so with their heads in a single line the women's necks were all caught and noosed, to make them die the most piteous death. For a little while their feet kept writhing, but not for long.

As for Melanthius, they brought him out to the entrance and the courtyard; they cut off his nose and ears with the ruthless bronze, tore out his parts to be eaten raw by dogs, and in savage fury lopped off his hands and feet.

Then, having washed their own hands and feet, they joined Odysseus in the hall with their task accomplished. Odysseus turned to Eurycleia: 'Now, old nurse, bring sulphur to cleanse away this pollution; bring fire as well, so that then I may purify the house. Then ask Penelope to come here with her waiting-women, and tell all the other maidservants to come back here as well.'

Eurycleia the nurse replied: 'Yes, my child, all that you say is well said. But let me bring you a cloak and a tunic to put around you. You must not stand any longer here with no more than rags round your broad shoulders; that is something you might be blamed for.'

Odysseus answered: 'In the first place, let a fire be made for me in the hall.'

The old nurse did not neglect his words. She brought fire and she brought sulphur, and with this Odysseus thoroughly cleansed the hall and the palace and the courtyard.

Then Eurycleia went back through the hall to give the message to the women and make them come quickly. They came from their quarters, torch in hand; they fell on Odysseus and embraced him, kissing his head and shoulders, seizing his hands. And a tender longing came upon him to sob and weep, because he knew all of them once more, knew them from the heart.

LAUGHING loud, the old nurse set off for the upper rooms to tell the queen that her own husband was in the house. Her knees moved fast, her feet bustled on till she stood at the bedside of her mistress. 'Penelope, wake from your sleep, dear child, and see now with your own eyes the sight you have coveted day after day. Odysseus has come; he has lingered long, but now he is home. And he has slain the suitors besides, the braggarts who infested his house and devoured his substance and overrode the will of his son.'

But wise Penelope answered her: 'Dear nurse, the gods must have crazed your wits. They have power to make a wise man foolish, and again they set a weak-witted one on the path to wisdom. Your own mind was once well-poised; they have warped it now. Why do you mock my sorrow thus, waking me now to hear this folly and robbing me of the pleasant sleep that had wrapped me round and closed my eyes? Never before had I slept so well since Odysseus left me to visit that evil city Ilium whose name is an abomination. No; go back, go down to the hall again. If any other of all my women had roused me from sleep with such a message, I would quickly have sent her back repentant; but your grey hairs shall save you from that.'

But Eurycleia answered again: 'Dear child, in no way am I mocking your sorrow. In sober truth Odysseus is here; he is home again, just as I said. He is that same stranger whom everyone mocked at in the hall. Telemachus knew of his presence early, but in his wisdom he kept his father's designs hidden, to assure his vengeance on these overweening violent men.'

So she spoke, and her mistress was overjoyed. She leapt from her bed and embraced the old woman with many tears. Then her words came forth in rapid flight: 'Dear nurse, if indeed he is home again as you say, tell me truly how he mastered the shameless wooers; he was one man, and they were always a multitude in the hall.'

Eurycleia answered: 'I did not see; I was not told. I could only hear men's dying groans; we women were crouching terror-stricken in a corner of the room, locked in behind the close-fitting door, till your son Telemachus called me out; his father had sent him to summon me. Then I found Odysseus standing among the corpses of the slain. They lay around him, one above another, over the hard-trodden floor; your heart would have rejoiced to see it. And now the suitors lie all heaped up at the courtyard gates, and Odysseus has had a great fire lit and is purifying the place with sulphur; moreover he told me to summon you. Come down with me, then, so that you two after all your sorrows may tread the pathway of heart's gladness. Your hope deferred is fulfilled at last. He himself is living, is home and is at the hearth; he has found here both you and your son; and as for the suitors who did him wrong, he has taken vengeance on them all in his own house.'

But wise Penelope answered her: 'Dear nurse, do not laugh and exult so soon. You know how welcome the sight of him here would be to all – welcome to me above the rest, and to the son born to us both. But the tale you tell cannot be the truth; it must be some god who has slain these haughty-minded suitors, in anger at their outrageous pride and their evil deeds, since they had regard for no man, good or bad, who might come their way; and so by their own presumptuous follies they brought on themselves this evil end. But Odysseus has lost his chance of homecoming – Odysseus himself is lost, far away from the Achaean land.'

Eurycleia answered: 'Child, what words are these that have passed your lips? Your husband is here, he is at the hearth, and still you say he will never come home again; but your heart has always been unbelieving. Wait – there is something else. I can offer you certain proof – the scar that the boar's white tusk gave him long ago. As I was washing him I spied it, and was eager to tell you of it yourself, but he in the cunning of his heart clutched at my jaw and forbade my speaking. But now come down. I will stake my life on it; if I prove a liar, kill me with the most pitiable of deaths.'

Wise Penelope answered her: 'Wide though your wisdom may be, dear nurse, it is hard for you to probe the purposes of the eternal gods. Nevertheless, let us go down to join my son. I would gladly see these men in death, and the one who has brought death upon them.'

With these words she began descending from her room, much wondering whether to stand apart and question her husband thus or whether to go up close to him and to clasp and kiss his head and hands. But having entered, having crossed the stone threshold, she sat down by the further wall, with her face in the firelight towards Odysseus. He was seated against the tall bearing-pillar, looking down and awaiting what words his wife might utter, now that she had set eyes upon him. But she sat for a long time in silence, with bewilderment upon her heart, because as her eyes searched his face she thought him one moment like Odysseus and then again could not see him so because of his miserable rags.

Then Telemachus spoke to her reproachfully: 'Mother – but with that ungentle heart are you indeed a mother? – why do you shun my father thus? Why not sit beside him, ask him, question him? No other wife would be heartless enough to keep aloof from her husband so, when after much trial and tribulation she had him again, in the twentieth year, in his own country. But you have always been stony-hearted.'

Wise Penelope answered him: 'Child, the heart in my breast is dazed. I can neither frame a greeting for him nor ask a question nor look him in the eyes. But if indeed this is Odysseus, home again, we two shall soon know each other better, because we have certain secret tokens, known to ourselves but hidden from all others.'

King Odysseus smiled at her words. Then to Telemachus he said: 'Telemachus, leave your mother now to make her own trial of me here; before long she will know me better; but because I am still filthy, because I still have these wretched rags about me, for that reason she disesteems me and does not yet think I am the man. And now for ourselves – we must think what action will serve us best. When in any country someone has killed one man – one man who does not leave behind him a body of champions for his cause – even then he will leave his land and kinsmen and make himself an outlaw. But we for our part have killed the bulwark of the city, the noblest of all the youths in Ithaca. These are the things I bid you think of.'

Thoughtful Telemachus replied: 'Dear father, look to all this yourself. You have the name of the deepest counsellor in the world; no mortal man can vie with you there. Then the rest of us will follow you eagerly. Our help, I promise, shall not be lacking, as far as our strength allows.'

Odysseus answered: 'I will tell you then what seems best to me. First of all you must bathe and put fresh tunics on, and tell the maidservants in the hall to get fresh clothes as well. And then let the heaven-taught bard with his ringing lyre lead our steps in the cheerful dance, so that anyone listening from outside – a passer-by or one of our neighbours here – may think that it is a wedding feast. No talk of the slaying of the suitors must spread through the town till we have gone out to our wooded farmland. After that, we will ponder whatever stratagem the Olympian may put into our minds.'

So he spoke, and the others obeyed him faithfully. They bathed and they put fresh tunics on, the women decked themselves out, the heaven-taught bard took his hollow lyre and roused in them the desire for happy music and graceful dancing. So the great hall resounded now to the steps of men and of slender-waisted women taking their pleasure thus. And outside the house some townsman catching the sound would say: 'Doubtless one of her many suitors has married the queen at last. Heartless woman! She had not the grace to keep to the house of her true husband until he came.'

So men talked, the truth of it all being hidden from them. But inside Odysseus' house itself Eurynome the housekeeper had bathed the king, had anointed him with oil and had put a fine cloak and tunic on him. Athene too now shed great handsomeness over his head and shoulders. It was as when a man adds gold to a silver vessel, an artist taught by Hephaestus and Athene to master his craft through all its range, so that everything that he makes is beautiful; just so the goddess gave new nobility to the head and shoulders of Odysseus. As he left the bath he looked like one of the Deathless Ones; then he came and sat on the seat he had risen from, opposite his wife. And now he spoke to her: 'Wayward woman, surely the dwellers in Olympus have given you a heart more hard to melt than any among all womankind. No other wife would be heartless enough to keep aloof from her husband so, when after much trial and tribulation she had him again in the twentieth year in his own country. Nurse, come now and make me a bed where I can lie alone; plainly the queen has a heart of iron.'

Wise Penelope answered him: 'Wayward man, I am not proud and I am not scornful; I am not much bewildered; I have not forgotten how you looked when you sailed from Ithaca in the long-oared vessel. Come, Eurycleia, make a bed for him in the bridal room that he built so skilfully himself. Fetch out a bedstead, you and the other women, and then put the bedding on it, fleeces and blankets and shining rugs.'[1]

So she spoke, putting her husband to the test. Then Odysseus in sudden anger said to his faithful wife: 'Your words have wounded me to the quick.[2] Who can have put my bed elsewhere? That would task the most cunning workman, unless a god whose will can make all things easy should come in person and set it down in some other place. No mortal on earth – no, not if he were in his prime – would find it easy to shift that bed, because a strange secret lies in its fashioning. I was the maker, no one else. Inside the courtyard there was a bushy long-leaved olive tree in its prime and pride; it was as thick as a pillar is. Round this tree, using close-set stones, I built a bedroom from start to finish and carefully roofed it in above. I added faultlessly-fitting doors. Then I lopped the olive's leafy branches, rough-hewed the trunk from the root upwards, then trued the surface till I had made a bedpost of it; I handled the bronze as a workman should, and where holes were needed I used my auger. Working out from there, I shaped the frame complete, inlaying it with silver and gold and ivory and stretching across it bright crimson oxhide. There is my story of that secret. I do not know if the bed still stands untouched, or if by now some man has cut the olive-tree's trunk below and moved the bed to another place.'

So he spoke. Her knees failed her, her heart melted then and there as she knew for truth the undoubted tokens Odysseus gave her. Then in tears she ran across to him, and throwing her arms

1. In interpreting the famous test of the marriage bed I follow the opinion of a minority. On any view, Penelope is deliberately suggesting something that would be nonsensical to one who knew the secret. On the view I take (which implies the change of one Greek letter to give the sense 'inside' instead of 'outside') she does not suggest that the immovable bed should be moved outside but that a movable one should be put in the space already occupied by the immovable bed.

2. At the beginninng of this speech, and again half-way through line 203, Odysseus addresses Penelope with a vocative which may mean 'woman' or 'wife' or 'queen'. I dare not commit myself, and have preferred omission.

about his neck she kissed his head and began to speak: 'Odysseus, do not be angry with me now; you were always the most understanding of mankind. It was the gods who sent us misery, grudging us a life with each other, grudging us the happiness of our prime and the passage thence to the threshold of old age. But do not hold it against me now, do not nurse your anger, if I did not lovingly welcome you as soon as I had set eyes upon you. Deep in my heart I always have had misgivings that some strange man might come and beguile me with his words; schemers of dark designs are many. There was Argive Helen, child of Zeus; never would she have lain with a foreign lover if she had but known that the warrior sons of the Achaeans were to carry her back again to her own land. But the god impelled her to do the shameless deed; not till then did her mind conceive the fatal folly that was the beginning of distress not only for her but for us also. But now – you have told me beyond all contradiction the secrets of how our bed was built, though no one ever set eyes upon it but you and I and that one maid, Actoris, whom my father gave me when first I came here and who kept the door of that strong-built room. Now indeed you have won my stubborn heart at last.'

Thus she spoke, and quickened in him the mood for tears; he wept as he held the true-hearted wife in whom his soul delighted. As land is welcome to shipwrecked sailors when out at sea Poseidon has struck their gallant vessel – the sport of tempest and swelling waves – and now a few of them have swum out from the whitening waters to a refuge on shore, their bodies all encrusted with brine – as welcome as is the dry land to those when they set foot there with all their miseries behind them – so welcome to her was the husband she kept her gaze upon, and her white arms about his neck would not even now let him go. Rosy-fingered Dawn when she appeared might have found them still in melting mood, but Athene of the gleaming eyes turned her thought to another stratagem. She held back the night to linger long at the horizon, checking Dawn of the broidered robe at the edge of Ocean and bidding her not to yoke as yet the rapid horses that bring men light, Lampus and Phaethon, the young steeds of Dawn.

At last Odysseus spoke again: 'Wife, we have still not come to the end of all our troubles. There is vast labour, long and vexing, in store for me; I am bound to endure it till the end. Such was the prophecy that I had from the spirit of Teiresias on the day I went down into Hades' house in search of homecoming for my comrades and myself. But come now, wife, let us go to bed and seek our repose and pleasure in welcome sleep.'

Thoughtful Penelope answered him: 'Your bed shall be ready as soon as you desire it, now that the gods have brought you back to your own land and your pleasant-sited house. But since you have just recalled the thing – since the god has put it into your heart – tell me of this forthcoming trial. Sooner or later, I surely must learn what it is to be. If I hear it now, what harm?'

Odysseus answered: 'I fear you are over-anxious to make me repeat the prophet's words. Well, you shall have them without disguise, though like myself you will find them cold comfort. He said I must pass through many cities, holding in my hands a balanced oar till I came to men who know nothing of the sea, who eat food unseasoned with salt and are unacquainted with ships and their crimson cheeks or with balanced oars that are to ships as are wings to birds. And the prophet gave me a token that could not fail; I will reveal it to you now. When another traveller falls in with me and takes the thing upon my shoulder to be a winnowing-fan, then, Teiresias said, I must plant my oar in the ground and offer to Lord Poseidon the noble sacrifice of a ram and a bull and a boar that mates with sows; then I must turn home again and make offering of sacred hecatombs to the deathless gods whose home is wide heaven itself, to each one of the gods in turn. And death is to come to me far from sea, a gentle death that will end my days when the years of care have left me frail while my people round me enjoy all happiness. All this, he said, was to come to pass.'

Wise Penelope answered him: 'If indeed the gods are to grant you a happier old age, you may well hope to find at last a refuge from tribulation.'

Such were the words that passed between them. Meanwhile by the light of burning torches Eurynome and the nurse were giving the bed its downy coverlets. When their busy hands had covered the firm wood all over, old Eurycleia went back to her own room to sleep, while with torch in hand Eurynome as their chambermaid walked before the two on their way to bed. She

brought them to their own room and left them, and they passed
on with much content to where as of old their bed awaited them.[1]
As for Telemachus and the cowherd and the swineherd, they
rested their feet from dancing now, told the women to do like-
wise, and themselves then lay down to rest in the shadowy halls.

The two in their room enjoyed the delights of love, then pleased
one another with recounting what had befallen each. The queen
told how much she had suffered in these halls, seeing always
there the pernicious multitude of suitors who in wooing her had
slaughtered so many beasts, fat sheep and oxen, and drawn so
much wine from the great jars. The king told of harm he had done
to others and misery he had endured himself. Penelope listened to
him enraptured, and sleep did not fall upon her eyelids till he had
told his tale to the end.

He related first how he overcame the Cicones, then how he
reached the fruitful land of the Lotus-Eaters; the crimes of the
Cyclops and afterwards his own vengeance on him for the brave
comrades pitilessly devoured; his coming to Aeolus, who received
him gladly and sent him upon his way, though his homecoming
was still barred by fate, and a tempest caught him up again and
drove him in lamentation over the teeming sea; his putting in at
Telepylus, where the Laestrygonians destroyed his ships and
comrades. He told moreover of Circe's wiles and deceitfulness, and
how he voyaged in his vessel to the dank dwelling-place of Hades
to question the spirit of Teiresias, and there saw not his comrades
only but his own mother who bore and reared him. Then how he
heard the Sirens singing and came to the Wanderers, to grim
Charybdis and to Scylla, whom no man ever passed by un-
scathed; how his comrades slaughtered the cattle of the sun and
Zeus struck the ship with a reeking thunderbolt so that all his
comrades perished there although he himself avoided doom; how
he came to the island of Ogygia and to the nymph Calypso, who
kept him there in her arching caves, desiring him to be her hus-
band, lavishing every care upon him and offering him deathless-
ness and agelessness – yet all this without winning his heart to it.
Then how after long toil he came to the Phaeacians, who hon-
oured him as they might a god and sent him by ship to his own
land with ample presents of bronze and gold and garments. This

1. Many good scholars, ancient and modern, have held that the
original *Odyssey* ended here.

was the last thing that he told of; then sleep overcame him, sleep that soothes limbs and anxious hearts.

Then Athene, goddess of gleaming eyes, moved her care to another thing. When it seemed to her that Odysseus had had his heart's content of both love and sleep, forthwith she roused up Dawn of the broidered robe from Ocean to bring light to mankind again. And Odysseus too roused himself from his soft bed and instructed Penelope in these words: 'Wife, we have both had our fill of troubles, you in this house shedding tears of longing over my perilous voyage home, I abroad while Zeus and the other gods thwarted my craving with misfortunes and kept me far from my own land. But now that we two have come together in the bed we set our thoughts upon, you must keep watch in the house itself over all the possessions left to me. As for the flocks the proud suitors ravaged, much of the loss I mean myself to retrieve by pillage, and the rest our Ithacans shall make good till they have filled all my folds again. But now I must go to the wooded farmland to see my father – he has been in sorrow for me so long. And to you, my wife, wise though you are, I leave this bidding. At early sunrise, news will be spread abroad of the suitors that I killed in my halls. Do you therefore go to the upper room with your waiting-women. Sit there, look at no one and question no one.'

With these words he settled the armour about his shoulders, roused Telemachus and the cowherd and the swineherd and told them also to take in their hands the weapons of war. They obeyed, they armoured themselves with bronze, they opened the doors and issued forth, Odysseus leading. By this time light was over the land, but Athene cloaked the four in darkness and swiftly led them out of the town.

BOOK XXIV

THE SUITORS JOIN THE GHOSTS – ODYSSEUS
AND LAERTES – THE BATTLE RENEWED AND ENDED

CYLLENIAN Hermes began to summon the suitors' ghosts; he held in his hand the golden rod that he uses to lull men's eyes asleep when he so wills, or again to wake others from their slumber; with this he roused them and led them on, and they followed him, thinly gibbering. As in a recess of some eerie cave a chain of bats may be hanging downwards from the rock, but one of them drops from the clinging cluster and then all the rest flit squeaking round, so did these ghosts travel on together squeaking, while easeful Hermes led them down through the ways of dankness. They passed the streams of Ocean, the White Rock, the Gates of the Sun and the Land of Dreams, and soon they came to the field of asphodel, where the souls, the phantoms of the dead, have their habitation.

There they found the soul of Achilles and those of Patroclus and great Antilochus and Aias, who of all the Achaeans was noblest in form and aspect after the son of Peleus himself. These were gathered about Achilles when there came towards them the sorrowful soul of Agamemnon; round him were those who together with him met doom and death in the palace of Aegisthus. Achilles was the first to speak: 'Son of Atreus, we thought that of all our warrior princes you were always dearest to the Thunderer because you commanded so many brave-hearted men in the land of Troy where we Achaeans endured so much. Yet deadly fate, which no man, once he is born, can shun, was appointed to visit you thus early. Would that, in all the glory you mastered then, you had met your doom and death at Troy! Then all the Achaeans would have heaped up a cairn for you, and for your son as well as yourself you would have won great renown in after-times. But instead it was fated that you should fall by the most pitiable of deaths.'

And the soul of Agamemnon answered: 'Son of Peleus, godlike Achilles, happy were you to have died at Troy, far from home, while all around you the noblest of Trojans and Achaeans were being slain as they contended for your body. Majestic always, at that hour also you lay in majesty, there in the eddying cloud of

dust, and horse and chariot were nothing to you now. The rest of
us fought there all day long, nor should we ever have ceased from
the battle if Zeus had not put an end to it by sending a great
tempest down. We carried you then from the battlefield to the
ships, placed you on a bier, cleansed your fair flesh with warm
water and with unguents, and the Danaans stood all about you
with hot tears falling and hair shorn. Having heard the tidings,
your mother herself rose from ocean with other divinities of the
waters; over the sea there now came forth an unearthly lamen-
tation, and shuddering fell on the limbs of the Achaeans. And
indeed they would have started up and made for their ships, had
they not been checked by one who was rich in ancient wisdom
and whose counsel had been proved best before. This was Nestor;
eager to help them, he now cried out: "Stand there, you Argives;
do not turn to flight, young Achaean warriors. This is the mother
of Achilles; she is coming now to her dead son's side, and with her
are other divinities of the waters." At these words the Achaeans
checked their flight; the daughters of the ancient sea-god stood
round about you, wailing piteously, and clothed you with celestial
garments; and nine Muses sang your dirge with sweet responsive
voices. Not one Argive could you have seen there who was not
weeping, the clear notes so went to their hearts. For seventeen
days and seventeen nights we lamented for you, immortal beings
and mortal men; on the eighteenth day we committed you to the
flames and slaughtered round you many fat sheep and oxen with
curving horns. You were burned in garments such as gods have,
with plenteous unguents and with honey, and throughout the
burning, many armoured Achaean warriors in chariots and on
foot made their swift and resounding way about your pyre. When
the flame of Hephaestus had consumed you, at break of day we
gathered your white bones, Achilles, and steeped them in pure
wine and unguents. Your mother gave us a golden urn that had
two handles – given her, she said, by Dionysus, and made by re-
nowned Hephaestus himself. In this your bones now lie, Achilles,
mingled with those of dead Patochus but apart from those of
Antilochus, whom you cherished more than all other comrades
after dead Patroclus himself. And over the bones our mighty host
of Argive spearsmen reared a tall cairn on a jutting headland
above the broad Hellespont, to be descried from far out at sea by
men now living and men who shall live after us. Then in full

view in the place of contest your mother laid out prizes for the
Achaean chieftains; she had begged the gods for them, and most
noble prizes they were. In your lifetime you witnessed the funeral
games of many warriors, games that honour the death of princes
when the young men gird up their loins and prepare for contest;
but had you but seen these gifts, you must needs have wondered
more – these noble prizes, set out in your honour there by your
mother Thetis the silver-sandalled, because you were very dear to
the gods. And thus not even in death have you lost your name,
but for all time among all mankind the fame of you will be great,
Achilles. But for me what such comfort is there, after winding up
the skein of war? At my return Zeus plotted a horrible end for
me at the hands of Aegisthus and my accursed wife.'

While such discourses passed between them, Hermes the
Radiant One drew near, leading down the souls of the suitors
who had fallen by Odysseus' hand. Amazed to see this, the two
heroes moved straight towards them. Agamemnon's soul at once
knew Amphimedon, who had entertained him in other days at his
house in Ithaca. The son of Atreus was first to speak: 'Son of
Melaneus, what disaster has brought you all down to this land
of darkness, all of you men of mark, all of you of one age? One
who was seeking a town's best warriors would make no other
choice. Did Poseidon destroy you in your ships, raising up rough
gales and towering waves? Or did hostile men strike you down
on land as you drove off their flocks and herds or as they defended
their town and women? Answer me, for I call myself your guest.
Do you not remember how once I came to your house in Ithaca –
King Menelaus was with me also – to urge Odysseus to join with
us and to sail to Ilium? A whole month it was before we ended
our passage overseas; it was hard to win over Odysseus the city-
sacker.'

The soul of Amphimedon answered him: 'King, I remember all
you speak of, and I in turn will tell you unswervingly of our sad
end and the manner of death that overtook us. Odysseus had
long since been gone, and we were now wooing his wife. She
neither refused outright a marriage she detested nor yet would
she let it come to pass, but all the while she was planning death
and dark doom for us. Here is one scheme that she devised. She
set up in her hall an ample web, long and delicate, and began to
weave. At the same time she addressed us: "Young men who

after Odysseus' death have come here to woo me, you are eager for this marriage with me; nevertheless I ask your patience till I have finished weaving this robe, so that what I have spun may not be wasted and go for nothing. It is King Laertes' burial-robe, for the time when he is overtaken by the grim doom of distressful death. I dread reproach from Achaean women here for allowing one who had gathered great possessions to lie at his death without a shroud." So she spoke, and our wills consented. From that time on she would weave the great web all day, but when night came she would have torches set beside her and would unravel the work. For three years on end this trickery foiled the trusting suitors; but when seasons passed and the fourth year came, one of her maids who knew the secret revealed the truth, and we came upon her undoing the glossy web; so with ill grace she finished the work perforce. With the weaving over, she washed the great web and then displayed it; it shone out like the sun or moon.

'But at that same time some spiteful god brought Odysseus back – who can say from where? – brought him to the edge of the farmland and to the swineherd's cottage. The king's son found his way there too after sailing back from sandy Pylos. The pair of them plotted the suitor's death – an evil death – and then took their way on to the town; or rather, Telemachus went first and Odysseus followed him, led by the swineherd and wearing tattered garments, in the shape of an old, wretched beggar, stooping over a stick and with dismal rags about his body.

'Not one of us could tell him for what he was, this newcomer, not even the older ones amongst us; we assailed him with insults and pelted him, and for a while he bore patiently with the jeers and blows in his own halls. But the will of Zeus roused his mettle, and then with Telemachus to aid him he took down the weapons in the hall, put them away inside the store-room and shot the bolts. Then in his cunning he told his wife to set out in the hall before us suitors his own bow and the axes of grey iron; these were to be the means of contest and then of death to our doomed selves. Not one of us could stretch the string of that mighty bow; we all fell far short of it. But when the great bow was about to pass into Odysseus' hands, we all clamoured loudly that he should not be given it, however earnestly he might ask; only Telemachus urged the contrary, and ordered the bow to be handed to him. King Odysseus took it, strung it easily and shot through the iron. Then he leapt up on to the great threshold and took his stand there; with ruthless face he poured out the arrows in front of him, and struck and killed Prince Antinous. Then he began to send deadly shafts at others of us also; he took straight aim, and they fell down one upon another. Plainly some god was helping him and those who were beside him, for they swept in their fury down the hall, killing to this side and to that, and as men's heads were dashed on the ground a hideous groaning rose up from them and all the floor streamed with blood. In that fashion we perished, Agamemnon, and our bodies still lie uncared for, inside the palace of Odysseus, since as yet the kinsmen of each of us are still in their homes, knowing nothing; kinsmen would wipe the dark gore away from the wounds, lay out the bodies and make the mourning the dead have earned.'

Then the soul of Agamemnon answered: 'Happy Odysseus, how virtuous was the wife you won! How single-hearted was your incomparable Penelope, how faithfully did she keep remembrance of the husband she had wedded! And therefore the fame of her virtue will never die, and the Deathless Ones will see to it that men on earth have a lovely song in honour of chaste Penelope. Not so will it be with the daughter of Tyndareos. She plotted evil, she slew her wedded husband, and the song of her among mankind will be one of loathing; she will bring ill fame on all her sex, even on the virtuous.'

Such was the discourse of these two phantoms in Hades' halls, in the secret places of the earth.

Odysseus and his companions descended from the city and soon came to Laertes' fine well-farmed land. In years gone by the old king himself after much labour had rescued it from the waste; his house was here, and beside it a range of outhouses where the bondsmen who had to do his pleasure could take their meals or sit or sleep. There was also here an old Sicilian woman who tended her aged master faithfully on this estate away from the town. Then Odysseus said to his son and servants: 'Go inside the house at once yourselves and kill the fattest hog for our meal. I for my part intend to make trial of my father. Will his eyes tell him who I am, or will he not know me after so long a separation?'

With these words he handed his armour to his servants. They

and his son went indoors at once; Odysseus, continuing his quest, walked on towards the fruitful garden. As he went down to the great orchard, he found neither Dolius nor his sons nor any of the bondsmen; they had gone elsewhere to gather stones for a garden wall, with aged Dolius leading the way. His father he did find – alone in that well-tended plot, levelling the soil round a tree and ignobly dressed in a patched and dirty tunic. Round his legs he had oxhide leggings, likewise patched, to save him from thorns; on his hands he had gauntlets against the briars, and on his head was a goatskin cap; he was cherishing his sorrow. As patient Odysseus caught sight of him – an age-worn man with melancholy at heart – he halted beneath a tall pear-tree and shed a tear. Then he wondered inwardly whether to kiss his father, to embrace him and tell him all the tale of his coming home to his own land again, or to question him and make thorough trial of him. As he pondered, it seemed the better thing to make trial first with bantering words. With this in mind, Odysseus walked straight towards him. Laertes had his head bent down as he still kept hoeing round the tree. His son came up and accosted him:

'Old friend, you have no lack of skill in the keeping of a garden. Everything here is tended well; not a thing that is growing in this plot, not a vine or fig-tree, not an olive-tree or pear-tree or seed-bed is left uncared for. But then – let me say this too, and I ask you not to take it ill – you yourself are not cared for so. Beyond the burdensomeness of age, you are sadly unkempt and meanly dressed. Your master cannot suppose you idle and hence deserving of such neglect. No one who saw your height and presence could find anything slavelike in you; you might be one of a royal house. Such a man should be free to bathe, eat well, sleep in a soft bed; some such thing is due to the old. But tell me now, and hold nothing back. Whose servant are you? Whose is this orchard you are tending? And tell me too – I wish to make sure – whether this place I have reached is indeed Ithaca. On my way here, a short while ago, I was told as much by a man who crossed my path; but he was not very courteous, he did not trouble to answer fully or hear me out when I asked whether a former guest of mine were alive still or were dead now and in Hades' house. I will tell you everything – listen, and mark my words.

'I was once host in my own country to a man who reached our

palace gates – the most welcome guest from a foreign land that ever came there. He claimed that by birth he belonged to Ithaca, and said that his father was Laertes son of Arceisius. I brought him in and gave him warm welcome, entertaining him well from my ample stores and offering him at his departure the presents that such a guest deserved. I gave him seven talents of worked gold, a mixing-bowl, all of silver and patterned with flowers, twelve single cloaks with as many rugs and fine robes and tunics, and besides all this, four women of his own choice, handsome and skilled in all proper tasks.'

His father answered him, shedding tears: 'Stranger, the country you have come to is the one you have been asking of, but the men who command it now are violent and lawless. As for all the gifts you bestowed so lavishly on your guest, they were given in vain, though had you found him alive in Ithaca he would have responded with equal gifts and warm hospitality before he let you depart; such return of kindness is just and right. But now tell me this without concealment. How many years ago did you entertain him? For yourself, this man was a luckless guest, but for me – so help me heaven! – my ill-fated son. By now, I fear, fishes have eaten him in the sea, or birds and beasts have made him their prey on land, far from his friends and his own country. We his parents – the mother who bore him, the father who begot him – never made the ritual lamentation or shrouded him for the grave; his wife of the many bridal gifts, chaste Penelope, never closed her husband's eyes or wailed for him on his bed of death, as would have been right and fitting – such is the honour owed the dead. And tell me plainly – I long to know – who you are and from where you come. Where are your city and your parents? Where is the ship that brought yourself and your comrades here? Or were you a passenger on the ship of others – men who put you ashore and then sailed on?'

Subtle Odysseus answered him: 'I will tell you everything truthfully. I come from Alybas; my palace is there, and I am the son of Prince Apheidas the son of Polypemon; my own name is Eperitus. I sailed from Sicania; some god drove me off my course and brought me against my will to Ithaca. My vessel is not far off, but away from the town, near the fields. As for Odysseus, it is four years now since he parted from me and left my country. Unhappy man! And yet when he went he had birds of good omen on his right. We were glad to see them, he and I – he departing and I bidding him farewell – and the hearts of both of us were confident we should meet again as host and guest and offer each other noble gifts.'

So he spoke. His father, caught in a sudden black cloud of grief, took the grimy dust in both hands and scattered it over his hoary head, sobbing passionately. Odysseus' heart was stirred, and a keen pang shot through his nostrils as he looked at his beloved father. He leapt forward and clasped and kissed him and said: 'I am the man you are seeking, Father; it is my very self that you see, returning in the twentieth year to my own native land. Put aside your sorrow and tears and lamentation. I have news for you – but the time is short. I have slain the suitors in our palace; I have taken revenge for their hateful outrage and wicked deeds.'

Laertes answered: 'If indeed you are my son Odysseus, at home at last, tell me of some undoubted token to make me sure.'

Odysseus answered: 'There is first this scar – cast your eyes on that; a boar's white tusk gave me the wound upon Parnassus. I had gone there because you and my mother sent me to visit her father Autolycus and claim the gifts that he solemnly promised me when he came to Ithaca. And then, let me tell you the trees that you gave me once in this very plot that shows your care, when I was a little child following you about the garden and begging for one tree and then another; we walked through them all and you named them one by one. You gave me thirteen pear-trees, ten apple-trees, forty fig-trees, and you promised, yes, to let me have fifty rows of vines, each of them bearing fruit in turn; there were clusters on them of every degree of ripeness as the seasons of Zeus shed down their influence from above.'

So he spoke. As for Laertes, his knees failed him, his heart melted as he knew for truth the undoubted tokens Odysseus gave him. He threw his arms round his dear son, and wellnigh swooned as Odysseus clasped him close. When he came to himself and his spirit entered his breast again, he in his turn uttered these words: 'Father Zeus, now I am sure that you gods still reign in high Olympus, if indeed the suitors have paid the price of their monstrous insolence. But my heart has a terrible foreboding that the Ithacans, one and all, may at any moment assault us here and send out messages everywhere to the cities of the Cephallenians.'

Subtle Odysseus answered him: 'Take heart; do not let such
thoughts weigh down your mind. But your house is near the
orchard; let us make for it now. I have sent Telemachus there
already with the cowherd and the swineherd to prepare a meal as
soon as may be.' And upon these words the two of them set off
to the house. Arriving there, they found Telemachus and the
herdsmen slicing the plenteous meat and mixing the glowing
wine. Before the meal the Sicilian maid bathed her master in his
own room, anointed him with oil and then put a handsome cloak
about him. Moreover, Athene approaching him filled out the
limbs of this shepherd of his people and made him appear taller
and ampler to all who viewed him; so that now when he came
forth from the bath, his own son was amazed at him, so godlike
in presence did he appear. He said to Laertes: 'Father, it must be
that one of the everlasting gods has made you taller and hand-
somer to our eyes.'

Laertes answered: 'Would to Zeus and Athene and Apollo that
I might have been yesterday what I was when as lord of the
Cephallenians I sacked the city of Nericus, nobly sited just where
the mainland ends – would I might have been in that likeness
yesterday in our palace, with armour upon my shoulders, might
have taken my stand and beaten the suitors back; then in those
halls I should have loosened the limbs of many, and your own
heart would have rejoiced to see me.'

Such were the words that passed between them. When the
others had finished their preparing and had the meal ready, they
all took their places side by side on stools and chairs. As they
were putting their hands to the food, there appeared before them
old Dolius and his sons, tired with the farmwork that they had
left when the old Sicilian went out and called them – she was the
mother of the young men; she looked after them and lovingly
tended their father Dolius now that old age had fastened on him.
When they saw Odysseus – when their hearts told them who he
was – they stood stock-still there in bewilderment; but he spoke
to them in words that would put them at their ease: 'Old friend,
sit down to table; forget your astonishment, all of you. We have
been waiting here this long time, ready enough to begin our meal
but expecting you.'

Such were his words. But Dolius, opening his arms, ran across
to him, seized his hand at the wrist, kissed it and said: 'Dear

master, we had hoped against hope for your return, and now you are here and the gods themselves have brought you. So I bid you welcome and wish you happiness; may the gods give you every blessing ! But tell me one thing I long to know – does wise Penelope know beyond doubt by now that you have returned, or ought we to send her a messenger?'

Odysseus answered: 'Old friend, she knows already; trouble yourself no further.' Dolius at this went back to his seat, while his sons, too, at the great man's side, gave him their own words of greeting and clasped his hands; then they took their seats in order, next to their father Dolius.

But while in the house they were busy with their meal, Rumour as herald was speeding hotfoot through the city, crying the news of the suitors' hideous death and doom. Listeners here and listeners there moved forward with one accord to the fore-court of Odysseus' palace, wailing and lamenting. Groups of mourners brought out their own dead from the house for burial; the dead who had come from towns elsewhere they put on ship-board and sent back under seamen's escort, each to his own home. Then the mourning kinsmen made their way to the assembly-place, and when they were all duly gathered there, Eupeithes stood up and spoke among them; quenchless grief lay upon his heart for his son Antinous, the first to be killed by King Odysseus. With tears for this youth Eupeithes spoke among them : 'Friends, what a mass of evil things this man's devices have brought upon us Achaeans ! Many of us, all men of courage, he took away with him in his ships; he lost the ships and he lost the men; and now that he has come back again he has killed the noblest of all the Cephallenians. Come then; before he can make swift escape – perhaps to Pylos, perhaps to Elis where the Epeians rule – let us up and go ! If not, we shall be shamed for ever after. We shall be disgraced among all posterity if we leave unpunished these murderers of our sons and brothers. For me at least, life would have no savour; I would rather die now and join the fallen. Be quick; or else these men will have crossed the water and thwarted us.'

So he spoke with tears, and compassion filled the Achaeans' hearts. But suddenly there advanced towards them Medon the page and Phemius the bard; they had left the palace when sleep released them, and now they stood in the midst of all this throng.

Amazement came upon everyone; then Medon spoke these words of wisdom : 'Listen to me, you men of Ithaca. It was not without the gods' consent that Odysseus planned and did these things. I myself saw a deathless god standing by Odysseus in Mentor's likeness. This same immortal showed himself now in front of Odysseus, urging him on, and now again rushing down the hall and driving the suitors wild with fear till they fell down one upon another.'

So he spoke, and ashy terror seized on them all. Then old Halitherses addressed them all, the noble son of Mastor. He alone among them could look to things past and things to come, and he now exhorted them for their good : 'Men of Ithaca, listen to what I have to say. Friends, it is your own weak wills that have let these things come to pass. You would not hear me, you would not hear Lord Mentor; you would not turn your sons from their reckless ways. Yet they worked great harm by their evildoings; they squandered the wealth of a great lord, they humiliated his wife, because they thought he would not return. So now let this be the decision – be ruled by me, do as I say. Let us not set forth, or some may find they have brought new evil upon themselves.'

So he spoke; but though some of them remained standing there together, more than half of them leapt from their seats with a loud war-cry because his words were not to their mind and Eupeithes was the one they followed. They hastened away to get their armour, and when they had fitted the glowing bronze about them, they formed a troop at the entrance to the town. Eupeithes in his folly led them; he thought to avenge his son's death; instead, he was never to return, but to meet his doom in the place of battle.

Meanwhile Athene was speaking thus to the son of Cronos: 'Father of all of us, son of Cronos and sovereign king, hear my question and say what purpose your mind conceals. Will you carry further this deadly warfare and hideous strife, or do you mean to bring reconcilement between these foes?'

Zeus who masses the clouds made answer : 'Child, why pursue this anxious questioning? Was it not you who framed this plan, so that Odysseus at his homecoming should be revenged upon the suitors? You may work in any way you please, but I will tell you what way is best. Now that the king has taken his vengeance on the suitors, let both sides make a solemn covenant; let Odysseus

reign there all his days, while we ourselves bring about forget-
fulness of the slaughtering of sons and brothers. Let them all be
friends as they were of old, and let there be wealth and peace in
plenty.'

His answer inflamed her zeal the more, and down from the
summits of Olympus she sped to earth.

In Laertes' house they had eaten their fill. Then Odysseus spoke
to his companions: 'Let someone go out and look; perhaps they
are close to us already.' Hearing his command, one of Dolius'
sons went out and stood upon the threshold. He saw them all
near at hand, and said to Odysseus instantly: 'Yes, they have
come; they are all but here; let us arm at once.' So they leapt up
and put on their armour – Odysseus and the three around him,
and the six sons of Dolius also; and Dolius and Laertes too put
their armour on – grey-headed both, but ready to fight when
fight they must. Having fitted the glowing bronze upon them,
they opened the doors and issued forth, Odysseus in front.

Then there came towards them the daughter of Zeus, Athene
herself, taking the form and voice of Mentor. King Odysseus
rejoiced to see her, and said forthwith to his son Telemachus:
'My son, when you enter the battlefield where warriors prove
their mettle, you need not be told not to shame the lineage of
our fathers. In courage and manliness we have long been fore-
most, the whole world over.'

Thoughtful Telemachus replied: 'Father, if you are minded
so, you shall watch me in my present spirit by no means shaming
the lineage that you speak of.'

So he spoke, and Laertes in his joy cried out: 'Dear gods, what
a day is this for me! What happiness, when my son and my
grandson are vying for the prize of valour!'

Then Athene herself stood by his side and spoke to him: 'Son
of Arceisius, dearest by far of all my comrades, pray first to the
Maid of gleaming eyes and to Father Zeus, then poise at once
your long-shafted spear and hurl it.'

So Athene spoke, and breathed mighty strength into him. Then
he made his prayer to the daughter of sovereign Zeus, poised the
long-shafted spear and hurled it. He struck Eupeithes' bronze-
cheeked helmet; it did not keep out the spear, and the bronze went
right through. Eupeithes fell crashing down, and his armour

rattled over him. And at this Odysseus and his son fell upon the first rank of fighters, thrusting with swords and two-edged spears. And now they would have destroyed them all and taken away their hopes of home, had not the daughter of Zeus cried out and held back the whole throng: 'Men of Ithaca, cease from the toil of warfare; separate at once, and shun bloodshed.'

So spoke Athene, and ashy terror seized on them all; in their dismay the weapons flew from their hands and dropped on the ground as the goddess sent forth her voice. They began to turn back towards the city, eager to save their lives. But Odysseus, with a terrible cry, gathered himself and swooped upon them like an eagle from high in air. Then Zeus sent a thunderbolt from heaven. Reeking, it fell at his daughter's feet, and the goddess of gleaming eyes spoke to the king: 'Son of Laertes, Odysseus of many subtleties, now make an end, now halt the strife of inexorable war, lest Zeus the Thunderer should be angry with you.'

So Athene spoke, and with joyful heart the king obeyed. Then a solemn covenant was made between those who had been at enmity. The contriver of it had the form and the voice of Mentor now, but this was no other than Athene, daughter of Zeus who holds the aegis.

EPILOGUE

ON TRANSLATION

Such is our Pride, our Folly or our Fate
That few, but such as cannot write, translate.
                John Denham to Richard Fanshawe (1647)

There are many who understand *Greek* and *Latin*, and
yet are ignorant of their Mother Tongue.
                John Dryden, Preface to *Sylvae* (1685)

SOMETHING over forty years ago, having been invited to illus-
trate an episode from the *Odyssey*, Eric Gill was glancing through
his Butcher and Lang when his eye lit upon a phrase attributed
to Penelope: 'That were indeed unmeet.' Throwing the book
aside, he took down the version of T. E. Lawrence, which gave
instead: 'It would never, never do.' Having thrown aside this
book also, he appealed to me somewhat later: 'Can't they manage
something better than that?' This translation and epilogue are a
diffident answer to his question.

I propose to discuss at some length the difficulties of transla-
tion in general and of Homeric translation particularly, speaking
first of all to the many readers who are well at home with Eng-
lish idiom but have little acquaintance with foreign languages.

Every region of speech abounds in words and in word-
arrangements overlapping with those elsewhere but not alto-
gether coinciding. Every language works out its own differentia-
tions, trivial or interesting or very important indeed. In the mere
use of tenses, one language may offer a single formula while
another imposes choice between two or three. If I am to translate
into English the French present tense *Je vais*, I must choose
between 'I am going' or 'I go' or 'I do go (but . . .)'; if instead I
am to translate into French the English past tense 'I went', I
must choose either *J'allais* or *Je suis allé* or else *J'allai*.

In English it seems natural to us to speak of a pretty girl, a
beautiful cat, a lovely rose, a good-looking man, a handsome old
lady, a fine piece of printing. In French or Italian one could dis-
tinguish at least between 'beautiful' and 'pretty', but in fact
many Frenchmen or Italians would be likely to keep in every
case the very same adjective drawn from Latin *bellus*. If a French

or Italian novelist, keeping this word, were to describe how in one half-hour someone met all these variants of what pleases when seen, an English translator would have either to use customary English distinctions, which might blunt the point, or else to repeat one adjective ('beautiful'? 'handsome'?) which with most of these nouns would pass quite comfortably but at least once would probably be discordant.

Again, English is specially rich in verbs that express at the same time a particular movement and a particular sound or attitude – 'The cart rattled off', 'He limped to the window.' In other languages one might have to say something like 'The cart moved off with a rattling noise', 'He approached the window limpingly.'

The examples just given have shown differences of method in describing persons and things, actions and situations that in themselves are common to many countries. But when customs or institutions, features of landscape or building, national character or conventions are markedly different between one country and another, new difficulties arise in the effort to describe them outside the context to which they belong. In his powers and duties, a French *juge* is both like and unlike an English judge. In its placing and its use, a Spanish cathedral *coro* is both like and unlike an Austrian or Belgian cathedral choir. An Englishman in Italy may wonder whether to tell his countrymen that 'The *podestà* left the *municipio*' or just that 'The mayor left the town hall.'

These difficulties occur in the language of common talk and of the simplest statement or narrative. New risks appear when we pass to poetry or imaginative prose, because there we must deal nót only with denotations but with connotations, not only with plain undisputed meanings but with the sounds of words and with thoughts and memories linked for some persons with some words. Mathematicians and scientists are expected to stick to denotation. I suppose that in all languages a triangle is simply a triangle. I suppose again that in botany the international Latin words mean just the same thing to botanists everywhere; yet for plants and flowers in different countries the native names carry different suggestions with them. The *vinca* of the professional is called in English a periwinkle – a cheerful and childlike sort of name; the French *pervenche*, with its very different sound, may perhaps evoke a languorous and romantic feeling, and was fittingly recollected by the sensitive Rousseau.

Nearly all that I have written above has some bearing on Homeric translation, but every language has its own problems in every period of its development. Homer did not merely compose in Greek, he did so about three centuries before the age which is loosely called 'classical', and this not merely in verse, not prose, but within a convention of bardic poetry that was far from familiar to Sophocles or Plato and is quite unfamiliar to most modern Europeans. His language moreover is deliberately archaic or archaising and is chiefly used to describe a real or fancied heroic age many generations earlier. His translator is concerned in the first place with Greek, the language of a society very remote from ours and with corresponding divergences in the flexibility and extension of certain words; beyond this, he is concerned with poetry of a high order, framed in a pre-classical idiom and recalling images of a vanished world.

Let me begin with classical Greek. A case important to the historian of ideas is that of the adjective *dikaios*, for which the most general English equivalent is 'just' or 'righteous'. But not only is this Greek word used where we should be more likely to say 'honest', 'fair', decent', 'dutiful', or simply 'good' or 'virtuous'; it is also used with an alteration of active and passive that is quite foreign to our ideas. Thus the judge who sentences a thief is *dikaios* to convict him, but the thief also is *dikaios* to be convicted. To convey this in English, the best we can do is perhaps to say that the judge is the right kind of person to pass sentence and the thief the right kind of person to be sentenced. In certain arguments where *dikaios* is a keyword, it may be disputed whether a writer, wilfully or unconsciously, has used the same word in different senses, or whether he saw an underlying unity of ideas ('In these conditions, justice prevails') which has since been blurred by grammatical distinctions.

A second instance concerns forms of address, and this involves not only linguistic but social usage. In classical Greece it was customary for strangers and slaves to address a man by the same single proper name that his close friends would use. In Plato's writings, the slave whom Socrates guides in geometry and the slave-gaoler who brings the hemlock agree in calling the master 'Socrates', precisely as his disciples do. If a translator also says

'Socrates', the modern reader, expecting something like 'Sir', might think that these slaves were making themselves very familiar or else that Socrates as a philosopher discouraged conventional class distinctions – in either case a mistaken supposition. If the translator says 'Sir', the reader possibly will be closer to the general atmosphere of the scene but will miss one detail of Greek life that is interesting in itself. Here one might keep 'Socrates' but add a note on the difference of conventions.

In the *Odyssey* there are various forms of address that put the translator in a dilemma. I pause over two. The same word *xeinos* (*xenos* in later Greek) may be used not only of a 'guest' – this very frequently – but also of a 'host' – this very seldom. (A similar ambiguity in modern French and Italian and Spanish does not cause much embarrassment.) What is more important, this word (especially in the vocative), besides meaning 'guest' (something courteous), may also mean 'friend' (affectionate) and 'stranger' (sometimes neutral, sometimes welcoming, sometimes hostile). Time after time, Odysseus is so addressed by friends and by enemies and by neutrals, sometimes ambiguously. In the interview of Book XIX between Penelope and Odysseus, does the use of this word allow any shift in meaning as the wife listens more and more to her husband in his disguise? In line 350 she adds the word 'dear'. Is she moving from 'stranger' to 'dear stranger', from 'guest' to 'dear guest', from 'friend' to 'dear friend', or perhaps from 'stranger' to 'dear friend'? I wish I knew, but I am far from understanding the mind and moods of Penelope, though on each occasion I ought to commit myself to either 'stranger' or 'guest' or 'friend'.

More slippery still is the vocative *gunai*, for which the first dictionary rendering is simply 'woman'. But then, like the French *femme*, it is also the commonest word for 'wife'. And then again it often replaces other forms of address to women, with every degree of meaning from sheer contempt to humble homage. It is used in anger by Odysseus when he scolds the shameless girl Melantho. But queens in Homer are so addressed by their husbands and their subjects, and obsequious Persian courtiers in Aeschylus call the Queen Mother this, though they also call her something like 'Sovereign Lady'. In the Greek of the Gospels, Christ uses the same word to his mother and to Mary Magdalen.

In Book XIX Odysseus disguised calls Penelope *gunai*. To her it would have the force of 'Queen', but to him it would have the force of 'Wife' as well, and Homer's audience would doubtless have relished the ambiguity. Here I have chosen the rendering 'Queen'. In Book XXIII Odysseus uses the word again when Penelope even now denies recognition. She is still a queen, she is still his wife, but at the moment she is also an object of indignation, and the word might be a resentful 'Woman!'. Here I have been cowardly enough to omit the vocative altogether.

This by no means exhausts the difficulties in forms of address, and I shall return to the subject later. Meanwhile I pass to a more fundamental question. Given that Homer's work is not only verse but among the most celebrated verse in the world, what excuse is there for translating it into prose?

I should say that any verse worth notice is bound to lose when turned into prose, but how much it loses depends on the kind of verse it is – I do not mean its greatness or slenderness but its matter and its manner, its general structure, the units it is made from. Verse in which narrative is central and vivid, verse which portrays character, verse with a continuous important argument may leave a great deal for the translator even when metre is cast aside – witness Hague's *Roland*, Sinclair's *Divine Comedy*, Barnett's *Gītā*. Narrative power in the *Odyssey*, richness of incident, variety in the characters drawn – these leave the translator much that may be expressed in prose and is surely worth expressing thus. Moreover, the length and pace of the narrative let him construct, if so he wishes, fresh units of composition that are natural in themselves and yet do not falsify the original units of the poem. This is something difficult or impossible in a prose rendering of certain other verse forms. The elegiacs of Greek and Roman poets, with their usually independent couplets, are scarcely reducible to any convincing shape in prose. Their general effect seems inseparable from a strict metrical form, and this in English has usually meant rhyme as well. In the Greek Anthology there is a two-line epigram of uncertain date which the Loeb translation renders thus: 'The rose blooms for a little season, and when that goes by thou shalt find, if thou seekest, no rose but a briar.' Conscientious, straggling, flat. Dr Johnson, using the couplet to head an essay, had made this of it:

> Soon fades the rose; once past the fragrant hour,
> The loiterer finds a bramble for a flower.

The details there are not closely kept to, but the English couplet, like the Greek, is a visible unit conceived as verse; it has concision; it has its touch of pathos. Call it paraphrase or call it free translation, it is good.

To translate the *Odyssey* into prose should be a more rational undertaking than so to deal with Propertius or the Anthology. Yet to lose metre is to lose very much indeed, and the best translation imaginable would naturally be in verse. It should not be time wasted to glance at some English verse translators and see what they made of their opportunity. Five are of the seventeenth or the eighteenth century, and my footnotes to the text have offered quotations from them all, some exemplifying felicities that prose could never equal, others displaying notions of ancient epic that seem implausible to ourselves but illuminate part of English literature and indirectly contribute something to our understanding of Homer himself. As a Chinese scholar, E. R. Hughes, has said regarding his own province, 'What those people thought about the book becomes part of its relevance to us.'

Our first translator is George Chapman. Between 1598 and 1611 he had turned the *Iliad* into English 'fourteeners', a metre not to be simply despised but lending itself to ramblingness and monotony. Chapman did not escape these hazards. For his *Odyssey* (about 1615) he changed to the normal rhyming couplets which have come to be miscalled 'heroic', and a decade afterwards kept this metre for *The Crowne of all Homer's Workes*, Batracho-myomachia, *or the Battaile of Frogs and Mise* (this being a mock-heroic poem written a long time after Homer but palatable enough to readers of the Renaissance).

Chapman had gifts, and lived at a time when poetic freshness was in the air. He is full of happy turns of speech, it may be to characterise Penelope's 'lovely-wristed Ladies', it may be to lend to Homeric formulas the hint of a spirit of youth in England:

> ... But when Aurora rose
> And threw the third light from her orient haire,
> The winds grew calme, and cleare was all the aire.

Passages like this, and others recorded in my footnotes, explain well enough the regard for him that Keats expressed in a celebrated sonnet. But Chapman's virtues are not sustained. His style is undisciplined and uneven, and he could not control and

vary his chosen metre as Chaucer and Marlowe did. He inserts
feeble conceits of his own, and makes ill-contrived experiments in
his hyphened renderings of Homer's compounds – 'the King/
Good-at-a-martiall-shout' or 'the white-and-red-mix'd-fingerd
Dame'. A second look into Chapman's Homer is likely to bring
disenchantment.

After Chapman we have John Ogilby, who in 1660 dedicated
an *Iliad* to the returning Charles II and in 1665 followed it with
an *Odyssey*, having been meanwhile appointed 'Master of his
Majesties Revells in the Kingdom of Ireland'. Ogilby is a rather
bad poet who I think has been rather harshly done by. He was
satirised first by Dryden and then by Pope, though Pope was not
above borrowing lines from him here and there. Ogilby's verse is
often rough; his tone is colloquial and sometimes descends to
slang. Nevertheless he has vivid moments, a few good couplets,
attractive anachronisms (like his evident obsession with passports,
illustrated here on p. 217). There are times when his vigorous
Baroque seems nearer Homer than Pope's elegant Rococo, and he
gives a certain view of the *Odyssey* which might perhaps have
been shared by Samuel Pepys. Pepys, I think, with his naval in-
terests, would have enjoyed in Book I the change from Athene's
vague 'ship' to the careful designation 'a nimble vessel of the
second Rate'. Here from the same book are four characteristic
lines from Ogilby :

> Others the boards with pory Sponges dri'd
> And Tables cover'd, serv'd up Cates divide.
> Her first Telemachus, 'mongst the debosh'd
> Corrivals sitting, saw as she approch'd.

The roughness and clumsiness are conspicuous, but then we
have also 'pory Sponges' – much better, surely, than the 'porous
sponges' of Chapman and most translators. The sound is
smoother, and the ending has a homely expressiveness that recalls
Hardy's phrase for stringed instruments, 'All of our glossy gluey
make'. I have borrowed 'pory' for myself, and confess that I have
some weakness for Ogilby.

About 1675 the now very aged Thomas Hobbes published an
Iliad and *Odyssey*, in what frame of mind I cannot guess. Did he
hope that admirers of his philosophy would also admire his
English verse? Was he anxious to prove that his faculties were

not quite decayed? Did he intend to satirise Homer? In any case,
Hobbes translated the *Odyssey* into quatrains with a markedly
workaday vocabulary (he writes, for example, 'rats' for 'pirates').
There are a few good plain lines, but the general level is that of
contemporary tombstone poets, with more than average awk-
wardness in the placing of ordinary pronouns. With him as with
Samuel Butler later, one wonders if some absurdities are due to
facetiousness or just to insensitiveness – for instance:

> *Ulysses* half a Chine of Pork and fat
> Cuts off, and in the Squires hands putteth it,
> And said unto him, Give the Singer that.

With great relief I turn to the *Odyssey* of Pope, published in
1725–6 and still, I suppose, the best English version. (Pope trans-
lated twelve books himself and revised the verse of his colleagues
Broome and Fenton, who had already modelled their style on his.
Simplifying things, I speak of the whole work as Pope's, but make
quotations only from books that are all his own.) This Homer,
like many other works of Baroque and Rococo art, is sometimes
magnificent, sometimes absurd, sometimes both at once. Pope's
verse is technically accomplished, in certain passages brilliant or
powerful; at moments it becomes musical. But he lived and flour-
ished in a society that admired itself far too much to enter
seriously into dialogue with ages or artists whose thought and life
were fundamentally different from its own. It felt at ease with
Ovid's *Epistles* and Pliny's *Letters*; the polished epigrams and con-
ceits, the glibness and blandness here, the servility or the cyni-
cism there – with all these things our eighteenth century was in
tune, and for such authors its own translations are not likely to
be improved on. But what age could be worse equipped to trans-
late either Sappho or Catullus, either Dante or Thomas à Kempis?
Contemporaries of Pope could admire Chaucer, admire Shakes-
peare, admire Homer, but with prudent reservations. These were
all great men – Homer a very great man indeed – but they lacked
refinement and often talked about humble things, often fell short
of the sublime. To achieve the sublime there were now well-
proved recipes, and Pope undertook to help Homer out. He
blurred the picture of Homer's world by varnishing it with a false
gentility; he blurred the structure of the poem by using a con-
vention of verse that often suggests false emphasis and also false

units of composition. And yet he gains by his obstinate self-assurance. His free transposition of the *Odyssey* is a work conceived throughout as verse, often dignified, often vivacious, achieving its own consistency and sustained by unusual mastery of both rhetoric and metre. It cannot be blotted from English literature.

The last of this group of verse translations is perhaps the most disappointing, since its author has some claim to be thought the best poet of the five. William Cowper, whose *Iliad* and *Odyssey* appeared together in 1791, was a man of great sensibility who in certain hymns and lyrics gave simple words a strength and poignancy such as Wordsworth perhaps never equalled. In satire, again, he could coin a line as telling as one of Pope's – on clerical patronage, for example:

> The parson knows enough who knows a Duke.

Yet when, to counter his mental miseries, he set himself to translate Homer, he seemed to forswear his own best gifts, endeavoured to write Miltonic blank verse and showed just as much misunderstanding of Milton's style as the generation of Pope himself. He tried the same short cuts to sublimity – adjectives for adverbs, inversions and general pompousness:

> Ulysses, joyful at the sight, his steps
> Turn'd brisk toward her, whom he thus addressed ...

> Philoetius, chief intendant of the beeves,
> Served all with baskets elegant of bread ...

Cowper had excellent things as well – not only lines but whole passages. He is also a good deal more faithful than any of his predecessors, who apart from misunderstanding details allowed themselves to add or omit whole lines at will. But it is sad that he should have spent seven years in elaborating this long work in a manner opposed to his own genius.

The nineteenth century (and the early twentieth) brought a new crop of verse translations which I would gladly have disregarded, did not certain of them raise a question that deserves to be considered. Homer's hexameters make long lines – they may have as many as seventeen syllables. The standard metres of English drama and narrative are of only ten or eleven syllables –

the blank verse of Shakespeare and Milton, the rhyming couplets
of Chaucer, Marlowe, Keats. There were those who thought that
an English verse translation would better reflect Homer's move-
ment if it used a longer line, and especially if it offered an equiv-
alent of the original Greek hexameter. Elizabethans had made
some efforts to adapt Greek and Latin metres to English purposes,
and in the nineteenth century these classicising experiments
were renewed. Here I only speak of hexameters, and it seems to
me that early and later attempts in this direction have all in the
end come to grief through confusion of quantity with accent,
pitch accent with stress accent, and English spelling with English
pronunciation. To simplify a quite complex matter, let me say
only that Homer's verse rhythm relies in the first place on quan-
tity – a certain sequence of long and short syllables – while Eng-
lish verse rhythm relies in the first place on a certain sequence of
stressed and unstressed syllables. Logical transposition of Greek
hexameters into English should mean that long and short syl-
lables in Greek should be replaced by stressed and unstressed in
English, and this indeed seems to have been the usual aim of
experimenters. (The much subtler 'quantitive' hexameters written
by Bridges are outside my present terms of reference.)

In Homer's own lines the first four feet may be either dactyls
(one long, two shorts, -　　‿) or spondees (two longs, - -),
though dactyls predominate; the fifth foot is usually - ‿ ‿ , occa-
sionally - -; the sixth and last is either a spondee, - -, or a trochee,
- ‿. In exchanging quantity for stress, an accentual equivalent
for the dactyl should easily be found – one stressed syllable, two
unstressed. Even there, I fear, some Victorians practised subter-
fuge, though quite humble technique can carry accentual dactyls
onward, leaving an accentual trochee for the last foot, for in-
stance:

> Here in the depths of the valley, or there at the crest of
> the mountain.

The dismal line scans accentually. Trouble begins with spondees.
In Greek metre a series of longs may in theory never end at all.
In practice it was easy for Homer to begin a line with five longs,
making two and a half feet. The accentual equivalent of a
spondee ought to be two equally stressed syllables, but English
does not allow continued stresses as Greek allows continued longs.

English words that in isolation are clearly stressed may easily lose
that stress in the context of a sentence, and this simple truth has
been the downfall of many a professional classicist and amateur
versifier. To get five continued and equal stresses one must have
recourse to monosyllables, and these again need pauses between.
'No!', delivered slowly, might offer a decent counterpart: 'No!
No! No! No! No!', but this could not be kept up for long.
Victorian Hellenists with their 'English hexameters' cheated the
reader or cheated themselves. In his Oxford lectures, Matthew
Arnold pronounced this metre to be aptest for 'preserving the
general effect of Homer', and buttressed his case with his own
versions of a few passages from the *Iliad*. As a counterpart of five
Greek longs he offered such sequences as these: 'And he shook
his head'; 'Of all living things'; 'For that day will come'; 'In the
bloody dust'. For complete hexameters I may quote:

For than man, indeed, there breathes no wretcheder creature

And yet not that grief, which then will be, of the Trojans

and

For by no slow pace or want of swiftness of ours.

Not all Victorian hexametrists wrote so uncouthly – Arnold
himself quotes lines from Hawtrey that are more accomplished
that his own; but time, I think, has not vindicated any of such
experiments.

Might not more natural English rhythms be used in design-
edly long lines, rhymed or rhymeless? Either way there are
difficulties. Rhyme helps to define rhythm, but in a poem of epic
length various long rhyming metres that suit a lyric are likely to
grow as tedious as old fourteeners. Long unrhymed lines are much
more difficult to control than normal blank verse, and easily lose
rhythmical outline through the shifting of individual accents
inside the structure of a whole sentence. Thanks to a very sensi-
tive ear and to some help from private spellings, Bridges could
write 'loose alexandrines' that are seldom ambiguous, though the
gentle meditative metre that served him well in the *Testament of
Beauty* could scarcely be turned to heroic narrative; nor can one
expect his technique to be recaptured. The 'free six-beat line' of
Richmond Lattimore in his interesting and scholarly versions of

Iliad and *Odyssey* seems to me insufficiently controlled. As with much original modern verse, the rhythm intended is obscured by the ambiguities of stress, and 'beats' that seem obvious to the writer will seem elusive to the reader, who may reasonably be undecided between two choices or even three.

But indeed I think that the search for longer metres may in any case be mistaken, since the *feeling* of length in a given line depends not just on the number of syllables but on the sounds of a given language, the nature of the pauses, and the proportions of word-length and verse-length. English, rich in significant mono-syllables, can fill out a line of ten or eleven syllables to make as marked an effect of amplitude as a longer, more rapid line in Greek, where strong monosyllables are few and polysyllables are abundant. 'So clomb this first grand Thief into God's Fould.' In a way entirely proper to English, Milton's line has as much weight and fullness as many a Greek hexameter.

I cannot prophesy the future of English verse forms. Perhaps in the next fifty years an unrhymed metre will have been found that is quite distinct from older blank verse, yet with firm outline and definition. Meanwhile I may cherish the belief that the English Homer somewhere laid up in heaven has a manner and metre much like this:

> Come not to me againe, but say to Athens
> *Timon* hath made his everlasting Mansion
> Upon the Beachèd Verge of the Salt Flood.

I resume the theme of prose translations, where we have the contrast of Butcher and Lang, archaisers, and Samuel Butler and his descendants, modernisers. Homer looked backward to genera-tions of earlier bards, Butcher and Lang to the Bible of 1611 (whose translators had themselves looked backward to various preceding versions). To most modern readers such a procedure is alien and distasteful. In the last half century so many things have changed so much that we need to restore these authors to their own setting.

They were not eccentric. They wrote at a time when to many Englishmen the prose of 1611 was a second language, familiar through weekly hearing in church, sometimes through daily read-ing at home, and imitated by Nonconformists in frequent extem-porary prayers. Moreover it was widely accepted that all serious ancient poetry should be rendered in some kind of backward-looking English, verse or prose. This convention lasted till well within our own century. Schoolboys as late as in the thirties were praised for using *thou* in their versions. The *Herodas* of A. D. Knox (1929) is much more elaborately archaic than anything in Butcher and Lang. I myself am guilty of archaising translations published before the war.

All these things appear very distant now. The great and continued influence of a new school of poets, notably Ezra Pound and Eliot, has led many to take the view that poetry ought to keep the words and word-order of common speech (with no archaisms, no inversions) and rely for its effect on freshness of imagery and rhythm, on the sequence and concentration of thought. A change in the theory of poetry invites a change in the theory of translation (including prose translation), but we shall do well to ask if the principles just alluded to are to be accepted as true universally or only as the most valid for ourselves after our own experience and disillusionment. If we say that we ourselves never feel at ease except within such conventions, well and good – we must write accordingly. If we say that all poetry must conform to them, we cancel at once a great part of the poetry of the world. We may particularly enjoy some poems whose diction is not merely simple (for simple diction may also be grand) but positively colloquial, and yet refuse to make this the standard for poetry in general. There is one poem that begins:

> What's become of Waring
> Since he gave us all the slip?

There is one that ends:

> And so they went on till the train came in –
> The convict, and boy with the violin.

I admire these poems and their writers as much perhaps as anyone does, but what critic believes that every poem ought to be written so?

Greek critics at least did not – Aristotle, for instance, applauds the use of a rare word instead of the customary one, and the artificial lengthening or shortening of words to lift them above colloquial level. As for Homer's own practice, let me quote three distinguished modern authorities. 'Whatever its origins, Homeric

Greek was not a spoken language' (C. M. Bowra). 'The language of Homer is an artificial amalgam of elements from different regions and different periods, including many forms invented by the singers themselves' (G. S. Kirk). 'The remarkable but totally artificial dialect of the poems, which no Greek ever spoke but which remained permanently fixed as the language of Greek epic' (M. I. Finley). Later Greek literature throve on conservatism of language, and poets under the Roman Empire did their best to imitate the diction and prosody of ancient epic or elegy.

If then a writer translating Homer decides to keep to the common spoken language of his own time, he may well be doing what for himself is most natural or most honest, but he is moving one step further away from the bardic tradition which Homer follows. It is noteworthy that when Pound himself made his version of certain lines from the *Odyssey*, he chose neither a modern manner nor a Jacobean; he chose a modified Anglo-Saxon manner:

> Men many,   mauled with bronze lance heads,
> Battle spoil,   bearing yet dreory arms . . .

> Stand from the fosse,   leave me my bloody bever
> For soothsay . . .

It might be a profitable labour (though one not possible for myself) to work out under what conditions, in various languages, some kind of archaism has prospered, whether through very scrupulous imitation or through the judicious keeping of earlier elements among later. The trouble with Butcher and Lang's *Odyssey* is not, I think, that they wrote in the manner of 1611 but that they failed to do so. They were less at home in classical English than they thought. Their sense of rhythm was insufficient; they invented phrases quite out of keeping with their model ('a fair twy-eared chalice of gold'); anxious not to lose dignity, they regularly preferred the more ancient of two word-forms ('gat' and 'drave', though King James's scholars used 'got' and 'drove' as well) and studiously avoided the many short homely words that a Jacobean certainly would have used for a text not specifically sacred.

Reacting to what he thought the Wardour Street English of Butcher and Lang, Samuel Butler in 1900 published a version of the *Odyssey* in would-be 'plain prose', with some leaning, as he confessed, to the English of Tottenham Court Road. 'Plain prose', 'plain English' – how often translators have used such words to commend their travesties of some admirable original ! Butler, consumed by a bourgeois craving to shock the bourgeois, makes a king address his fellow-rulers as 'Aldermen and town councillors' and says later that when assembled 'They set the steaks to grill and made an excellent dinner' – phrasing which does not give a more honest picture of a court banquet in a heroic age but intrudes instead a distracting image of municipal Victorian guzzling. Side by side with his drab modernity, Butler had various archaic formulas ('if haply', 'ere ever') – not, I think, as representing a mixture of styles in Homer but through mechanical reminiscence of the conventions of his schooldays. (T. E. Lawrence, if I do not misunderstand his preface, designedly mixed his styles in English to echo what he called Wardour Street Greek – hence such clashes as 'Wherefore let us whip up the thrill of battle.')

Other prose translations of Homer over the last forty years or so have followed much the same lines as contemporary translations of the Bible, choice among which is indeed embarrassing. Authors of these profess to write a 'twentieth-century English' which everyone is to understand. But what is twentieth-century English? In its most familiar and typical forms, it is manifestly debased English – that of journalists, publicity agents, politicians. (Other groups, of course, make their own wrenchings of the language – a linguistic philosopher is likelier than his charwoman to use the word 'infinitely' in the sense of 'somewhat'.) Yet amidst all these aberrations there have persisted other quite different forms of English – among them the narrative and reflective prose of Herbert Read in *The Innocent Eye* and *The Green Child*, the prose-poems of David Jones, the stylised dialogue of Miss Compton-Burnett. This is work of the twentieth century and no other, yet it seems to have taught nothing whatsoever to translators who assume in readers a general feeblemindedness and a deep distaste for serious language on serious matters, the more trivial word being thought more genuine. Distress, for example, grief, anger and indignation remain common human experiences, and their natural names puzzle no one, but these translators prefer to describe human beings as depressed or worried, upset or annoyed – suffering only from such misfortunes as advertisements undertake to cure. This widespread technique – applied to the Bible or to Homer – degrades the writer while it insults the reader. Homer did not sing down to his audience.

I now pass on to defend my own translation. It is made in prose because such verse as I can command is quite inappropriate for a heroic narrative. Prose, then, with words of the present century, but not the language of careless day-to-day talk and writing; a certain formality seems needful if the reader is to have some inkling of Homer's own much greater formality. The gap between verse and prose vocabulary remains a wide one, but I have borrowed one resource from the procedure of Samuel Butler. At times he incorporates in his prose a phrase from Shakespeare or Milton or the Authorised Version (with which, like some other Victorian sceptics, he was enviably familiar), and in this I have gratefully followed him. I think a translator has the right to interpolate among his own words any phrases from an English classic that without aid from inverted commas might be quoted or adapted now by a novelist or an essayist. It is from *Macbeth* that I take the concept of light that thickens, and the castle's 'pleasant seat' has been used for the formula 'pleasant-sited'.

It will be asked if this is a literal translation or a paraphrase. Like 'Classical' and 'Romantic', these two expressions are difficult to avoid but also difficult to apply. I myself prefer to call a translation 'close' or 'free', but these words too are relative and subjective, and what to one critic may seem a natural freedom may seem to another an intolerable licence. Any translator, I suppose, is inclined to one side or the other, yet it is common sense to control one's inclination by reference to the particular passage in hand (paragraph, sentence, single phrase). 'I began', says King Alfred translating St Gregory, 'to turn into English the book called in Latin *Pastoralis*, sometimes word for word, sometimes meaning for meaning'; that seems a pattern for all translators. There are times when the closest translation is the best (every word keeping the original order and given the first equivalent from a dictionary). There are times when a close translation is inadequate or absurd, and a whole sentence must be recast. There are times when a free and a close translation are reasonable alternatives.

Faced with the last line of the *Divine Comedy*, any beginner in Italian will naturally arrive at the strict translation:

The love that moves the sun and the other stars

which makes an English verse line not likely to be improved on. Faced with the first four words of the *Odyssey*, I dare not begin 'Man me tell Muse' though that is the nearest I can get to a word for word translation. Lastly, when, at the opening of Book IX, Odysseus describes the site of Ithaca, he says, in Butcher and Lang's translation, 'Many islands lie around, very near one to another.' That keeps faithfully to the Greek, and I have nothing to say against it. But remembering a dictionary definition of 'cluster' as 'a number of things close together', I render the words 'Round it are clustered other islands' and consider this an idiomatic alternative.

I should call my translation rather free; some may think it unduly so. I need scarcely apologise for the occasional transference of a phrase to another position in a passage, for the insertion of a definite noun when a pronoun would be ambiguous, or for some exchange between parts of speech when a verb or noun is obliquely rendered by an adjective or adverb. These are commonplaces of translation. I am more likely to be reproached for sometimes adding a few words where I think that otherwise the sequence of thought or the emphasis might be missed. Thus in my translation the fourth paragraph in Book I has this: 'The tale begins when ...'. For these four words the Greek has the one word 'then', but I wished to make plain to English readers what Homer's listeners knew without further telling – that the formal prologue was complete and the main narrative about to begin.

Other points affecting translation are directly linked with the oral and traditional character of Homer's two epics, which visibly separates them from the written poems of later ages. That Homer composed in different circumstances from Pindar or Sophocles is not a new observation, but the many consequences of this have only recently been explored. The American scholar Milman Parry (1902–35) quite changed the face of Homeric studies when he made a first-hand investigation of oral epic as it survives today (for example in Yugoslavia and Central Asia) and used his discoveries in this field to illuminate the technique of Homeric verse-making. For a full, wide-ranging account of such research and its implications, there are now available the collected papers of Parry himself (*The Making of Homeric Verse*, 1971) and

Bowra's *Heroic Poetry* (1952). These are long and learned discussions of the subject; there is a good clear summary in Bowra's short *Homer* (1972). Certain problems remain unsettled, and I have no private solution for them. My sole concern here is with those now established points which a modern translator must consider.

(i) The bard does not seek to be original. He hopes to enter fully into a tradition, and if he achieves that, the imprint of his own personality matters to him very little.

(ii) He draws on familiar themes, choosing this or that version of a story and perhaps varying his version for various audiences. His memory holds a great fund of phrases, often half-lines, that will fit many different situations. He builds up his verse very largely through such existing formulas, redistributing them at will as later poets redistribute existing words at will.

(iii) His epithets – adjectives or nouns – are normally of an obvious nature and usable again and again. They are sometimes misapplied. The choice of epithets is much influenced by metre.

(iv) Whole lines, and sometimes whole passages, are repeated for repeated occurrences – sunrise, feasting, a guest's arrival, preparations for a journey.

(v) Brevity is seldom aimed at, a leisurely pace being more comfortable both for the bard and for his listeners.

These constant features of improvised verse are so unfamiliar to most of us that they need some pausing over. A cautious comparison with music might possibly be illuminating – music as improvised either by modern Asians or by Handel and by Mozart; but that would take us too far afield. Better to seek a very rough parallel from the history of English verse. Homer inherited from his bardic ancestors an elaborate and exacting metre. It may perhaps be non-Greek in origin; certainly it precludes the use of many ordinary Greek words. One line with its six feet offers room enough for several distinct points, but the circumstances of oral recitation encourage the bard instead to amplify one point at a time. Imagine some Tudor tale of war written in drab fourteeners. The long line could take in four points:

> Says France: 'To arms! The foemen come, and John is at
> their head.'

But the author, though writing instead of improvising, might feel he was squandering his resources; the reader might feel he was being hurried. So the versifier might use one line in amplification of 'says France' – either by adding verbs of speaking:

> Then chided them the King of France, and thus he spoke
> and said

or by dwelling on nouns with their set adjectives:

> Then spoke that high and noble knight, the king of lovely
> France

after which another line or two would tell how one or the other side was sore bestead or full boldly did advance, as history or as rhyme suggested. In his own grand way, Homer constantly does something comparable.

The claims of rhyme in a great deal of English verse have some affinity with the claims of metre in Homer's verse. Metre has claims in English verse also, but many readers who pay little heed to this are attentive to the use of rhyme. They see that rhyme is bound to affect the choice of words but rightly resent the abuse of it when meaning is distorted. With bad poets, distortion is common, but it does appear with good poets too in moments of carelessness or fatigue. Wordsworth spoiled one of his best sonnets by gross misuse of the word 'boon'; Spenser translating Tasso spoiled a fine passage by a false ending –

> Gather the Rose of love whilest yet is time,
> Whilest loving thou mayst lovèd be with equall crime –

where the last three words are an addition quite out of tune with the mood of the original.

The internal rhyme which occasionally is found in Homer has no effect upon composition, but a strictness of metre with no direct English equivalent imposes checks on his word-choice and word-arrangement that recall obliquely the checks imposed by the laws of English rhyme. Milman Parry in his analysis overstressed the exigencies of metre, minimised the remaining power of choice, and treated almost as meaningless any word that made no interesting addition to the main sense. Yet although either rhyme or metre is bound to influence vocabulary, neither should simply determine it, and if sound and sense cannot somehow be recon-

ciled, the poet has either not learned his trade or is lapsing from
its accepted standards. But again, the standards themselves allow
a rational flexibility. They must exclude what is contradictory or
absurd, but they need not enforce a rigid code of economy and
concentration such as is observed in some European metaphysical
poetry or – so I suppose – in the Japanese poems of 31 or of 17
syllables where every syllable must be made to tell. There is also
a place for leisureliness of many kinds. Homer's verse is in some
ways leisurely; in other ways much English Augustan verse is
leisurely. An unfriendly critic might mock Pope's line:

> But anxious Cares the pensive Nymph opprest.

Does this mean more, such a man might ask, than 'The anxious
girl was made more anxious by anxious anxiety'? The answer is
that what in logic may seem superfluous may nevertheless rein-
force the meaning and help to define a certain mood. Again, to
quote from an earlier and greater period of English verse, the
'obvious' adjective *sad* in Webster is perhaps more moving than a
new and ingenious one would be:

> I am acquainted with sad misery
> As the tan'd galley-slave is with his Oare.

The great frequency of obvious epithets, the recurrence of
formulas taking a half-line or a line, the repetition of longer pas-
sages describing familiar sequences of events or actions – these
are things taken for granted in the oral and traditional style of
Homer but likely to disconcert those accustomed to twentieth-
century conventions. Confronted with such unmodern elements,
the translator is bound to make decisions. Should he, in deference
to his original, reproduce all these features as faithfully as he can?
Should he just omit whole classes of them so as not to discourage
otherwise willing readers? Has he the right to treat differently
different examples of things that at first sight seem to belong to
the same class?

My own answers to such questions involve a good deal of
compromise. I think it wrong simply to oust certain features that
do not at once recommend themselves to a modern public. Indeed,
one attraction of good translations is that of blending convinc-
ingly the familiar with the unfamiliar, some things in them be-
longing to human experience generally, others only to the

country or age or culture from which a particular work has issued. This holds good for conventions of composition as well as of behaviour, and things that at first do not seem acceptable may endear themselves to us later on. But I do not think the translator is bound to use repetition at every point where his author does – that method may have for the modern reader a deadening effect not felt by the bard's own audience, so that would-be faithfulness may prove in the end unfaithful. Honour is satisfied, I should say, if the reader is constantly reminded that Homer's narrative is in some respects akin to a tale for children read at the fireside (where the audience enjoys certain repetitions and may protest if a tired adult tries to leave them out) rather than to a modern short story that aims very consciously at concision (beginning, for instance, with some such phrase as 'Ten years later he saw her again'). If in this translation the reader finds one epithet used eighty times for the same person when modern custom would let it appear only once or twice, then I think I have given him guidance enough on how Homer handles epithets. If the guardian of some computer proceeds to ask if Homer himself did not use this epithet 215 times, I shall return no answer. It is not my mission to lessen the labours of computers.

I must now recall the commonplace that in any language the same word or the same phrase will sometimes be used with a different emphasis or a different sense; and the special importance in oral epic of fixed epithets and repeated formulas does not place Homer's language outside the range of this general principle. Consider in English so common a word as the adjective 'nice'. The big *Oxford English Dictionary* gives fifteen main senses for it, divided not quite equally between the obsolete and the modern; and there are many subdivisions. Then we have words used mostly now in a single sense, but sometimes keeping a vestige of older senses; a 'fond mother' may be merely affectionate or may be a besotted mother – and there the adjective has retained an older and now dialectal flavour. And then we have also formulas belonging to proverbs or quotations, sometimes used with full consciousness of their meaning, oftener not. Campbell's half-line, 'few and far between', is still much quoted, but usually just as a strengthened 'few', even if the few things in question came close together.

Thus in Homer also we should expect that the same word or phrase will in different contexts mean different things, and in that case it is more important for the translator to make the sense clear on each occasion than to look for some English word whose meaning might be equally flexible. A common Homeric adjective, *kakos*, is a rough equivalent of the English 'bad', but may be used more specifically in the senses of 'base-born', 'cowardly', 'ugly' or 'unskilled'. In a given passage one might use 'base' to cover both of the first two meanings, and yet this might hardly be worth while. Clarity should be the first concern. Again, a word or phrase that in one context may be powerful may in another be plainly weaker, and then elsewhere may become so weak as barely to need translation. There is, for instance, a frequent phrase, metrically convenient, whose 'literal' meaning is 'in (one's) halls'. This is sometimes used with great emphasis – one king is murdered, another becomes a beggar, in his own halls. Sometimes it comes in the weaker sense 'at home', sometimes with no more emphasis than a simple 'here' or 'there'. The word *philos* means in the first place 'dear' or 'friend', but is used too of one's 'kith and kin', one's 'own people', even if unfriendly, and then more widely of things that belong to one – perhaps a strong 'his own' or 'your own', perhaps a quite weak 'his' or 'your'. The word *klutos* begins as 'famous', but passes into a vague general word of praise, now replacing something like 'good' or 'fine', now, it would seem, a mere metrical stop-gap of two syllables.

For my present purpose I group together single repeated epithets and longer repeated phrases, agreeing with Bowra as against Milman Parry that 'the phrase takes its colour from the situation', but admitting of course that a phrase or epithet may from time to time be misused. Before illustrating this position from particularised Homeric instances, I should like to make a partial comparison with Shakespeare's use of one phrase. The last act of *The Merchant of Venice* ends its first line: 'In such a night as this'. In the following lines the four words 'In such a night' are tossed to and fro between the lovers. Lear on the heath and in the storm says also 'In such a night', and then reinforces it – 'In such a night as this'. For the tragic scene as for the idyll, no phrase could have been more surely chosen.

Among Homer's most repeated adjectives are those describing the usual qualities of familiar things – the swiftness of ships or arrows, the glitter of a metal, the good workmanship of a palace's furnishings. Some scholars mistrust any epithets used so lavishly,

perhaps disliking repetition as such, perhaps resenting the space
allowed to unexceptional useful objects – a pair of sandals, a table,
or what Hobbes calls 'a brave Pot or Pan'. But the sharp distinc-
tion of use from beauty taken for granted in an industrialised
society had not been thought of in Homer's days because it was
still unfounded (witness the relics of those days now treasured in
our museums), and the bard needed no exhortation to praise
whatever was well made. As Augustine expected an iron stylus
to be functional and beautiful too, so Homer and his characters
and his audience would expect a 'well-wheeled' wagon both to
run smoothly and also to please the eye, a result still worth re-
cording even although familiar.

Certain ancient critics thought it irrational that a 'swift' ship
should be at anchor or that 'lovely' streams on the Trojan plain
should be defiled by a mass of corpses. We need not share their
short-sightedness; after all, the Rome Express may be standing at
a platform and a friend's dog may have left black pawmarks all
over a spotless carpet. But sometimes Homer does indeed use con-
flicting epithets – notably so in the *Iliad* with the simile of stars
and watch-fires:

> As when in the sky the stars round the bright moon
> Shine very clear ...

Conceivably the first line was an unconsidered borrowing from
an earlier bard who contrasted, as Sappho later did, the moon
herself with the 'meaner beauties of the night':

> As when in the sky the stars round the bright moon
> Are clear no longer, for she outshines them ...

But in any case, Homer distorts the sense through a formula mis-
applied. What should the translator do here? Tell the truth and
shame the devil, some scholars will say, and certainly it would be
dishonest to emend 'bright' to 'pale'. But surely a case can be
made for Tennyson, who omits the first adjective altogether:

> As when in heaven the stars about the moon
> Look beautiful, when all the winds are laid ...

I think this a sensible attitude for any translator who is sure
that for one reason or another his author has said what he did
not mean. I have specified already cases from Spenser and from

Wordsworth where words were manifestly misused for the sake of rhyme. I may add that both Chatterton and Browning misused the word 'slughorn' (an early form of 'slogan'), not for rhyme but in sheer ignorance, believing this thing to be a musical instrument. If I had to translate these offending passages into some other language, I should merely ignore Spenser's 'crime', I should treat Wordsworth's 'boon' as if it were something like 'bargain', and should replace the slogan with some real sort of horn or trumpet. This seems to me simply common sense, though some may prefer to call it impertinence.

In my dealing with Homer's adjectives, I have lessened repetition of some, not to improve on the original but to ease my reader's acquiescence in an unfamiliar convention. I have also varied translation of the same adjective when the shifts of sense it could bear in Greek seemed without parallel in English or when the development of our language has brought differentiations which our ancestors did without but which, once made, can scarcely be disregarded. (The flexible 'fair' and 'goodly' of earlier English – or of Butcher and Lang – were in their time very serviceable words, but we cannot now give them back that once ample range.) Thus the constant epithet of Odysseus commonly rendered 'much-enduring' appears to me to invite some distinction, since the verb it is drawn from is sometimes used of active daring or hardihood, sometimes of passive tolerance or submission, so that in differing contexts 'patient', 'much-tried', 'bold' or 'dauntless' may all be reasonable translations.

I have seldom used what I think is my right to omit an adjective altogether when it seemed no less of an intrusion than the English rhyme-words discussed above. The epithet 'greaved' is used with precision in the *Iliad*, where it refers to a piece of armour which distinguished Greeks from Trojans. In the *Odyssey* it occurs twice in reminiscences of the Trojan war, and there I have kept it in translation; I have omitted it in three alien contexts where I consider it meaningless. For one other epithet, time after time applied to the crew or comrades of Odysseus, I have kept nearly always the usual translation 'trusty', but in Book XII I have omitted it when it comes just after the men have betrayed their leader by killing the cattle of the sun. Just possibly this might be bitter irony, but I doubt if Homer meant it so.

Certain other adjectives, I think, have been assumed to be

misapplied when a critic has rashly supposed identity between some ancient and modern categories or has failed to recognise evolution in the overtones of English words. These adjectives most often express some form of praise, and it has been forgotten that such words are likely to shift their meaning according to the subject discussed and the scheme of values held by this or that person or group. The simplest of all words of praise, the adjective *good*, used of any persons or things that are what they ought to be, has very great differences of meaning in varying contexts and times and places. In England its reference is often moral (upright or pious or kind). It is also used of many skills (a good archaeologist, a good cricketer; Richard Wilson is very good). Again, it may indicate social standing, and on different lips the phrase 'a good school' may stress the quality of the teaching or the quality of the parents. Other turns to *good* are almost endless. In the classical epoch of Japan, a simple *good* might imply an expert calligrapher, and Mr Belloc once said to me: 'The squire here is a very good man. He understands claret.'

The normal Greek word for *good* is *agathos*. In Homer it often means 'well-born', often 'brave', often 'skilled' ('a good doctor' or 'good at boxing'). Two centuries after him it becomes extended to moral virtue. But the words I am concerned with now are compound adjectives which often have been conventionally translated as 'great-hearted', 'great-souled', 'high-minded', 'blame-less' or the like and then denounced as hopelessly false in application. But the Greek words thought of as 'heart' or 'soul' or 'mind' are by no means exact equivalents of that English; they include, according to the dictionaries, such different senses as 'seat of life or passion or feeling', 'will' or 'desire' or 'anger'. As for the 'great' or 'high' that precedes them, it has been forgotten that these and suchlike compounds in English have often had other overtones than their present ones. 'High-minded' in Coverdale's *Psalms* is a synonym for 'proud'; Talbot in Shakespeare uses it to insult Saint Joan. 'Great-hearted' has meant 'implacable' or 'unyielding', and 'magnanimity' in Sir Thomas Browne is parallel to 'vainglory'. But a villain or a ravening lion may be as 'bold-hearted' as a hero, and we should not exploit unnatural English to disparage the natural Greek of Homer. As for the negative *amūmōn* which has called forth many learned pages, one need only say that its first meaning is almost certainly 'faultless' or 'irreproachable', but that its application depends upon its context. In its most obvious and general sense, it fits Nausicaa like a glove when Odysseus in Book VII asks the king her father not to reproach a girl who in every way is beyond reproach. But some of its uses are less straightforward. Dancing of course may be 'irreproachable' either socially or technically, but how can one call Aegisthus 'faultless' or 'irreproachable', when he is best known for his murder of Agamemnon? I think we have here another instance of social eminence looming larger than moral eminence. Just as *agathos* might mean 'well-born' without meaning 'virtuous', so *amūmōn* may mean 'noble' without any rider that 'noble is as noble does'. As Gibbon might more elegantly have put it, his lineage was pure though his manners were flagitious.

A particularly evasive epithet is *dios*, which seems in the first place to be used of the bright clear sky and of the sky-god – an adjective meaning 'bright' or 'celestial' or 'divine'. And since in early societies everywhere it is normal that all kings and queens, whether virtuous or wicked, should be hedged about by divinity of a kind, this epithet may naturally be attributed to any sovereign, and by extension to any great noble. It may then be reasonably translated as 'king' or 'queen', 'kingly', 'queenly', 'royal' or 'noble'. But when in the *Odyssey* the swineherd and the goatherd are given the same epithet, what shall be said then? The most honest answer is that the word has been misused for the sake of metre; the translator may choose to reduce its meaning to something like 'good' or 'worthy', or else to reject it as misapplied. To return to traditional uses of the same word, we are left in doubt in certain cases whether the prevailing notion is that of brightness or that of celestialness and unearthliness. Is Circe a radiant goddess or a mysterious one? Is the dawn bright and the sea sparkling, or are both of them 'numinous'? (And this last adjective is an excellent example of a word that in modern poetry might be used to great effect but that in a translation of ancient poetry would be utterly out of place, since it does not express at first hand the feelings of a primitive people but interprets those feelings at second hand as understood by a modern scholar.) Alternative versions are obviously defensible.

For the gods themselves, as also for rulers and for nobles, there are of course many other epithets which offer more problems in translation. The gods have a multiplicity of titles, some of which are obscure to us and may have been so to Homer. (Hermes is given one epithet which means perhaps 'the slayer of Argus' but perhaps instead 'the Radiant One'. The goddess Dawn perhaps had a golden throne, perhaps a robe embroidered with golden flowers.) In any case, for the poet and his like-minded listeners, all such titles were in themselves theologically correct, so that if he began by telling them that Athene said or did this or that, it could not be wrong to round out a line with some such addition as 'the Unwearied One' or 'goddess of gleaming eyes' or 'Driver of Spoil' or 'Daughter of aegis-bearing Zeus'. Nevertheless, the alliance of cult and metre sometimes appears a hollow one, and the modern reader may feel uneasy to be told first that 'Athene led the way' for Telemachus and then in the very next line that 'the gleaming-eyed goddess Athene addressed him thus'. I have made the same compromise for these titles as for other Homeric epithets, translating them all often enough to make the convention clear, but thinning out repetitions of them.

Men of exalted station are likewise given many honorific epithets which prudence may persuade one to modify or to use more sparsely. Kings and princes are taken to have divine origins or at least a special divine protection, and tradition makes them strong and wise. This, with an idiom using some nouns for adjectives, lets Homer say what in 'literal' English might be rendered 'The sacred strength of Telemachus spoke to them.' To assimilate this to such later periphrases as 'His Worship the Mayor' or 'His Sacred Majesty King William' seems to me a considerable mistake, and although I enjoy both the scholarship and the eccentricities of Bérard, I think he was ill advised to translate this phrase 'Sa Force et Sainteté Télémaque leur dit'. A once sacred formula, already half-secularised in Homer, has probably no genuine equivalent in a modern language, and here it seems better to say no more than 'Prince Telemachus spoke to them', letting the reader enrich the bare title 'Prince' with the overtones he feels appropriate for an ancient hieratic society.

One epithet very freely given to anyone of high rank is a word which would literally be 'godlike'. That English word might be kept in a translation if interpreted in a Victorian sense, as when Trollope praises in a ne'er-do-well hero 'the perfect form of his almost godlike face'. It has no suggestion in Homer's verse of the 'godlike reason' that Hamlet brooded over. In a context where appearance is dwelt upon, one might speak of something like 'godlike countenance', or more simply call a man 'young and handsome'. Where the word seems a mechanical adjunct of rank, one might replace it by 'King' or 'Lord' or omit it altogether.

The rendering of some titles and forms of address is made more difficult because Homer does not mark precisely the lower and higher degrees of rank or the mutual relationship of his characters. He has two main words for 'king', one of which appears sometimes stronger, sometimes no stronger, than the other. His society seems now feudal, now not. Odysseus in Ithaca, Alcinous in Scheria are certainly the chief rulers there, but not the only rulers; there are other sceptred chiefs or princes. The men who form the crew of Odysseus are sometimes felt as being his subjects, sometimes much more as comrades or near-equals. The girls who wait on Nausicaa have the white arms and braided hair that define them as ladies of the court; they are usually called something like 'attendants', but once they are called something like 'slaves'. These shiftings of view are of great concern to archaeologists and historians, but for a translator the lesson would seem to be that he should not attempt to codify where Homer did not, but rather practise that easy to-and-fro which allowed Shakespeare in the same scene to call the same person 'king', 'prince' and 'lord'. It will be less misleading than rigid observance of modern etiquette.

One final point affecting the theory of translation. Homer is fond both of doubling and of varying words that are much alike. I mean by 'doubling' the use of like words in immediate succession and with parallel construction; I mean by 'varying' the use of like words in phrases more detached from each other. 'He begged them to let him go' gives a clear sense, and 'begged' is already stronger than 'asked'. If I want further strengthening, I may say 'he earnestly begged them' or 'he begged and begged them', or finally 'he begged and implored them'. This last procedure is common in Greek and Roman oratory and in the English Prayer Book ('erred and strayed', 'sins and wickedness'). It may be abused, it may become a mannerism, but in itself it is very natural, and Homer believes in it.

Different from this is the use of like words in separate phrases with deliberate avoidance of repetition. This is the device whose frequent abuse in journalism was mocked by Fowler under the name of 'elegant variation'. His strictures have possibly done more harm than good, since he failed to remind his often too trustful readers of the very honourable past history of variation used rationally and effectively by great masters of prose and verse. I briefly observe that the 'parallelism' of ancient verse in Israel and in China is one illustration of this device ('Jacob shall rejoice, and Israel shall be glad'); that orators in classical Greece like to use such formulas as 'knowing this and aware of that'; that Tacitus is particularly ingenious in contriving new variants; and that there is nothing ridiculous in Milton's 'fresh Woods and Pastures new' or in Johnson's 'vain to blame and useless to praise him'. Homer is fond of this device. In one passage he has in successive lines a close equivalent of 'townwards' followed by 'to the city'; in another he has in the same line the equivalent of 'arrows' followed by 'shafts'. He ranges freely among four words for 'sea' although he has only one word for 'ship' (later Greek poets discovered more).

When an author thus exploits the use of synonyms and near-synonyms, I should claim a latitude for the translator to follow his text religiously or to condense it freely, or again to replace variation by repetition or repetition by variation, according to the idiom of the two languages or the emphasis of a given passage. I shall be reminded that Homer's variants are linked with metre. Of course they are, but that does not mean that they gave no pleasure in themselves. I have been reluctant in this translation to multiply verbs of speaking, but have freely exchanged 'sea' and 'ocean' (keeping Ocean with a capital for the great river encircling the earth and for its guardian god). I have often varied 'ship' with 'vessel' when Homer could not; I have had not scruple in using such variants as 'cave' and 'cavern' to avoid an unwanted rhyme, a conspicuous verse rhythm or a jagged ending to some sentence. Prose, no doubt, is a humble medium; nevertheless it has its own decencies, and concession to these may be forgiven in view of the bard's ampler concessions to the exigencies of verse.

Such have been my principles in translation; I may at times have departed from them. The Greek text that I have translated has been in the main that of T. W. Allen, but I have adopted a few modern emendations which it seemed absurd to disregard, and have omitted certain lines which scholars of eminence have seen as merely displaced by copyists. On my own account I have made neither emendations nor omissions.

I should like to add, for what they are worth, a few suggestions to those who read Homer's narrative in this form. In a sense, each reader as well as each translator makes his own image of the story and its significance. (Samuel Butler thought that women in the *Odyssey* were 'so well and sympathetically drawn' that its author must have been a woman. T. E. Lawrence found in the author an 'infuriating male condescension towards inglorious woman'.) There are clearly many approaches to the poem, and one familiar approach today is that of the detective – who may be the learned specialist, accounting in one way rather than another for the many loose ends and inconsistencies in the poem, or may be the genial amateur, reckoning up the various improbabilities of a single episode – for example, that of Penelope and her web. Such exercises are always innocent, sometimes praiseworthy and instructive, but not the most likely to aid understanding of the poem. The folktale of the web, for instance, might much more readily come alive for someone venerating in Durham the Anglo-Saxon braids and embroideries given by Athelstan to Saint Cuthbert's shrine. In certain ways, the two centuries or so that link us with the Industrial Revolution are a greater barrier to understanding Homer than the three millennia or so that divide us from Mycenae.

In any case it should be accepted that Homer (or 'the Homeric author') simply disregarded many details of narrative that later authors have led us to expect. It would be quite vain to attempt a methodical reconstruction of what things happened at what moment in what part of the Cyclops' cave. Homer had neither the higher imagination of a Dante or a Shakespeare, embracing everything in a single glance, nor the conscientiousness of a nineteenth-century French novelist composing slowly and reconciling details at leisure. He had instead many good conventions (comparable, one might say, to the 'open-roof' convention in classical Japanese painting) which, once agreed on, are seen as admirable. Vividness is one of his gifts, but it is fundamentally different from the naturalism which so often and in so many ways has bedevilled European art.

Greeks of the centuries after Homer approached his poems divergently. For some of them, 'fundamentalists', he was a universal sage whose incidental utterances on theology or strategy, on doctors' remedies or on chariot-racing, must be acquiesced in as permanently valid – a view that called forth Platonic satire. For others he was a scientist in disguise. For others again he was a teacher of moral virtue, presenting the pattern of an Odysseus who was proof against Circe and the Sirens and combated the base instincts of his crew. At a loftier level, the neo-Platonist Porphyry considered Athene in the Cave of the Nymphs to have taught Odysseus detachment from earthly goods and expounded the doctrine of transmigration.

In all this interpreting of Homer, we must keep apart two opinions – that the poet himself meant certain things or that what he meant as simple narrative might well be given a second and higher meaning. No less than his philosophical opponents, Porphyry wrenches his author's text, presuming in him a knowledge of ancient mystery cults which is incompatible with the whole tenor of the poem. I take it that in the Homeric world some knowledge of these things had survived, but that in the poet's own environment it had almost altogether faded. The *Odyssey* keeps many vestiges of older traditional religion – one would be perplexed if it did not. The Cave of the Nymphs with its human and its divine entrance is indeed a natural place for initiation; the four paradisal streams on Calypso's island belong of course to ancient cosmogony, but for Homer these things seem no more numinous than 'Cubit the Pretty Ploughboy' for a nineteenth-century country singer. Homer's religion is more simple – the homage paid to the water-nymphs in Book XVII, the patriarchal ritual and sacrifice in Book III, the sacred relation of host and guest set forth in vain by Odysseus to the Cyclops: 'Zeus himself is the champion of suppliants and of guests; "god of guests" is a name of his; guests are august, and Zeus goes with them.'

It is one thing to believe that Homer himself intended his poem as a continuous allegory (like, say, the esoteric *Bird-Parliament* of Attar, nobly paraphrased by Fitzgerald); it is another thing to believe that what was in the first place a narrative is an admirable foundation for allegory (perhaps a private one of the reader's, preferably one that lights up the meaning of a wide and genuine tradition). The capacity to allegorise without distortion (to find tongues in trees and sermons in stones) is a mark not of simple-mindedness but of wisdom. There exists a pattern of endurance against adversity which some may recognise in the natural world as they consider the salmon battling against the stream, others in human history with the example of some explorer or inventor. The same pattern may be found in certain works of imagination, among which the Odyssey stands high, although not highest.

In the early centuries of the Church, some theologians rejected classical books generally as a temptation of the devil; others delighted to find in them a prefiguration of Christian truth. Some of these latter turned especially to the Odyssey, not only because they found there a general parable of the human voyage through perilous seas to a spritual harbour but because they saw the ship of voyagers as the Church itself, and again Odysseus bound to the mast as an image of Christ nailed to the Cross. (Consult for such things Karl Rahner's book on Greek Myths and Christian Mystery.)

Long afterwards, some scholars of the Renaissance, aware that Plato had allegorised and assuming that Homer had done no less, made their own restatements of his purpose in terms of morals or of theology. Chapman in England followed this lead. No one now is likely to accept his belief that the Odyssean descriptions of certain countries 'have admirable allegories besides their artly and pleasing relation', but any of us might do far worse than conclude with him that the traveller's hope is to arrive 'at the proper and onely true natural countrie of every worthy man, whose haven is heaven and the next life, to which this life is but a sea, in continuall aesture and vexation'. Those for whom such thoughts are idle must be content to recognise in the Odyssey the power inherent in beauty of every kind to keep warm men's wits to the things that are and to console them among their miseries.

W. S.

GLOSSARY AND INDEX OF NAMES

THE aims of the following list are modest, but a little information is much better than none. To take the glosses first: it would be possible usefully to append to the *Odyssey* large sections of a full-scale classical encyclopaedia, but here the briefest of entries are provided, sufficient to make clear whether the name in question is that of a person, a place, or whatever, and to give the most immediately relevant additional information. Phrases after a new comma refer afresh to the main name, not to a name in the previous part of the entry. The reader who is in search of more is referred to Lemprière's *Classical Dictionary*, or to the *New Larousse Encyclopedia of Mythology*. As for the page-references, these list all the occurrences of the name itself (with the exception of 'Odysseus'), as well as of the main descriptions that sometimes stand in for it; most descriptions indexed in this way are entered in quotation marks at the beginning of the gloss.

There are many different systems for the spelling and pronunciation of Greek names. Conventional usage follows none of them consistently. The spellings and stresses adopted here are (at least) usual in contemporary English. Hyphens separate two syllables which might otherwise have been taken as one.

Place-names mentioned in the glossary are entered on the maps on pages 347–9 unless the places are mythical or of uncertain location.

ACÁSTUS, king of the western Greek island Dulichium, 172
ACHAÉA, another name of Greece, 62, 131, 147
ACHAÉANS, collective name of all Greek-speaking peoples, 3, 6, 7, 8, 9, 10, 12, 13, 14, 15, 16, 17, 18, 19, 21, 25, 26, 27, 28, 29, 32, 37, 38, 40, 41, 43, 46, 54, 86, 90, 96–7, 100, 105, 113, 136, 138, 139, 140, 160, 161, 170, 173, 181, 184, 192, 194, 196, 199, 205, 211, 214, 216, 222, 223, 231, 232, 233, 240, 246, 247, 250, 256, 257, 259, 261, 262, 263, 264, 266, 279, 282, 286, 287, 288, 289, 295
ÁCHERON, river in the underworld, 126
ACHÍLLES, son of Peleus and Thetis, hero of the *Iliad*, xviii, 25, 27, 35, 42, 62, 86, 138–40, 286, 287, 288
ACRONÁ-US, a Phaeacian, 87
ÁCTORIS, maid of Penelope, 282
ADRÁSTE, maid of Helen, 37
AE-AÉA, island home of Circe, 116, 129, 143
AE-AÉAN, inhabitant of Aeaea, 99, 149
AE-ÉTES, brother of Circe, 116, 144

HÉRMES, 'Radiant One', god, son of Zeus and Maia, messenger of the gods, guide of souls to the underworld, x, 2, 3, 55, 56–8, 59, 79, 92–3, 120–1, 142, 152, 175, 185, 237, 286, 288

HÉRMES' HILL, hill above the town of Ithaca, 201

HERMÍO-NE, daughter of Menelaus and Helen, 35

HIPPODAMEÍA, maid of Penelope, 221, 222, 224

HÍPPOTAS, father of Aeolus (1), 113

HÝLAX, fictitious father of Castor (2), 169

HYPEREÍA, previous home of the Phaeacians, near the Cyclops land, 67

HYPERÉSIA, town of Achaea, 183

HYPÉRION, name used by Homer both for the sun-god himself, 1, 151–2, and for the sun-god's father, 146–7 and perhaps 149

I-ÁRDANUS, river in Crete, 30

I-ÁSIAN, epithet of Argos, 223

I-ÁSION, son of Zeus and Electra, 57

ÍASUS (1), father of Amphion (2), 134

ÍASUS (2), father of Dmetor, 212

ICÁRIUS, father of Penelope, 9, 13, 53, 54, 138, 200, 221, 223, 224, 240, 261

ICMÁLIUS, Ithacan craftsman, 229

IDÓMENEUS, king of Crete, 27, 160, 170, 174, 232

ÍLIUM, another name of Troy, 16, 98, 100, 113, 130, 131, 132, 163, 166, 170, 208, 223, 231, 232, 234, 242, 277, 288

ÍLUS, son of Mermerus, 7

ÍNO, sea-goddess, daughter of Cadmus (see also Leucothea), 63, 66

IÓLCUS, town in Thessaly, 133

ÍPHICLUS, king of Phylace, 134

IPHIMEDEÍA, wife of Aloeus, mother by Poseidon of Otus and Ephialtes, 135

ÍPHITUS, son of Eurytus, 254

IPHTHÍ-ME, daughter of Icarius, sister of Penelope, 53–4

ÍRUS, nickname of Arnaeus, a beggar in Ithaca, xi, 217–19, 222–3, 225

ÍSMARUS, city of the Cicones in Thrace, 100, 103

ÍTHACA, island off west coast of Greece, home of Odysseus, vii, viii, x, xi, xiii, xiv, 1, 3, 5, 6, 7, 10, 12, 13, 14, 16, 17, 18, 19, 20, 25, 39, 48, 49, 50, 54, 99, 111, 123, 124, 126, 128, 129, 130, 131, 136, 138, 146, 156, 157, 159, 160, 161, 162, 168, 169, 172, 173, 178, 181, 184, 189, 190, 192, 193, 196, 198, 200, 217, 231, 237, 238, 248, 251, 254, 256, 258, 260, 262, 265, 266, 270, 279, 285, 288, 291, 292, 293, 296, 298

ÍTHACUS, co-builder of a well on Ithaca, 206

ÍTYLUS, son of Zethus (2) and the nightingale-daughter of Pandareus, 240

MELÁNTHIUS, son of Dolius, goat-herd, xi, xii, xiii, 206–8, 210, 247, 249, 258, 260, 268, 269, 276

MELÁNTHO, daughter of Dolius, maid of Penelope, 225, 229–30

MÉMNON, son of Tithonus and Dawn, 39, 139

MENELÁUS, son of Atreus, brother of Agamemnon, husband of Helen, vii, xi, xvi, 8, 26, 27, 29–31, 35–49, 62, 97, 138, 163, 164, 176, 178, 179–81, 182, 203, 204, 205, 232, 288

MÉNTES, son of Anchialus, king of the Taphians, whose form Athene borrows on her first meeting with Telemachus, 3, 5, 11

MÉNTOR, son of Alcimus, friend of Odysseus in Ithaca, whose form Athene habitually adopts as a disguise, 17–18, 21, 23, 28, 50, 203, 270, 271, 296, 297, 298

MÉRMERUS, father of Ilus, 7

MESAÚLIUS, servant of Eumaeus, 175

MESSÉ-NE, district in south-west Peloponnese, 254

MESSÉNIANS, inhabitants of Messene, 254

MÍMAS, promontory in Asia Minor opposite Chios, 27

MÍNOS, son of Zeus and Europa, king of Cnossos in Crete, 135, 141, 214, 232, 264

MÚLIUS, Dulichian servant of Amphinomus, 227

MUSES (English word), nine daughters of Zeus, goddesses of poetry, song, dancing and all the arts, x, 1, 86, 96, 287

MYCÉ-NE (1), Agamemnon's city, capital of Argos, 30, 256, 264

MYCÉ-NE (2), legendary Achaean heroine, 15

MÝRMIDONS, people led by Achilles and after him by his son Neoptolemus, 27, 35, 139

NAÚBOLUS, father of Euryalus, 87

NAUSÍCA-A, daughter of Alcinous and Arete, ix, x, xix, 67–74, 76, 83, 95–6

NAUSÍTHO-US, son of Poseidon, father of Alcinous, 67, 77, 98

NAÚTEUS, a Phaeacian, 87

NE-AÉRA, mother by the sun-god of Lampetie and Phaethusa, 146

NÉ-ION, spur of Mount Neriton in Ithaca, 5, 25

NÉLEUS, son of Poseidon and Tyro, father of Nestor, 23, 25, 27, 29, 32, 133, 134, 183

NEOPTÓLEMUS, son of Achilles, 35, 139

NÉRICUS, town on west coast of Greece, 294

NÉRITON, mountain in Ithaca, 99, 162

NÉRITUS, co-builder of a well on Ithaca, 207

NÉSTOR, son of Neleus and Chloris, king of Pylos, ix, xi, 8, 23–34, 35, 36, 38, 39, 40, 42, 46, 134, 139, 179, 181, 182, 204, 287

NILE, river in Egypt, 46, 48, 171, 212

NÍSUS, king of Dulichium, father of Amphinomus, 199, 221

NO-ÉMON, son of Phromius, an Ithacan, 21, 49–50

PHÝLACUS, hero of Phylace, 183

PHÝLO, maid of Helen, 38

PI-ÉRIA, district north of Mount Olympus, 56

PLEÍA-DES, a constellation of seven stars, 61

POÍAS, father of Philoctetes, 27

POLÍ-TES, companion of Odysseus, 118

PÓLYBUS (1), father of Eurymachus, 10, 16, 190, 198, 200, 252, 261

PÓLYBUS (2), man of Thebes in Egypt, 38

PÓLYBUS (3), Phaeacian craftsman, 93

PÓLYBUS (4), a suitor, 271

POLYCÁS-TE, youngest daughter of Nestor, 34

POLÝCTOR (1), co-builder of a well on Ithaca, 206

POLÝCTOR (2), father of Peisander, 224, 271

POLYDÁMNA, wife of the Egyptian Thon, 40

POLYDEÚCES, son of Zeus and Leda, brother of Castor (1), 135

POLYNÁ-US, father of Amphialus, 87

POLYPÉMON, fictitious father of the fictitious Apheidas, 292

POLYPHÉIDES, father of Theoclymenus, 183

POLYPHÉMUS, son of Poseidon and Thoosa, Cyclops, x, xvi, 3, 12, 103, 104–12, 117, 124, 130, 147, 162, 243, 284

POLYTHÉRSES, father of Ctesippus, 271

PÓNTEUS, a Phaeacian, 87

PONTÓNO-US, page of Alcinous, 80, 86, 155

POSEÍDON, 'Earthshaker', son of Cronos, brother of Zeus, god of the sea, x, 1, 3, 23, 24, 27, 31, 33, 44, 46, 61, 63–5, 73, 74, 75, 76, 77, 82, 92–3, 98, 106, 109, 111–12, 130, 131, 133, 135, 137, 145, 157–8, 162, 282, 283, 288

PRAMNÍAN WINE, used by Circe, 118

PRÍAM, king of Troy, 25, 26, 57, 137, 140, 161, 170, 270

PRÓCRIS, daughter of Erectheus king of Athens, 135

PRÓREUS, a Phaeacian, 87

PRÓTEUS, sea-god and sage, father of Eidothea, servant of Poseidon, whose seals he herds near Egypt, 43–8, 205, 287

PRÝMNEUS, a Phaeacian, 87

PSÝRA, small island near Chios, 27

PÝLOS, 'Neleian' (see Nestor), city in Messene on south-west coast of Peloponnese, x, xi, 3, 8, 17, 19, 20, 23, 24, 27, 34, 49, 50, 51, 55, 133, 134, 138, 160, 169, 179, 182, 183, 190, 191, 193, 194, 198, 203, 204, 256, 289

PYRIPHLÉGETHON, river in the underworld, 126

PÝTHO, sanctuary and oracle of Apollo on Parnassus, 86, 141

RAVEN'S ROCK, place in Ithaca, 163

RHADAMÁNTHUS, ruler in the Elysian Fields, 48, 83

RHEÍTHRON, harbour on Ithaca, 5

MAPS OF REAL PLACES

HOMER'S geography is an indissoluble amalgam of fact and fiction. Some places are clearly real, others clearly mythical. Most are a mixture – imaginary places embodying actual geographical details. The places and features marked on these maps of Greece in the classical period are real, and those whose names Homer uses may be the same ones he was referring to.

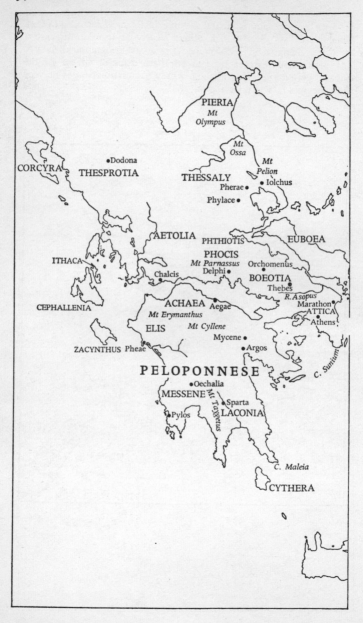

Bhagavad Gita

The Bible Authorized King James Version
With Apocrypha

Dhammapada

Dharmasūtras

The Koran

The Pañcatantra

The Sauptikaparvan (from the
Mahabharata)

The Tale of Sinuhe and Other Ancient
Egyptian Poems

Upaniṣads

ANSELM OF CANTERBURY   The Major Works

THOMAS AQUINAS   Selected Philosophical Writings

AUGUSTINE   The Confessions
On Christian Teaching

BEDE   The Ecclesiastical History

HEMACANDRA   The Lives of the Jain Elders

KĀLIDĀSA   The Recognition of Śakuntalā

MANJHAN   Madhumalati

ŚĀNTIDEVA   The Bodhicaryāvatāra

Women's Writing 1778–1838

JAMES BOSWELL	Life of Johnson
FRANCES BURNEY	Cecilia
	Evelina
JOHN CLELAND	Memoirs of a Woman of Pleasure
DANIEL DEFOE	A Journal of the Plague Year
	Moll Flanders
	Robinson Crusoe
HENRY FIELDING	Joseph Andrews and Shamela
	Tom Jones
WILLIAM GODWIN	Caleb Williams
OLIVER GOLDSMITH	The Vicar of Wakefield
ELIZABETH INCHBALD	A Simple Story
SAMUEL JOHNSON	The History of Rasselas
ANN RADCLIFFE	The Italian
	The Mysteries of Udolpho
SAMUEL RICHARDSON	Pamela
TOBIAS SMOLLETT	The Adventures of Roderick Random
	The Expedition of Humphry Clinker
LAURENCE STERNE	The Life and Opinions of Tristram Shandy, Gentleman
	A Sentimental Journey
JONATHAN SWIFT	Gulliver's Travels
	A Tale of a Tub and Other Works
HORACE WALPOLE	The Castle of Otranto
MARY WOLLSTONECRAFT	Mary and The Wrongs of Woman
	A Vindication of the Rights of Woman

The Oxford World's Classics Website

www.worldsclassics.co.uk

- Information about new titles
- Explore the full range of Oxford World's Classics
- Links to other literary sites and the main OUP webpage
- Imaginative competitions, with bookish prizes
- Peruse the Oxford World's Classics Magazine
- Articles by editors
- Extracts from Introductions
- A forum for discussion and feedback on the series
- Special information for teachers and lecturers

www.worldsclassics.co.uk